P[illegible]

THE WOMAN [illegible]EL

"From the author of *The Invincible Miss Cust* comes another powerful novel about a woman bringing change, this time to the world of the internal combustion engine. *The Woman at the Wheel* by Penny Haw is the story of Bertha Benz, wife of the automobile pioneer Carl Benz. In 1872, Bertha and Carl marry, and she alone believes in his dream of creating a horseless carriage. Supporting him with her love, encouragement, visionary ideas, and even her dowry, Bertha's behind-the-scenes contributions assist Carl in producing the first two-stroke engine, which led to the creation of the first automobile. Once again, Penny Haw has created a commanding tale of a woman who follows her heart and succeeds in accomplishing her dreams. Readers will be thrilled to get to know this inspirational woman."

—Julia Bryan Thomas, author of *For Those Who Are Lost* and *The Radcliffe Ladies' Reading Club*

"Penny Haw makes us care for Bertha from the first page: she's a smart, gutsy, determined heroine, whose love for her inventor husband pervades this glorious novel. The nuances of their marriage are explored in a way that feels fresh and realistic. I enjoyed learning about the technical challenges of building the first-ever motorwagen and yearned for it to be a success. This is fine historical writing, transporting us back to another era while telling a compelling adventure story about characters we feel we know. A triumph!"

—Gill Paul, *USA Today* bestselling author of *The Secret Wife* and *The Manhattan Girls*

Praise for

THE INVINCIBLE MISS CUST

"A girl with unusual spunk and an innate love for animals becomes a woman determined to forge her own destiny in Penny Haw's beautifully written novel. In a world where women are relegated to needlepoint and parlor chairs, Aleen sets her sights on barns and veterinary surgery. Her journey to become the impossible is inspiring, heartwarming, and ultimately triumphant."

—Lisa Wingate, #1 *New York Times* bestselling author of *The Book of Lost Friends*

"I loved *The Invincible Miss Cust*. The book is an important reminder of how hard women have had to fight for the right to work and study. From Ireland to France, I enjoyed every moment of Aleen Cust's unpredictable journey. What a remarkable woman—and what an enthralling story!"

—Janet Skeslien Charles, *New York Times* bestselling author of *The Paris Library*

"*The Invincible Miss Cust* is an absolute delight, an exceptional, immersive work of historical fiction set amid the beautifully detailed landscapes of Ireland and England. Readers are sure to adore and admire Aleen Cust for her compassion for animals as well as her courage as they follow the unpredictable twists and turns of her enthralling story."

—Jennifer Chiaverini, *New York Times* bestselling author of *Switchboard Soldiers*

"I loved this gripping and inspirational book! Aleen Cust's story is one of a heroine for all ages, defying family censure and social barriers to fulfill her ambition. Her courage and independence of spirit shine through on every beautifully written page as she faces life's triumphs and tragedies. I cheered her on every step of the way."

—Fiona Valpy, bestselling author of *The Dressmaker's Gift*

"A skillfully told story of an extraordinary woman's grit, determination, and devotion to her dream of becoming Great Britain's first female veterinary surgeon. Haw brings Aleen Cust to vivid life, from her aristocratic but stifled childhood to her difficult days at school, to her eventual acceptance as a highly skilled vet—all the while fighting a patriarchal system designed to thwart her every step. Detailed and evocative, *The Invincible Miss Cust* is an engrossing read."

—Shana Abé, *New York Times* bestselling author of *The Second Mrs. Astor*

"A vivid, compelling story of a daring and determined woman. Emotionally rich and bringing light to an incredible life and legacy, you won't want to miss this inspiring novel of England's first female veterinary surgeon."

—Audrey Blake, *USA Today* bestselling author of *The Girl in His Shadow*

"An amazing story! *The Invincible Miss Cust* introduces readers to Aleen Cust, Britain and Ireland's first female veterinary surgeon, and we are better for the acquaintance. Haw's descriptive prose and deft characterizations lead us through Cust's remarkable life, setbacks, and triumphs, and leaves us in awe of her perseverance, determination, and loyalty."

—Katherine Reay, bestselling author of *The London House* and *The Printed Letter Bookshop*

"A gripping story of one woman's unrelenting quest to treat and care for our four-legged friends. Readers will be rooting for Aleen as she comes up against and triumphs over a mountain of obstacles. A must-read for all animal lovers."

—Renée Rosen, *USA Today* bestselling author of *The Social Graces*

"A fascinating true story of a woman determined to become a veterinarian in the late 1800s. Aleen Cust is everything I love in a heroine: fiery, determined, confident, and smart. No matter what life threw at her, Aleen continued to pursue her passion. We could all learn a thing or two from Aleen Cust."

—Martha Conway, award-winning author of *The Physician's Daughter*

"*The Invincible Miss Cust* is the gripping true story of a young woman who dreams of becoming a veterinary surgeon. Aleen Cust is a determined free spirit whose love for animals surpasses the challenges and hardships faced by a woman pursuing a profession in the 1890s, a time when women were rarely allowed to dream of an education or a career. Readers of James Herriot will find this a delightful, inspiring read."

—Julia Bryan Thomas, author of *For Those Who Are Lost*

"This work of historical fiction is a powerful portrait of an inspiring woman whose stubborn determination and passion for her calling drove her to defy her family's wishes, stand up to the sexist norms of society, and take the reins of her own life no matter the cost. Bravo!"

—Samantha Greene Woodruff, author of *The Lobotomist's Wife*

"Penny Haw takes us deep into the heart and choices of Aleen Cust, who defied convention to become Britain's first woman veterinary surgeon. A vivid, beautifully written, and compelling novel."

—Louisa Treger, author of *Madwoman* and *The Dragon Lady*

ALSO BY PENNY HAW

The Invincible Miss Cust

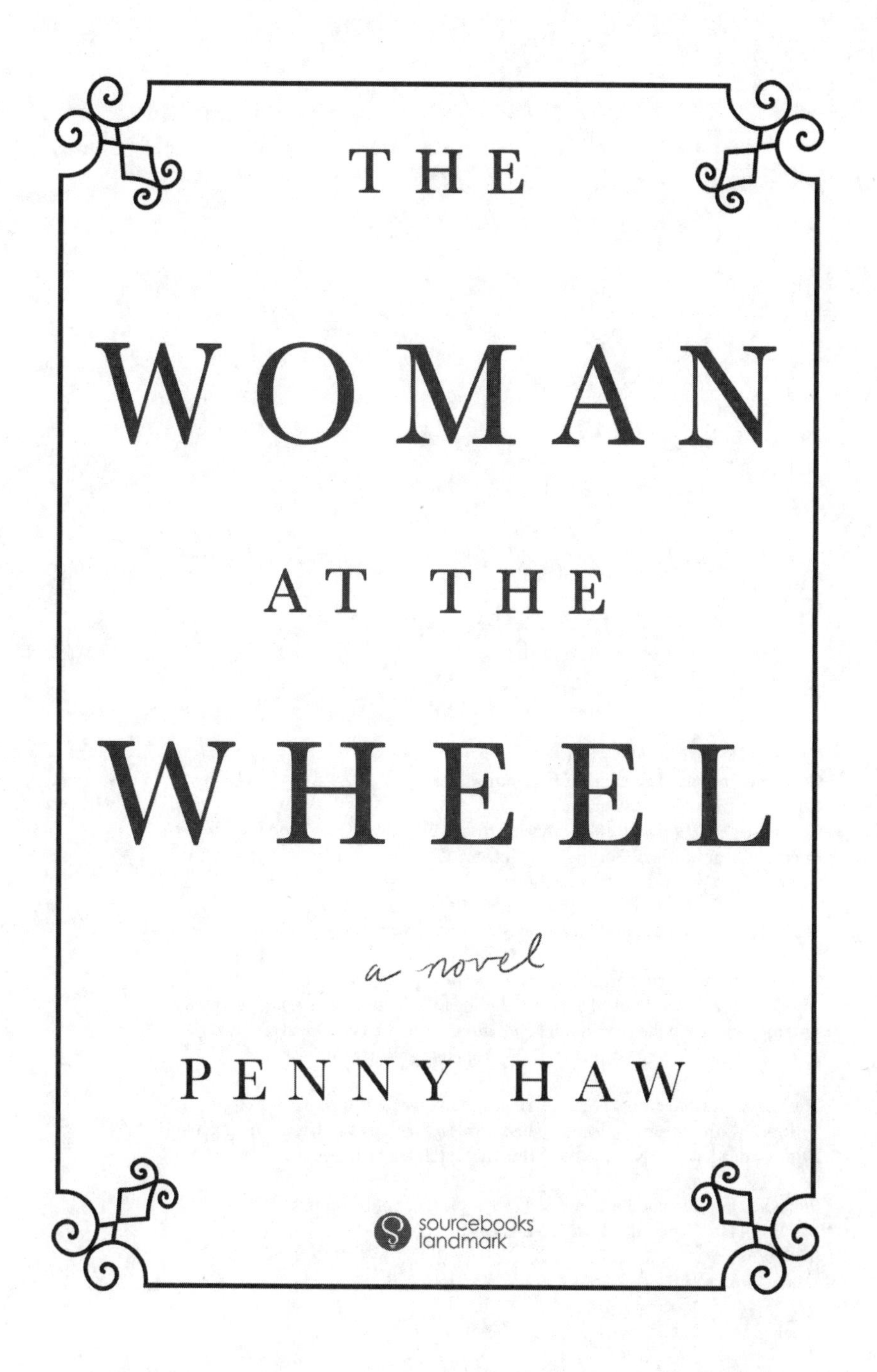

THE WOMAN AT THE WHEEL

a novel

PENNY HAW

sourcebooks landmark

Cover design by Chelsea McGuckin
Cover images © Ildiko Neer/Arcangel, Jaroslaw Blaminsky/Trevillion Images
Internal images © ChrisGorgio/Getty Images, Christine_Kohler/
Getty Images, paseven/Getty Images

Published by Sourcebooks Landmark, an imprint of Sourcebooks
P.O. Box 4410, Naperville, Illinois 60567–4410
(630) 961-3900
sourcebooks.com

Cataloging-in-Publication Data is on file with the Library of Congress.

Printed and bound in the United States of America.
LSC 10 9 8 7 6 5 4 3 2 1

To Claudia, may your ideas forever sparkle and your heart always dance

CHAPTER 1

1859
Pforzheim, Germany

I WAS TEN YEARS OLD WHEN I FELL UPON FIVE WORDS THAT CHANGED THE way I saw the world.

At the time, my parents, Karl and Auguste Ringer, had seven children. Our number would rise to nine when Thekla was born in 1862, followed by Julius in 1864. Given how occupied our father was as Pforzheim's preeminent master builder, it might've seemed incongruous that he had the energy to spawn so many of us. Certainly, Vater had little time to spare.

Pforzheim was already so entrenched as the hub of Germany's jewelry and watchmaking industries that it had been dubbed the "Golden City." Our town, on the northern edge of the Black Forest, was also abuzz with preparations for inclusion on the Karlsruhe–Mühlacker railway line. Accustomed to dodging businessmen checking their pocket watches in the streets, we were also growing used to the increased clatter of trolleys, carts, and carriages carrying materials to build the new transport system.

As they were leaving Vater's study one day, my father and his colleagues spoke about what the railway might mean, not only for Pforzheim but also for Germany. I was halfway down the stairs when I heard them agree that the train was much more than a method of transportation.

"It'll open new worlds to many," said the tallest, leanest man among them. As they walked toward the front door, he explained that, whereas only the wealthy and powerful could afford to travel by horse and coach, the locomotive would allow many others to move across the country with greater ease.

I peered over the wooden handrail and saw my father and the others nodding.

"It doesn't matter that few understand how it works," continued the man. "When people lose their fear of the locomotive and recognize the advantages it offers, everything will change for them. Already, things are changing."

There was more nodding and some affirmative grunting before the group disappeared, leaving me with thoughts of hordes of men, women, and children clambering into train carriages, in search of new worlds. It *was* exciting.

Indeed, business was booming in Pforzheim, and Vater was making the most of it. Most days, he was gone before dawn sprinkled its early light on the Enz River. He came home after the streetlamps were lit. However, when our father was with my mother, siblings, and me in the large, fashionable house he'd built us, he was generous and affectionate. Vater was also forthcoming, if rather self-engrossed, and inclined to talk primarily about his work.

His lengthy discourses about his clients (mostly wealthy), projects (largely elaborate), building materials (typically expensive), and new techniques (always brilliant) were acknowledged with indistinct mumbles and nods from my mother and sisters. My brothers were too young to feign interest. I, however, was fascinated by Vater's work and his stories about it. I'd listen for as long as he'd talk, interrupting to beg for more details and to ask questions, which he neither shirked nor responded to with impatience.

Often, he and I became so absorbed in conversation, we'd only notice that the others had left the room when the fire dwindled and we grew cold. I didn't understand their indifference. How was it possible they were not enthralled by the buildings Vater created, the people he met, or the role he played in the development of Pforzheim? He knew people who were establishing factories, inventing tools, and designing machines. He was watching the future of the world as it was rolled out. How exciting I found it. My mother and siblings' disinterest made no sense to me. On the other hand, my curiosity about Vater's work and his eagerness to satisfy it created what I believed to be a special bond between us.

"Building houses, factories, shops, and churches is only part of what I do," he said as I walked alongside him down Karl-Friedrich Street one afternoon, a week or so after I'd overheard him and his colleagues talking about the locomotive. "I'm also an appraiser. That means I must examine the work of other builders."

"Why should you do that?" I asked, slowing my skipping to match his step.

"Because if buildings are not constructed with care, they fail. An appraiser checks on the quality of the work," he said.

"What kind of things do you have to check?" I asked, spotting—a moment too late—a pile of freshly deposited horse manure on the cobblestones. It was rare for me to accompany Vater on a business outing. In my excitement, I'd forgotten my mother's rule that we should *always* walk on the pavement. I'd have to clean my shoes before she noticed the evidence of my carelessness.

Vater removed his hat and used it to fan his rosy cheeks. At almost sixty and burdened by a belly that seemed to expand by the day, my father was not as agile or fit as he had been.

"I'll explain when we arrive," he said.

We walked on without talking, crossing the small bridge toward the town square, where the pavements bustled with afternoon shoppers and the roads rattled with carriages and carts. Finally, down a quieter side street, we rounded a corner to our destination. Vater stopped in an open doorway, stomach rising and falling as he filled and emptied his lungs. The building, a jewelry workshop that was being extended, was made up of two large rooms. There was a strong smell of brick dust and wood, but aside from a few tools propped up against a wall and a low pile of planks on the floor, the rooms were bare.

"Physical activities be damned," muttered Vater. "I *will* take the carriage next time."

Finally, breathing restored, he lifted his cane and pointed to the floor. "The first thing I examine is the foundation. Without solid groundwork, a building is doomed."

From there on, my father described his duties as an inspector. He explained how the weight that the walls needed to support was calculated and how builders fortified them accordingly. Vater told me how window frames were fitted, edges squared, and floors sealed. He gestured at the beams and described how poles and planks were selected and treated.

I followed him into the second room, staying close so as not to miss a word. He continued talking until he was distracted by two men who—wearing glossy shoes, hats, and dark suits so tailored and neat they might've been painted on their bodies—entered the room.

"Stay here," said Vater.

The three men shook hands and exchanged a few words before my father led the way around the first room. I followed, this time at a distance. The younger of the two carried a ledger and, as my father spoke, made notes with a pencil. It pleased me to see how the men—though more polished than Vater in their expensive-looking outfits, complete with gold watch chains swaying against their hips—listened and nodded attentively as he spoke. My father's words carried weight.

The younger man seemed particularly engaged, leaning toward Vater as he spoke and then recording his words in the book. *What is he writing?* I wondered. Whatever his role, it appeared important. I pictured myself following my father around his construction sites, making notes about what he saw and asking questions when I was unsure. I would be important too. I'd do something useful. The only time I'd ever seen my father writing was shortly after my mother gave birth to Erwin four years ago. As I'd passed the study door, I saw Vater, quill in hand, bent over his desk. What role did writing play in his work? I was curious and decided that, at the first opportunity, I'd sneak into the study—we were not allowed to go in there alone—and see if I could find his notes. If I was going to help Vater with his work, I'd need to know what writing he required.

An hour or so later, my father heaved a sigh of gratitude when the older of the two men offered us a lift home in his carriage. As we climbed in, I examined the coach with new interest. *How was it made?* I wondered. Did its construction require the same deliberation as was necessary for the workshop we'd just examined? It made sense since the carriage had to be strong to carry passengers over roads, many of which would be rutted and rocky. I peered at the latch that held the door closed, marveling that someone had come up with the idea and had made and fitted it to the carriage. Would it have been a metalworker or a carpenter? As we returned along Karl-Friedrich Street, I stared out at the buildings, seeing them afresh. That so much consideration, knowledge, and skill had gone into creating each one intrigued me. How interesting life was. How much there was to learn and do.

"You took your favorite to work with you?" said Mutter, glancing up from her needlework as I followed Vater into the drawing room a short while later.

He sat down heavily in one of his favorite plushily upholstered chairs near the door and rested his cane against his knee. "Just a quick inspection close by." He looked up. "She was the only one who chose to come."

My older sisters, Emilie and Elise, sat on either side of Mutter, their heads bent over large sections of white cloth, through which they dipped their needles and threads in silent industry. At fifteen and thirteen respectively, my sisters were, Mutter insisted, running out of time to complete their trousseaux.

"She should begin preparing for her future like her sisters are," said Mutter, her eyes on her needle.

Karl, who was a little over a year younger than me, sat at Emilie's feet, untangling a ball of cotton. The three little ones—Herbert, Erwin, and Amelia—were upstairs with the nurse.

Mutter glanced at Karl. "Did you not want to accompany your father, my son?"

"I was busy," he replied, holding up the cluster of cotton. "I shall go with you next time, Vater."

"You should," I said as I pulled up a stool and sat near my siblings. "It's *so* interesting. Vater can show you how he digs and fills foundations, and how carpenters shape wood so that the beams slide into each other and are held together."

"What is that on your shoe, Bertha?" asked my mother.

I crossed my feet, placing the clean shoe over the soiled one, and slid them beneath the stool.

"It's too late for that," she said with a small scowl. "Go and clean it."

Emilie caught my eye and shook her head.

As I walked toward the scullery, I noticed that the door to Vater's study was ajar. I thought again about the man with the ledger. With everyone in the drawing room, it was a good time for me to slip into the office, have a look at my father's records, and see what I might be called upon to write one day when I worked alongside him.

The study—with a large, dark desk and matching chair on a burgundy rug—was sparsely decorated. A gold clock, encased in the same dark wood as the other furniture, hung behind the desk. Rather than the rows of books and records I'd expected to find, there were a few neat piles of letters on a small bureau against the wall. The only things on Vater's desk were a quill, a pot of ink, and the big leather-bound Bible, from which he sometimes read aloud to us after dinner.

I went to the desk and lifted the book's heavy cover without real purpose. My thoughts were elsewhere. The clues I'd hoped to find in the study did not exist. I'd have to ask Vater about the note-taker's role. I absent-mindedly turned a page. There, on one of the first blank pages of the Bible, my father had written his name, *Karl Friedrich Ringer*, in blue ink. When I turned the page, I saw that he had listed the birth of each of his children in order of our arrival. I read, running a finger beneath his spidery cursive.

Emilie Auguste Louise Ringer, born 11 December 1845.

Elise Mathilde Miethe Ringer, born 3 June 1847.

I stopped reading, my breathing suspended when I came to the third entry. The record of my birth had an addendum.

Cäcilie Bertha Ringer, born 3 May 1849. Unfortunately, only a girl again.

I stared at the words. My heart seemed to beat in time with the clock but louder. I closed my eyes for a moment, hoping that when I opened them, I'd see that I'd imagined the addition. It didn't help; it was still there.

Unfortunately, only a girl again.

I leaned against the desk. The wood was hard and cold. The happy curiosity that had carried me into the room had vanished along with the strength in my legs. My thoughts swam in several different directions but arrived at the same conclusion: my arrival had disappointed my father. Our bond was a sham. There was no special connection.

Unfortunately, only a girl again.

Even the ink for those five words was heavier, as if my father's misery had flowed through him, out of the quill and onto the page, thick and fast.

Only a girl.

What did Vater mean by that? I was not *only* anything: I was Bertha. I was the girl who listened when he reminded us—as he did frequently—how he'd been raised a parson's son, poor and uneducated, and how he had built his business from nothing. He would describe how he'd not allowed himself to become distracted from his goal until he amassed the wealth, reputation, and enough future projects to add *find a young wife and start a family* to his list of tasks. Hard work and patience, he said, rewarded him—and even if he was well into his forties before he had time to attend to matters familial, look how well we lived. Vater could not have built this home for us, have us attended to by servants, and send us to school if not for his resolve. How I admired him for that. How I wanted to be like him. It had never occurred to me before that it would not be possible. Now, though, having read that I was *only a girl*, I saw how foolish I had been.

Instead of going to the scullery to clean my shoe, I went to the backyard to look for Affie. Acquired by Vater about a year ago to help keep the rats out of the stables and granary, Affie was an affenpinscher—or, as some preferred to say, a "monkey terrier." Certainly, with her short, mustached muzzle; fluffy, round head; and bright eyes, she had the face and playful, curious attitude that one might associate with a monkey.

When Vater had arrived with the tiny black bundle of fur, he was stern about the fact that the puppy had a practical purpose and insisted we were not to pamper her or turn her into a pet.

However, with Vater gone so much and Mutter as enchanted by Affie as her children were, there was little chance of the dog *not* becoming a pet. Indeed, before long, Affie had the run of the house while our father was at work. The instant her keen ears heard the tapping of his cane on the front path, the dog jumped up, trotted down the passage, and disappeared into the scullery or yard. Even if she was stretched out in front of the fireplace in cozy slumber, Affie's hearing never let her down. We were confident that Vater was oblivious to the dog's indoor indulgences.

Now, as I stepped into the yard and called her name, Affie ran to me. I picked her up and crept upstairs to the bedroom I shared with Elise. The dog looked pointedly at the door as I placed her on my bed.

"I know he's here, but he's tired and won't come upstairs now," I said, shutting the door.

Affie pressed her flat nose against the bed covers, sniffed about for a bit, turned around three times, and lay down. I stretched out alongside her, running my hand over her curved spine.

"You are not *only* a dog, Affie," I whispered, my father's words still vivid in my mind. "I would never think, say, or write that. And yet I am *only a girl.* I might go to school, know more than Karl, and want to help Vater with his work, but I am *only a girl* and there is nothing I can do about it."

The dog sighed.

"I might as well begin working on my trousseau. At least Mutter will be pleased with me."

Affie lifted her head, ears raised. There was a light tap at the door.

"Bertha, it's almost suppertime. Mutter says to wash and come downstairs," said Elise.

"I'm not feeling well. I'm already in bed," I called out, drawing a small blanket over Affie and myself.

Elise opened the door. "Shall I ask Mutter to come to you?"

"No. It's only a small headache. I just want to sleep. It'll be gone in the morning."

Although Vater had not written *only a girl* alongside Emilie's and Elise's names, it applied to them, too, did it not? Did they know our lesser status? If they did, did they care? Or had Vater still been so buoyed by the novelty of becoming a parent when they were born that he didn't experience the same disappointment that he did when I arrived?

"I see Affie, Bertha," said my sister, her tone light.

"She's keeping me warm. Please don't say anything to Vater."

Elise approached, placed her fingers on my forehead, and squinted at me. I gave her a small smile. Mutter said Elise and I were friends the moment she helped one-year-old me toddle from my crib to the nursery window. Now she patted the dog through the blanket. Affie's tail wagged slowly against my leg.

"Why would I?" asked Elise as she left and closed the door quietly behind her.

CHAPTER 2

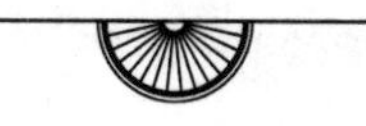

1861
Pforzheim, Germany

JUST AS ELISE NEVER MENTIONED THAT AFFIE WAS IN OUR ROOM THAT NIGHT, I did not reveal what I'd seen in Vater's handwriting in the Bible. For a while, it was hard to bear, and as one feels about an itch that screams to be scratched, there were times when I ached to disclose my pain. What, though, would I have achieved by doing so? How would sharing my suffering ease it? I said nothing. Instead, I watched my father closely, looking for signs of dissatisfaction with me. I found none. Sometimes I wondered if I'd imagined what I had read. Then I'd pass the study; see the book on the desk in big, solid reality; and again experience the cold whip of truth.

I held my shame close, but it didn't shield me from my affection for Vater. I'd cared for him all my life, and when the shock of his words wore off—as it did—my love for him remained. So, too, did my interest in his business. He was unaware that anything might've changed, and for as long as I was attentive, Vater regaled me with the details I hungered for. His projects intrigued me, and as he spoke, I became so caught up that my questions tumbled out like a waterfall in flood. Even if I'd been inclined to sulk, my inquisitiveness did not allow it. I was still Bertha; it didn't matter that I was *only a girl.*

So it was that, for almost two years, nothing around me seemed changed even if, when I gave in to reflection, I knew everything had. Then Vater began taking Karl to work with him regularly.

"I see how hard it is for you," said Mutter when she came upon me in the hallway one morning.

Vater and Karl were closeted in the study, examining—I guessed—the building plans for the cellar my father had described to me some weeks earlier. School was closed for summer, and although I'd begun work on my trousseau, I didn't feel like being indoors and was on my way to the drawing room to try to tempt Elise to walk along the river with me. I was surprised by my mother's comment.

"What do you mean?" I asked.

Mutter took my hands in hers. Although she wasn't yet showing evidence of it, my mother was pregnant with Thekla. She'd broken the news while Emilie, Elise, and I were alone with her the previous day. Vater, she had said, was overjoyed. An eighth child! What a woman he'd married, he'd exclaimed. *How weary she looks,* I'd thought. She might've been twenty-two years younger than Vater, but it seemed she aged faster with every child she brought into the world.

"It worried me when your father decided that you and your sisters would attend secondary school. I warned him it might make you restless," she said, her eyes searching mine. "The others seem to have escaped unscathed, but I see I was right about you."

She'd alluded to her concerns before. While Mutter agreed that learning French and English was helpful for girls—indeed, she wished she'd had the opportunity to learn both—she believed that everything else we studied at school was pointless. What were women to do with arithmetic, geometry, nature studies, science, calligraphy, and bookkeeping when bearing children and keeping house would be their duties?

I tried to object. "I'm not restless."

"You're not longing to know what's going on in there?" she asked, tipping her head toward the study.

I glanced down. She knew me well.

"I was on my way to find Elise. I wanted to go for a walk before it gets too warm," I said.

Her response was unexpected. "Let's go. Just you and I."

The walk would be shorter and slower with Mutter than it would've been with my sister. However, the novelty of being alone with her, particularly out of the house, made up for the deficit.

"I'll fetch Affie," I said.

—

My mother's spontaneous proposal to accompany me on a walk might've been unforeseen, but that she turned south as we stepped onto the street was not. A journey from the house with her inevitably passed the equestrian arena a block away.

Mutter did not often speak of her childhood, but we knew she was born and raised on a farm, where taking care of animals was one of her favorite responsibilities. She understood, loved, and missed them. It was undoubtedly one of the reasons Affie was so indulged and surely why she chose her routes according to where she was likely to see the most animals gathered.

We approached the equestrian center to see a line of carriages of various shapes and sizes assembled along the edge of the main paddock. Inside, several strings of horses stomped their hooves and flicked their tails in the morning sunshine. Some were led back and forth while two or three were ridden around the enclosure. Breeders, riders, coachmen, and businessmen were gathered, stepping forward here and there to run their hands down the shoulders and legs of the animals or pry open their lips before peering into their mouths. The low babble typical of marketplaces, where aspects of quality and price are quibbled, filled the air.

As we drew closer, the smell of sweaty horses, leather, and dust grew stronger. Mutter raised her shoulders and walked faster. It was likely, I realized as we approached, that our walk would go no farther than the equestrian center. Indeed, she led Affie and me to a bench with a clear view of the arena and sat down. I settled alongside her.

"That's a Hanoverian," said Mutter, pointing to a dapple gray with a broad chest and muscled flanks, led by a man wearing remarkably white jodhpurs. "Bred in Holstein from English Thoroughbreds for their ability to gallop long and far without getting tired."

My mother's knowledge of animals was extensive. It made me think about what she'd said earlier about the education my sisters and I were receiving.

"Why, when you know so much, does it worry you about what my sisters and I learn at school? Is learning, no matter where you do it, not still learning?" I asked.

There was no reply. I persisted.

"How is our education in a classroom different from what you learned on the farm?"

She didn't take her eyes off the horses. "What I learned had practical purpose. I might—if I had not married a builder—have married a farmer. I needed to know about animals. It made sense. Most of the subjects you are taught will do you no good as a wife and a mother."

"So we must sew and learn to manage servants and run a house?"

"Ja, that's right," she said. "Everything else a girl learns is useless and, for some, misleading."

I looked at her. "Misleading?"

"It makes you wish for a life that is not possible."

"But don't you think that an education can also show a girl what *might* be possible?" I asked.

Mutter gave a small chuckle. "Oh, Bertha, you are so young. You don't understand yet. One day, you will."

She was right; I didn't understand. I thought about the Bible and wondered if Vater's disappointment in me might somehow be connected to my mother's misgivings about our education. *Only a girl* needed to learn enough to run a house and raise children—unless she was a farmer's wife and needed to understand animals. But if Vater believed the same, why did he send us to secondary school?

"What does Vater say when you argue that education is unnecessary for me and my sisters?" I asked.

"He doesn't argue."

"But why—"

"He likes the idea of you being among the daughters of the wealthy. He's pleased that he can afford to send you to such a prestigious school, believes it will help your chances of making good marriages. Perhaps to the brothers of your classmates."

I stared at her. She was still watching the horses. Vater sent us to an expensive secondary school, not strictly to be educated but because he thought it would improve our chances of meeting affluent suitors. It had never occurred to me that he would be thus motivated.

"Is that why Vater encourages us to accept so many invitations?"

She lifted her hand to point. "Look. The gray stallion has broken free!"

We watched as the muscle-bound Hanoverian, having torn the reins from the hands of the man in white pants, bolted toward a group of three horses tethered to a pole. The trio lurched in fright, pulling apart as far as their harnesses would allow. Two grooms rushed at the gray. He spun around, reared, and tossed his head in their direction, as if daring them to give chase, before taking off once more.

With his bridle flapping against his face and neck, the horse galloped across the arena toward us, hooves thundering and nostrils flaring. Men scattered. The stallion's tail was raised like a hirsute flag, the sunshine glistening through its strands as if ablaze. I felt a furry weight against my ankle; Affie had taken refuge beneath the bench. It made sense: the horse was hurtling toward us at pace. His power and energy suggested he would vault the wooden poles that separated us from him, placing us directly in his pathway.

Without thinking, I snatched my mother's hand. She gasped and I turned to look at her. She was transfixed by the horse, her smile wide and her cheeks flushed. Affie whined.

"Mutter!" I yelled.

"It's all right," she said, squeezing my hand.

I didn't believe her. Still, the horse galloped. He showed no sign of slowing. Affie whined again. I held my breath. The ground trembled. The stallion might have even touched the barrier as he skidded to a halt. He stood before us, trembling, pawing the earth, and snorting. I exhaled and reached down to pat Affie.

"What an animal," whispered my mother. "That is how he should always be. That is how *they* should always be. Free to run. Free from carriages, plows, mills, and riders. Free from the cavalry. Free to be horses."

I had never seen her eyes so bright. For the first time, I pictured her as a girl on a farm.

"Free?" I echoed.

She exhaled loudly. I'd broken the spell. "If you ever see horses at rest or at play in the countryside, you'll understand," she said.

There was a great deal I didn't understand that day, it seemed.

"It's unfortunate that we've made slaves out of them, harnessing and whipping them into submission," said Mutter.

"But we need transport. We need their power," I replied.

The man in the white jodhpurs, scowling now, approached the horse, snatched the reins, and led him away. Mutter stood.

"Yes. *We* need their power," she said, sighing again as she led the way home.

CHAPTER 3

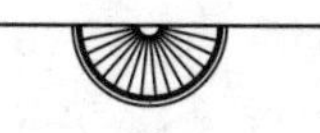

1863
Pforzheim, Germany

Vater's instinct that enrolling his daughters in Pforzheim's premier secondary school for girls would advance our stakes in marriage soon rewarded him. Two days after her eighteenth birthday, Emilie married a classmate's brother, Gustav. He was the second son of an eminent goldsmith, and so pleased was our father by the match that he abandoned his cane for the wedding day. That night, however, Elise told me something that I feared might have our father leaning more heavily on his stick in the days to come.

"Don't mention it to anyone else yet, but Emilie says Gustav is eager to move to America," she said as we prepared for bed.

"America? Oh! But why?" I asked, feeling a ping of excitement on our older sister's behalf.

"Why does anyone go there? For opportunity," said Elise, weaving her long, dark hair into a plait. "Gustav wants the freedom of starting a business of his own, away from his father and older brother."

"Will they go soon?" I asked, looking over my sister's shoulder at her reflection in the mirror.

She shrugged. "Emilie doesn't know. Her husband will decide and tell her."

"Really? Will she have no part in the decision?" I thought about how Emilie *always* had the final word. She made decisions for her siblings and often even helped Mutter reach conclusions.

Then it occurred to me. "Does our sister *want* to go to America?"

Elise stood and climbed into her bed. "She didn't say. It doesn't matter, Bertha. She's married, and if Gustav wants to go, so must she. Don't you want her to leave?"

"No, it's not that. I think it would be a wonderful adventure, but maybe Emilie feels differently. She seemed pleased that they would live close to us. So did Mutter and Vater," I said.

My sister snuffed the lamp on the table between us. "It's not about what Mutter and Vater want for her now; it's about what Gustav wants." She fluffed her pillow. "Good night."

I lay down, but my mind was restless. It seemed strange that my oldest and most responsible sibling would now live her life according to the whims and wants of a man whom, I realized, we barely knew. Gustav was quiet and friendly. He didn't appear unkind and, according to Vater, "came from a good family." But what did we really know about him? What did Emilie know? What could one know of another with whom they had rarely been alone?

"Do you like Gustav?" I said in the dark.

I heard Elise turn toward me. "Yes, I think so. He doesn't say much, but I can't see fault with him. What about you?"

"I feel the same. Does Emilie know him much better? Than we do, I mean."

"I hope so," said my sister. "Why do you ask?"

"She's going to spend the rest of her life with him."

"So, they have many years to get to know each other. Go to sleep, Bertha. You're creating unnecessary worries," said Elise, in a tone that confirmed it was the end of the conversation.

Still, I did not sleep. It wasn't just that Gustav was a stranger that concerned me. As the oldest, Emilie had long ago assumed the role of the most conscientious and dependable of the Ringer children.

Emilie chivvied us when we were late. She reminded us to button up our coats and pointed out the puddles as we walked. She encouraged me to learn to read before I joined her and Elise at school and insisted that I do the same for Karl when he was old enough. Emilie praised us when we were well behaved and reprimanded us when we were not. She kept a calendar of everyone's birthdays and planned celebrations. Even my parents stood back when Emilie was organizing her siblings. It was Emilie who had finally convinced Vater that using a cane would not only help him get around more easily but also added stature and gravitas to his image. She was one of the columns that held our family aloft.

I rolled onto my side and closed my eyes, but sleep evaded me. Elise must be mistaken. I couldn't imagine Emilie taking orders from anyone else. Also, why should she? My sister was intelligent, practical, and capable. Her ideas and decisions were sound. Gustav was fortunate to have her at his side. He would be wise to invite *and* listen to her opinion. Finally, I fell asleep, thinking that I would only marry a man who agreed to hear what I had to say about decisions that would affect our lives.

—

A few months later, Gustav and Emilie joined us for Sunday lunch. In from the rain, they took off their coats and briefly said their hellos as we gathered in the hallway.

"I must talk to you about something, please," said Gustav to my father, glancing at the study.

They went in and closed the door. Mutter, Elise, and I looked at Emilie. She turned away and walked into the drawing room. We followed.

"Are you—" said Mutter.

"No," said Emilie.

She picked up the tablecloth Elise was working on and studied it. "Lovely," she said, giving Elise a tight smile. "You're much better at embroidery than I am. So clever with color. Will you make a set of napkins too?"

They discussed embroidery, whether Elise should make twelve or sixteen napkins, and how the colors of the flowers on the cloth would match the curtains for the dining room Elise imagined one day decorating. With its familiar solid furniture, heavy drapery, fireplace, and walls dotted with tapestries and paintings, the drawing room was my favorite room. It was the spacious and comfortable place where many of the most important conversations of my life had taken place. It was the location of family debates, laughter, and quiet togetherness. Today, though, the room had the taut, stifling air of a chamber whose inhabitants longed to be anywhere else. I went to the window and looked out.

The street was dotted with puddles, and the rain, though more of a drizzle than a shower, cast a gray shadow over everything, making it seem much later than it was. A carriage went by, hooves clattering, harnesses jingling, and wheels splashing as it rolled through pools of water. It was a cool day, but I was warm. I tugged at the collar of my dress and leaned my ear against the window, hoping that the sound of the rain would drown out the voices in the room. I didn't want to discuss embroidery, curtains, or dining room decor. It was an artificial conversation, words to detract from the real discussion that was going on in the study. The rain was too soft to mask the chatter. I couldn't bear it, so I turned toward my mother and sisters.

"What is Gustav talking to Vater about?" I asked.

Elise frowned at me. Mutter looked at Emilie, who hid her face by lifting the embroidery as if to examine it more closely. They didn't speak.

"Well?"

Elise narrowed her eyes. "Bertha, not now," she said.

"Why? Why can't we discuss what's going on? Why can't Emilie tell us what's happening in *her* life? Why do we have to wait to hear it from Gustav?" I asked.

Mutter stared at me and then at Elise, her forehead furrowed. "What's going on?"

We looked at Emilie. She turned her back to us, but her heaving shoulders gave her away. I couldn't remember ever having seen my oldest sister cry.

"Look what you've done," said Elise, glaring at me.

We heard the shuffle of shoes at the door. Vater stood there with Emilie's husband at his shoulder.

"Gustav has some news," said my father, his tone unconvincingly cheerful.

There was a hush. Emilie turned to face us, brushing her fingertips across her cheeks.

"We are leaving for America next month," said Gustav.

"America?" said Mutter.

"Yes. My uncle has settled in Milwaukee. He believes there are good business prospects for me there."

My mother turned to Emilie. "Mil...Mil—where?"

"Milwaukee," said Gustav, as if not trusting my sister to respond. Or perhaps he didn't think she could pronounce the name either. "It lies on the shores of a large lake and is a growing town with many needs and opportunities."

A short while later, in the dining room, lunch was a quiet affair. The matter was settled: Gustav and Emilie would move to Milwaukee within a month. I didn't look at Emilie, for fear of what might happen if I caught her eye. Would she cry again?

Elise glanced at me, and I saw that she understood. If she and I had been alone, I would've spoken my mind. I would've told her how unfair it was that Emilie no longer had any say in her future. I would've argued that Vater should insist his daughter be given choices. Elise would've listened and then calmed me with every other possible perspective. Where Emilie was my conscience, Elise was my balm. Now, though, I guessed Elise was as unsettled as I was by the thought that we might never see our sister again. Mutter kept her eyes on her plate. Even Vater, who would've applauded the gumption of beginning a business in a new country in anyone else, was subdued. It was one thing for his daughter to have married well but another that a consequence thereof should be her relocation to another part of the world.

—

Silence settled in the Ringer house during the weeks leading to Emilie's departure. Even the little ones who were too young to understand what was going on were quiet. Mutter moved around as if mute.

"We've lost two voices," said Elise.

"Hers will return, won't it?" I asked.

My sister shrugged.

I tried a different approach. "If Mutter is upset about Emilie leaving, why doesn't she object? Why doesn't anyone in the family say anything about the fact that our sister hasn't breathed a word about whether she wants to go to America? What happened to her voice when she got married?"

"Everyone fears change. That's all it is," said Elise. Her manner was thoughtful rather than certain. I wasn't convinced.

"Change? What change are you talking about? The change of countries or the way *she* has had to change who she is simply because she's now a married woman?"

Elise held my gaze. "Emilie hasn't changed—she's adjusting. That's what people must do as their circumstances alter and life progresses. You'll see, Bertha. That's just how it is."

"Is Gustav adjusting too?" I asked.

"I don't know. Probably," she replied without further explanation.

—

Though no one admitted it, it was almost a relief to hear the train hiss, see its wheels roll, and watch the trail of steam disappear down the tracks when Emilie and Gustav left. We waved from the new Pforzheim station platform, as smooth and clean as marble beneath our feet, until the smoke dissolved. When Mutter turned to Vater, she was dry-eyed and had found her voice.

"Who was the young man you were talking to?" she asked.

"Werner Miethe. A friend of Gustav's. He wants to talk to me about a tool he's designed for carpenters. His father works for the city. A lawyer. We should invite him to the house."

"The father?" asked Mutter.

"No, of course not—the son, Werner," said Vater, his eyes on Elise, who walked ahead, herding Herbert and Erwin toward the carriage.

At first, we received a letter from Emilie every two or three months. Establishing a home in Milwaukee was not easy, particularly without a maid or a cook. When the first baby was born, the letters arrived further and further apart.

In Germany, the railway network continued to expand. The steel industry and other businesses flourished with it. Vater explained that, while there was talk of nationalizing some of the large businesses to support the industrialization, it was unclear how it would be done.

With Karl having broken the news that he was more interested in making furniture than constructing buildings and the other boys too young to be of any assistance yet, our father was as busy as ever. Karl's indifference to our father's business also left Vater looking for another interested ear. He was pleased to find mine still disposed. Although he no longer invited me to visit his projects—"It is no place for a young woman"—he was happy to talk to me about his work and that of other businesses.

Elise completed her schooling and assumed Emilie's role at Mutter's side. She moved into Emilie's old bedroom, and our younger sister Amelia took her place in the room we had shared.

"She's terribly noisy," I complained as Elise and I walked Affie along the Enz River one afternoon. "Are you sure you don't want to move back?"

"It's the excitement of being with her older sister. You were the same when you moved in with me," said Elise.

The river flowed dark and slow as we followed the path beneath the Romanesque arches of the St. Michael's Church clock tower. The bells were still, and with evening fast approaching, there was no one else around. It was peaceful until Affie sniffed out a pair of ducks, who squawked in fright, flew across the water, and landed near the shore on the other side. She gave a few sharp yaps before bounding through the long grass on the riverbank in search of other unsuspecting creatures.

Elise hooked her arm through mine. "We're all moving up a place, moving on," she said.

"Yes, I know. I don't really mind. It is just that—"

"I'm not only talking about Amelia."

I looked at her. "What do you mean?"

"Werner is going to talk to Vater."

"Werner? Talk to Vater? You mean, you and Werner..."

She smiled and nodded.

In the months that Emilie and Gustav had been gone, Werner had been a regular visitor to our home. I'd suspected, from what I'd overheard Vater say at the station, that he believed the man to be a potential suitor for Elise.

How had I missed what had subsequently happened? Why had my sister not confided in me?

"But when did this happen? Why didn't you say anything?"

She squeezed my arm. "Mutter said it would be better not to say anything until—"

"Until?"

"It was certain."

"Why not?"

"We didn't want to upset you."

I pulled my arm from hers and turned to face her. "Why would it upset me? Do you… Do you like him?"

"Yes," she said, smiling but unable to meet my eye.

"Then why? I would've told you immediately. You would've been the first person I told," I said, aware as I spoke of how childish I sounded.

"I know," Elise said, her voice low now.

"Then why?"

"Because Werner and I are also going to move to Milwaukee."

CHAPTER 4

1869
Pforzheim, Germany

WHEN, SHORTLY AFTER THEIR WEDDING, SHE AND WERNER PREPARED TO LEAVE Pforzheim to join Emilie and Gustav in Milwaukee, Elise promised that she would write every second month.

"Even when the babies come, I shall write to you," she said, taking my hands in hers as if to secure the pact as we stood on the same shiny platform from which we'd waved goodbye to Emilie and Gustav.

There was no reason to doubt my sister's intentions, but I couldn't help thinking about how scarce Emilie's letters had become. In the past year, we'd received just one at Christmas. In it, our oldest sibling had complained how, despite the growth of Gustav's toolmaking business, there was little time for her to do anything other than take care of the family and their home.

> *Gustav does not believe that I need help in the house. Even if he did, it would be difficult to find the kind of servants we knew in Germany. I only realize now how fortunate we were.*

It wasn't only the prospect of receiving ever less news from Elise as the months and years added to the distance between us that worried me but also the fact that I was losing my closest confidante. Although the house still contained six other siblings, it wouldn't be the same without Elise. I would miss her perceptiveness, camaraderie, and easy laugh. No one else could oust my doubts and worries with calmative logic the way she could. Elise was the one who would join me and Affie on walks along the Enz River in all kinds of weather. She was the person who furtively took my needlepoint from me and, without Mutter noticing, completed the stitches I couldn't get right. Who would whisper witticisms in my ear in church when the sermon benumbed my brain and then squeeze my hand to help suppress my giggles?

As I watched her and Werner leave, I doubted I would ever find so fine a friend as Elise again. She was not only my dearest sister and friend but also the tinder that lit my soul. When her letters from America came—true to her word, every second month, initially—they affirmed my fears. She was irreplaceable. However, while they could never be as satisfying as having Elise alongside me, the missives were folded leaves of joy.

Unlike Emilie's sporadic lists of woes from Milwaukee, Elise's letters spilled over with color, adventure, and life. She wrote how the morning sun rolled out a golden pathway across Lake Michigan, which she described as "an endless expanse of turquoise water, so large it could be the ocean that separates Europe from the Americas." She described beaches with white sand and forested fringes, saying that she and Werner were determined to explore a new one every month. On one of their weekend outings, they encountered a herd of deer grazing quietly near the water.

We lay low in the bushes and watched them. There were several energetic young fawns among them, which could have been Thekla and Julius chasing each other in the park in Pforzheim. Who knew wild creatures found such joy in play! I wish you could have seen them, Bertha.

Elise described the expanse of their new country, the distances between towns, the bustle of Milwaukee, and the joy of meeting different people and experiencing new things. The sky in Pforzheim seemed low and life predictable by comparison. My sister's excitement was infectious, and I responded accordingly.

Perhaps when you and Werner have children, I will be able to convince Vater and Mutter to send me to you. I will argue that you need help and that Vater should pay my fare to America. I long to experience Milwaukee alongside you.

Elise was disappointingly circumspect in her response.

It would be wonderful to have you near me, dear sister, but you cannot do that. It is neither wise nor safe for you to travel alone or to come here as an unmarried woman. You will be beset upon by all manner of desperate and unsuitable men, few of them gentlemen. Marry a good man from Pforzheim, convince him to bring you here, and we will raise our children together.

Pressure to get married was not what I'd wished from Elise. There was enough of that from closer quarters.

"Surely she met *someone* at school who has a suitable brother or cousin," I overheard my father say. "She is twenty years old. Emilie and Elise were married and living in America at that age."

I did not linger to hear my mother's response. The more impatient my parents became to see me wed, the less inclined I grew. Weren't there more important matters to contemplate than finding me a husband? Increasingly, it seemed not. Vater returned from work several times a week with a different man at his side. Some were invited in for a drink and others to stay for dinner. They were indistinguishable. It was not only that the men did not appeal to me—every introduction and the accompanying anticipation in my parents' eyes reminded me that my worth would be measured according to the man who would have me. What I had learned at school and from my father, and who I was and how that might affect my future, didn't matter. I was *only a girl,* and unless I married well, my father's disappointment would prevail.

One morning, after another evening of awkwardness with an uneasy stranger at the dinner table, I offered to fetch the cotton my mother needed from a shop in the center of town. Affie and I took the longer, picturesque route along the river. Two young women walked by in the opposite direction.

Their heads were nestled so closely together in conversation that they didn't notice me step aside to allow them to pass. *Are they sisters?* I wondered. *What are they talking about? Are their parents as dedicated to marrying them off as mine are?* I imagined what advice Elise would've offered had she been there.

"You're inclined to be contrary when people try to persuade you to do things, Bertha. It's as if you're stubborn because you dislike being directed as a matter of principle rather than what the direction might mean for you. It could work against you. Perhaps you could try being less reactionary," she might've said.

I picked up the soppy, half-chewed stick Affie had dropped at my feet.

"She's right," I told the dog.

Affie bounced backward in front of me, her eyes never leaving the branch.

"I should try and be more agreeable. What do you think, Affie? Shall we agree to go to the picnic at Maulbronn Monastery next weekend and socialize with some of Pforzheim's finest?" Affie gave a sharp yap. "What? Oh, you agree, but you'll only come with if I throw your stick immediately."

—

Vater had come across the advertisement in the newspaper a few days earlier.

"You might enjoy this, Bertha," he'd said. "The Eintracht Social Club has organized an outing to the Cistercian monastery, with a musical performance followed by a picnic on the grounds."

He handed me the newspaper. I glanced at the notice and put it down. Mutter took it.

"Ah. 'Carriages leave from the equestrian center'," she read. "A refined affair. I shall accompany you."

"I've been to Maulbronn Monastery. You showed me the Gothic tower years ago, Vater, and explained how it was built," I replied.

"Ja, but this is a social event. You won't be inspecting buildings; you'll be meeting, erm, people," said my father, tugging his waistcoat over his stomach.

"A day in nature will do us both good," said Mutter.

"I'll think about it," I'd replied, making for the door. "If we go, we should take Affie. She likes to be in nature too."

Vater had sighed while Mutter gave me a tiny smile.

As it emerged, it was not altogether convenient to have Affie with us on the outing. Mutter and I stood with the other attendees at the equestrian center at the appointed time when the director of affairs from the Eintracht Social Club—a small man with the neatest, blackest mustache I had ever seen—flapped his hands in our direction.

"*You* will have to wait and travel in the last carriage on your own," he said. "I do not want to upset anyone by insisting they share their seat with a dog."

"Seat? Naturally, our dog will stay on the floor," said my mother.

"Even so," he replied, turning his back to talk to a woman in a frothy blue gown.

I took Mutter's elbow, and we stepped away, allowing others to move ahead of us.

"Really," she said, her nostrils flaring and her hat askew. "Such a scene about a little dog. City people are becoming more fastidious by the day."

"There's no rush, Mutter. The monastery has been there for centuries. It's not going anywhere. It will be peaceful to have a carriage to ourselves."

"This is meant to be a *social* outing, Bertha," she said.

We watched from a distance as the carriages lined up and, drawn by pairs of horses—most of them matching—rolled to where the picnickers were assembled. Harnesses jingled, hooves clip-clopped on the cobblestones, and cabs groaned and squeaked as men, women, and a few children clambered aboard.

With every horse brought before us, the expression on my mother's face relaxed. The furrow that had appeared on her forehead when Herr Neat Mustache shooed us to the back of the queue disappeared. Her mouth was soft, and her lips moved every so often as if in silent speech.

I bent to stroke Affie. "It's the horses," I whispered. "They bewitch her."

The crowd had thinned and there were only three carriages remaining when one of the dark bay horses harnessed to the coach in the middle grew agitated. She emitted a cry—more of a squeal than a neigh—and reared as far as the breeching and shaft of the carriage would allow. The horse alongside her stumbled, the cart shook, and the coachman roared.

"Halt! Halt, you dumb beasts!" he shouted, battling to stay seated.

The troubled horse screeched again, pawing the air with her front hooves, and collided into her partner. Clinging to his seat with one hand, the coachman raised his whip and brought it down on the horse's rump. Once. Twice. Three times. The animals jostled in fear and again, the unsettled animal tried to rear. The coachman lifted his arm once more.

"Enough! Stop! Stop it now!"

It was Mutter. Skirts raised, she hopped off the pavement and ran to the horses. For a moment I thought the coachman was going to bring down the whip on her, but he froze, rod in the air as the leather straps fell onto the roof of the carriage. The horses, now alarmed by the arrival of my mother, jerked backward, eyes rolling. Mutter grabbed the agitator's reins in both hands.

"Quiet," she said, leaning toward the animal. "Quiet."

The horse grew still. My mother reached out to take the reins of the other animal too, brought their heads closer together, and whispered something that only she and they could hear. Finally, she lifted her eyes to glare at the coachman.

"Look," she said, jerking her head toward the horse's chest. "Her belly band is twisted. The buckle is stabbing the poor animal. Get down and fix it while I hold them."

—

A while later, when we climbed into the last carriage, my mother was still breathing heavily. She flopped onto the seat and took off her hat. Affie lay at her feet.

"It's appalling," said Mutter, "what we do to horses. That man shouldn't be allowed near any animal. How could he not see that the horse was in pain? What good would whipping her do?"

I nodded, still stunned by how quickly she'd spotted the problem and calmed the horses. I sat opposite her and spread out my skirts. It had turned warm, and I thought again how convenient it was to have the carriage to ourselves. A voice at the door indicated this was not the case.

"Good morning. What a relief. I thought I was late!"

A tall, lean man filled the doorway and, removing his hat, crouched to avoid bumping his head on the roof. He glanced at Affie—and my skirts spanning the seat—and sat alongside Mutter.

"Good morning," said my mother, fanning herself with her hat. "You *are* late. We were held up by an incompetent coachman."

"Oh. I'm sorry about that but also grateful," said the man, catching my eye fleetingly. "I mean, I would've missed the outing otherwise."

Mutter took in his dusty shoes, slightly too-short trousers, and unfashionable jacket with sleeves so long they almost reached his knuckles. Certainly, he didn't reflect any of the polish and promise she and Vater had hoped I might encounter that day.

The carriage lurched, and we were on our way. The man felt about in his jacket pockets, eventually retrieving not one but two watches. He held them side by side, scrutinizing them as if comparing their reliability. I took the opportunity to examine him more closely.

His narrow face was smooth and clean shaven but for a symmetrical, English-style mustache that seemed to flow from his nose, which, long and straight, reminded me of those featured on the faces of Greek statues I'd seen illustrated in schoolbooks. His dark, glossy hair was combed back to reveal an expansive forehead and deep-set, serious eyes. He might've been shabbily dressed, but the stranger was handsome. As Elise might've said, he was "well assembled." He put the watches in two different pockets, glanced up, and saw me staring. I looked away.

He cleared his throat. Mutter looked at him. "Thank you for sharing your carriage," he said. "I am Herr Benz. Carl Benz."

"Frau Ringer and my daughter Bertha," she said.

He glanced at me again. Our eyes met briefly. This time, we smiled.

"What—if you don't mind me asking, Frau Ringer—caused the delay?" he asked, eyes back on Mutter. "You mentioned a coachman."

I rubbed my neck, twitchy at the thought of my mother's wrath at the coachman being reignited. Sure enough, she sat upright and, fanning her face with her hat once again, recounted the incident. She described in minute detail what had happened, pausing occasionally to ensure that Herr Benz was keeping up. He nodded encouragingly as she fumed about the ineptitude of the coachman and his rough treatment of the distressed horse, and the way horses were treated in general. Her voice rose and her nostrils splayed. Affie stood and slunk closer to me.

"Every time I venture into the streets, I'm dismayed again by how horses are maltreated by the very people who rely so heavily on them for their daily business," she finally concluded. "It's distressing, infuriatingly so. Something should be done."

"Horseless carriages," said Herr Benz when Mutter paused long enough for him to interject.

We stared at him.

"Horseless carriages?" my mother echoed, as if she, too, thought she might've misheard him.

"Yes. Horseless carriages. A vehicle like the locomotive but without the rails. A self-driving vehicle for the road that doesn't need tracks. A carriage, like this," he said, gesturing to the space around us, "but without the horses. A horseless carriage. That's what we need."

Mutter leaned back, staring at him, her eyes narrow. "Yes. Well, I do not—"

"It's my plan. To invent and build horseless carriages to carry two, three, or four people. Imagine, every home and place of business might have one," he said.

Mutter sighed and began fanning herself once more. We hadn't yet reached our destination and she seemed exhausted.

"But how?" I asked, unable to curb my curiosity. "How do you imagine that's possible? Will your horseless carriage be powered by steam? Like a locomotive?"

Herr Benz looked at me. His eyes were bright, much brighter than I had realized.

"You understand how trains are powered?" he asked.

"Yes, of course. I *am* educated. Also, my father is a businessman. I listened when the process was explained to him many years ago. Well?"

He blinked and seemed uncertain. I was disappointed. He didn't have a plan.

"No, erm, the carriage will not be powered like a train. I want to invent a machine that runs under its own power like a locomotive but not on rails. Rather, it will move like a wagon, simply, on any street."

Mutter had had enough. "I dream of a world where horses are not enslaved for our convenience, Herr Benz, but I fear your dream is even more impossible than mine."

He leaned forward and tried to respond. "It could be—"

She ignored him. "Even if you had a solution—and I see you do not—your idea of an unnatural machine like a horseless carriage for every house and business would not be accepted by others. Not by many, anyway. It's artificial. Goes against nature. Against God," she said.

"Ah, but, Frau Ringer, did God not give us the means to create? Are we not doing God's work by using our brains and hands to invent and build new things? Is the train not an example of this?" he asked.

Mutter shrugged. "I'm just warning you about how others will respond to your ludicrous…I mean, *ambitious* idea," she replied, looking out the window as if that was her last word on the subject. Or perhaps she'd lost interest. I had not.

"So, if your carriages will not be powered by horses or steam, how will they move?" I asked. "Will we pedal them ourselves like velocipedes?"

"It's possible they'll be powered by gas," he said.

"Gas?" I echoed.

"Yes. A few engineers are already working on the idea. I have some ideas sketched out myself."

"Are you an engineer?" I asked.

He nodded. "I am a foreman at the Gebrüder Benckiser Engineering Works in the city."

"Is that where you are inventing the horseless carriage?" I asked.

His cheeks reddened. "No. Bridges. I design bridges."

Mutter turned to him, her interest suddenly revived. "Bridges?" she repeated.

He nodded.

"Hmm," she murmured. "Are you meeting friends at Maulbronn?"

Herr Benz glanced at his feet. "No. I came alone."

"Ah! So would you like to join us at the picnic?" she asked.

CHAPTER 5

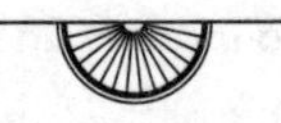

1869
Maulbronn Monastery, Germany

Mutter would say later that she invited Herr Benz to picnic with us despite his outmoded attire and tardy timekeeping because she'd never seen me so interested in a man. Moreover, he was educated and designed bridges. That promised something, didn't it? It was possible, she reasoned, that he and my father might share business interests.

She was right that I was fascinated by Herr Benz. He was nothing like Gustav, Werner, or any of the men Vater had invited to the house. With their prescribed civility, measured opinions, and ordinary ideas, those men were interchangeable, forgettable. Herr Benz, on the other hand, was remarkable, particularly when he spoke about the horseless carriage. I'd never encountered anyone as excited by an idea. As if discerning a fizzing in the air, even Affie raised her head from the carriage floor as Herr Benz described his fantasy self-driving road vehicle. Regrettably, his fervor dwindled when we arrived at Maulbronn.

Mutter led the way between the chalky walls of the medieval monastery as we went to join the rest of the party. I followed, inhaling the cool, musty aroma that spoke of darkness; damp, poor ventilation; and old age. Herr Benz was some distance behind. I'd been before, but the stature of the Romanesque arcades, elevated ceilings, rows of ornate pilasters, and massive Gothic stained-glass windows fascinated me anew. What visionaries the twelfth-century Cistercian monks had been. What skilled craftsmen they must have engaged as builders. Or had the monastics done the work themselves?

As we approached the cloister hall, where the others were already seated for the music performance, I paused to wait for Herr Benz. He walked slowly, looking left, right, up, and down, his expression impartial.

"Have you been here before?" I whispered, hoping to reignite some of the energy I'd admired earlier.

He shook his head, saying nothing as we took our seats. The choir, accompanied by an organist, began singing, the sounds bringing the chamber to life. As one melody faded and another began, I glanced at Herr Benz. He stared ahead, still impassive. Where was the excited inventor? What an unusual man he was.

A blossom-covered magnolia tree monopolized the courtyard where the picnic was to be held. After she'd walked around the tree, leaning in to breathe in the lemony scent of the pink flowers, Mutter asked Herr Benz if he'd enjoyed the music.

"Ja," he said without further elaboration.

I wondered if he'd been to such a concert before. Perhaps he lacked the words to describe whether the performance had moved him or not. Or maybe music didn't touch him at all. My mother glanced at me and gave a dismissive shrug. We were an awkward trio.

"The food awaits!" called Herr Neat Mustache from the far side of the courtyard. "You are to serve yourselves."

The spread, arranged on a wide wooden table in the center of the lawn, was substantial. There were delicate bread rolls topped with smoked trout, and combinations of celery, cheese, and ripe tomatoes held together with creamy dressing. Two large platters of sausages—I counted six varieties—were quickly depleted, as were several plates of hard-boiled eggs, slices of ham, and portions of roast fowl. There was beer and wine, and the meal ended with sugary-topped apple cake and coffee. The picnickers were more earnest than one might expect of a gathering where the purpose was to socialize, and there was little mealtime conversation. It was as if the holy setting commanded dedicated and silent mastication.

As Mutter swallowed a final bite of cake and dabbed her mouth with a napkin, her eyes rested on Herr Benz, who leaned against a wall, his head bowed over a plate and his jaws champing. I saw her bosom rise and fall. Was she wondering how to relay the disappointment of the outing to my father?

I looked around for Affie. She was tiptoeing across the grass as if to avoid the fallen magnolia blossoms. The dog was also sniffing purposefully.

"I shall take her out that way," I told my mother, pointing to a gate that opened onto a grove of trees.

"Yes. Quickly," she said, acknowledging the urgency of Affie's nosing.

A vineyard grew on the hillside behind the trees. I'd not meant to walk far, but Affie ran ahead, and I followed her up a track alongside the vines. The grapes had recently been harvested, and, where a few had fallen from the baskets and been trampled, their splattered remains created syrupy gatherings of insects. I paused to watch their industry. How purposeful they were. When I looked up, I saw the dog rummaging in the long grass at the top of the hill.

"Affie!" I called. "Come! We must go back."

She ignored me and disappeared into the undergrowth. I continued my ascent.

The view from the crest unfolded in a series of green meadows, orchards, and vineyards. Cattle dotted some of the paddocks, and in the distance beyond the glistening waters of a lake, I saw the dark fringes of the forest. Two roads, one of which we had probably taken to reach the monastery, cut through the landscape like sandy ribbons going north to south and east to west.

"Ah. The view. That's why you didn't come when I called," I told Affie as I lowered myself to sit on the grass. She wagged her tail and leaned against my arm.

Drawn by a white pony, a cart filled with fruit or vegetables—exactly what, I could not discern from so far away—rolled up the road silently, turned a corner, and disappeared. Would I have heard it if it were operated by a machine? There would no doubt have been noise and smoke. How would that have detracted from the peace of the countryside?

"I wondered what you hoped to find up here."

It was Herr Benz. He stood a few meters away as we looked into the valley for several minutes. It was silent but for the call of a dove somewhere in the trees below. The sun was warm on my back and the breeze cool on my face. Eventually, I rose, dusting my skirt.

"I should return."

"Would it be inappropriate for me to accompany you?" he asked.

"Probably."

He hesitated.

"But just as inappropriate for you to allow me to wander around the countryside alone," I added.

He fell into step with me. I felt tiny beside him.

"I was watching the road, trying to imagine what it might be like to see a horseless carriage traveling there," I said.

"Do you mock me?" he asked, his voice low.

"No. I'm intrigued by your idea. You seem determined. I wonder, though, if determination will be enough. It's...well, an ambitious idea, and you seem unsure about the details."

He scowled, glancing at me from beneath his eyebrows. I'd insulted him.

I tried to make amends. "Obviously, every invention begins with uncertainty. It's just—"

Herr Benz cut me off. "My father was one of the first men to operate a train on the line between Karlsruhe and Heidelberg. When people first saw the locomotive, some insisted it was impossible for it to move without the help of horses. They examined the tracks. Even dug up sections. They suspected teams of horses were somehow concealed below ground and harnessed to the train. That the train moved independently of horses was inconceivable to them. Just as the idea of a horseless carriage is inconceivable to you."

"No, you misunderstand me, Herr Benz. It's not that I find it inconceivable; it simply hasn't been done yet. But are *you* the man to do it?"

He chuckled, sounding uncertain rather than amused. "Why not?"

Because you design bridges, I thought but did not say. There didn't seem to be a way of answering directly without being even more impolite. I changed tack.

"Does your father still operate a train?"

"No. He died when I was a baby," he replied.

"I'm sorry, but how—"

"My mother spoke about him throughout my childhood. He was excited by the locomotive and by what might come afterward. He was fascinated by the possibilities. My mother raised me alone, determined to honor what my father hoped for me. No standard school was good enough if I was to follow his footsteps. Though I still wonder how she afforded it, my mother sent me to the finest lyceum school in Karlsruhe and, when I was sixteen, to university. I was educated so that…well, the way I see it, I can live out my father's legacy."

I was intrigued. "What do you mean?"

"My father's father and his grandfather were blacksmiths. His brother too. The family was angry when my father left them for the city, wanting to work on the train. They called it 'the devil's car.' My father wanted to be part of the future and not the past. He didn't want to equip horses to pull carriages like his grandfather and father did. He wanted to be part of whatever came next in transport and travel. I want to do the same."

"And so you dream of a horseless carriage?"

"Yes. A self-driving vehicle that travels not on rails but on the road."

"This carriage, you said, will be powered by gas. How will that work?" I asked.

He turned to examine my face for a moment, as if to assess the seriousness of my question before continuing.

"As you rightly said earlier, the answer to that is not clear. I imagine, though, that it will have an engine. A combustion engine. Not like the external combustion engines used by trains, which rely on coal burnt outside the engine." He stopped to look at me once more. "Do you understand how a steam engine is powered to draw a train?"

"I do," I replied, wondering if he hadn't believed me earlier. "As I mentioned, I'm educated, and understood when my father and his business colleagues discussed it."

Herr Benz nodded, urging me on like an eager tutor. I took a deep breath and recited what I'd learned.

"Burning coal heats water, and the engine uses the force produced by steam pressure to push a piston back and forth inside a cylinder. This is transformed into rotational force by a connecting rod and crank to turn the wheels," I said, hoping he wouldn't ask for more detail.

He stared at me, silent for a moment.

"Ja. There are hundreds of other parts necessary even for the smallest locomotive, but that's right," he said as we began walking again. "Well, there is another kind of engine invented by a Frenchman, Monsieur Lenoir. The locomotive has an external combustion engine where the heat is created outside of it. The internal combustion engine—Monsieur Lenoir's machine—works differently. Here, instead of heating up the fuel on the outside, a mixture of gas and air is inserted into the engine and ignited to cause tiny explosions, or combustions, in an enclosed space. The energy produced by this compels movement and can be used the same way energy caused by steam in a locomotive is."

"And this, erm, this internal combustion engine is the one you believe could move your horseless carriage?" I asked, trying not to smile at the pleasure I felt listening to him describe the machine in such detail. He knew I understood.

"Yes, I believe so. There are many things to work out, but it's possible. Of that, I'm certain!"

I glanced at him, increasing my pace to keep up. He walked with energy and purpose. His eyes were bright. The fire that had disappeared at the monastery was back.

—

The carriages were lined up near the gates by the time Herr Benz and I returned. Mutter peered over several hats and beckoned to me. I hurried to her side.

"Sorry. Affie went a little—" I began.

She shook her head as if to quiet me.

"There you are, Bertha," she said in an uncharacteristic singsong voice. "Let me introduce you to Frau Volk and her son, Eberhard. Frau Volk is Werner's mother's sister, so Eberhard is Werner's cousin. Imagine! They have recently moved to Pforzheim. It's as if we are family already."

I'd noticed Frau Volk earlier when we ate. She was a petite woman with hair so blond it was almost white. Wearing a pale-yellow dress with matching gloves, she made me think of the canary one of my mother's friends kept in a bamboo cage. I wondered if Frau Volk could sing. I'd seen Eberhard at her side, too, but hadn't pictured them as mother and son. His pristine black suit and white shirt might've been worn by a clergyman. Add to that a dense black beard and small round spectacles, and he looked old enough to be her brother.

We greeted one another and exchanged chitchat about Werner and Elise. Frau Volk said she was sorry to have missed the wedding. She was pleased to hear that my sister and her husband had settled well in America. Eberhard stood mutely at her side, blinking as if unaccustomed to the sunshine. I tried to appear interested while furtively looking about for Herr Benz. He'd disappeared.

"Perhaps we could travel home together, get to know one another better," said Frau Volk, smiling at my mother.

"Yes. That would be splendid," she replied.

Eberhard looked at me, eyelids still fluttering.

I glanced at Mutter. "We should not forget—"

"I'm sure he will be perfectly fine with someone else," she said.

"We should not forget *Affie*," I repeated, gesturing to the terrier at my feet.

Frau Volk and Eberhard looked at each other. He opened his mouth as if to speak at last, but she beat him to it. "Oh, how sweet! We are fond of dogs. Are we not, Eberhard?"

He blinked faster.

It was settled: Mutter, Affie, and I would share a carriage with the Volks. I looked for Herr Benz again. I didn't want to leave without explaining or saying goodbye. I wondered what I might say to him to convince him to call on me in Pforzheim. Still, he was nowhere to be seen. One or two carriages had left. Had he already gone?

Mutter took my arm, and we followed Frau Volk and Eberhard.

"They're a prominent family," she whispered. "Herr Volk owns several businesses in Mannheim, and this is the oldest son. He seems pleasant."

"Hmm," I replied.

"Please, Bertha. Let the day not be a *complete* waste. You nearly ruined it by walking unchaperoned with Herr Benz. Thank goodness he's so easy to overlook."

I pulled my arm away and looked at her. "That's untrue and unkind, Mutter. He might not wear the finest outfit, but he is interesting and intelligent and nothing like—"

"Bertha!" she hissed.

I said no more as a carriage pulled up and Eberhard helped Frau Volk get in. He held a hand to my mother.

"No, no, no!" came the voice of Herr Neat Mustache as he trotted toward us. "I'm afraid the dog cannot go in that cab."

Eberhard looked at Mutter as if expecting her to argue. She held his gaze, willing him to be gallant and protest on her behalf.

"Erm, well, we do not mind," said Eberhard with little conviction.

The organizer waved his hands. "That might be so, but as I explained when we left this morning, the ladies with the dog will have to wait for the last carriage. I want everyone to travel home the way they arrived this morning," he said.

Mutter stepped forward. "That's unreasonable. These people are family!"

Herr Neat Mustache ignored her and hastily propelled two other women ahead of us, practically shoving them into the carriage with the Volks.

Frau Volk poked her head out of the window and called to Mutter. "I shall stop by next week to arrange something," she tweeted, reminding me again of the canary.

Mutter's nostrils flared. "Affie will stay at home in future," she said.

At last, the final carriage drew up and we got in. My mother collapsed onto the seat, took off her hat, and leaned back. Affie lay at her feet, and I sat opposite. The carriage rocked.

"Just in time!" said Herr Benz, ducking his head as he climbed in. "I was examining the wine press and forgot to check my watch."

—

That night, I wrote to Elise, explaining in the final paragraphs of my letter:

I thought for a moment that Mutter was going to emit a loud groan when she saw him, but she was too exhausted to do anything more than roll her eyes. We'd barely left when I heard a light thump. Her hat had fallen to the floor, and she was sound asleep. It meant Carl—he insisted I use his first name—and I were able to talk freely again.

I wanted to ask him about his mother. What a remarkable woman she must be to have raised and educated him alone. However, he began talking about Professor Ferdinand Redtenbacher—it was very important to him that I got the name correct—who was director of the Polytechnic University of Karlsruhe, where Carl studied. It was the professor who convinced Carl that steam power is a thing of the past and that engineers must find other means of running engines. Carl said that he and Professor Redtenbacher discussed many different ideas, at least one of which he believes could lead to inventing a horseless carriage. When I asked him if he was still in touch with the professor, he looked stricken for a moment. Alas, the teacher was dead. Carl was among the students to carry his coffin. It was an awkward moment, and I feared I'd spoilt our talk, but he recovered, and our discussion continued.

As I listened to him talk and saw his excitement, I realized that it is indeed conceivable that Carl will invent a horseless carriage. What imagination, Elise! It occurred to me as he spoke that one cannot achieve anything that one cannot imagine. Is that not what holds many of us back? A failure of imagination? He has imagination and such passion for the idea. He has what it takes to be an inventor. I've never seen such a thing in any other person! And that he spoke so freely to me about his ideas, never questioning that I might not understand him because I am a woman! It was the most wonderful day.

But he insists that it's not just that he is excited about inventing a machine that will replace horse-drawn carriages. Despite his dedication to physical fitness, mostly through gymnastics and rowing, Carl says his legs grow tired from pedaling his velocipede, which he refers to as 'the boneshaker.' He imagines adding an engine to it so that he can ride it wherever, whenever he wants. And why not?

"I'd rather wear out a machine than my legs!" said he.

Elise, Carl might be the most earnest man I have ever met, and yet he made me laugh. I asked him if he would bring his boneshaker to the house so that I could see the contraption that threatens to wear his legs out. He said he would, so it seems that I will see Carl Benz again.

CHAPTER 6

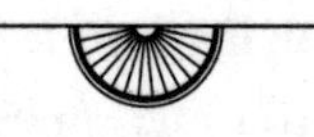

1869
Pforzheim, Germany

I SAW CARL'S BONESHAKER. NOT ONCE BUT SEVERAL TIMES. THE FIRST TIME he rode it to the house, Mutter, Herbert, Julius, Thekla, and I gathered in the courtyard to examine it. It was a spindly contraption made of wood and iron, with a tall front wheel and a smaller one at the back. I looked closely to see that, while the wheels and their spokes were made of wood, a thin band of metal was fitted to the outer parts of each wheel to protect the timber from the roads.

"Why is it so tall?" asked Herbert.

Carl pointed to the pedals, which were attached to the center of the front wheel. "So that the rider can get further with every stroke. If the front wheel was small, you'd have to pedal a great deal more and much faster to get anywhere."

Herbert nodded.

"The larger wheel helps make it a little less bumpy too," added Carl.

I looked at the wooden seat fitted on top of a small spring. Carl explained that the spring was there to provide comfort from the vibrations caused by bumpy roads. Surely, I thought, a wider seat would be more comfortable? I was about to suggest as much when the gate swung open. It was Vater. If Mutter had told him about Carl, neither had mentioned it to me. As it was, my father was so intrigued by the velocipede that he paid scant attention to its owner.

"You can ride this machine?" he asked, finally acknowledging Carl when Mutter introduced them.

"Yes, Herr Ringer," said Carl. "It took some practice. Would you like to try? I shall hold it for you."

Herbert and Julius exploded with laughter. "Do, Vater, do!" shouted Julius.

The idea of our father with his short legs perched on the machine was comical, and I looked away to conceal a smile.

Mutter shushed the boys, and Vater walked around the machine, pausing to test its weight. It was, he grunted, heavy.

"If you don't want to ride it, can I?" asked Herbert.

"Nobody is going to ride it," said Vater. "Most certainly not on the cobbles."

He looked at Carl. "Did you practice on it in a meadow? Learn how to balance and pedal it on the grass in case you fell?"

"No. Grass is too soft. It creates too much resistance and makes it harder to pedal. I learned on a country lane, where the road was smooth but not too sandy. As it was, it took me more than two weeks to master," said Carl.

Vater nodded. "And when you want to stop?" he asked.

"This is the brake," said Carl, pointing to a metal lever on the underside of the frame below the handles. "When you pull it like this, it presses this wooden pad against the back wheel."

"I see. That's clever, but it must be tiring. Pedaling and doing all the work yourself, I mean."

"It is. Particularly going uphill. That is why I imagine fitting an engine to it. And another wheel, perhaps, so that it is not as difficult to balance."

My father straightened, put a hand to his hip, leaned back, and looked at Carl as if truly seeing him for the first time.

"Engine?" he asked.

That was Mutter's cue to round up my brothers, sister, and me and insist we go inside to prepare for dinner.

"But it's too early," said Herbert.

"Inside!" she said, looking directly at me. I tried to catch Carl's eye, but he was looking at his boneshaker.

When I came downstairs a little later, my parents were in the hallway.

"You invited him to dinner on Friday? Why?" asked Mutter.

"He has interesting ideas."

My mother's voice had risen a pitch or two. "What? The engine? The horseless carriage? Is that what you're interested in?"

"No. Certainly not. That is youthful fantasy. I'm not a fool. About using iron to reinforce arched doorways. He also has useful knowledge about equipment to lift heavy materials. He's in the bridge-building business," replied my father.

"I know, but—"

She stopped speaking when she saw me, shrugged, and walked away.

Vater glanced at me with a frown. I smiled. If Mutter *had* voiced any concerns to him about my interest in Carl following the picnic, my father had clearly forgotten them.

So it was that Vater, not I, invited Carl to our home again. It was an easy evening. My father had many questions for him. They spoke about building—new techniques and different materials and how designs for bridges could be adapted to construct better buildings and vice versa. The meal was nothing like the lunch we'd endured at the home of the Volk family the previous weekend, when Vater and Eberhard had found nothing in common beyond their fondness for beer. That event had been saved by Frau Volk and Mutter, who, determined to maintain a semblance of conviviality, had kept the gathering animated with their chatter about various family members we had in common.

Now, with Carl at the table, Mutter was quiet and eventually stopped watching me. I kept my eyes averted from our guest but listened closely. It's possible my mother imagined that I'd grown bored with Carl. Nothing could've been further from the truth. I was particularly intrigued by how excited he became when he told Vater about his recent visit to Vienna and the city's preparations for the World's Fair in 1873.

"The gates to the Herausgeber Technical Museum are under construction," he said. "What a combination of art and engineering they are. It's worth the trip just to see them, Herr Ringer. The entrance will frame the rotunda, which is where the machines will be exhibited."

"I've heard it said that Vienna will be transformed by the fair. Such is Emperor Franz Joseph's ambition that the event should outshine the previous one in Paris," said Vater.

"Ja. There's an enormous amount of work underway, with no expenses spared. New designs and materials will be used by some of the world's best designers, engineers, and artisans," said Carl.

"Is your company involved?" asked Vater.

"Yes, but unfortunately it's only a small project, and I won't have the chance to visit Vienna again soon. However, I hope to go there for the fair."

"Perhaps, since it is currently the center of engineering developments, you should look for other work in Vienna. It would surely be an exciting experience for a young engineer like yourself," said my father, expressing the same thoughts I'd been having.

Carl did not respond.

"Why not?" asked Vater.

"It's not that I haven't considered it. However, it'll take me far from my mother, who is not in the best of health," he replied quietly.

"Ah, your mother. There's no one else to take care of her?"

Carl shook his head and briefly explained how he and his mother had been alone after the death of his father. My father stopped chewing to listen and, when Carl stopped speaking, said, "I understand. I, too, did not know my father."

—

Later that night, as I lay in bed, I thought about Carl's reluctance to go to Vienna. If I were his mother, I would want him to go. Had she not done everything she could to ensure he received the best-possible education? Would he, without his mother's determination and inevitable sacrifice, have become an engineer? Now, with the world's finest scholars, inventors, and businessmen in his profession gathered in Vienna to create machines and techniques that would shape the future, he should join them. Surely, if she knew, his mother would insist upon it. Would she not be disappointed that he chose, rather, to stay in Pforzheim and accept the boredom of designing bridges? He wanted to be an inventor; I was certain that she would support his ambition. It was, I decided, my responsibility to convince Carl that his mother would want him to pursue his dream.

The opportunity arose a week later, when Herbert and I accompanied Carl to meet my father at one of the buildings the company was working on. Vater wanted Carl's advice on reinforcing the doors. Mutter was not home that afternoon to object to my going to a building site.

"Have you given any more thought to working in Vienna?" I asked as I sat opposite Carl in the carriage.

He and Herbert peered at me as if I were speaking a foreign language.

"You sounded eager to go," I continued, holding Carl's gaze. "I can't imagine why you would think your mother would not want you to. Is she not your greatest supporter?"

"Yes, but—"

"Have you spoken to her about it?"

"No, it's not something that I would discuss with her."

"Why not? Because she's a woman? You don't believe that she, the one who worked so hard to give you the best-possible future, deserves to know that you are letting an opportunity like Vienna pass you by?"

Herbert turned away to look out the window. He was embarrassed by my brazenness. I didn't care. I'd seen Carl's passion when he spoke about the horseless carriage. It excited me and I wanted to see it again.

"It's not that," said Carl, leaning toward me. "She is unwell and showing no sign of recovery. My aunt is taking care of her in Gondelsheim. I can visit on weekends. I couldn't do that if I was in Vienna."

"But—"

"I know," he said, his eyes on mine. I saw sadness there. Also love. "But she is... Without her I'm alone."

"No," I whispered, allowing my heart to speak. "You're not."

CHAPTER 7

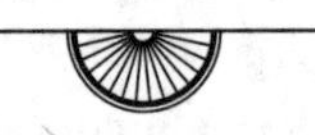

1870
Pforzheim, Germany

Herbert was officially responsible for Carl's next few visits to our home. After he'd badgered him for days, my brother convinced Vater that he should receive boneshaker lessons from Carl. The idea was that Herbert would get his own velocipede when he turned eighteen.

"Imagine how helpful it will be for business, Vater," my brother had reasoned. "I'll be able to pedal around town and help when you need things done quickly."

By then, with his oldest son having accepted a permanent position at a furniture-making company, Vater had laid to rest any lingering hopes that our brother Karl might change his mind and join the family business after all. He now hoped Herbert would succeed him instead. As such, the boy's argument about the velocipede's usefulness as a business tool convinced Vater that Carl should indeed teach him to master the machine.

That was my cue to enter the discussion. It would, I insisted, be safer for two people to hold the contraption while Herbert was learning, which was why I should also attend the lessons.

In fact, it did not take Herbert long to steady himself above the two wheels, and soon he was riding away, leaving Carl and me alone. We didn't discuss Vienna again during that time. Carl did, however, show me his drawings of the trackless, horseless vehicle he imagined one day assembling.

"Early on, while I was still studying, my thoughts were dictated by ideas of creating a smaller version of the train. You can see it here," he said, opening his large brown notepad and pointing to a sketch of a locomotive perched far off the ground on wheels that could've been those of a carriage. "But even then, my machine was free of the rails. Whatever it ends up looking like, it will rule the streets on all sides—left to right, up, and down. There'll be no tracks to restrict it."

I examined the drawing. "It looks top-heavy. As if the wheels might not be able to support it."

He looked at me, blinking as though he'd forgotten how much I understood. "Yes, that was one of the problems." He turned the pages. "That's why, when I got the boneshaker, I began working on ideas based on the velocipede being powered by an engine. Human power must be replaced by machine power. Steam, gas, or something else. But what exactly, and how? That's what keeps me awake every night."

Several pages of the notebook were covered with intricate sketches of velocipedes with various rough attachments. Not all the detail made sense to me, nor did I recognize many of the parts he'd drawn. Carl had made notes alongside his sketches, but the words didn't clarify everything for me either. What was clear was how fascinated he was by the invention. I pictured him sitting in a small, poorly lit room at night, bowed over his book, his large, slender hand moving furiously as he recorded his thoughts on the page.

"And then this?" I said, pointing to a diagram that looked nothing like a velocipede.

"That was when I saw that my machine could not have two wheels. Learning to ride the boneshaker is not easy for everyone. Some think it's frightening. Too few people would be brave enough to make the effort to learn."

"So you gave it four wheels?"

"At that point, yes. I'm certain of nothing yet, but I realized that, in addition to how difficult the two-wheel machine might be for most people to master, it could be uncomfortable and limiting too. My machine should accommodate passengers. Most importantly, to be used on the streets and go wherever there are roads, it needs to be like a carriage and able to compete with the most elegant of cabs when it comes to comfort," he said.

"That makes sense."

Carl closed the book. "Yet the problem remains: How will it be powered? How will it be steered without rails to manage its wheels?"

"You're an engineer, an inventor. That's up to you work out, isn't it?" I asked.

He sighed. "My invention will, I'm afraid, have to remain a paper one. I lack everything necessary to actually create it: money, time, and opportunity."

"Now, yes, but that will surely change."

"Not while I'm at Gebrüder Benckiser Engineering Works," he said. "It's not just that I'm interested in designing machines and not bridges; it's also the frustration of working for bosses who have no vision for the future and having to motivate workers who are only interested in the money they receive each week."

"But isn't your job as a foreman to ensure that the workers do what's laid out before them every day?" I asked, thinking about how Vater had described the hierarchy of employees in his business.

Carl ran a hand over his head. "Why should I have to stand over them, check everything they do, and ask them to work faster? Don't they know that that's what is expected of them, day after day, week after week?" He grimaced. "It's why they're employed and paid. If they did what was asked of them without having to be urged and managed every hour of the day, I'd be able to work on new designs. I could come up with the ideas and answers that my bosses are incapable of imagining and inventing," he said.

It occurred to me that, raised as an only child, Carl was unaccustomed to being among people whose habits and methods were different from his. Unlike me, he hadn't experienced life with sisters and brothers whose ways, moods, likes, and dislikes varied. Carl hadn't learned that, while others might do things differently from him, it didn't necessarily mean that they and their ways were wrong. He was intelligent, educated, and ambitious. He'd attended university when he was just sixteen and had graduated quickly. Being clever and scholarly didn't mean he understood everything, though, did it?

"My father says a business is like a body," I said. "There are many different parts to it, each undertaking different actions and responsible for different things. The legs cannot do what the arms and hands do, or the other way around. If one part fails, it affects the functioning of the whole body. If you injure your foot, your whole body slows down."

He smiled and stepped closer, reaching for my hand. "Well, perhaps, but—"

"Wait. I'm not finished," I said, moving away. "You, your bosses, and the workers are different parts of the company. You each must do your own jobs to make the business a success. You must also remember that everyone is different. We don't have the same thoughts or the same ambitions."

"I know," he said, no longer smiling. "It frustrates me that people don't think the same way as I do."

I stared at him.

Carl exhaled. "You're right: it's unreasonable of me," he said.

I stepped toward him. How I wished we could always be so close. Carl took my hands in his. He'd become bolder recently. "I promise I'll be more tolerant, more patient, if only for you, Bertha."

That wasn't exactly what I wanted to hear. In fact, I wanted to object and say that he shouldn't do it for me but for himself. At that moment, though, there was a whoop and rattle as Herbert pedaled into sight. Carl and I stepped apart.

—

To my disappointment, I never met Carl's mother, who died in Gondelsheim a few weeks later. I was curious about the widow, who, despite being poor and uneducated herself, had worked and saved to educate her son. Although Carl and I didn't discuss it, I suspect she never knew that he had thought about going to Vienna. Despite my urging, he'd kept that dream from her. Isn't that what we do when we love people? Withhold truths to protect them?

Around the time that Frau Benz died, news of Germany's war against France loomed large, demanding our attention and, above all, eliciting fear. While Carl was exempt from signing up to fight because he was an only son, my brother Karl met the criteria for conscription. Our father might've been larger and slower than ever, but in this instance he acted fast. Within a week, Karl's journey to Milwaukee was booked and paid for.

"I didn't work this hard to raise a family and reputation so that my heir could die fighting a war I don't understand," said Vater, ignoring Mutter's worried shushing. She was, I'd overheard her saying to him earlier, afraid he'd be accused of sedition.

The walls of the house themselves seemed to breathe a sigh of relief once we'd bid our brother farewell. The war would go ahead, but no Ringers would take up arms. That afternoon, Herbert appeared in the doorway of the drawing room, where I was with Mutter, Amelia, and Thekla.

"Bertha, can I show you something? Out here," he said.

I followed him into the hallway. "What is it?"

"It's Carl. He's here to see you," he said, his voice low.

I glanced toward the drawing room.

"He asked me not to announce him. Wants to see you alone," Herbert explained. "I'll tell Mutter you went walking with someone. One of your friends from school. Take Affie. Or I'll come, too, and—erm—chaperone."

It was unlike Carl to initiate our meetings. Moreover, he disliked clandestine dealings of any nature. He'd never acknowledged that my helping him with Herbert's boneshaker training was simply a wily excuse for us to be alone. It's possible he rationalized that it could not be secretive because *he* wasn't in on the secret. This time, though, I didn't want to sneak out to be with him. It was a significant step for Carl to visit and ask to see me alone. My pulse raced. It was time to be candid with my family.

"No. No lies," I told Herbert, taking my coat from a hanger.

I pulled it on as I went back to the drawing room.

"Mutter, I'm going to walk Affie—with Herr Benz," I said.

She stared at me. "What? Herr Benz? No. I do not think that's a good idea."

"I'm not a girl, Mutter. It's not inappropriate. All will be well. I'll tell you and Vater all about it when I return," I said, turning to leave.

Carl looked up, eyes wide and uncertain, after Affie had greeted him at the door and I followed.

"We'll walk along the river," I said. "I presume you have time?"

"Yes, but—"

"I explained to my mother. We're not children."

We walked without talking until we arrived at the path that took us away from the road toward the Enz River.

"Thank you for the letter," said Carl. "Your sympathies were kind."

I'd seen little of him in the aftermath of his mother's death, and never alone. As such, I'd written to him. I wanted him to know that he was in my thoughts—always.

"How are you?" I asked.

"Better. Much better. I thought I was prepared; she was ill for so long. But I was mistaken. I'm getting accustomed to it, though."

"To her absence from this world?"

Carl nodded. "To her being gone."

"You'll—"

"No, please, Bertha. Don't say that she and I will be reunited in heaven."

It was not what I was going to say, but I didn't explain. We walked in silence once more, chuckling when Affie—now stiff-legged with old age—saw a field mouse in the grass and, long after it had disappeared, executed a halfhearted pounce in the direction the rodent had fled.

"I don't know what to do," said Carl eventually, giving a tuft of grass an unenthusiastic kick.

I didn't respond. He needed to do the talking.

"Gebrüder Benckiser. I can't work there any longer. I didn't study to be paid to be bored. The hours are long, and I have no time to work on my invention. When I do, my arms and hands are tired from the day's work, and my eyes suffer in the poorly lit factory."

He scuffed his shoes on the sandy path.

"I haven't added to my sketches in weeks. My bosses don't want to hear about my ideas, and the workers don't care if I tell them the same thing every day. The salary isn't good enough for me to save so that I can one day start my own business."

My stomach felt hollow, and my head whirred. There was a rushing sound in my ears. It wasn't the river. When I'd told my mother that I'd explain everything to her and Vater on my return, I'd imagined coming home having agreed with Carl that he should ask my father if we could get married. I'd been practicing my responses to their objections before I fell asleep for months. It hadn't occurred to me that Carl wanted to talk to me—again—about how miserable he was at work. I took a deep breath, rubbed my ears as if to rid them of the noise, and gave him my full attention.

"You should go to Vienna," I said.

Carl stopped. "What?"

I walked on.

"What did you say?" he asked, striding to catch up.

"I said you should go to Vienna. Find work you enjoy there. Learn as much as you can. Meet people who can help you work on things that interest you. Work on the design of your horseless carriage," I replied.

"But Vienna?"

"The only reason you didn't go was because of your mother. There's nothing holding you back now."

He stepped ahead and turned to face me, preventing me from walking on.

"Do you mean that? Is there *nothing* keeping me in Pforzheim?" he asked, his eyes searching mine.

"What do you mean, Carl? Can you say it?"

He looked at his shoes as if he might find the courage there. "If I go to Vienna, I will not have you."

"No. I will not be there, but that shouldn't stop you from going."

"But—"

I didn't have the patience to draw it out of him. "I'll be here, waiting for you. Waiting until you're ready—until we can afford to get married, and then I'll join you," I said.

He blinked. "Married?"

I nodded.

Carl glanced at his feet again. "Would you?" he asked.

"Why wouldn't I?" I replied, noting a tiny bump of doubt. Had I misunderstood how he felt about me? Why was it so hard for him?

He took my hands. "I'm poor, Bertha. You are… Your family is not. Your father has high expectations."

"Yes, he does. So do I. I have high expectations of you."

He pulled one of his hands from mine and rubbed the nape of his neck. We were silent for a moment. Eventually, Carl took a deep, shaky breath. "But what if I disappoint you?"

"How's that possible?" I asked, gently squeezing his fingers. "The day we met was the day I realized what it is in life that I hope for. When you told me and my mother about the horseless carriage, I recognized a fire in you. One that burns in me too. I don't want to stand by and watch your fire. I don't want to have to fight to keep mine burning. I want to be with you so that our fires can burn together. The only way to disappointment would be to allow our fires to dwindle and die. I don't believe that'll happen—if we're together."

—

Vater might have admired Carl's intellect and his willingness to share his engineering knowledge, but he didn't like the idea of him as a son-in-law.

"I tried to warn you," said my mother when, back from our walk, Carl and I told them that we were betrothed.

My father sat down, his cane falling to the floor. "But what about Eberhard Volk?" he said.

Carl shuffled his feet and glanced out the window. I touched his elbow, as if that might stop him from fleeing. He knew about Eberhard and how I felt about the other man, but I was ashamed that my father would ignore how his comment might affect Carl. It was unlike Vater to be cruel. I glared at him. He ignored me, so I transferred my look to Mutter. I'd repeatedly told her I wouldn't consider marrying Eberhard.

She ran a hand across her forehead and spoke without conviction. "Ja. He would be a better match."

"Herr Volk is *no* match," I said. "He doesn't want me, and I don't want him."

My mother wasn't ready to give up entirely. "It's not true that he doesn't want you, Bertha. You haven't given him a moment to get to know you."

"At least Eberhard can afford to keep you, Bertha," said my father. "Do you have any idea how much it costs to keep a house like this? The clothes? The carriages? The servants?"

"Emilie and Elise don't have servants," I replied, glancing at Carl. He shrugged.

My mother cast her eyes at the ceiling. "They live very differently. Are you going to go to America?"

"No. Carl is going to Vienna. When he's settled, we'll get married and live there."

Carl hadn't said a word since the initial announcement. I looked at him, hoping he would endorse our Viennese plans, but he didn't. I pushed on.

"It was your idea, Vater, that Carl should go to Vienna. It'll be a chance for him to work with great designers and engineers. He can gather the experience, knowledge, and money he needs to work on the horseless carriage. To become an inventor."

"You are not serious about *that,* are you?" asked my father, looking at Carl.

"Yes, Herr Ringer. I am. I know that it will require—"

Vater lumbered to his feet. "Then it's worse than I imagined," he groaned.

Mutter handed him his cane, and he hobbled from the room.

I wrote to Elise that night:

When Carl left, Mutter tried again to convince me that our betrothal was a bad idea. She argued that he might disappear in Vienna, which would be humiliating for me, particularly if Eberhard had found someone else by then. It was difficult not to laugh. Then she wanted to know why, if I cared so deeply for Carl, I was so eager for him to go to Vienna. You might wonder the same. So I shall explain.

There is nothing as important to Carl as his dream of creating a horseless carriage. I cannot compete with that dream. I want to be part of it. His eyes light up when he talks of it, and he is never more eloquent. Do you remember how Mutter explained how priests and nuns are "called by God" and how they willingly give up everything to serve Him? This dream calls to Carl. It gives him life. Going to Vienna now is the best chance he has of learning more about the equipment and designs that will help him create the machine. He is an inventor. He must invent. It is because I care so much for him that I want him to go. I will stand by him, support him, and encourage him at every point on his way to making his dream come true—regardless of how long it takes. That is my calling.

CHAPTER 8

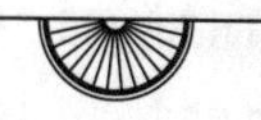

1871
Pforzheim, Germany

It didn't take Carl long to find work in Vienna, which was promising. His skills were clearly in demand. That would make him happy, I thought, picturing him bouncing on the balls of his feet as he executed an uncharacteristic strut on his way to work between rows of tall, modern buildings every morning. Vienna was, Vater insisted, the epitome of style and innovation.

However, Carl's letter, written but two weeks after he first hung his hat on the rack at his new place of work, dispelled my hopefulness. Working at the iron-construction company in the other city, he wrote, was no better than designing bridges at Gebrüder Benckiser. The owners were blinkered, the workers dispirited, and the work tedious. As he had complained in Pforzheim, the hours were long and left him no time to meet other engineers, examine different projects, or devote any thoughts to his own designs. Adding to his woes, Carl was unable to find a Viennese gymnasium or rowing club he could afford. He was frustrated, bored, *and* increasingly unfit.

I didn't bother to disguise my disappointment when Vater, having intercepted the letter from the carrier at the front door earlier, asked for news. He listened, puffing his cheeks, as I listed Carl's grievances.

"He's only twenty-seven and yet so impatient," said Vater. "Doesn't he *want* to learn from others?"

I glared at him. "Obviously, he does. As you know, that's why he went to Vienna: to meet other engineers and see new things so that he could work on his design, start inventing the machine in earnest."

"Ja, inventing his machine. Hmm. Don't you see that the problems he had here are recurring in Vienna? It's a new city, new company, new people, and different products. The only thing that's the same is Carl, and yet..." He lifted his cane to accessorize a shrug.

I understood his point but said nothing.

"You know, I think *he* is the problem, Bertha," said my father, mistaking my silence for ignorance or denial.

I went to the window and gazed out onto the street. It was early evening, and the town was quiet. A laundry wagon pulled by a large black-and-white horse clattered by as three boys scampered down the street in the other direction. Their shrill shouts and laughter lingered as they disappeared. When Carl had left for Vienna, I imagined following him soon after. Now I wondered if I'd ever leave Pforzheim. Vater lumbered to my side.

"There is no doubting Carl's intelligence and ambition," he said. "We know that. However, he needs to accept that he must work with others, *for* others until he can afford to set up something himself. Is he too stubborn to acknowledge that? I worry for him, but mostly I worry for you. It's not too late."

"Please, Vater, not again," I said, stepping around him to leave the room.

I didn't want to hear once more how it was not too late for me to break off the engagement. My parents dragged the idea into every conversation they could, despite my unswerving response that *nothing* would induce me to give up Carl. The twinges of frustration I experienced at his restlessness didn't diminish my love for him. No one held my attention the way Carl did, nor—without ever having said as much—had me believe that my voice was and always would be equal to his. I was eager to share his life. However, I couldn't deny that my father was right about my betrothed's aversion to working with others, and how it hindered him and might affect our future. I'd seen it before; neither tolerance nor patience came easily to Carl. At the same time, the distance between his dream and reality was immense. The only way to reduce it would be for him to keep working for others, save what he could, and remain inspired by his dream until he could afford to devote himself to it. I wondered what I could do or say to encourage him to be more tolerant of others and to learn patience without belittling him or sounding officious.

That evening, I wrote to Carl, telling him how much I loved and missed him. I described what a warm summer we were having and explained how much Herbert enjoyed riding his new velocipede. Erwin and Julius were eager to try it, but Herbert wouldn't let them near it. I described how thin and listless Affie had become and how old age seemed to have suddenly seized her. My letter contained none of my worries about him. Perhaps it was cowardly, but I couldn't express my concerns with so great a distance between us. I sealed the letter and tried to convince myself all would be well. Carl just needed time to settle in Vienna, didn't he?

As it was, he came up with an alternative. Indeed, Carl's next letter, which arrived just a week later, could've been written by another man. Whereas the previous one had been two pages of inked complaining, the words of the new one—a full four pages—contained so much energy and optimism they risked hopping out of the envelope of their own accord. It's possible he was now truly bouncing on the balls of his feet as he walked the streets of Vienna. What had changed? Carl had met August Ritter.

—

I was introduced to August Ritter two months later when he and Carl were in Pforzheim. By then, Vienna was a thing of the past. Carl and Herr Ritter—also an engineer—were to establish their own company, Carl Benz and August Ritter Mechanical Workshop.

"Like yours, his father is a master builder," said Carl as we waited for his business partner to arrive at my parents' house. "But in Mannheim. Herr Ritter Senior will help us set up the business, but August and I will be the owners. It's a full partnership. We're looking for premises."

"Where?" I asked.

"Mannheim. It makes sense because that's where August's connections are. And those of his father. It's where our customers will come from."

It *seemed* to make sense, but I didn't know Mannheim. The city, little more than one hundred kilometers away from Pforzheim, was much closer to my hometown than Vienna, but it was foreign to me. I'd imagined living in Vienna. I'd pictured it and looked forward to it. The notion of going to Mannheim was new. All I knew about the place was that the harbor, built on the Rhine less than forty years previously, had brought a great deal of business there and that it was growing.

"It's a beautiful city," said Carl, sensing my uncertainty.

Before I could reply, there was a knock on the door: Herr Ritter had arrived.

"Fräulein Ringer! At last!" he said, gliding across the floor as if on skates. "I feel I know you. Carl speaks of nothing else!"

I glanced at Carl. He pulled at his collar and looked at his shoes. We both knew that it wasn't true; Carl would've mentioned me but no more than that. He didn't easily talk of personal matters. I wondered why his new business partner felt it necessary to pretend otherwise. However, it wasn't the time for scrutiny, and I stepped forward to greet him.

August Ritter was a head shorter than Carl, but his stance was not that of a smaller man. His thick, blond hair was combed away from his face, creating a glossy helmet that bobbed as he spoke. His eyes were an unusual light blue, and his expression was that of someone who was accustomed to being admired. He was sleek, self-assured, garrulous, and nothing like Carl.

At dinner, August—as he insisted we address him—provoked a blush in my mother when he complimented her on the meal and again, moments later, when he admired the "most intricate work I have ever seen on a tablecloth." His theatrical descriptions of Vienna and the city's zealous flurry to prepare for the fair had my father almost choking with laughter.

"I mean no disrespect, but it's as if the place is being dressed and coiffed to attend a ball," said August, assuming an exaggeratedly serious expression. "And we all know what happens to the gowns, finery, and flamboyant hairstyles once the ball is over."

He even cajoled Carl into delivering an unusually verbose description of their plans for the new business in Mannheim. I couldn't remember so lively a dinner since Elise left.

"You were very quiet tonight," Carl said later as I walked with him to the front door to say good night.

I smiled. "What could I say to improve the already dazzling company?"

He frowned. "You don't like him?"

"I don't know him," I replied.

"Bertha, this is the opportunity we've been waiting for. August and I will work together to create a successful business. One that'll allow us to get married and me to work on the horseless carriage. It's exciting. We're on our way," said Carl, placing his hand on my arm.

"It *is* exciting," I said, allowing the tingle that raced through me at his touch to dispel my speculative misgivings that August might not be everything my beloved hoped.

Later, in bed, the doubts returned and kept me from falling asleep. I tried to assure myself that my worries were unfounded, caused only by how different Carl and August were. Even so, I spent a restless night.

At first light, I gave up the idea of sleeping, got up, dressed, and went downstairs. A walk with Affie would calm me, I thought, but the little dog wasn't in the scullery.

"No, I haven't seen her this morning," said Cook, who was scooping coals from the stove. "She was in the yard yesterday when I left."

I went outside, calling Affie's name quietly. She was nowhere to be seen. I opened the gate out of the yard and looked down the street. It was unlike her to leave the property but not impossible for her to have slipped out when the servants arrived earlier. The street was bare, and I returned to the yard to search. Eventually, I found her little body, curled up and motionless, behind the woodpile.

Herbert helped me wrap Affie in a small rug and carry her near the river. I sat, my hand on her lifeless body, while Herbert dug a deep hole beneath a large weeping willow, whose branches cast a dark shadow over the water. I thought about how many times I'd walked there with Affie—often with Elise, sometimes with the boys and my mother, and occasionally with Carl. I pictured her pouncing on insects in the grass, rushing at the ducks as they paddled on the river, and stretching out in the shade when we sat to rest on warm days. She'd been my comfort when my sisters left for America.

Pforzheim wouldn't be the same without her. Her death marked the end of an era for me. Perhaps it was also a sign confirming that Carl's move to Mannheim was for the good. We'd have a new start in a place I'd not always expect to see Affie.

—

Some weeks later, my mother and I took the train to Mannheim to look at the property Carl and August had purchased with money August borrowed from his father. I looked out the window as the train groaned, sighed, and hissed to a halt in the station. Carl had warned me that Mannheim station had been damaged during a recent storm. The building had been partially and haphazardly restored as a temporary structure while a new station was under construction elsewhere. Carl and August hoped that they'd be called upon to supply materials for the replacement building. I wondered what it might look like. Had Carl seen the plans? The old station seemed to have been built primarily of wood and was nothing like the shiny, marble-clad structure we knew in Pforzheim.

"It was a good life," said Mutter, getting to her feet to leave the train.

I looked at her, confused.

"You've been thinking about Affie. I see it on your face, and you've barely said a word all morning," she said.

"Oh. No. I mean—yes. Affie had a good life, and it's not the same without her, but I was not… Yes, you're right. I miss Affie," I said.

Indeed, I felt the dog's loss deeply, but it wasn't Affie I'd been thinking about on the train that morning. On the other hand, my preoccupation was easier explained by her death than by the truth: I was worried that Carl and August had gone into debt to buy land before they had any work on their books.

As it emerged, the seven-hundred-and-fifty square meters at Square T6, Number 11, Mannheim was a fine piece of land on the left bank of the Neckar River, which surprised me by being almost as large as the Rhine. Although it was on the edge of town, Carl and August's property was accessible to other businesses and not too far from the harbor. The area was a great deal less built up than what I was accustomed to in Pforzheim, which pleased me. Green fields and woody thickets suggested new beginnings and fresh opportunity. The misgivings I'd experienced were replaced with excitement, and as Carl showed us the site, I laid my hand on his arm and smiled at him. It had surprised me how much I'd missed him when he went to Vienna. It was, after all, at my insistence that he go. Now, in Mannheim, he was closer, and things were progressing. I longed to be with him permanently, to wake up alongside him, make a home with him, and work toward his dream every day. I loved his ambition, his brilliant mind, and his earnestness. Mostly I appreciated how certain I was of our love.

"You see, Mannheim is not that bad, is it?" he said, beaming down at me.

Carl unrolled the plans he and August had drawn up for the workshop on the road alongside the carriage. Because it was to be built quickly, the building would be constructed of wood. Carl pointed to the largest room, in which he said they would work on clients' designs and materials. They planned a slightly smaller workshop for Carl's horseless carriage.

I was surprised. "Really? You're going to start work on it soon?"

Carl ran a hand over his head as if his hair needed tidying before he replied. "Well, yes. As soon as possible. I mean, August agrees that as soon as we can afford it, I should get started."

"Hmm," murmured Mutter.

Carl glanced at her and then at me. I ignored them both and placed my finger on the plans, pointing to a tiny chamber adjacent to the workshop. "And this?" I asked.

"My living quarters," said Carl. "August will stay with his parents in town, but we agreed that I'll live here. It'll not be luxurious but suits me because it'll save money and allow me to work whenever I can."

My mother squinted at the drawing; her nose wrinkled. "You don't expect Bertha to live there when you're married, I hope," she said.

Before Carl could answer, the thudding of hooves drew our attention. It was August, on a large bay. He dismounted with a flick of a leg and landed on the road with a light hop. I couldn't help noticing how tailored and new his jacket was. Carl was wearing the same one he'd worn when we met on the way to Maulbronn two years ago.

"Frau Ringer! Fräulein Ringer!" August swooped his hat from his head and bowed theatrically.

Mutter nodded, her eyes on the horse.

"What an honor to have you visit our humble place of business. You approve, I hope?" he asked, looking at me.

August's energy and enthusiasm were affecting. It was difficult not to return his smile, nor did we turn down his offer to take another tour of the property. He strode ahead of us, waving his arms expansively as he described how the workshop would be set out and drawing our attention to the view toward the river and across the town, where the buildings seemed stacked close together and the streets were barely visible between the bricks. Carl was quiet but smiled when I caught his eye.

On the way back to the carriage, Mutter walked ahead with Carl, and August slowed to walk alongside me.

"Your betrothed showed you the plans, then?" he asked. "What do you think? We've allocated ample space for his dream machine, have we not?"

I looked at him, trying to gauge whether there was any scorn in his comment, but his expression was serious.

"Yes. To be frank, I was surprised to see that you've devoted a separated area to the carriage," I conceded.

"Oh, indeed! It was among his conditions of the partnership. And I wouldn't have it any other way," he said. "I've never seen anyone as passionate about a project as Carl is about his horseless carriage. He becomes a poet when he talks about how autonomous travel will revolutionize our lives. His dream of people climbing on machines and heading off whenever they want to without having to harness horses or direct coachmen is exhilarating. As is his determination to achieve it."

"We agree on that," I said, once again pleased that I'd made the trip to Mannheim.

"Has he shown you his latest sketches? Of the carriage?" he asked.

"Yes," I replied, although I couldn't be sure. Carl modified his plans and diagrams often. It was possible he'd come up with new ideas since I'd last seen the drawings.

"Adding more spokes is an excellent idea. It will mean he can increase the weight of the rest of the design," said August.

I didn't know about the spokes. However, I nodded and tried not to feel envious about August not only being more up to date with Carl's work than I was but also probably understanding it better than I did. Carl was impatient to begin his own business and have time to work on the carriage. I was impatient to marry him and know more about his work and dreams than his business partner—or anyone else, for that matter.

CHAPTER 9

1872
Pforzheim, Germany

Little over six months later, I wrote to Elise:

> *You once suggested that I marry someone who would bring me to you in America. Before I met Carl, I imagined how you and I would live as neighbors; our husbands would become friends (perhaps even business partners), and we would raise our children together. I admit that the dream disappeared when I fell in love with Carl. He is so absorbed by the idea of inventing a motorized carriage that there is no space in his thoughts for moving to another country. I have never even suggested it to him. Now, however, I wonder if it might be the answer. Let me explain, Sister, and then please give me your counsel.*
>
> *The business in Mannheim was originally called Carl Benz and August Ritter Mechanical Workshop, but they renamed it Factory for Sheet Metal Machines because August felt that emphatically naming the business as being a factory for machines for sheet metal working would draw more customers. However, it has not prospered and shows no signs of doing so.*

As I explained in my previous letter, the land they bought is beautiful and seemed ideal. They built a fine-looking workshop and, with the little money left over, equipped it with some tools. Carl lives frugally in rooms alongside the workshop. He works every hour of the day and often at night. Unfortunately, most of the projects he is working on are his own ones. He's designing and making tools he hopes will help artisans. These are yet to sell. The little paying work that comes in does not even cover repayment of the loan to August's father. He and Carl are deeply in debt, and there is no indication that things will get better.

Carl argues that August is not trying hard enough to find work. He even wonders if August bothers to leave his parents' comfortable home some days. August says he has exhausted his contacts and that there are too many engineers in town offering the same services and materials. This makes Carl even angrier because August insisted, before the partnership was established, that he knew Mannheim well and that he and his father would ensure there was more than enough work for the business.

Another thing Carl discovered after the fact was that August borrowed more money for tools—with the land as surety. He did not discuss the viability or whether in fact the tools he purchased were essential for the business with Carl before finalizing the deal.

As if that is not frustrating enough for Carl, he learned from Herr Ritter Senior recently that, in soliciting the loan, August had assured his father that Carl's horseless carriage was, to borrow from Aesop, "the goose that would lay the golden egg"! The truth is that the partnership explicitly excludes the motorized carriage because the machine is still in such early stages of development. What's more, Carl holds the idea too close to his heart to consider sharing the designs freely at this stage.

I have not told Vater and Mutter about Carl's difficulties, but it will not be long before they find out. Vater is too well connected for the news to remain hidden. I would like to find a solution before things get worse. The longer Carl is indebted to the Ritters, the harder it will be for him to extricate himself from them. I have told him that he should look for a way out. August is not the partner Carl thought he would be, neither is he the one who stands to lose if the business fails. August still has his father's backing and does not seem inclined to dissolve the partnership with Carl. Why would he? He knows that if work suddenly does appear, Carl will do it and he will benefit. For Carl, though, time matters. His debt is growing, he is not free to explore other options, and our wedding day continues to evade us.

You know me, Elise: I want to find a solution. Do you think that coming to Milwaukee could be the answer for Carl? Will there be work there for him? Will he be able to continue to design his carriage? Will you ask Werner his opinion? I do not want to propose the move if it is not the best solution, so I beg your haste and look forward to hearing from you.

My letter might not even have sailed yet when matters came to a head in Mannheim. I heard the details when Carl arrived unexpectedly in Pforzheim on a Wednesday afternoon.

Thekla found me upstairs, where I was helping Mutter fold linen. "Carl is here. You should come quickly. He doesn't look well," said my youngest sister, who, at ten years old, was becoming more and more like Elise both in looks and temperament every day.

I lifted my skirts and ran down the stairs. Carl was not inclined to spontaneity. For him to have interrupted his workday—however frustrated he might be with the tasks at hand—to travel all the way to Pforzheim indicated that something critical had happened. He stood in the hallway, moving his hat from hand to hand. His lean face was taut, and his jaw twitched as he ground his teeth.

"Come," I said, taking his elbow to steer him toward the drawing room. "Sit. Let me get you something to drink."

"No. I'd rather walk," he replied, pulling away. "If you don't mind."

We took the normal route to the Enz. This time, there was no Affie to entertain us, and Carl needed no encouragement to speak his mind.

The previous day, August had ridden to the workshop, which, said Carl, was something he had begun doing less and less frequently in recent weeks. He'd seemed excited, if a little nervous, as he told Carl that a master builder on the other side of the city wanted to meet them on-site the next day to discuss a significant order of metal sheeting.

"He couldn't give me any numbers or specifics on materials," Carl told me, "but indicated that the order would be a change of fortune. August was fidgety, even more so than normal, but I put that down to excitement. I was also excited. This was what we needed. He gave me the address and time for our meeting the next day—that is, this morning—mounted his horse, and rode away."

Determined not to be late for once, Carl had left early, pedaling his velocipede across town. When he arrived at the designated place—with time to spare—he saw not a building site but a house, which showed no signs of having been built recently. He was not immediately concerned, reasoning that August must've misunderstood the prospective client and that the meeting would take place in his home. August was to meet him there, so Carl leaned his velocipede against a tree and waited.

The appointed time came and went. August did not appear. Carl decided it would be rude to make the client wait any longer. He knocked on the door. It was opened by a maid, who not only explained that her employer was out for the day but also that he was a banker and not a builder of any sort.

"Still, it did not occur to me that I'd been misled," said Carl. "I checked the address, which I had written down. Perhaps the number was incorrect. I tried several houses on the street, but no one knew the man I was looking for. Neither did they know of any master builders in the area."

By now, Carl's patience was dwindling. He'd exhausted his inquiries and was beginning to attract suspicious looks. He climbed back on his velocipede and rode to August's parents' house, which was several blocks away. Frau Ritter said neither her son nor her husband was home.

"It is a workday, ja?" she said, looking at Carl through slanted eyes as if he was an idler.

Herr Ritter was out of town, and no, she had no idea where August had gone.

"He is a grown man, Herr Benz," she said. "I do not have to keep track of his whereabouts anymore."

There was nothing for Carl to do but head back to the workshop. He hoped that August had found the building site and that the meeting would proceed without him. When he saw August's mare and another horse he didn't recognize hitched to the fence at Square T6, Number 11, he was relieved. His partner and the client had come to find him.

"But the two men were not in the main part of the workshop," Carl explained. "As I rested my velocipede against the wall, I heard their voices. They were in the other room—my room—where they were discussing my drawings of the carriage. *My* drawings, Bertha! The ones, as you know, I keep secure in a wooden chest to avoid mice and anything else getting to them."

I glanced at Carl. He clenched his fist and ground it into the palm of his other hand. I'd never seen him so agitated. Was it possible he'd hit the other man? I hadn't known Carl to be violent, but this was unlike any incident I'd heard about.

August knew, as I did, that Carl didn't like anyone to examine his designs, particularly without him being present. He insisted that it was because, without his explanations, the designs could be misunderstood. I knew, though, that they were Carl's most precious possessions, which he didn't want examined by strangers. Why would he, given all the years, contemplation, and time he had spent on them? Indeed, Carl's designs were *not* for public viewing—that he had once trusted August enough to show him the designs was remarkable enough.

"What did you do?" I asked, a ball of dread knotting in my stomach.

"I listened at the door for a while. I heard August tell the man that if he bought into the company, he'd be part of the future and that he'd make thousands with the horseless carriage."

I put my hand to my mouth. It was worse than I'd imagined.

"That was not what angered me most, though," Carl continued, running his hands through his hair. "August was not only proposing that the other man buy into the company; he was trying to get him to buy *my* shares, which would come with *my* designs."

"Buy your shares?"

Carl nodded and went on, "I was overcome by rage, ran into the room, grabbed the lapel of August's jacket, and thrust him against the wall."

He stopped to face me, breathing heavily. "I wanted to lay into him, Bertha. I even raised my fist," he said, closing his hand and lifting his arm as if it was necessary to demonstrate the move.

"You did not, though," I said, placing my hand over his knuckles.

"No. Suddenly, it was as if I saw myself from somewhere else in the room: a desperate man acting without control. Without dignity. I released him—but not without once more shoving him against the wall. The other man was gone; I hadn't noticed him leave. August stuttered an explanation...said he was trying to save the business."

"But if—"

"I wouldn't hear it. If he was trying to save the business, he should've spoken to me about his idea. Instead, he invented a client, lied to me to get me away from the workshop, and, like the thief that he is, broke into my chest to get to my private papers. I told him I want nothing more to do with him. There's no trust between us."

There was no arguing about that—the partnership was over. The problem, however, remained: What about the debt? We walked without speaking for a moment. Carl seemed weary, as if recounting the day had depleted his energy.

I went over what had happened in my thoughts. It seemed implausible that August had imagined that someone would buy Carl's shares and plans. There was no business to speak of, and I knew enough about Carl's work to know that, while he'd labored long and hard over them, his designs were still fledgling concepts. He'd recently explained to me the limitations of the gas engine that had won a gold medal at the 1867 Paris Exposition for Eugen Langen and Nicolaus Otto.

The medal-winning machine was, according to Carl, still too much of an unreliable oil glutton and—as an imitator of the steam engine, with the addition of a slide control to allow a mixture of air and gas to be drawn in place of steam—far too cumbersome to power any kind of road vehicle that Carl might imagine. While he recognized its shortcomings, he hadn't come up with a solution. Weaknesses of the gas engine notwithstanding, Carl's drawings of the hypothetical frame for his contraption were rudimentary sketches of carts that could have been the offspring of a velocipede and a Berlin carriage. Would anyone truly consider spending money on them? Were they worth anything yet? Carl's genius wasn't on paper; it was safely locked away in his mind. I wondered, not without shame, whether an offer for Carl's shares and incomplete designs might not be a small price to pay for the debt, trouble, and mistrust that came with August. I knew better than to propose it as a solution, though.

"Will you try to sell the land? The workshop?" I asked instead. "Is it possible you will be able to cover the debt you've incurred?"

"I proposed that, but August rejected it. If I want to end the partnership, he insists I buy his share. With what, though? I have nothing. The market is down, and we'll not make a profit by selling the property. He says he's in no hurry to sell it. His father agrees that it's not a good idea."

"What's his share worth?"

"I estimated nothing more than four thousand one hundred marks. He insists he deserves more, but I disagree. He's done nothing for weeks—months, perhaps. Not that it matters. I don't have the money."

"But what are you supposed to do until things improve? If you cannot work together, how are you to proceed?" I asked.

"I don't know. I'm willing to work, but we have no clients. I've built tools hoping artisans will buy them, but they haven't sold. I'm without more ideas and without hope. I'm worse off than I was as a bridge designer."

Carl stopped and stared across the river. His arms hung at his sides, and his shoulders were stooped, making him seem much shorter than he was. I'd never seen him so dejected. He was thin and his clothes hung from his body. He looked older than twenty-eight. I took his hand. He didn't seem to notice. I knew in that instant what I had to do.

"Let's go back," I said. "You need a good meal and sleep. I have an idea, which we can discuss when you've rested."

—

It took three days to convince my father to give me my dowry *before* I was married. This was essential because it would only be possible for me to buy August's share in the Factory for Sheet Metal Machines and become Carl's business partner while I was single. Once I was a married woman, the law would prohibit me from acting independently and investing in a company.

"But if you get married and Carl has access to the money, can't he buy August's shares?" asked my mother.

"That's not a solution, because it would make Carl the sole proprietor, which would change the nature of the company and incur additional administrative costs. We can't afford it," I replied.

"Your dowry won't solve everything," said Vater. "It's not enough for what you require."

"I know," I said quietly. "I hoped you might add my inheritance to it."

Mutter shook her head and left the room.

My father sighed. It was a sound of surrender, but he didn't own up to it immediately. "You're not married, yet you want your dowry. I'm not dead, yet you want your inheritance," he said.

"Yes," I replied, placing my hand lightly on his forearm.

"What is it that makes you so different from your sisters, Bertha? That's a question I have asked all your life, and still I'm no closer to an answer."

Several things occurred to me. Perhaps I was different because reading his words *only a girl* when I was ten years old compelled me to prove there was no such thing. Or maybe it was because I'd always been greater than what the words implied, and nothing could change that. Or could it simply be because my sisters and I were different, and what distinguished me from them was more prominent than the other way around? I thought this all but said nothing.

So my father finally yielded, insisting, though, that Carl and I sign a prenuptial agreement. "There will be no money if a wedding does not follow shortly thereafter!"

It was almost as difficult to get Carl to agree to the idea of me using the money from my father for the business as it was to get Vater to give it to me.

"Your dowry? Your inheritance? That's for you to invest in your family and home, not a business," said Carl.

"You're my family. And without you, I'll have no home," I replied.

"You know what I mean," he replied.

"Do you love me?" I asked.

"Of course I do. You know that."

"Then I don't want to discuss the dowry or inheritance anymore," I said. "I want to free us from August Ritter. I want to get married and start a life with you, one in which we can work towards our dream of building the horseless carriage and raising a family together."

He placed his hands on my shoulders and looked into my eyes. "You are the one person in the small ship of life who stays with me even when the boat seems destined to sink. Bravely and resolute, you set the new sails of hope. I love you, Bertha Ringer."

—

Carl and I agreed that he should stay away from the Ritter family, so I asked my father to accompany me to Pforzheim to conclude the deal with August.

A silent butler led us down a long, wide passage to a study, which I took to belong to Herr Ritter Senior. August turned from the window and greeted us coolly, keeping the large desk between us—as if Vater and I might throw him against a wall. Gone were the smiles, jokes, and compliments he had been so generous with previously.

"So, the big man has sent a small woman to do his work?" he said.

"For your own safety, August," I said, handing him the agreement Carl and I had drawn up.

His eyes flicked from the top of the page to the bottom.

"It's not what I asked for," he said, not looking up.

"It's what your shares are worth," I replied.

The four thousand two hundred and forty-four marks my father had given me as early settlement of my dowry and inheritance were more than Carl believed August's shares were worth and fifty-six marks less than what August had demanded.

"I'll take the tools as settlement for the rest," he said.

"You'll do no such thing," I said. "We need the tools to keep the business running. This is the final settlement."

He put the agreement on the desk. My father stepped forward; I placed my hand on his arm. We'd agreed earlier that he'd allow me to do the talking.

"It was suggested that we involve a lawyer," I said, ignoring the thumping of my heart, "to investigate your unlawful access to Carl's plans and for revealing them to an unauthorized party."

He snorted.

"One of my clients took the legal route after a similar abuse of confidentiality," said my father. "It cost the other man a great deal—not only financially. He's yet to recover his reputation."

August snorted again.

"Let's leave this behind us," I said. "Sign it, take the money, and we can *all* get on with our lives."

No more was said as August signed the document. He didn't respond to my farewell.

Vater had asked the coachman who had brought us from the station to wait. As we made our way across the porch toward the carriage, a woman with the same glossy hair and smooth walk as August appeared, a shiny black-and-brown dachshund at her heels.

The woman smiled. "Herr and Fräulein Ringer, I assume? I'm August's sister, Ava. Good morning."

We greeted her.

"I'm sorry to hear about your trouble with my little brother," she said, in a tone that sounded more cheerful than apologetic. "He thought for a while that he'd struck gold. I warned him that it seemed too good to be true."

"We've resolved matters," I replied, curious about what she meant but also eager to leave.

She tilted her head. "You have? So quickly? Well, in that case, well done."

"What do you mean by 'struck gold'?" asked my father.

Ava gave a light laugh. "Well, Herr Benz, of course. August says he's a genius."

Vater glanced at me. "It's a pity, then, that your brother didn't do his part."

She laughed again. "If by 'part' you mean *work*, then you should know that's not one of the many pursuits August likes to indulge in."

We said goodbye and left, but I thought about the exchange on the way to the station. There didn't appear to be any malice in the way Ava had made light of her brother's behavior. She didn't know what lengths we'd gone to in order to free ourselves of August. She certainly didn't know that we'd invested our future in his dalliance with the company. Was Carl a genius? I believed so, particularly when it came to the horseless carriage. Yet he'd been misled by August.

CHAPTER 10

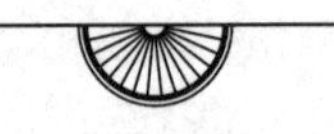

1872
Mannheim, Germany

We were married in the Schlosskirche in Pforzheim on the twentieth of July in 1872 and left the next day to set up home in the rooms that Carl had prepared for us alongside the workshop in Mannheim.

As my husband—my husband!—opened the door and ushered me in, I remembered my mother's expression of dismay when Carl had shown us the plans for Square T6, Number 11, and she'd asked whether he expected me to live there. It had seemed unlikely at the time, but now, as I looked around, I couldn't think of anywhere else I'd rather be. I described our new home in a letter to Elise:

> *I had no idea that Carl would alter his living quarters so much to accommodate me. He has more than trebled the size of the area and partitioned it so that the sleeping, living, and cooking areas are closed off from one another. Furniture is sparse, but we have comfortable places to work, read, sleep, cook, eat, and bathe. In other words, we lack nothing. Carl made most of the pieces himself but, unbeknownst to me and at Mutter's invitation, he also brought a small table and four chairs that our parents stored*

in the barn in Pforzheim for many years. My favorite place is the kitchen, where we also eat. The small woodstove heats the entire room. Affie would have loved being here, in the warm room with frequent company.

Carl hung a clock in every room. Each has its own story, he says. The one in the living room is the first clock he repaired. His mother—she was a cleaner—brought it home when one of her employers declared it irreparable and told her to discard it. Carl fixed it. He was eight years old. The clock in the kitchen was a gift from him to his mother, paid in part with money from his first salary. The third, in the workshop, reminds Carl of the clock on the wall of Professor Redtenbacher's office at the Polytechnic University of Karlsruhe.

As Mutter might have told you, my husband is a great collector and repairer of timepieces—as was his father. Carl inherited five pocket watches from his father and says that one of the reasons he understands machines is because he learned "the language of interlocking gears in watches." Our mother might also have told you that all the clocks and watches in the world do nothing to improve Carl's timekeeping. I have accepted that I will be responsible for hurrying him until death us do part.

When we left Pforzheim, and despite knowing we couldn't afford it, Mutter beseeched me to find a cook in Mannheim. She was sure we'd starve otherwise. Granted, my cooking repertoire is limited, but so is our budget. We shall eat plenty of potatoes and sauerkraut, and my breadmaking skills will no doubt get better. I think about how you and Emilie said that taking care of a house without help was a great deal of work. I suspect, because we have so little, it is easier and quicker for me than for you, which has the advantage of allowing me to help Carl in the workshop.

—

It didn't take us long to unpack the few cases that I'd brought from Pforzheim.

"What's in here?" Carl asked as he lugged the final and largest chest indoors. "More clothes?"

"A few, but mostly linen."

"Linen?" He placed it on the floor and put his hands on his back, straightening with an exaggerated wheeze. "All of it?"

I unbuckled the chest and lifted its heavy lid. Carl leaned forward to look. Carefully folded and separated with tissue paper, the tablecloths, napkins, doilies, place mats, aprons, dish towels, sheets, pillowcases, bedspreads, quilts, towels, handkerchiefs, and a few sets of sleepwear that I'd cut, stitched, hemmed, and embroidered—mostly under Mutter's watchful eye and often with Elise's help—over more than a decade seemed to exhale in expectation. I wondered what the items would've thought if they could think and see their modest surroundings.

"Is this—"

"My trousseau," I said, struggling to suppress a giggle as I held Carl's gaze. "For our home."

He peered into the case, lifted his head, and—as if he might find the room with its two small windows, wooden walls, and scant furniture miraculously changed—looked around.

"But where will we put it?"

"That'll be no problem," I replied, reaching into the chest and removing one of the pieces from near the top.

Carl stared at me, his brow furrowed. I folded back the tissue paper, letting it slip to the floor, and held up the soft summer nightgown, which fell to its full length. Carl blinked and swallowed deeply as he took in the scooped neckline with its ruffle and bow, the lacy band across the midriff, and the sheerness of the fabric.

"Oh," he said, blinking again as I held it against me.

I smiled and laid the garment across a chair. "As for the rest, I propose we leave it closed in the chest, place the container against the wall, and use it as a table."

"The rest? There are more? They are all like that?" he asked, with an uncharacteristic stammer.

Imagining my mother's response to such a notion, I could no longer contain myself and erupted with laughter.

"No," I said, trying to control my spluttering. "Tablecloths, bedding, curtains, and the like. You can't imagine my mother directing the production of a chest full of nightdresses, can you?"

"But that," he said, pointing to the chair.

"Emilie, Elise, and I made it and similar others when our mother was out." I giggled, recalling how creative we'd become, not only at finding material and time to make the flimsy nightgowns but also at keeping them hidden from Mutter.

Carl shook his head and chuckled. His cautious amusement set me off again, and we laughed together, louder and without restraint, until our cheeks were wet with tears and my stomach ached. I'd never seen Carl give in to hilarity. Just as he understood when to apply the brakes of his velocipede, he was typically judicious about controlling his emotions. This time, though, he seemed to be freewheeling. It was a joy to watch and provoked more laughter. I put my hand on a chair for support. Carl placed his hands on his hips and bent forward. The small room reverberated with mirth.

Eventually, exhausted and gasping for breath, we quieted. Carl took me in his arms.

"One day, we'll unpack everything, and you'll be able to use it in the kind of home your mother imagined for you," he said. "One day…in the not-too-distant future, I hope."

"Until then, we shall have to be content with that," I replied, tipping my head toward the nightgown on the chair.

—

During the first months of our marriage, I spent many hours helping Carl in the workshop, where I became accustomed to the searing heat of the forge, the loud clanging of metal upon metal, the swooshing and heaving of the bellows, the dense smell of coal and metal, and my husband's low voice explaining what we were doing and why. Most of our work involved making iron fittings for the building trade, but there were also some more inventive projects for other artisans, including those who built wagons, made leather goods and clothing, and farmers.

As we worked, I found myself comparing Carl to my father. They were naturally very different. Vater was never more garrulous than he was when surrounded by others; Carl was never more reserved. Status was critical to my father; he'd worked his way out of poverty and valued his wealth. Innovation was everything to Carl; he wanted to shape the future, the way he believed his father had dreamed of doing. He focused on the work and skills that would accomplish invention. Being liked and admired were priorities to my father; being received indifferently troubled him. Carl didn't notice one way or another. It only mattered if the person mattered to him—and truly, he'd ask, how many people matter *that* much? Indeed, Carl and Vater were as different in character as they—one short and round, the other tall and lean—were physically.

My husband and father did, however, share one characteristic that I found crucial: they enjoyed talking about their work to me. Just as Vater had, Carl always responded to my questions, mostly at length. His descriptions of his work and ideas were as exhaustive as my father's had been. The men's reverence for their respective occupations was comparable, even if Carl's manner was much more contemplative and technical than my father's. At times, it was as if my husband was solving problems as he spoke. He would deliberate out loud, change his mind midway through an explanation, and offer an alternative. On occasion, it occurred to me that there were multiple Carls in his head. They'd debate issues, suggest different ways of doing things, and challenge one another to do better. Perhaps, because he'd spent so much time alone, he found it easier to talk to himself than to others. Now, however, I was there to listen—and I did so with pleasure.

Most of the time, working alongside Carl was like I imagined it would be to have signed up for an apprenticeship. It was easy to do. Not once did Carl imply that anything about me might impede or bar me from understanding and doing the work. At other times, being in the workshop was like attending a lesson, demonstration, or professional debate. Moreover, because I was his wife and *not* his student, I could interrupt him, ask for clarification, and even disagree if I noticed a contradiction or anomaly. It was an excellent training ground and, as the days went by, I was pleased to find how helpful I was becoming in the workshop.

"I assured Herr Schuster I would deliver his stretching pliers to him at the shoe shop by the end of the day. Can I leave you to make the other three?" said Carl one morning, after I'd heated the metal bar for the first of four brackets ordered by one of Mannheim's busiest wagonmakers, Herr Braun, and watched Carl turn it into the finished product. It was the second of what we hoped would become many jobs that we'd done for the wagonmaker. While the items were simple—the kind a blacksmith could make, Carl said—the work was quick and profitable.

"I can't imagine what my father might've said if he had seen me doing this," he said. "He was determined to get away from his family's blacksmithing business and make a career out of the future, yet here we are, doing the kind of work his father and grandfather did. He would've been appalled."

"I disagree. Your father would've been proud that you are prepared to do whatever necessary to work toward your dream," I said, not bothering to add that the slow demand for our services meant we had to be grateful for *any* work that came our way. Besides, the uncomplicated components required by the wagonmaker gave me the opportunity to improve my skills.

The three sections of flat bar were already cut to size. I arranged the coal in the forge, adding some extra pieces so that I'd have enough heat to complete the set, and jiggled the first metal bar into place. Carl had taught me to gauge the temperature of the metal by watching the color change. Underheating it would make it difficult to work with, and overheating could weaken it. I felt his eyes on me briefly as I positioned the glowing bar on the anvil and took up the hammer. His scrutiny didn't unsettle me; he'd only interfere if I made a mistake or was unable to complete the task. I bent the metal to the measurement Carl had specified, heated the ends, punched the necessary holes, and quenched the bracket. As I wiped the perspiration from my brow and checked that there was no scale on the part, I pictured my mother, sisters, and me doing needlepoint in the drawing room in Pforzheim. What would Mutter make of me scrabbling about in the embers and wielding a hammer like a blacksmith? She might've learned to take care of horses and cattle in her youth, but I couldn't picture her in a workshop.

I finished the final bracket and watched Carl work on the pliers for the cobbler. When Herr Schuster had told him what he wanted, Carl had proposed adding a tack hammer to the tool. As he made a quick sketch of the idea, the cobbler's face lit up.

"What an excellent idea, Herr Benz," he'd said. "As long as the additional cost is less than the price of a new tack hammer."

Carl had assured him it would be, and the cobbler left the workshop smiling.

"I'm going to think of some other ideas for tools and machinery that might make Herr Schuster and other cobblers' work easier," Carl had told me. "If customers are not coming to us with requests for machines, we need to go to them with ideas. It's the only way we'll increase the income of the workshop."

As I watched Carl test the tool's pivot point, I wondered how it would ever be possible to find the time and money to work on the horseless carriage if we had to invent tools and machines for others to earn our daily keep. My thoughts were interrupted by a loud knocking at the workshop door. I washed and dried my hands, pushed my hair from my face, and opened the door to a boy bearing a letter addressed to Carl.

"Open it," said Carl when I showed him the envelope.

It was from a lawyer representing August Ritter. We were, it demanded, to pay August an additional fifty-six marks to make up the difference between what I'd paid him and what he believed his shares in the company were worth by the end of the month. If the payment was not made, we'd be summoned to court.

"How dare he," I said.

Carl took it from me and read it again, his jaw twitching and his eyes narrow.

"He wants to ruin us," he said, crushing the letter in his fist and walking toward the fire.

I grabbed his wrist. "Wait," I said. "Give it to me."

—

Later that day, I walked to town to deliver the brackets and pliers while Carl worked on another idea he'd come up with for the cobbler. As the streets grew narrower and quieter, the air became heavy with a mix of dust, drains, and horse manure. Herr Braun was at the door of his workshop when I arrived.

"So quickly," said the wagonmaker when I handed him the brackets. "I thought Herr Benz would need another day at least."

"He has some help in the workshop," I replied, peering at the half-assembled carriage in the shed behind him. "What a fine-looking landau. It reminds me of the one my husband created door locks for recently."

"He makes locks too? That, I did not know," said Herr Braun as he paid me for the brackets.

"He does. Should I ask him to come by so that you can discuss what you might need from him?" I asked.

"Yes, do that."

Herr Schuster was not in when I arrived at the shoe shop, which was in a prettier part of town that smelt of leather and slightly damp cobblestones. The shoemaker's assistant barely grunted and didn't look at me as he paid for the pliers, and I left, having had no opportunity to bid for more work.

Although I lingered to breathe in the delicious buttery smells that emanated from the bakery a few doors away, fantasizing about the day we might afford to buy a fresh cake or tart, the quick transaction at the cobbler's rooms meant I arrived at the Ritters' house earlier than I had expected. I was there to confront August. The agreement we'd signed when my father and I visited months earlier stipulated that the offer was full and final. That he was now paying a lawyer to hound me and Carl for more money was unlawful and immoral. August knew that we didn't have the money to hire our own lawyer to contest the case. Or did he hope that we would somehow find it and pay him because he knew how stressful Carl would find his prolonged involvement in our lives? Was he cruel? I'd not seen *that* in August. I knocked on the door, steeling myself to do battle.

The silent butler I'd met previously led the way to a large drawing room, where he told me to wait and left, closing the door behind him. I assumed he'd gone to fetch August. I looked at the heavy curtains and solid furniture. So imposing were the tables, chairs, wall hangings, and light fittings that it occurred to me the walls might've been built around the decor. There was an air of permanence about the place and everything it contained. It might've been there forever; the Ritters had been born to it, not it to them.

I was peering at a large tapestry, which depicted a forest and rows of deer and made me think of Elise and the animals of America, when the door swept open. I looked up to find not August but Ava with the dachshund at her feet.

"Frau Benz," she said, her tone welcoming. "I didn't expect to see you here again so soon. Or ever, really."

"Good afternoon, Fräulein Ritter. I'm—"

"Ava, please. I have not been Fräulein Ritter for several years. I'm the Widow Fischer, but I prefer Ava."

"Oh, I didn't know. I'm—"

She cut me off once more. "No. How would you know? One day, Rudolf and I were married. The next, he went to war. Two months later, I was a widow. Our army might've won the Battle of Sedan, but I lost my husband. Here I am, back in my childhood home, a woman in limbo, pitied by all and loved by none—except this sweet little creature, Marta." She looked down at the dog and smiled. "However, I've always been Ava. At least that has not changed."

What an unusual woman August's sister was. There was no melancholy in her tone. No distress or cynicism. I wasn't sure how to respond. She didn't seem to notice my uncertainty.

"You came to see August, but I'm afraid he's not here," she said. "Is there anything I can do for you? At least have coffee with me."

"Thank you, but this is a matter I need to talk to August about. Do you expect him home anytime soon? Perhaps I could wait for a bit?"

"Expect him? I'm afraid I have no idea when he'll be home, but you are welcome to wait. Please have coffee with me. My mother buys her beans from an Arabian supplier, and though I've not admitted it to her, the brew is delicious."

She pointed to a large chair. "Please! I've had such a boring day, and it would improve matters greatly to have your company."

So it was that my expedition to the Ritter house became not the confrontation I'd anticipated but a pleasant chat with Ava, a cup of coffee, and a slice of butter cake—the very kind I'd fantasized about earlier.

We spoke about Marta and the fearlessness of the dachshund breed. I told her about Affie and how I missed her. We agreed that the coffee was particularly smooth and flavorsome and, as if Carl and I could afford it, Ava told me where I could buy the beans. She asked me briefly about how I had settled in Mannheim and how the city compared to Pforzheim. She crinkled her nose when I told her that we lived in rooms alongside the workshop and asked if she could come and visit. I hesitated, not because I was ashamed but because I couldn't imagine welcoming August's sister in our home. She seemed to understand my reluctance and didn't press the matter.

"What did you want to talk to August about, Bertha? Are you sure I can't help? I know my brother better than anyone," she said.

I told her about the letter we'd received from August's lawyer. She shook her head.

"You might not believe it—after everything he's put you through—but that doesn't sound like something August would do."

I took the letter from my bag. It was still slightly wrinkled from being crumpled in Carl's fist. "There's no mistake," I said, handing it to her.

"Ah. Yes. The lawyer, Herr Jäger," she said, distinguishing the stationery immediately.

I leaned forward to rub Martha's ears while Ava read.

"I see what you mean. This purports to come from August, but I recognize my father's hand," she said, placing the letter on the table. "Herr Jäger is my father's lawyer."

"And also August's," I said.

She gave her head a little shake. "Perhaps, but I suspect that when our father heard about your agreement with August, he was appalled that his son had let anyone—let alone a woman—browbeat him into accepting less money than he wanted. I believe my father bullied August into suing you."

"Does it matter?" I asked. I looked at the clock. It was getting late, and I wanted to get home before it was dark. I folded the letter, put it in my bag, and stood. "The point is that August is suing me and Carl. It's unwarranted and unacceptable."

Ava sighed. "Can I organize the carriage for you?"

"No, thank you," I said. The letter had reminded me why I'd come, and I felt uneasy once more.

"Will you come back?" she asked as we walked to the door. "To see August, I mean?"

"Do I have a choice? Perhaps you can tell me when I'm most likely to find him at home."

Ava smiled. "Come early. He's seldom out of the house before ten every morning."

As I walked home with others returning to their houses after a day in town, taking the shortest route across the square and over the bridge, I thought about

Ava's husband, who'd died in the war against France, which my brother Karl had escaped by going to America. I shuddered and was grateful that Carl had avoided conscription. I was also grateful to leave the close confines of town and climb the hill toward home, where the trees and grass were green and the air clear.

—

I'd not told Carl that I planned to visit August after I'd delivered the brackets and pliers, and since he didn't notice how late I returned, I didn't mention it afterward either. He was bent over his notebook at the table when I arrived home. I hoped that he'd found a moment to work on the horseless carriage; it would take his mind off August's letter and our financial problems.

"Have a look," he said, sliding his notebook toward me. "It's a sewing machine for cobblers. Herr Schuster complained that it's difficult and time-consuming to get the thread through the sole and the leather."

Carl placed a finger below a sketch. "This is a pedal-operated machine, which would move the needle up and down when you push your foot here. It would speed up the process considerably."

I peered at the drawing. The contraption was made up of several levers and wheels, a foot pedal, a shoe holder, and a sewing machine fitted to a metal table. I was sorry that Carl was not able to work on the carriage, but he was being inventive and practical. We needed to make money urgently if we were to save the business.

"What an excellent idea," I said. "Will you show the drawing to Herr Schuster so that he can offer his suggestions?"

Carl stared at me. "Go into a partnership with him? No. I'll make the machine, and if Herr Schuster doesn't like it, I'll sell it to another cobbler. I'm not going to allow others to interfere with my business like I did with August."

I shook my head. "No, not a partnership. Herr Schuster is the one with experience in making shoes. He knows what tools and machines he needs. A simple discussion with him about your proposition could make all the difference to the usefulness and value of your machine."

"I'll think about it," he said, reaching across the table to retrieve the notebook. "But I don't want to delay. Perhaps this machine will help us get rid of August Ritter once and for all."

I felt a fresh charge of anger at August. Although we'd been struggling to keep the business afloat before his letter arrived, it had seemed possible that we'd overcome our problems. We'd been working on components for carriages, farming equipment, buildings, furniture, and various other things for several months. Carl rarely turned away work and, if necessary, worked through the night to ensure that parts were ready for clients. Even so, there was too little paid work, and Carl and I spent hours talking about mechanisms, tools, and machines we could invent to sell to others. More recently, though, after supper—potatoes and cabbage again—Carl had begun looking at his designs for the horseless carriage. It filled me with joy and anticipation. Without money to invest in building and testing the horseless carriage, progress on the project would be slow, but at last, it had again seemed possible. Now, with August demanding more money, our hopes had been halted once more.

CHAPTER 11

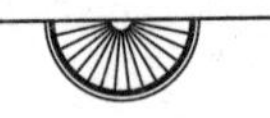

1873
Mannheim, Germany

Before I fell asleep that night, I resolved to walk across town again and confront August about his demands as soon as possible, but the next two days brought enough work to keep me in the workshop. As usual, when we received orders, Carl and I began working on them immediately. Completed projects meant money, which might allow me to buy meat for a meal once or twice a week. The faster we worked, the quicker it came. On the third day, when finally there was nothing to keep me in the workshop, I awoke feeling inexplicably weary but rose anyway, determined to get to the Ritter house before ten.

"You're dressed for town," said Carl when he came in for breakfast. He got up before dawn every morning to work for at least two hours before I awoke.

"I am," I said, surprised that he'd noticed I was wearing one of the dresses that I favored when visiting customers or going to the market. "I have some errands to do."

He gestured to the window. "You might want to wait a few hours."

I hadn't noticed but, indeed, it was raining.

"Tomorrow, then," I said, accepting that I wouldn't get to the Ritter house on time unless I was prepared to get wet.

Carl squinted at me as if expecting an explanation. I sat down at the table opposite him and said no more.

Later, as I placed a loaf of bread in the oven, I noticed movement outside—a carriage drew up. Hoping it was a customer with an order, I washed my hands, took off my apron, and opened the door. The rain had subsided, but the short path was peppered with puddles. I pictured the paving my father had laid to our front door in Pforzheim. Perhaps Carl and I could collect river stones to create a similar effect, which might make a better impression on customers.

The coachman tipped his hat at me and opened the door. The leg that emerged was not, as I'd expected, trousered but swathed in skirts. It was Ava. I watched as she navigated her way around the pools of water, holding up her skirts in one hand while clutching what looked like a bundle of peach-colored cloth in the other.

"Good morning, Bertha," she said when she reached the door. "I come bearing…this!"

She held the bundle toward me. A pair of shiny, dark eyes peered at me from a tiny black face with a tan muzzle and matching flecks above each eye.

"A dachshund," said Ava.

"Yes, but—"

"She's Marta's sister. The most recent litter. I saw how you were with her the other day, and you said how you missed your affenpinscher. So…" She shrugged and placed the tiny animal in my hands.

The puppy wriggled her torso. Her black tail shot out of the cloth and whipped about. I held her up, and when she opened her mouth to give me a pink-tongued smile, I smelt the distinctive sweet puppy breath, warm with innocence and hopefulness.

"Is she weaned?" I asked, marveling at her tininess.

"Yes," said Ava. "Two weeks ago."

The puppy, tail still wagging fiercely, twisted her head and sank her needlelike teeth into my thumb.

"Hey!" I cried, trying to extricate my digit from her mouth.

"Look," said Ava. "You're already attached."

We went inside, where I was too distracted by the puppy—who, once on the floor, pitter-pattered around the room, sniffing curiously—to worry about what Ava might think about our home. Eventually, I turned to her.

"She's lovely, but we cannot afford to buy a puppy."

Ava raised her hands in mock horror. "Buy? No. That's not what I meant. She's a gift. From me."

"A gift?"

"Yes. Are you not familiar with the concept? It's when one person gives another person something for the simple pleasure of doing so. In the best cases, dual enjoyment ensues. One person gets pleasure from giving and the other from receiving," she said.

I laughed. It felt good.

"Thank you. She's adorable," I said.

"I hope she'll bring you as much joy as your childhood dog in Pforzheim did. If she's anything like Marta, I know she'll be delightful," she replied.

I wondered, as I took the bread from the oven, if the puppy was Ava's way of apologizing for her brother's behavior. Or was it a simple offer of friendship? She'd said she was bored when we'd had coffee three days previously. I was new to Mannheim, a stranger unrelated to her past—which, although I knew little about it, must've been sad and difficult for her. Perhaps, just as the puppy's breath seemed to hint at fresh beginnings for me, I promised something new to Ava. But what would Carl think? Because I knew he'd try and talk me out of confronting August, I still hadn't mentioned my visit to the Ritter house or that I'd planned to go again. I remained sure that it was the best immediate course of action. Now I wondered if I could convince Carl that Ava was nothing like August. Even if I couldn't, it wasn't possible for her and me to be friends without him knowing.

"Come," I said, taking the puppy from the floor and placing her soft body in the crook of my arm. "Let me introduce you both to Carl."

"We met once when he came to see August at the house shortly after they'd set up the business. I'd like to see him again, but in a while," said Ava, remaining seated at the table. "First, we need to name the puppy—and I have to tell you something."

"Tell me something?"

"First a name."

I placed the puppy back on the floor and sat down. She tottered to the mat near the oven. It was the exact spot where I'd imagined Affie lying. The dachshund stretched her tubby, sausage-like body to its full length; opened her pink mouth; and yawned. She looked like she was about to fall asleep, but then she caught sight of a broom I'd left against the wall. The puppy squirmed to her feet and pattered across the floor to investigate it.

"Tapsen," I said, thinking of the German word for *pitter-patter*. "Tapsen. No. Tappie. Her name is Tappie."

"Tappie! That is perfect," said Ava, clapping her hands. Tappie, startled, turned and looked at her. "She knows it already."

We watched as Tappie resumed her toddle toward the broom. She sniffed it and began chewing the bristles. She was, I knew, going to add to my work, but the companionship and entertainment she'd offer would make it worth every minute. I pictured the walks Carl and I would take with her.

Ava interrupted my thoughts. "Good. We've settled on a name. Let me give you the news."

I turned to face her.

"Remember I said that I didn't think that demanding more money from you and Carl would've been August's idea?" she said.

I nodded.

"I asked him. And I was right. He was ready to move on to other things. However, when our father found out about the settlement August agreed upon with you, he was furious. He insisted August take it up with the lawyer. Unsurprisingly, the lawyer encouraged August to take legal action," she said.

"But our agreement specifies that the money I paid is the final settlement," I said. "That's why it makes no sense for August to insist on more."

"I know. But no one spots so-called opportunities like a lawyer. That's what they are trained to do."

"Opportunities?" I echoed.

Ava went on. "Ja. Herr Jäger saw that there was no witness signature on the document. That, he says, could be grounds to discredit it."

"Witness? But we were both there. We signed the agreement together. First August and then me. My father was also there."

"That might be so, but if your father's signature is not on the document, there's no proof of him being there, and the agreement can be contested in court."

I stared at her. I couldn't believe that August would go along with such deceit. Even if it was because his father bullied him, it was appalling.

"So we have to go to court," I said. "We'll need my father to testify on our behalf. Undoubtedly, it will call for a lawyer. Even if the case goes our way, it'll cost us money we don't have."

"No," said Ava.

"No?"

"No, you will not need to go to court."

I was confused. "But—"

"Remember I was there the day you and your father visited?" she asked.

"Yes."

"Marta and I were outside my father's study when you and August signed the agreement. Your father was there and so was I."

"You were?" I asked, wondering how it was possible that none of us in the study had noticed Ava outside that day, particularly given how much time August had spent looking out the window.

"I was. I saw it happen. I mean, I saw you and August signing the papers. I saw your father standing at your side. I told my father and August as much and said that I would testify in court that I witnessed not only the signing of the agreement but also the witness—your father—witnessing the event," she said.

"You would?"

"If I had to."

"If?"

Ava chuckled. "My father is furious. It would embarrass the family enormously. August pretends to be angry, too, but I think he's relieved."

"You mean—"

"Yes, they've instructed Herr Jäger to withdraw the case."

"They have?"

She smiled, nodding.

My eyes prickled. "I don't know what to say," I said. "Thank you, Ava. Thank you. You cannot imagine what a relief this is."

"I have some idea," she said, removing an envelope from her small purse. "However, I wasn't satisfied. I insisted on a letter signed by August, my father, and the lawyer. It confirms that the matter is final and that the agreement stands. Here's your copy."

I took the envelope. "Why did you do this? For us? My gratitude is immense, but we've only recently met."

She gave another small laugh. "I love my brother. Indeed, I even love my father, but he's a bully," she said. "August is not a wicked man, but he's weak and in our father's thrall. He's also indebted to Father. His and Carl's partnership isn't the first time he's borrowed money from our father and failed with it. It makes it difficult for my brother to get out of our father's grasp. I wanted August to stand up to Father himself, but he wouldn't, so I took it upon myself to shame them both."

"But, for us? I mean, you barely know Carl and me."

"When August told me that you were going to buy his share in the business using your dowry, I was intrigued. I don't know any other women who would do that. I wanted to get to know you. Since my husband's death, I've felt like I don't belong among the people I've known since I was a girl. When Rudolf was killed, I was uncertain for the first time in my life about what life holds for me. It scared me, until I heard your story and realized that not everything goes according to plan. Husbands die young and leave their wives alone. Women use their dowries to buy businesses." She shrugged. "I'd like us to become friends."

I smiled. "Come. Let me introduce you to Carl."

We left Tappie where she'd fallen asleep, curled up against the broom, and I led the way to the workshop.

Carl looked up as we walked in, his eyes flicking from Ava to me and back again. He wasn't typically quick to recognize people he'd only met a few times.

"You remember Ava, August's sister?" I asked.

He blinked several times as if that might clear the confusion. "Oh, yes. How are you, Frau Fischer?" he replied, surprising me by remembering her married name.

"Oh, call me Ava, please."

I told Carl about Tappie. If he was surprised or confused, he hid it well.

"But that wasn't the only reason for Ava's visit," I said. "She also came to say that August has withdrawn his claim for more money."

This time, he didn't withhold his astonishment. "He has?" he said, staring at her. "That's excellent news, but why? What made him change his mind?"

Ava glanced at me. "I'll let Bertha explain when I've left, Herr Benz. Let's simply celebrate that sanity prevailed."

Carl looked at me.

"Sanity and a persuasive sister," I said.

Ava and I chuckled.

"It's good to see you again, Herr Benz, but I must be on my way," she said.

"Call me Carl, please," said my husband with an uncertain smile.

—

Carl's response to my explanation about how August had come to withdraw his claim was one of muted puzzlement.

"Why didn't you tell me what you planned to do?" he asked.

"Because you would've tried to stop me."

"Is she to be trusted, August's sister?"

"Ava. I've only met her on three occasions, but what could she possibly gain?" I said.

"Her brother was beguiling," he said.

"We are not entering a partnership of any kind with Ava," I replied.

He gave that a moment's thought.

"But a puppy?" said Carl eventually.

"Yes. Tappie. Isn't she wonderful?"

That evening, as I prepared our meal of spaetzle and mushroom sauce, Carl lifted Tappie and lay her on her back in his lap. At first, she squirmed, trying to right herself, but when he began scratching her soft, pudgy stomach, the puppy relaxed and looked back at me over her ears as if to say, "This is surprisingly pleasant."

"How big will she grow?" asked Carl.

"No taller than a chicken, says Ava, but much longer. The breed was created to hunt badgers, but these days, with more people keeping them indoors as companions, they're bred smaller," I said.

"An elongated chicken," said Carl, continuing to tickle the puppy.

I chuckled. "You do know that the way you begin with a dog is the way they learn to be for the rest of their lives."

"You mean the way your father insisted when she arrived that Affie wasn't a pet?" he replied, his chortle startling Tappie.

—

Ava's unexpected involvement in our lives, our budding friendship, and Tappie's arrival were not the only surprises sprung upon us that winter: I also realized I was pregnant.

"The timing couldn't be better," said Ava as she and I walked across the field down to the Neckar River one cold but unusually cloudless Sunday afternoon. Marta and Tappie bounced along the path ahead of us, their tails flicking fast as if to power them. "The baby will arrive in April or May, am I right? Tappie will be much calmer by then and the weather warmer."

She was right about the puppy and the weather, but with business still not having improved, the timing of the baby wasn't ideal. I didn't share my doubts with Ava. The truth, though, was that while Carl and I continued to take on almost every project that came our way, there still wasn't enough income to afford the materials he needed to start work on the engine he hoped would one day power a carriage.

"The good thing is that I will have exhausted all possible thinking, sketching, and planning before we are able to build it," Carl said that evening, after he'd told me again how convinced he was that the way to power the horseless carriage was to develop a gas engine, despite the enthusiasm others reserved for steam engines. "When Herr Schuster sees what I have invented for him and other cobblers place their orders, we can celebrate and soon thereafter afford to begin working on the carriage in earnest."

Indeed, Carl had gone ahead and built the machine he'd invented to mechanize stitching leather to the soles of shoes. Despite my hoping that he would discuss the machine with the cobbler before spending the time and money required to assemble it, Carl had remained convinced that the shoemaker would see things his way and jump at the opportunity to improve production. As such, and against my wishes, Carl had borrowed money from the bank to build the stitching machine for Herr Schuster.

"If he doesn't take it, another cobbler will," he insisted.

For several nights leading up to the completion of the machine, Carl came to bed hours after I'd fallen asleep and was gone before first light every morning as usual. I'd wake briefly to the sound of him stoking the wood oven and chatting to Tappie in the kitchen.

"We're getting there, Tappie. This is the machine that'll free us to invent the real thing."

Finally, one afternoon, the contraption was complete, and Carl called me to the workshop to demonstrate it in operation.

"You'll see," he said, stepping aside as I came through the door so that I could see it. "This is the machine that'll allow us to get to work on the horseless carriage."

Built on a solid iron table, the apparatus included a pedal, flywheel, material holder with a vise, and a stitching machine. It was designed to allow the operator to stand and comfortably activate the needle and thread with one foot while having both hands free to adjust the leather as necessary. Carl took up the position and set it in motion. The machine was not only quiet, quick, and easy to use, but it also looked elegant, with its curved iron and shiny components. I stepped forward and watched as the leather ran smoothly beneath the needle and emerged from the other side with a neat row of stitches solidly in place.

Carl's stitching machine was impressive, and despite my previous doubts, I felt a jolt of excitement. My husband was a genius and his workmanship clever and precise. It was an excellent piece of engineering that was bound to find favor. This was the breakthrough we needed.

"Herr Schuster will be here tomorrow," said Carl, stifling a yawn. "I'll go to bed early tonight so that I don't fall asleep while I show him how it works."

I helped him tidy the workshop, and we tested the machine once again to ensure that everything was in place. Carl was asleep before I was that night, and as I tucked myself around him and pulled the bed covers over us, I felt excited and hopeful.

—

I watched from the doorway the next morning, flushed with pride, as Carl led Herr Schuster and his assistant to the machine. Wearing his smartest shirt—the pristine white one my mother had presented to him for our wedding, which he reserved for special occasions and had never previously worn in the workshop—Carl looked handsome and rested. His eyes sparkled as he glanced at me.

"So, this is it," said Herr Schuster, who was a small, wiry man with a friendly smile and an unruly head of graying hair that looked like it was fleeing his head. "It's very shiny and much larger than I expected."

The men followed Carl around the machine as he pointed out the components and described what they did.

"It looks good," said the cobbler. "Show us how it works."

Carl eased himself into position and set it in motion. Herr Schuster bent closer to inspect the result. "That is clever," he said.

"And so easy," said Carl, stepping aside. "Try it yourself."

The cobbler nodded and smiled as the leather ran smoothly beneath the needle. He moved away, and his assistant tested it. Carl caught my eye and smiled. Things were going well.

Indeed, the machine would, said Herr Schuster, speed up production. His assistant nodded energetically. How smart it was. How robust. How well designed.

"What is the price?" asked the cobbler.

Carl gave him the figure.

Herr Schuster stopped smiling. His assistant looked out the door beyond me as if suddenly interested in being elsewhere.

"But that's ridiculous," said the shoemaker.

"It's a fair price, given the cost of the materials and the time and effort it took to invent and build—not to mention the time and effort it will save you," said Carl, his voice low and his tone affable.

"I could hire a boy to do the stitching at a fraction of the price," said Herr Schuster, running his hand over the metalwork as one might caress a cat. "Your talent is too expensive, Herr Benz."

He lifted his hat from where he'd left it on Carl's desk and moved toward the door.

"Perhaps I could reduce the price a little," said Carl. "But I need to cover the cost of the materials."

The cobbler paused. "What's the lowest you could go?"

Carl gave him another figure.

Herr Schuster placed his hat on his head. "I would have to increase the prices of my shoes so much to cover the cost that even Mannheim's wealthiest families would buy their shoes elsewhere. We are, it is said, facing a recession. I cannot put up my prices and lose my clients to the competition."

Carl exhaled loudly. "But you'll recover the price of the machine in no time. If you hire people to do the stitching for you, you'll have to continue hiring and paying them. The machine won't get tired or ill or need a salary," he argued. "You will never need another. I will service it for you as necessary."

"Maybe so, but I cannot afford the outlay. It'll take me too long to recoup the cost. You're right about it doing a good job and making life easier for me, but I've managed the stitching by hand until now, and I'll manage it that way in future. Some things don't require change, Herr Benz."

Carl ran a hand over his head. His jaw twitched. He avoided looking at me as he walked Herr Schuster to the door.

—

That night, Carl and I stayed up, creating advertising flyers that featured drawings of the stitching machine and instructions on how to use it. The next day, while Carl made locks for carriage doors for the wagonmaker, I visited all the other cobblers I knew of in the city and handed them copies of the flyer.

"It'll increase the speed at which you produce shoes and reduce your labor costs," I repeated.

Their response was almost identical to that of Herr Schuster: the contraption was clever and would be useful, but it was too expensive. Late that afternoon, I came home via the post office, where I posted several copies of the flyers to Herbert, who was working with Vater in Pforzheim.

"Please ask one of your workers to distribute these flyers to shoemakers," I wrote in a note to accompany the advertisements.

When I arrived home, Tappie greeted me at the gate, her torso wriggling and her tail whirring. I found Carl in the workshop and told him about my day, trying to ignore the big stitching machine that stood against the wall. Carl took me in his arms.

"Enough, Bertha. No more knocking on doors. You've done everything you can. It's my mistake. I'll work to recover the loss. We'll use the material from the stitching machine for something else and pay back the bank," he said.

As we walked, hand in hand, to the house, I thought about how long it had been since I'd seen Carl's eyes light up with excitement the way they did when he spoke about the horseless carriage. The stitching machine had failed, but there had to be a way to afford to start working toward our dream.

Two days later, my father paid an unexpected visit from Pforzheim while Carl was out. Vater leaned heavily on his cane and stopped twice to recover his breath on the short walk from the gate to the door. My mother had told me that he spent three out of five workdays in his study nowadays, leaving the visits to sites, customers, and suppliers to Herbert. Even so, I hadn't realized how frail he'd become.

I settled him at the table, and we exchanged some trivial news. My father didn't mention the flyers I'd asked Herbert to distribute, but his conversation made it clear that he knew about them.

"Business is difficult for us in Pforzheim too," he said, accepting a cup of coffee. "Matters were bad enough when the banks lent money too freely because of the immense growth they anticipated from the expansion of the railways. Now, with silver being removed from our currency, things are even worse. How it will end, we do not know."

"The building business in Mannheim is also slow," I said.

Ava had told me that her father was concerned about his company and that August had left the city to look for work in Munich.

"In hindsight, the downturn must surely have played a role in things going so badly for Carl and August. If only they'd known," said Vater.

"I don't think it would've changed the outcome," I said, reluctant to discuss the failed partnership again. However, my father might've had a point. Regardless of what happened between the two men and even if the full extent of the recession was only felt a year later, it hadn't been a good time for Carl and August to establish a new business.

A few days after Vater's visit, I received a letter from Elise. She wrote that while Werner and Gustav agreed Carl's skills *might* be valued in Milwaukee, it was impossible to guarantee anything. Things changed very quickly in the new land, she warned, and America was not immune to the looming depression.

I'd still not told Carl that I'd asked Elise to solicit opinions on his prospects for work in America. His confidence had taken a knock when the partnership with August failed. The disappointment of not selling the stitching machine was a further blow. I did, however, show him the newspaper cutting about American inventor George B. Brayton's engine that Elise sent with the letter. Carl read the article and quietly examined the two sketches that accompanied it for several minutes.

"I wonder what Herren Otto and Langen have made of this," he said. "Herr Brayton's engine is much safer than theirs. I've no doubt that when our countrymen learn of this, they will work even harder to improve on their machine."

"As will you," I said, placing a hand on his shoulder.

Carl gave me a wistful smile. "If only we could afford to *really* join the race."

"Didn't you say that your plans and designs will put you ahead when you're able to begin manufacturing, assembling, and testing your machine? You might not have anything to show for it yet, but remember how you once explained how you trained for rowing when you were a student?"

He frowned.

I went on. "You told me that sometimes the results of training are invisible until the day of the race, but then the rowers who have put in the most effort beforehand win."

CHAPTER 12

1873
Mannheim, Germany

By the time the Vienna Stock Exchange crashed in 1873 just days after the opening of the World's Fair in the city, the hands and feet of our firstborn, Eugen—named for Herr Eugen Langen—had lost their bluish tinge and turned pink to match the rest of his body. I was adjusting to nights of interrupted sleep and days dictated by his cries. Eugen's arrival did not, however, change the circumstances of our lives at Square T6, Number 11, in any other way—nor did it shield us from the recession.

For a while, Carl was distracted by newspaper reports from the World's Fair in Vienna about inventor Siegfried Marcus's wooden cart, which was propelled by an engine that used illuminating fuel.

"We think alike," said Carl, having studied another article on Herr Marcus's cart one evening. He seemed surprised, as if it was exceptional to come across a like-minded individual. "Herr Marcus hopes his self-propelled carts will one day be used to transport people to railway stations."

"So only short distances? I thought you were more ambitious," I said.

"We all have to start somewhere," he said.

Our dream, though, demanded more patience. As the days passed, Carl's jaw twitched more frequently, particularly when he completed a job and there was no other work awaiting his attention. It gave me no comfort that we were not alone with our struggles. At the market on Fridays, I saw worry etched in the lines of practically every face I encountered. Even the clouds over the market square seemed lower. It was small consolation that I wasn't alone in selecting the cheapest vegetables and smallest cuts of meat.

Given that so many people and businesses were struggling financially, the banks begrudgingly extended loans, including ours. I suspected the amount we owed made little difference to their coffers. The extension brought us temporary relief but also prolonged our concern about how we would repay it, particularly with less work coming in.

With Eugen on my hip and another baby due just seventeen months after his birth, it was more difficult for me to look for opportunities for work for Carl the way I had prior to becoming a mother. Some weeks, the only jobs—mostly small projects like creating new tools, repairing old ones, and making small components—came via Ava. She, it emerged, surreptitiously told her father's contacts and anyone else who might be interested about Carl's ingenuity at every opportunity.

The upside of the recession was the revitalization of Carl's determination to develop a gas engine for the horseless carriage. He'd never stopped working on his designs, but now, with fewer demands from customers, he had time to design and make engine components from whatever materials he could find.

"I can see it, Bertha," he said, with an intensity that reminded me of the young man who had clattered into the carriage en route to Maulbronn years previously. "An atmospheric gas engine around which I will eventually build, refine, and assemble the carriage."

—

Months passed and we struggled on, grateful for every opportunity to earn enough to keep our family warm and fed. Carl's commitment to building an engine never faltered.

"I don't question his dedication to his dream, but I wonder if Carl is approaching it in the most effective way," said Ava, who was shelling peas while

I nursed our second born, Richard, who'd arrived in autumn 1874. It amused Carl that Ava so willingly helped me with chores in our home while the same tasks were taken care of for her by a team of servants in the Ritter household.

"What do you mean?" I asked her.

She was quiet for a moment, as if examining her words before speaking. "When my brother and Carl were partners and August mentioned the horseless carriage, there was often ridicule. You are surely aware of what people say about him, aren't you?"

I nodded. Of course I was. I'd discovered how peculiar people thought Carl was shortly after I arrived in Mannheim. It was market day, and I'd been wandering between the stalls, daydreaming about the meal I'd cook my new husband that evening and how he would take me in his arms afterward and declare his satisfaction. After I had placed a handful of potatoes in my basket, paid, and turned to make my way to the butcher, I overheard someone say in a low voice, "Is that the bride of the eccentric engineer?"

I'd slowed to hear the response, which came with a sneer from another man. "Ha! 'Eccentric engineer'? I think he's a tinkering crank. A crazy inventor. What kind of madman would imagine removing the horses from a carriage and expect it to move? I mean, he might've fooled young Ritter into believing it, but no one else will fall for his fantasy!"

The men had exploded with laughter.

"Perhaps his bride will knock some sense into him," the one with the low voice had said.

Their mirth amplified.

I'd wanted to tell the men how unimaginative they were. How backward-looking and uninventive. Didn't they know that the carts they used to get their vegetables to market were created by resourceful people with imagination and ambition like Carl's? By inventors? What about the tools and implements they used to plant and harvest their vegetables? Were those not the inventions of creators who might once have been considered eccentric, tinkering cranks? I'd wanted to argue with them and defend my husband. However, I knew that that would only fan their ridicule. It had made me even more determined to work alongside Carl. I wanted to prove the naysayers wrong.

We'd encountered similar scorn on several other occasions. It was one of the reasons Carl and I agreed that we wouldn't discuss the horseless carriage when strangers were within earshot. We'd hoped that the derision August's careless chatter about the horseless carriage had incited would eventually be forgotten. Now, though, Ava's words indicated otherwise.

"August told me several people said the notion was blasphemous," she said. "That it goes against nature and is at odds with God's will. It might even be black magic."

I moved Richard to my other breast. "Yes, we're aware of that sentiment. But it doesn't matter. Carl is now devoted to getting a stationary gas engine operating, one that might be used for various purposes—other than moving carriages, I mean," I said, reluctant to defend the notion of the horseless carriage again.

Ava glanced at me. She wasn't fooled by my insinuation that Carl had stopped working on the horseless carriage, but she let it pass.

"One of my father's dinner guests recently spoke of how profitable patents can be. I wondered if Carl wouldn't prosper if he focused on different inventions, patented them, and then earned money by licensing them or receiving royalties when others make use of the invention," she said.

I thought about the stitching machine he'd built for the cobbler. It had failed at great cost to us, but perhaps Carl could find other industries for which to provide successful inventions. Might it, as Ava suggested, be more profitable for him to become an inventor of many different products? Then I remembered how indifferent Carl was about many of the projects he undertook. The passion he had for the horseless carriage was unprecedented. It was on his mind when he went to sleep at night, and it was the first thing he thought about in the morning.

"It's possible," I said, lifting Richard and laying him against my shoulder. "But he is working on the engine now. He doesn't have the time to invent other things."

"Might he not consider *making* the time for it if it means providing better for you and your sons?" said Ava, her eyes on the peas.

"I wouldn't ask it of him," I replied. "It's one thing to make small items and do repairs for customers to put food on the table, but I can't imagine Carl being driven to invent other things at this time."

"But—"

"Carl's dreams make him who he is. The man I fell in love with."

Ava glanced at me with a smile.

Does she pity me? I wondered.

I mentioned the conversation to Carl later that evening.

"She's correct: patents could be a means of making money. They work for others. However, I won't invent things simply for the sake of registering patents. Everything I do must take us another step closer to the engine that will one day provide the power for the carriage. Once the engine is going, all my efforts will be directed to creating a carriage that is driven by it. If opportunities for patents arise from that, then we will take that step. Not before that," he said.

Not before that.

What did those three words mean? How long would it be until the engine was running? When would the carriage be ready? How long would it take for the engine and carriage to be successfully incorporated?

Carl and I often discussed the many things that would still have to be done once the engine was running: He needed to work out how to attach the engine to the carriage and how to transmit the power from the engine to rotate the wheels. How would we keep the engine running and yet stop the carriage? Horses were guided by coachman via harnesses, bridle bits, and whips. Also, the animals instinctively followed the road. How would we steer the carriage and control its speed? There were so many things to think about, experiments to do, and parts to develop that it was sometimes difficult to imagine it would ever happen. Also, being poor didn't necessarily ruin the dream, but it certainly helped keep it beyond our reach.

—

Some months later, Ava was visiting again—she came by several times a week—when a boy arrived with a telegram.

`Vater gravely ill. Come quickly. Herbert.`

Eugen was napping. Baby Richard, less inclined to sleep routinely, was crawling after Tappie. I left him in Ava's care to go to the workshop.

"You should go," said Carl when I relayed the news. "Take the boys."

"Yes, I know, but you should come too," I replied.

"I should work," he said, not meeting my eye.

"You have a commission? Something a customer needs urgently?" I asked, looking around for evidence of a project I didn't know about.

"No, but I'm at a crucial point with the—"

"Herbert wouldn't have sent for us if it wasn't serious. We need to go. Both of us," I said.

"The train fare," said Carl quietly.

"Yes, but we have to go."

"It's not possible, Bertha," he said, swallowing deeply and raising his eyes to meet mine. "We can't afford it. I had to buy iron. I needed it now. There's enough money for you to travel to Pforzheim, but not for both of us."

"You—"

"There's a plow coming in for repair in a few days. We'll have money again this time next week but—"

"My father might not need me this time next week," I snapped.

"I know," he said, quiet again. "That's why you must go."

I turned and left the room.

Ava held Richard while I packed.

"Where's Carl?" she asked as I placed the boys' clothes in my case.

"He's not coming."

She was quiet for a moment. "Would you like me to come with you? To help you with the children."

Ava's kindness nudged me to the edge, and my eyes brimmed. She placed Richard on the floor and took my hands in hers. Burning with shame and tears running freely, I explained why Carl couldn't accompany me. I felt I should be angry with him, but how could I be? He'd spent money on the machine that we believed would one day change our circumstances.

"He *must* go with you," said Ava. "I'll lend you the fare."

I shook my head.

She squeezed my hands. "I'll not hear otherwise. I know you'll insist on paying me back when you can. Leave it at that. Finish packing. Go and tell Carl. I'll take Tappie home with me. Marta will be delighted by the surprise."

We laughed, knowing that Marta, who was extraordinarily possessive of Ava, would most certainly *not* be the least bit pleased by Tappie's visit.

—

Although he thanked her, Carl didn't hide how humiliated he felt about accepting Ava's money when we were alone.

"How amusing the Ritter household will find this," he said as Eugen thrust his tiny hand against the glass, trying to grab the smoke beyond the train window. "August will surely applaud the fact that not only did I have to depend on my wife to rescue our business but also on his sister for the train fare to Pforzheim."

"I don't believe Ava will mention it to anyone," I said, hoping I was right. "Anyway, August lives in Munich and has no interest in us."

"I shouldn't have come," he said, as if to himself.

A wave of irritation washed over me. "Your pride would get in the way of visiting Vater? We'll pay back Ava as soon as we can. You said yourself that there'll be money next week."

He took Eugen onto his lap, and they looked out the window together. "Yes."

"We'll visit my father, confirm all is well, and come home." I placed my hand on his knee, ashamed of my impatience. "Where, as ever, we will work and not despair."

Carl nodded but didn't look at me. He and Eugen watched the countryside speed by, their quiet chatter inaudible to me.

With Richard asleep in my arms and Carl carrying Eugen, we clambered from the train in Pforzheim and hastened in silence on foot from the station to the house. If I'd arrived alone with the children, I would've taken a carriage from the station and asked one of my brothers for the fare when we arrived, but I didn't want to further humiliate my husband. As sleeping babies are wont to do, Richard seemed to double in weight in my arms, and I felt a trickle of perspiration run down my back despite it being a cool, gray day. The distance between the station and my childhood home seemed to have stretched.

The front door was ajar. Herbert, Erwin, and a man in a black suit were huddled in the hallway, murmuring their conversation. Amelia, Thekla, and

Julius were perched on the stairs behind them. I knew Mutter was elsewhere; she wouldn't have tolerated the youngsters' undignified stations. Thekla looked up, jumped to her feet, and threw herself at me, waking Richard, who emitted a piercing wail. The man in the suit gasped in fright and clutched his chest.

Vater had died a little over an hour before we arrived.

"I should've called the doctor weeks ago," said my mother, who was still at Vater's side when I went upstairs. "He complained about feeling unwell after dinner every evening. I said he shouldn't eat so many sausages."

"You couldn't have known, Mutter."

"Yet I added another sausage to his plate when he asked for it." She wiped her nose. "Would he have listened if I'd told him to see a doctor?"

I shrugged, picturing my father leaning against his cane. I couldn't remember a time when he'd not needed it, but indeed, he'd been particularly breathless and fatigued the last time I saw him. I searched my mind for some reassuring words for my mother but found none.

"He asked for you," she murmured. "Just last night. Said he wanted to tell you that he wished you were a boy. His firstborn son. You would've done him proud."

I caught my breath and the many words that rode upon its coattails. Right to the end, I had been *only a girl* to my father. I walked toward the static mound in the bed. His eyes were closed and his face waxen and expressionless. I bent and touched my lips to his forehead.

"I love you, too, Vater," I whispered.

Carl returned to Mannheim immediately after the funeral a few days later. I stayed on to help Herbert and Erwin get our father's affairs in order. Amelia, Thekla, and Julius looked on, pale and wide-eyed. For the most part, the house was hushed as we went about our business. We kept our voices and eyes low, as if looking directly at one another and speaking at normal volume would undo us. From behind closed doors, sometimes during the day but mostly at night, came the muffled sounds of crying. What was it about grief that shamed us so?

Mutter was essentially absent from us. She rose every morning, dressed in her mourning gown, ate breakfast, and then went to the drawing room, where she sat until we called her for luncheon. She spoke only when necessary, using few words. Thirteen-year-old Thekla was unsettled.

"Will she ever be the same?" she asked.

"I believe she will," I replied. I pictured our mother at the station when Emilie and Gustav left for America and she and Vater identified Werner as a prospective husband for Elise. "As soon as she has another project to fix her mind on, something to give her purpose, she will be herself again."

Sure enough, a few days before I was due to return to Mannheim, Mutter intercepted me on my way to breakfast. She'd already eaten.

"The state of your clothes and those of Carl, Eugen, and Richard distresses me," she said.

I glanced at my skirt. Once licorice black, it had faded to a dull charcoal. The fabric was visibly worn in places where the hem brushed the floor.

"We didn't pack expecting to stay," I said.

"I sent for some fabric. Amelia and Thekla can help me make a few items for you."

"Thank you, but it's not necessary."

"It *is* necessary," she said. "Anyway, it'll give you an opportunity to see how skilled your sisters are before you leave. Amelia's trousseau is complete, and she is but sixteen. Thekla is not far behind. They will be ready when the right men show themselves."

Mutter was back.

—

Tappie greeted the boys and me at the gate when I arrived home the following week. I was surprised to see her. I thought Carl might've left her with Ava until my return. It was possible, I'd imagined, that he would've arrived home and headed into the workshop without giving the dog a thought. It was not that he wasn't fond of her, but Tappie was always with me and the children—and she played no part in the progress of Carl's machine.

"I brought her home when I went to repay Ava," he said as he knelt to hug Eugen.

"You went—"

"To the Ritters' house, yes. I'm many things, but I am not a coward, and I don't like owing anyone anything. As soon as the farmer paid me, I sped across town to give her what we owed."

"Excellent," I said, trying to disguise my wonder. I knew how uncomfortable Carl was about owing money but had anticipated he'd leave the task of repaying Ava to me. I felt a bump of self-reproach for expecting less from him.

"Well, to be perfectly honest, I was relieved to find only Ava and her mother home. Frau Ritter greeted me coolly, and I declined Ava's invitation for coffee. I only went to give her what we owed," he said.

"And to fetch Tappie," I added.

"That's right...*and* to fetch the dog."

Being at home without the burden of shouldering my mother and siblings' sorrow allowed me to finally grieve my father. The emotions were immense and came in waves, crushing me without warning as I went about my day. Sadness would swallow me up as I watched the boys playing on the mat. They would never know their grandfather—nor he them. I felt it when I opened the door, looked down the path, and imagined him there, leaning on his cane, as he had on his final visit.

Grief also found me when, after supper and the children's bedtime, Carl and I returned to the workshop to labor over the engine, adding new components, adjusting existing ones, trying different approaches. By now the engine—which had the power of one horse and special air and gas pumps—was taking shape. Carl had also equipped it with a surface carburetor and a slide control to take care of the gas intake. With Carl having to manufacture every part himself, it was a slow process, but we knew that everything we did brought us a little closer to realizing our dream.

I mourned the fact that my father would never see the horseless carriage in action. He had taught me more than he would ever know. Even if he didn't believe I was as capable as my brothers, his conversations about business, construction, and new developments in the world had prepared me to be the best-possible partner for Carl. I'd fantasized about one day being able to say to him, "Look, Vater, I'm a girl, but that did not stop me from understanding the work of my husband and being not just at his side but partly responsible for this incredible invention."

Indeed, it was as I grieved my father that I came to see that my ambitions were every much as vital as Carl's. His dream was ours.

CHAPTER 13

1877
Mannheim, Germany

With the birth of our daughter, Clara, in 1877 came news that Herr Nikolaus Otto had been granted a patent for his engine. During the previous five years, he and his partners had built a large factory that produced engines to pump water, turn mills, and move farm equipment. The patented engine, for which there was great demand, was based on the one that had won Herren Otto and Langen the gold medal at the 1867 Paris Exhibition. Since then, however, Herr Otto had adapted it to use only one piston per chamber to spread the cycle of combustion over four strokes. This, Carl had explained to me, made the machine more efficient and less noisy and meant it could produce more power. It was this "four-stroke engine" that earned Herr Otto the patent.

"Perhaps we should have named Eugen 'Nikolaus' instead," said Carl. "Our next son, then?"

"You are not disappointed?" I asked, looking at him across the room from where I was feeding Clara.

"That we did not name Eugen 'Nikolaus'?"

I laughed. "Don't be silly. About the patent?"

He shook his head. "I can only work as fast as I am. Herr Otto has a large, established company and money. I can't compete with that. Not yet. Also, it helps me that other engineers are also working on engines. I can learn from them where possible, work faster, and make a better machine. Herr Otto's four-cycle machine is clever, but I believe that three cycles of the engine are wasted. After all, there is only one combustion stroke," he said.

"Would fewer cycles or strokes also require less material for the engine? Make it smaller?" I asked, knowing that one of Carl's objectives was to build a small engine, one that did not add unnecessary weight to the carriage.

"I believe so," said Carl.

I was relieved that, rather than discouraging him, the news of Herr Otto's patent had inspired him. With three children to take care of and—when time allowed—work to be done in the workshop alongside Carl, I didn't always have the energy to placate and motivate him.

Carl crossed the room and, with his hand on my shoulder, looked at Clara, whose fine, dark eyelashes brushed against her plump cheeks as she suckled.

"She is a quiet baby, this one," he said.

"Perhaps," I replied. "But I believe she's already wiser to the world than her brothers were at this stage and preparing to do great things."

Carl squeezed my shoulder and left the room.

The birth of our daughter—at a time when, following the unification of Germany in 1871, and with the theme of the Fatherland and issues around men remaining priorities—stirred me in a way that the boys' arrivals had not. Although no one wrote *only a girl* alongside Clara's name, I thought how little had changed since I read those words in the Bible in Pforzheim. I described my thoughts in a letter to Elise.

> *I see now, with a daughter at my breast, how alike babies are at birth. Her soft head, tiny hands, and plum-like lips could have been those of Eugen or Richard when they were newborn. No matter what gender, we arrive in the world with the same eagerness for life. We fill our lungs with the same air and our stomachs with the same milk. Why, then, is it that we are assigned different paths from the moment our gender is known? Are our brains and hearts already classifiable? What if, when they are older,*

Eugen and Richard would rather do needlepoint or learn to bake while Clara would prefer to work alongside Carl in the workshop or become a farmer like those in Mutter's family? Should they not have the choice? Is it different in America? Is life freer? Can children in Milwaukee choose their own paths when they are ready to do so?

Although she eventually wrote back, Elise ignored my questions. In fact, she didn't mention anything about gender at all. Did my thoughts make her uneasy? Why would they? She and I would've discussed such matters easily in the past. Had the years, like the ocean, come between us to such an extent that I could no longer freely reveal my thoughts to my sister? It saddened me to think that despite our best efforts, Elise and I might've grown apart.

—

It was a year and a half later that I raised the subject of gender with Ava. By then, Clara was old enough to toddle about behind her brothers. However, during Ava's morning visit on New Year's Eve in 1878, my daughter climbed onto my lap, laid her head on my breast, and fell asleep while the boys continued running in and out of the room. I brushed some strands of damp hair from Clara's forehead, which was hot from her efforts to keep up with Eugen and Richard.

"Did you ever wonder what your life might've been like if your parents had raised you the way they raised August?" I asked Ava.

"You mean, send me to school beyond the age of twelve and then pay for me to study at university?" she asked.

"*Twelve?*"

"Yes. Does that not explain why I don't always understand what you and Carl are talking about when you discuss things like *combustion* and *atmosphere*?"

"No. I didn't mean that."

"I'm teasing," she said. "The idea was I would continue my education at home with a governess, who would school me in the art of being a gentlewoman as well as teach me languages, music, and other subjects."

"That didn't take place?"

"No, my mother decided she could provide everything I required. I would've loved to have continued my education like you did. I don't know any woman who is better educated," she said. "Actually, after I stopped going to school, August showed me his books and told me what he was learning. So there was a little more. We hid from my parents, and he became my teacher. I realize now, seeing how much you know, that my brother wasn't a good teacher, but it was better than not learning at all."

Her words made me think about what I'd learned at school. Certainly, my education was better than that of many other women my age. However, much of my knowledge—particularly the practical information—had come from my father and Carl. I knew about business and machines because I asked them questions—and because they'd always answered and explained until I was satisfied.

"Will Clara go to school for as long as the boys?" she asked. "It is more widely accepted now than when we were children."

She was right. Much had changed. Teacher and writer Betty Gleim's argument that girls required the same public education as boys and the 1875 decree regarding girls' high schools had increasingly opened the way for girls to be educated beyond basic learning.

"She will," I replied. "I hope that by the time Clara completes school, girls will attend university and that she will be among them."

Ava narrowed her eyes. "Really? Do you think that will ever be possible?"

"I hope so," I replied, not adding that I also hoped that by the time Clara was ready to attend school, Carl and I would have enough money to educate her.

—

That night, Carl was warming his hands over the oven when I returned to the room having finally persuaded Richard—always the last of the children to surrender—to sleep. I cleared and wiped the table. So immersed in thought was he that Carl seemed as oblivious to my presence as Tappie, curled up on the mat alongside him, was. I placed a hand on his back.

"Shall we try one more time? It's Silvester and we'll be welcoming 1879 in a few hours. Imagine the children's joy if, when they awake, we can tell them that not only has a new year begun but that the engine is also running," I said.

"Imagine *my* joy," he said.

"Well?"

"One more time, then. Particularly since the tradition of Silvester requires that we do no work tomorrow."

I smiled and led the way to the workshop, knowing that nothing would keep Carl from working on his engine—not even an ancient German custom.

As envisaged, Carl's deviation from Otto's four-stroke engine had resulted in a two-stroke machine, which was lighter because it was made up of fewer mechanical parts. This not only reduced the weight of the engine—which was important for our eventual plan to use it for the horseless carriage—but also lowered the costs.

"It will be easier to manufacture and, because it does not use as many cycles, will also be less inclined to overheat," Carl had explained to me.

Certainly, the engine had many advantages, but despite having fired and started several times during the day, it almost immediately died. Carl had tried everything but couldn't get the pressure, fuel-air mixture, residual gas, and their interaction correct.

Now, as we looked at the machine on the final day of 1878, Carl explained the steps he'd taken earlier that day to try to keep it running beyond the few seconds it burst to life.

"I'm sure it's not the parts; I have cleaned and checked them multiple times. The fuel, too, is clean. Why the mixture is not creating the required action, I cannot say," he said, running his hands through his hair.

"You've checked the slide valve?" I asked.

"What do you mean?" he said.

I pointed at the valve. "If fuel can build up and affect the vaporization of the carburetor and its entry into the cylinder, isn't it possible that the slide valve could get dirty and not close properly?"

Carl looked at me and nodded slowly.

"Shall I clean it?" I asked.

"We could try that," he said.

As Carl dismantled the relevant parts, handing them to me to inspect by lamplight and clean with a soft cloth, I thought about how I had celebrated Silvester in the past. In Pforzheim before I met Carl, we typically spent the evening eating pancakes, drinking mulled wine, and playing games. Bleigießen involved melting and pouring lead to foretell what the year might bring. Another favorite was Bibelstechen, which required closing your eyes, opening the Bible to a random page, and pointing to a verse, which would offer typically indistinct guidance for the new year.

"What did you do as a child at Silvester?" I asked Carl.

He frowned. "I don't recall. Except for one year, when after I fixed a neighbor's clock, he brought my mother a fowl to roast," he said. "We had a feast. That was a memorable Silvester."

One day, I thought, *we will celebrate every Silvester with a feast of roasted fowl.* I held the lamp above his head as Carl reassembled the machine. Eventually, he straightened.

"Right. Let's try again," he said.

I stepped back slightly as he bent over the engine to start it. As it had previously, the machine gave a loud blast as the spark from the plug ignited the fuel. This time, however, the explosion evolved into a chugging sound.

Do, do, do, it seemed to sing. *Do, do, do.*

For once, it didn't stop singing.

Do, do, do, it continued.

The engine was running! I stared at it, holding my breath and not daring to move. It continued. Our eyes met across the machine; neither of us said a word for fear of interrupting the process. It went on and we left it to sing. Carl bent to examine it. I stepped closer. Vibrating and bathed in the golden light of my lamp, the engine seemed to dance. Carl looked at me; his lips moved.

"What?" I shouted. "I can't hear you."

He walked around the table, put his arm around my shoulders, and said, "This is better than roasted fowl. Much better. This is the most memorable Silvester I have experienced in my thirty-four years of life."

I laughed, but Carl hadn't finished.

"This is the music I have longed to hear all my life. I don't want to listen to concerts in monasteries or bands in the street. This monotonous song can do what no magic flute in the world will ever achieve."

CHAPTER 14

1879
Mannheim, Germany

ALTHOUGH THE ENGINE STARTED EVERY TIME AND RAN UNTIL WE STOPPED it, and Carl and I were confident that it was ready for reproduction by others for a license fee, the authorities rejected our first application for a patent.

"Too general!" said Carl so loudly when he received the notice that Clara ran to me and hid her face in my skirts. Tappie scampered to the other side of the room. They were unaccustomed to Carl raising his voice.

He flung the letter onto the table.

"The specifications, they say, are too close to those of Herr Otto's machine! What nonsense that is. The incompetence! They clearly don't understand the difference between four- and two-stroke operations," he said.

That was possible, I thought, but it wouldn't help our cause to insult the decision-makers. Nor could we afford to lodge objections and repeated patents at the Imperial Patent Office in Berlin. There had to be another way to ensure the success of the application. I thought about what my father had said about failed plans: "When the first plan fails, do not repeat it, hoping that you'll get lucky and succeed through repetition. Instead, come up with a different plan."

"Let's have a closer look at it when the children are asleep," I said, folding the letter and putting it in the pocket of my apron.

Carl glared at me before he finally shrugged and then marched from the room.

By the time we sat down by lamplight that evening, he was calm, and we were able to go through our application step-by-step.

"Perhaps we should add more information about what distinguishes our machine from Herr Otto's," said Carl. "We need to point out exactly how his engine and ours are *not* alike. That'll prove to them that they are wrong."

"That's one way of doing it, but what about a different approach? We could detail the individual and unique components and processes featured in our engine without making mention of any other machines. Our application could emphasize components like the oil-drip valves and fuel regulators, which are not used in other engines. Let's ignore what they resisted and present them with inventions the patent office has not seen before," I said.

"That might work," said Carl.

We mailed a revised application the next day and celebrated a successful patent for the two-stroke engine a few weeks later. However, while it was a significant achievement, it didn't immediately change our circumstances. We had an engine and a patent, but still we lacked the money necessary to further develop the horseless carriage. Once more, we had to call on our old friend, patience.

"The time will come," Carl said one morning when I took him coffee in the workshop. "I wish it would come sooner—but as I look at the engine, I know it will come."

"There must be a way to speed things up," I said.

"I think there is," he replied. "My heart belongs to the horseless carriage, but I believe the stationary engine is the key that'll open the door to it. I'm going to perfect this engine so that it is as uncomplicated and affordable to reproduce as possible, and inexpensive to run. We need to be able to build and sell the stationary engine quickly to generate profits. If we get it right, there'll be a good market for it among factory owners, millers, farmers, brewers, and town engineers."

So it was that Carl further refined the engine as a stationary power source.

Among the features he added to it was a system to ignite the compressed gas-air mixture quickly and effectively. Carl installed a spark inductor, which was connected to a small generator to generate the high-voltage electric current required to cause a spark and ignite the gas-air mixture. Every hour we spent working on the engine brought us closer to creating a machine that achieved the lowest-possible gas consumption per hour and the highest horsepower at full speed. However, all our dedication and hard work and Carl's genius were not enough. We needed money to build multiple engines to get them out into the world to demonstrate their worth so that they would attract further buyers.

"I cannot see a way around it, Bertha. We need the bank," said Carl at breakfast one morning.

It had been coming. We'd discussed how we might raise money for production costs for days, and as much as we loathed the idea of going into debt again, we realized it was necessary if we were to make money from the engine.

"There's no point waiting. I shall meet the bankers today," he said.

It occurred to me that I might go with him. Perhaps Ava would stay with the children for a few hours. I knew, though, that Carl, having made the decision, would be eager to get going.

"Yes. But don't feel rushed into a decision. Perhaps discuss what they offer, and let's talk about it before you agree to anything," I said.

Carl had barely pedaled away when I heard the clatter of a carriage pulling up outside. I looked through the window to see a large man with a thick, black beard disembark. He paused and looked around, buttoning his long, dark coat. His expression was one I was accustomed to from wealthy visitors: puzzlement. What is this place? A home? A workshop? A factory? I enjoyed how, as was usually the case with strangers, the confusion mounted when I opened the door with a child in my arms and two at my skirts. What was uncommon, though, was Tappie's response. She gave a low growl before launching into a frenzy of barking so robust that every woof raised her chest and front legs off the ground.

Richard lifted her into his arms. It put an end to her baying, but she stretched her neck toward the man, lifted a lip, and snarled. She was generally a friendly dog. Was it his size and the flapping coat that unsettled her?

I stepped in front of her and Richard. "Good morning. Can I help you?"

The man glanced at Clara, who was in my arms. His eyes lingered on my hand. And why wouldn't he stare? I'd not had a chance to scrub off the oil that had accumulated on my skin and under my fingernails earlier while I had worked alongside Carl.

"Frau Benz, ja? Good morning. I am Herr Emil Bühler, court photographer," he said. "I required some polished steel plates for my work. This is the place of Herr Benz the, erm, engineer, is it not?"

"It is."

"Good. I believe he might be able to make them for me. Can I speak to him?" he asked, craning his neck to look behind me.

"He's out, but please, tell me what you require."

"Thank you, but perhaps—"

"I will know if we—if he is able to help you," I said. "The workshop is this way."

Eugen and Richard ran ahead to open the double doors. I followed, carrying Clara, who peered over my shoulder at Herr Bühler. Just as I was accustomed to strangers being surprised by our home, I was familiar with them not expecting me to understand what they wanted from my husband. I never mentioned that it was possible that I might work on whatever it was they needed—although it did occur to me that Herr Bühler might wonder if that was the case, given the state of my hands.

I placed Clara on the floor. Eugen took her hand and led her across the room while I found Carl's notebook and a pencil. Herr Bühler was staring at the engine, which was on a workbench in the center of the room.

"What is this?" he asked.

"A turning machine," I replied as dismissively as I could. Carl and I had a few standard explanations about the engine for strangers who were unlikely to see any purpose for it. We very rarely mentioned the horseless carriage. The questions, skepticism, and scorn that that elicited were tedious. Herr Bühler, however, was not satisfied.

"What does it turn?"

"Mills. Factory and farming equipment," I replied, pencil poised. "Do you know the size of the steel sheets you want? What exactly will you use them for?"

"Does it work?"

"Yes," I replied.

"I'd like to see that. Would Herr Benz show me?"

"You'd have to ask him yourself," I replied. I could've fired it up myself, but why would I? Why would I waste fuel for the entertainment of a photographer who might or might not become a client?

"So, the steel plates, Herr Bühler. Give me as much detail as possible about what you want."

—

Less than a week later, Herr Bühler returned. Not only had Carl made and delivered the plates to his satisfaction, but my husband had also agreed to demonstrate the engine to him.

"What use does a photographer have for an engine?" I'd asked Carl.

"He is interested as an investor. He's wealthy and well connected. The banks will not lend us any money. I thought it might be worth hearing what Herr Bühler has to say. There's no risk in listening. We have no other options," said Carl.

Indeed, Carl had visited every bank in Mannheim, all of which turned down his request for a loan. None of the men Carl had spoken to showed any interest in the engine. They couldn't imagine that a gas engine might offer anything that wasn't already provided by a steam engine. Even Carl's illustrations of farms, mills, breweries, and factories using the engine had failed to raise their curiosity. They'd been distrustful of the idea and, Carl said, could barely hide their impatience to show him out of their offices.

So it was I opened the door to Herr Bühler once more. Again, Tappie objected vociferously. The big man glanced at her with the look of someone who could barely restrain his boot from shooting out and striking the little dog.

"How you tolerate such a noisy creature, I don't know," he said, not bothering to greet me.

"I thought it was your coat that upset her last time, but clearly it is something more," I said, taking Tappie in my arms. "My husband is in the workshop. You know the way."

The familiar blast, shudder, and clattering of the engine came a few minutes later. It ran for several minutes, long enough for Carl to have demonstrated its steadfastness. With Eugen having recently begun school, Richard and Clara played quietly while I cleaned our rooms. Although I couldn't hear their voices from the workshop, I imagined what Carl might be telling Herr Bühler. He was probably explaining, in minute detail, the exact chemical and mechanical workings of the machine, which few people seemed to understand and—unless they were fellow engineers—cared to understand. Perhaps, with his knowledge of photography and cameras, Herr Bühler might be different. But I couldn't find it in me to feel hopeful about the visit. It wasn't just that I felt uneasy about the man, but I also wondered why a photographer might be interested in investing in the engine. The visit would come to nothing, I thought. The only outcome would be a wasted and frustrating morning for Carl. I was wrong.

"Should we not draw up an agreement?" I asked when Carl appeared in the house and told me the news a little later.

He walked to the children and bent to pat their heads. His eyes were bright and his step springy. "You mean, like I did with August? No. I was very clear with Herr Bühler: I do not want a partner."

"So he'll give us money so that we can manufacture more engines, and we'll pay him back with interest? Surely even that needs some type of—"

"He'll provide nothing more than a means for me to make and sell engines. He'll earn more money from his investment in the engines than he would elsewhere, and we'll be on our way to earning enough to focus on the carriage," he said.

"Did you talk about the carriage? Does he know about it?"

Carl shook his head. "No. Herr Bühler's involvement has nothing to do with the carriage. I've learned my lesson, in that regard. We'll not mention it—not to him or anyone else until the time is right."

Emil Bühler wasted no time in returning with enough money for Carl to build four more engines. Tappie gave a low growl every time she caught sight of the photographer, but I couldn't deny that he—or rather, his money—was valuable to us.

"They are sold!" said Carl a day after he'd completed work on the four machines. The children, Tappie, and I were in the yard.

I was astonished. "So soon? How?"

"Emil's brother, Christian, is a cheesemaker. He's also investing in the engine and is well connected to factory owners. The four I built have gone, and we have orders for more, Bertha!"

I smiled, speechless.

"Did you hear me?" he asked, placing his hands on my shoulders. "Orders for more!"

The children gathered around us. Eugen and Richard each took one of Clara's hands. She giggled in anticipation. They formed a circle and began skipping, Tappie dancing between them as the dust rose around their feet.

"Orders for more! Orders for more!" they chanted.

CHAPTER 15

1881
Mannheim, Germany

No doubt others wondered why Carl and I chose to renovate our home at Mannheim, Square T6, Number 11, rather than move to a place with a more fashionable address when we could afford to do so. However, Ava was the only one who asked the question outright.

"It's beautiful out here, yes. You have a larger garden than you might have elsewhere, and the changes will result in a lovely house—but don't you want to be closer to the city center?" she asked after I'd explained how we planned to expand and improve the house. "You might even find it less expensive to move than to rebuild."

"I've no desire to be in the middle of the city. Neither does Carl. We're happy here," I said, moving Carl's sketches of the renovations from the table so I could set out the coffee things.

Ava persisted. "But what about the children? You could be closer to the school. To their friends. Think of the convenience."

"It wouldn't be convenient at all. Carl's work is here."

"Isn't that another good reason to move? Wouldn't you and the children see more of him if his work wasn't so conveniently close to home?" she asked.

How poorly my friend understood Carl. Indeed, the Mannheim Gas Engine Factory, which Carl, Emil, and Christian had established within months of selling the first four engines, occupied a large, new building on the other side of Carl's original workshop. There, where they now employed forty other men to build and sell engines, Carl worked from dawn to dusk. When the other men went home at the end of the day, he ate dinner with me and the children and then headed into his workshop to continue work on the horseless carriage. I often joined him when the children were asleep.

I handed Ava a cup of coffee. "He works in his workshop—which is not part of the factory—every night and during the weekend."

"I didn't realize he was still working on his other designs," she said, confirming once more how little she knew Carl. He would *still* work on our dream until it was realized. Even then, he'd inevitably work on improving it.

"Yes," I replied. "But even if he wasn't and didn't want a workshop here, we would probably stay."

"Probably," she echoed doubtfully.

We sipped our coffee quietly for a moment before Ava spoke again.

"I might have selfish reasons for wishing you'd move into the city," she said. "No, that's not true: I *do* have selfish reasons."

"But I thought you enjoyed the carriage ride to visit me here. Has it become tiresome?" I asked, half joking.

I rarely visited Ava at her parents' house in Mannheim. It was difficult for me to get away, with three children to care for. Also, I didn't feel at ease in the Ritter home, given Carl and August's history, not to mention the role Herr Ritter Senior had played in urging his son to set a lawyer on us.

"It's not that. Well, not entirely. It would be pleasant to have you closer by. It's just that…well, things might change," she said, smoothing her hair back in an uncharacteristically self-conscious way.

"What things?" I asked.

"I told you a while ago about Herr Adler. Do you remember?"

"Is that your father's colleague, the widow, who brings his small daughter to dine with you and your parents? The man your mother pities?" I replied, recalling how we'd laughed about how Ava's mother had accused Herr Adler's cook of underfeeding the man because he was so thin.

"Yes," she said, eyes on her cup as she laid it in its saucer with inordinate care.

"Well?"

She didn't respond immediately, and when she finally did, I had to lean forward to hear what she said.

"He's asked my father if he might propose marriage to me," she said.

I wasn't surprised by the idea of Ava marrying again. She was an intelligent, kind, and amusing friend. Like me, Ava was already in her thirties, but her satiny complexion, glossy hair, and liveliness made her seem younger. She had none of the heavy-footed hopelessness or disappointment one might expect of a widow. Ava was energetic and in good health, with many child-bearing years ahead of her. She was also the daughter of one of the city's most eminent families. Many men might want her.

"And?" I asked.

Ava shrugged. Still, she didn't look at me. "My father said he could."

"So?"

"I expect he will."

"What will you say?" I asked, suddenly aware of a strange whirring in my head.

"I don't know." Finally, she looked into my eyes. It was unusual to see her distressed. "What should I do, Bertha? What should I say when he asks? It could be this evening. He and his daughter—her name is Hannah—are coming to dine with us. Again."

"Will you move away?"

"What?" she asked, clearly bewildered.

My response surprised me too. It also explained the noise in my head. I was afraid that, as it had done with Emilie and Elise, marriage would take Ava away from me.

"If you marry Herr Adler, will you leave Mannheim?"

"No. He lives and works here. Why would you think that?"

I felt my face redden.

"Ah! Your sisters! No. I won't go to America or anywhere else. I will..."

Ava's words trailed off, and she reached out and took my hand.

"I haven't even decided if I'll marry him. You have to help me make the right decision," she said.

"But I don't know Herr Adler," I replied. I felt foolish about having allowed my fears to appropriate the conversation. But that didn't stop me from wondering if Ava knew for certain Herr Adler didn't plan to leave Mannheim with his daughter and new wife—and even if she had, would it make any difference? My sisters had had no say about going to America.

"How do you feel about him? About becoming his wife and raising his daughter?" I asked.

"Hannah is delightful, full of questions, playful, and good. He is, well—polite, quiet, and rather serious."

"But how do you *feel* about him?"

Ava shook my hand as if to wake me up. "That's why I need your help. I don't *know* how I feel about him. When Rudolf proposed, I said yes immediately."

"You were in love with him. That made it easy," I said, thinking about how eager I'd been to marry Carl.

"It wasn't just that," said Ava, leaning back in her chair and crossing her arms. "I can't remember if I loved Rudolf at that time. I loved him later, yes. But when he asked me to marry him, I was so excited by the idea of being married I didn't stop to consider much else. I wanted to be his wife, a wife."

"But now?"

"Now I've seen you and Carl together, the marriage you have. I'm older and I realize that being a wife isn't enough. I want to be with someone who interests me, whose work interests me, and who is interested in what I think," she said, her eyes bright and steady once more.

"Are you saying Herr Adler doesn't interest you?"

"I don't know him well enough to know that. He's so quiet. I haven't heard him speak about his work or anything that might interest him aside from Hannah. I have no idea if he might be interesting. How did you discover that you and Carl shared an interest? That you were as enthusiastic about what he does as he is?" she asked.

I told her how, when we met on our way to Maulbronn, Carl had described his dream of inventing a carriage driven by an engine. I recalled how intrigued I'd been, not only by the fantasy of the project but also by the fire in him. I had never met anyone with such passion for an idea.

"How did you know what he was talking about?" asked Ava.

"I don't know. I certainly had no idea how it might be done. Mostly, I was excited by his excitement and determination. And when he responded to my questions without condescension and was interested in—even asked for—my opinions, I saw for the first time a man who valued me, not as a girl or woman but as another person with thoughts and suggestions worth considering. And that those thoughts and suggestions were about machines, and the future was even more thrilling," I said.

Ava was silent for a moment before she said, quietly and with some melancholy, "I've experienced none of that with Herr Adler."

"Maybe it will come when you get to know him better," I said, feeling uncertain about whether that was possible or likely.

"But what if it doesn't? What if I marry him and find that nothing changes?"

I shook my head. "I don't know. Perhaps you could suggest that you get to know one another better before you agree to marry him. Is that possible?"

She chuckled. "Definitely not. He'd be insulted. My parents would be appalled. What man waits around to find out if he is good enough for a woman?"

"A man who truly wants you to be his wife might."

Ava stood. "You see! That's why I want you to move to the city. If we lived closer, you could guide me. You and Carl could get to know Herr Adler. He might see your marriage and be inspired by it."

"What are you going to do?"

"I don't know," she said, gathering her things to leave.

—

In fact, Carl and I had never contemplated moving. Being on the outskirts of Mannheim meant we were removed from prying eyes. Our neighbors were too far away to hear the sounds that came from the workshop, and when Carl tested his engine, he was able to do so without raising curiosity, criticism, and repugnance. Disparaging sentiment about Carl's work prevailed from those who believed that machines—any machines—belonged in a godless world and that inventions such as the engine were the work of the devil. As if that were not challenging enough, when he eventually told them about it, Carl's work on the horseless carriage was dismissed by his colleagues. I explained as much in a letter to Elise.

Carl had hoped that once the factory was going well, the Bühler brothers would agree that he could start working on the horseless carriage there. The equipment in the factory is more advanced than that in his workshop, and it would help Carl to have the assistance of some of the other men at times. However, when Carl decided the time was right and told them about his plans for the horseless carriage, Emil and Christian were aghast at the idea of anything other than gas engines being manufactured at the Mannheim Gas Engine Factory. Emil, it emerged, had heard rumors about Carl's ambitions and is adamant they shouldn't be indulged.

"No! No gimmicks and fantasies," he told Carl. "Don't chase after a phantom! Let us continue to build our fortune on the stationary two-stroke engine and not waste time and money on experiments on your unrealistic dream."

When Carl pointed out that the business only existed because of his experiments and hard work, Emil and Christian argued that it only existed because of their money. You can imagine how furious that made Carl. Fortunately, he restrained himself, and after further discussion, he was able to extract something of an assurance from the Bühlers that as soon as there was surplus income, some of it would be allocated to experiments on the horseless carriage. For the moment, there is calm, and, while he assured Emil and Christian that his attention will not be diverted from the engines at present, Carl continues to work on his project in his workshop during every spare hour he has.

—

I did not disclose to anyone how worried I was about Carl's relationship with Emil and Christian. Many of Carl's complaints about his colleagues reminded me about how things were when his and August's partnership began failing. His grievances about working at the Mannheim Gas Engine Factory with the Bühlers were also similar to those he'd had when he worked at Gebrüder Benckiser Engineering Works and in Vienna. He moaned about how inept the workers at the factory were and how blinkered the Bühlers' approach to business was. I couldn't escape the cold dread I felt when, one evening, he listed his objections once more. It made me wonder, not for the first time, whether Carl would ever be content to work with others.

"Every day, we have the same discussions about the same problems. Every day, I give them the solutions, but nothing changes," he said. "Emil and Christian don't know the difference between a flywheel and an exhaust, and they show no interest in learning. I'm the reason the business exists, and yet they don't take my advice."

"But still the factory has grown," I reminded him.

"Because I built a good engine, which works well for our clients and is increasingly replacing steam engines at more and more factories," he persisted. "Not because the Bühler brothers are good businessmen."

"But, for the time being, you can't afford to be without Emil and Christian."

"I did without them before," grumbled Carl.

"And you will again in time to come," I said, not reminding him how close we'd come to financial ruin before Emil arrived and brought Christian into the business. "At least while you are working at the factory, you can quietly work on the horseless carriage in your spare time."

"Yes, but what's frustrating me now is how close I am to being able to assemble the machine. I want to start testing it. You've seen how my drawings have evolved over the years. Look," he said, sliding his open sketchbook toward me. "Every morning, I wake up wishing that I could get started on it. Instead, I must go to a factory and do the same things I did the day before, with men who don't care about what could be but only what is."

I pulled the book closer and examined the drawing. It was the latest of the countless sketches of his design I had seen over the years. I thought of the variations that had come before. Day by day, the changes he made might have appeared minor. Over the years, though, they were immense. I studied the clean, definite lines and saw that Carl was right: the sketch of the carriage looked convincingly complete. As he had experimented and learned more about the engine and thought obsessively about the horseless carriage, his design had transformed from an idea to a plan, which—clear, in black on white—demanded that the next step be taken.

"Hmm. Horseless carriage," I said, thinking out loud. "It no longer resembles a carriage. You've created something unlike anything anyone has seen before."

"Ja," he said. "It deserves a proper name."

The most recent version of the carriage had evolved over several months after a businessman from the city, Herr Max Rose, visited Carl to discuss a tricycle for two people that he was contemplating ordering and selling from his shop. Nothing had come of the tricycle. Herr Rose had decided it would be preferable to sell high-wheel velocipedes instead. He'd told Carl that his wife had discouraged him from pursuing the idea of the two-person tricycle because she said that women would not want to pedal the machine alongside their husbands.

"I wonder how many women Frau Rose spoke to before arriving at that conclusion," I had said. "I can picture me and you riding through the countryside together with great enjoyment."

Carl had smiled. "Yes, surely as many women as men would like the freedom of climbing onto a machine and riding wherever they wanted without having to harness a horse to a carriage."

"Indeed," I'd replied. "The only thing more appealing would be to power the machine with an engine rather than one's legs."

So it was that the discussion about the tricycle had led Carl to adapt his sketches of the carriage once again. What emerged on paper now was a three-wheeled velocipede with a wooden platform for the driver and a passenger. Fixed on creating a machine that was simple to use, Carl had sketched a single front wheel, which was mounted on a fork fitted with a lever on a toothed rack. This would be conveniently located above the knees of the operator. The engine would turn the back wheels while the operator steered the front wheel using the lever to determine direction.

"As it is on the velocipede, the front wheel will turn with little effort," he explained.

Unlike most velocipedes, though, the machine had two much larger back wheels. The three-wheeled format not only stabilized the vehicle but also provided the space necessary for a seat for the driver and a passenger and, behind them, place for the engine and other components required to operate it.

"It might not look much like a carriage, but it's still a wagon in that it will carry people and, perhaps one day, also produce and materials. Perhaps it is a horseless wagon," I suggested as I inspected the drawing now.

He shook his head. "No, I don't think so. The word *horseless* makes it sound lacking, whereas it's the opposite. It'll be free of horses by gaining a motor."

"Is it a motor carriage?" I asked.

"Well, maybe… Or is it a motorwagen?" said Carl.

We looked at each other, nodding. *Motorwagen* was a good name.

I smiled. "So, we have a name and detailed drawings. Now we simply need to—"

He stood up and strode to the other side of the room, ignoring me.

"How can Emil and Christian not be interested in the motorwagen? How can they not see how it could change life for all of us? Why are they so blind? I feel held back by the very people who should have a vision for the future. That's not how it's meant to be!"

"As long as there are things you can continue to do from here, you're moving toward the dream," I said. "You could do it quicker if the Bühlers understood, but that's not the way things are, and we have to accept that even small progress is better than none."

"You're right," he said. "I shouldn't be impatient. I'll keep working on the carriage—I mean, motorwagen—and start undertaking as many experiments as I can afford in my workshop. Hopefully, when they see how it works, Emil and Christian will agree that we can assemble it in the factory."

—

For a while, Carl ceased his complaining. I hoped it was because he was more content at the factory. Another visit from Ava took my mind off the matter temporarily.

"I did it," she said without preamble when I opened the door to her.

"You agreed to marry Herr Adler?"

She swept passed me, pausing briefly to scratch Tappie's ears. "No, I took your advice and said I'd like to get to know him better before I decided."

"Oh. So?"

"He was shocked. I expected it. Remember?"

I nodded.

Ava sat down in what I had come to think of as her chair in our home. She placed her folded arms on the table and emitted a deep sigh. "But I didn't anticipate just how shocked he would be." She looked up at me. "It's early, I know, but can we have coffee? Please?"

We didn't talk again until coffee was brewed and poured, and then Ava continued as if we hadn't stopped.

"Herr Adler is not, it emerges, as quiet as I thought he was. He was outraged by my request and reprimanded me at length. Honestly, I'd not imagined him capable of chastising anyone with such vehemence," she said.

"What did he say?"

"As I predicted, he was insulted. He wanted to know what I suspected him of and exactly what he should do to prove himself worthy of me. I tried to explain that I believed it would be to our mutual advantage to get to know each other better first."

"Which seems reasonable."

"Eight times! Eight times he'd been to our house, he shouted. How many more dinners would it require before we knew each other, he asked."

"He counted," I said.

Ava giggled. "Yes, he counted. You know what the silliest thing is, Bertha?"

I shook my head.

"While Herr Adler was roaring in indignation, it occurred to me that he might be more interesting than I imagined. Just as you recognized Carl's passion years ago, I thought I saw some fire in him." She paused to take a long sip of coffee. "But then he said something that changed my mind again."

"What?" I asked.

"He said that any woman, particularly a childless widow like me, should be grateful for his interest, which, he concluded, he was summarily withdrawing."

"Oh, Ava! I'm—"

"Please don't say you're sorry, Bertha."

"Can I finish?"

She nodded with a tight smile.

"I'm relieved you didn't accept him. *His* is not the kind of passion that you want. It's good that you found out before it was too late," I said.

"Yes. I tell myself that, but as my parents pointed out in frustration, it'll probably mean I'll be alone for the rest of my life," she replied.

I wanted to say it might be better to be alone than to be married to an unsuitable man but didn't. How easy it was for someone who had a happy marriage to make such glib observations. It had taken Herr Adler's interest in Ava to open my eyes to the idea of her being lonely. Our friendship and her easy relationship with my family couldn't replace what she might hope for in love and motherhood. She might've read my mind.

"Don't feel sorry for me. I wouldn't change my response to his proposal even if I anticipated his rage. I'll miss Hannah, but I don't want her father. I took your advice because it was wise. Don't pity me or feel responsible. The only thing you are guilty of is having an extraordinary marriage and making me want the same," she said.

That evening, when I told Carl what had happened to Ava, he murmured his disapproval at Herr Adler's behavior with his characteristic indifference to other people's affairs. Or was he more withdrawn than usual? At dinner, I realized then that he no longer mentioned the Mannheim Gas Engine Factory in our conversations at all. He didn't appear sullen or ill-tempered, but I couldn't help wondering if he was withholding his grievances about the Bühlers and the business because he felt censured by my comments about how we couldn't afford to be without them. What kind of woman forces her husband to repress his conversation? Was this the marriage Ava admired? Whom could Carl talk to about his concerns if not me?

I followed him into the workshop after I'd put the children to bed.

"How are things at the factory?" I asked, sitting on what I thought of as *my* three-legged stool. "You don't mention the place these days."

He didn't look up from the workbench. "I didn't want to worry you unnecessarily."

"What does that mean? That there might be something to worry about, or there is no need to worry?" I asked, keeping my tone light.

Carl raised his head. "The latter, I hope. Christian has employed a salesman, who he believes will double our orders."

"I thought Christian was responsible for sales. What's his role now?"

"Apparently, he has exhausted his contacts. He wants to spend more time at his cheese factory and says that we need someone who is willing to travel further afield to demonstrate the engine."

"That makes sense, doesn't it?" I asked.

Carl nodded, but his jaw twitched.

"What is it, Carl?"

He sighed. "The new salesman knows nothing about engines. Just like Emil and Christian, he does not seem interested in learning. How will he be able to sell the machines if he doesn't know how they work?"

"Christian was able to sell them without understanding them. Is it not about *what* they can do rather than how they do it? How much do your customers need to know?"

Carl looked me, his eyes narrowing as he frowned. He was disappointed that I was siding with the Bühlers.

I leaned toward him, reminding myself how even the strongest, tallest, and smartest people have vulnerabilities. "I understand that you would like your colleagues to be as intrigued by your engine as you are, but is it necessary, Carl? You are an inventor and an excellent engineer. You've designed and built a machine that's safe and easy to operate. The Bühlers, their salesman, and your customers don't have to understand the engine like you do. They only need to value it and what it can do and put it to work in their factories and farms," I said.

Carl nodded. "You're right. It's just that I can't help wishing I could work with like-minded men. With engineers who understand what I'm doing and what I could do given the chance."

"Men like August Ritter," I joked.

He chuckled. "Ah, Bertha! I can always count on you to shake me awake and see what's real. Again, you're right. Like-minded men might not exist. That's why you and I should work alone."

"If only it was possible for just the two of us to build the kind of business and machines we dream of. But that will never be practical or financially achievable. We need others. We need a company," I said.

"Eugen and Richard will soon be old enough to work alongside us. Then it will be different."

"And Clara," I added.

—

What Carl and I didn't know when we spoke about the appointment of a new salesman was that the man had been employed under desperate circumstances. Not only had Christian run out of prospects, but the forecast for all future sales from the factory was decreasing. The business's primary competitor was the Cologne-based Gas Engine Factory Deutz AG with its four-stroke "Otto engine." Established by Otto, Langen, and fellow engineers Gottlieb Daimler and Wilhelm Maybach, the company was older and significantly larger than the Mannheim Gas Engine Factory.

"It's not easy to compete with a factory that's run by several engineers when yours has just one," muttered Carl. "Apparently, they're building about ten engines a week. We don't manage that in a month, and if we could, we couldn't sell them all anyway."

Despite assuring Emil and Carl that he was traveling extensively and visiting as many businesses and farms as he could, the new salesman did not find as many new customers as the Mannheim Gas Engine Factory needed to survive. Without income, the factory was stalling. Bills and salaries had to be paid, but the Bühlers had exhausted their investment and the banks were not prepared to lend them any more. Christian withdrew from the company completely, telling his brother that he must buy his shares from him as soon as he was able. Emil refused to spend another mark on the company. Unless Carl had an alternative, said Emil, they must find new investors.

"He says he knows several men who are interested and who could secure a loan from the bank that will save the business," Carl said one night as we prepared for bed, having agreed that it would not be wise to invest our small savings in the factory. "Emil will arrange meetings as soon as possible."

I wished I felt more positive about the news of potential investors. However, it came after a particularly snowy week and at a time when I was heavily pregnant with our fourth child. Although Eugen, Richard, and Clara were well behaved and helpful, having the children stuck indoors and restless all day had tried my patience. I was tired and uncomfortable.

Pulling the blankets over my distended belly, I forced myself to think of the advantages of new investors. That a different group of businessmen was interested in backing Carl and Emil's business upheld the belief that the future was promising. The new partners might think differently from Emil and allow Carl to start working on the motorwagen at the factory. However, there were also potential disadvantages. New investors would reduce Carl's and Emil's shares in the business. With that, their say in how the company was run would diminish too. Carl was already unhappy about having to answer to Emil. How would he cope with additional partners? I wished I didn't feel as encumbered by my pregnancy and that I was more alert to how we might manage the implications of new shareholders.

"Do you know the men?" I asked, unable to raise my energy and unscramble my thoughts to contemplate anything more useful.

"No. Emil said one is a banker. He described the other three as 'men of wealth.'"

"Do any of the men understand engines? Is it possible you might finally work with someone who understands technical matters?" I asked, hoping that Carl might at last have a colleague who, like August, was an engineer but, unlike August, also an astute businessman.

"Emil didn't know. I'll find out more when we meet," said Carl, sounding as unenthusiastic about matters as I felt.

CHAPTER 16

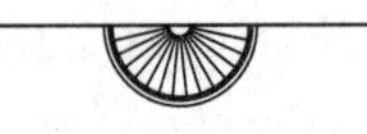

1882
Mannheim, Germany

The snow had melted, but the air was still heavy with the iciness of winter when our second daughter, Thilde, was born. She slid into the world quietly and with ease, which, said my mother—who'd come to lend a hand for a week or two—was the way of children born fourth or later.

"They know that their mothers are no longer excited by babies and that their place in the world has already been tested by their siblings," explained Mutter.

It was true that my feelings of anticipation had become more muted with the birth of each child. However, as I ran the tips of my fingers over Thilde's downy head, I felt warm with love for her.

"I hope each of my children test the world in their own way, however unconventional that might be," I said, thinking fleetingly about how our parents had unquestioningly decided on what my sisters and I would do with our lives, while our brothers were given license to choose their own paths.

At that moment, Clara, nearly five years old, walked into the room with Tappie, gray-muzzled now, at her heels. My daughter handed me a glass of water.

"The midwife said you must drink water so that the baby gets enough milk," she said, giving Mutter a self-assured look.

Clara was determined to be my dedicated helper and was a little unsettled by her grandmother's presence in the house. It reminded me how Emilie had assumed a similar role alongside Mutter when we were young. It helped Clara, though, that her brothers were older. At eleven and ten respectively, Eugen and Richard were helpful around the house and increasingly in the workshop too.

"You've raised such useful children," said Ava, when my mother had returned to Pforzheim and my friend came to meet Thilde. "Richard opened the door to me, and Clara said she'd make coffee."

"With Richard's help, I hope," I said, placing sleeping Thilde in her arms.

She nestled the baby against her breast and admired her sweet, round face. Ava had always been at ease with my children and they with her. Now, as I watched her gently rocking Thilde, I wondered whether they made her long to have her own. Even after the matter of Herr Adler's proposal, we'd not discussed whether she wanted to be a mother. Elise had argued when we were girls that "all women want children" and that those who did not were unnatural. Even then, I'd had my doubts. Women were all different. Why would we all want the same things? And if a woman didn't want to be a mother, why would that make her abnormal? What about women who became nuns? Did their devotion to God exempt them from being classified as unnatural? I wished it was something I could discuss with Ava. However, just as it seemed unfair that Carl and I had such a happy partnership and she was alone, it seemed cruel, with my four healthy children in the house, to pry into whether she wished to be a mother. Sometimes what one does *not* discuss with those they are closest to is what keeps them close.

After I'd fed and placed Thilde in her crib, Ava and I sat while Clara served us coffee, Richard hovering respectfully behind her.

"So, there have been changes at the Mannheim Gas Engine Factory, I believe," said my friend.

"Yes, there have."

I felt uneasy talking about the factory. Discussions with the new investors hadn't been finalized when Thilde made it known that she would arrive earlier than expected. When I had asked Carl about the outcome a few days after her birth, he'd been vague.

"All four have bought shares in the company," he'd said.

"So, you are satisfied with the outcome?" I'd asked.

He hadn't lift his eyes from Thilde, who was at my breast. "They say the investment will enable us to compete with Otto's business."

"Do you agree?"

"It's possible...in time," he'd said.

"Are any of the men engineers?"

He'd shaken his head.

"Is there an agreement? A written one?"

He'd nodded.

"Have you signed it?"

He'd nodded again.

Now, as Ava mentioned the factory, I felt my chest constrict with the same cold nub of concern I'd experienced when Carl and I spoke of the agreement. I didn't like not knowing the details.

"What have you heard?" I asked her.

Ava glanced at me, blinking. She wasn't accustomed to me sounding uncertain.

"I've been a little occupied with the baby and might not have paid as much attention to the factory as I usually do," I explained.

"My father's banker is one of the new investors. He's apparently very pleased with his involvement and the fact that one of the other men is the new chairman of the factory. That's all I know," she said, lifting her cup to drink as if to verify she had no more to tell me.

She was better informed than I was.

—

Carl confirmed later that one of the investors had, indeed, assumed the role of chairman of the Mannheim Gas Engine Factory. I asked him to tell me exactly what had happened during the negotiations that had taken place at the time of Thilde's birth.

He commenced with a sigh, telling me that during Emil's initial discussions with the four men who were interested in investing in the factory, the photographer had ill-advisedly disclosed their names to one another.

As a result, the men had come together and agreed to discuss the terms of their investment as a group rather than as individuals. The bank behind the necessary loan encouraged this. Moreover, it insisted that the Mannheim Gas Engine Factory become a corporation with an additional four directors on the board, taking the total board members to nine.

"This gave the new investors more power in their negotiations and meant that they were able to lay out other terms, which Emil and I couldn't counter," said Carl, unable to meet my eye.

"What kind of terms?" I asked, dreading his reply.

He ran his hands over his head. "Well, you already know that one of the men claimed the position of chairman."

"Yes. And?"

"My shares, and Emil's, have diminished. We own less than a sixth of the business."

My stomach churned. Carl's manner had indicated that matters were bad, but I'd not anticipated this. "Less than a sixth! But how can that be? You brought them a factory in operation, with a production line for an engine that has already proved itself. I don't understand it, Carl. How could you have signed such an agreement?"

Carl's voice was quiet and low. "I had no choice," he said.

"Surely—"

"We risked losing everything, Bertha. Emil and Christian hadn't disclosed just how bad things were, how much we owed. Surely you understand that I wouldn't have signed if there was an alternative. It was the only way to save the factory from its creditors."

There were many things I wanted to say. I had a head full of questions, leading with, *There* must *have been another way?* But it didn't matter. The deed was done, and now, looking at Carl, I could see what it had taken from him. Once again, our dreams were stalled. I didn't have to tell him that. I had to know one more thing, though.

"Did you discuss the motorwagen with your new partners? Do you think they'll allow you to work on it at the factory?"

He shook his head. "No, I didn't. I don't trust them to give them access to my plans or to work on it there. It's all we have."

—

It wasn't *all* we had, but it was close. Later that month, Emil cut all ties with the Mannheim Gas Engine Factory, but not before making a fanfare of presenting Carl with his portion of the shares.

"Naturally, I was grateful he *gave* them to me. Even if they're not worth a great deal at this point, Emil's shares give me more say in the business," said Carl, recounting what had happened the day Emil told him he was leaving the company. "But to go on and on about how generous he was being took all my pleasure away. The third time he said that he *'didn't have to'* give them to me, I felt like telling him not to."

"Perhaps he thought you weren't showing enough gratitude," I said.

Carl glared at me. "I thanked him. What did he hope for? That I prostrate myself before him?"

"Probably," I murmured.

"What I wanted to do was remind him that without me, he would've had *no* shares in the company to so generously bestow upon me. He's forgotten that," he said.

I nodded. There was no point reminding Carl that Emil and Christian's money had enabled him to establish the factory. For a while, things had gone well for them. Even if Carl still hadn't been given the time, money, and help he wanted to devote to the motorwagen, the Mannheim Gas Engine Factory had given him the opportunity to develop the stationary engine. The initial success had also enabled us to improve our home. Now, with Emil's shares added to his own, perhaps Carl might reconsider his initial reluctance to broach the subject and try to convince his new partners to shift some of the factory's efforts to the motorwagen. I suggested as much to him.

He grimaced. "Perhaps in a few weeks or months. I don't trust them enough to discuss the motorwagen with them yet."

His wariness was reasonable. Carl went into every business hoping that it would open new opportunities for the motorwagen. However, the only business partner who had shown any real interest and faith in the project was August—and his interest had been misplaced. Despite their initial admiration for Carl's ingenuity vis-à-vie the engine, Emil and Christian had never allowed

Carl to apply himself to other inventions at the factory. They had invested believing that the engine would be enough to secure their fortune. I'd hoped that the Bühler brothers would, in addition to their money, bring some of the business skills that Carl lacked to the partnership. It hadn't happened and everyone was disappointed. But perhaps, at the genesis of a new partnership, it might be advantageous to raise the matter of working on the motorwagen upfront.

"Or you could clarify your expectations now, particularly since you have more sway in the company with the addition of Emil's shares. If you do it now, your new partners will know what you're hoping to achieve with the company, and there will be no surprises," I said.

He frowned at me. "Do you mean show them the drawings? Describe everything I have done up to this point?"

"Not initially. See what their response is first."

Carl was pensive, but he didn't say anything more on the subject until the next day when he returned from the factory. As was the case most evenings, he found me and the children in the kitchen. Despite having added other rooms to our home, including spacious drawing and dining rooms, we still spent a great deal of time in the kitchen. It was warm and cozy, with a large new table, around which we regularly gathered. That evening, Clara and I were at the stove and Eugen at the table reading while Richard was on the floor, entertaining Thilde and Tappie. We looked up as Carl walked in.

"I went to the factory this morning determined to discuss the motorwagen, as you suggested," he said, barely pausing to greet us. "It made sense. We've laid the foundations and have the engine. All I need is time and money to finalize the project. It'll change the way people are transported forever. The investors are new to the business, still full of enthusiasm and hope. I decided it was a good time to tell them of my plans."

"What did they say, Vater?" asked Eugen, whose understanding of Carl's work had grown considerably in recent years.

Carl sat down. "They said they're moving the factory to Schwetzingen."

Eugen and Richard looked at me as if I might know what that meant.

"Schwetzingen," I repeated. "But that's so far away. We'd—"

"We'd have to move there," said Carl.

Eugen snapped his book shut. "But, Vater—"

"Don't worry. We're not going anywhere," said Carl.

He held my gaze for a moment.

"My time at the Mannheim Gas Engine Factory is over. They will move the factory, and I will continue working from here, without them."

I pulled a chair away from the table and sat down. How was it possible that this had happened *again*? Was there no hope that Carl might establish a successful partnership? First, things had gone wrong with August; then with Emil and Christian; and now with the partners whose names I hadn't even had a chance to learn. Was it my fault? If I hadn't been distracted by Thilde's imminent arrival when Emil began discussions with the investors, I might've prevailed upon Carl to be more cautious in the negotiations. But they'd been desperate. Would it have made a difference? Perhaps not, but I could've tried. I might've been able to help avoid the difficulties that now almost certainly lay ahead for us. We were a family of six. Clara would soon begin school. Richard had never worn a new pair of shoes but would soon be the same size as his brother and wouldn't fit in Eugen's old ones. The work that Carl had done for other customers in the workshop at home had dried up. There was no other means of earning an income. What had he done? I swallowed, forcing down the dread that rose in me like bile.

I raised my head to look at Carl. "But how—"

"How could I stay, Bertha? Today I discovered that they'd begun discussing the move to Schwetzingen before the agreement was even signed. It's close to the chairman's home. What does that tell you about how little they think of me and my involvement in the company? I'm meant to be a partner, but they didn't bother to mention the move to me until now."

"But you now have Emil's shares. Does that not compel them to involve you more?" I asked.

"Emil's shares make no difference. It's not just about them moving the factory. I told them I had another project and that I wanted to discuss setting aside some of the company's money to experiment on it. They didn't even ask what the project is. They are unified, and I have become an outsider in my own business. I am a puppet in the company I established. A puppet who is operated by a gang of puppet masters. I refuse to dance to their tune.

If I have no power at the Mannheim Gas Engine Factory, I want no part of it," he said.

"So..."

"So they will buy me out. They seem relieved to see me go. They can take the factory wherever they want. I will stay and work on the motorwagen."

"But how—"

Carl put his head in his hands. "I don't know, Bertha. We'll have to make do."

CHAPTER 17

1883
Mannheim, Germany

That the Mannheim Gas Engine Factory would move to Schwetzingen was not the final aftershock to come with the arrival of the new investors. On closer scrutiny of the agreement, Carl discovered that he and Emil had also signed away ownership of the tools and machinery at the factory. Everything belonged to the organization, which meant that the new owners were exempt from paying us out for the value of the equipment. Once again, we realized that, without the means to pay lawyers, Carl would leave with a small portion of what the company he'd established was worth. Not for the first time, I wondered whether it might not be better for us to seek our fortune in America than to resume our struggle in Mannheim. I wrote to Elise.

> *It's approaching doom. Once again, Carl's business partners have let him down, and he has left the factory he created almost as poor as he was when he started it. His collaboration with Emil and Christian Bühler failed just as his business with August Ritter did. The next, with new investors, barely existed before it crumbled. Mutter reminds me, as she*

might have written to you, that there is a pattern to what happens with Carl, regardless of who he works with. As if I might have forgotten, she recalls how unhappy he was at the bridge-building company in Pforzheim and how he could not work in harmony with his colleagues in Vienna. Mutter says it proves that contrary to what he says, Carl is the problem and not the others involved.

None of this is news to me, Sister. I am not blind to my husband's foibles. Who knows the traits and quirks of a man better than his wife? It is true that Carl is impatient and proud and has little tolerance for ignorant, greedy people, but he is also fair and principled. Above all, he is clever, ambitious, and driven by the dream of building the motorwagen. Must he be penalized for having a dream and fighting to realize it? Rather than working alongside him so that they can benefit from his brilliance, his partners fear it and rein in his inventiveness.

It doesn't matter who is to blame, though. Either way, we are so poor again that we have rented out some of the rooms we used for the factory to a farrier to help put food on the table.

If only we could cope alone. But alas, no matter how we look at it, there is no way we can continue without the investment of others. As reluctant as he is to risk entering another partnership, Carl acknowledges it is the only way we will ever afford to continue work on the motorwagen. He is anxious and says it is like being caught between two fires. The question is whether the heat of not being able to work on the motorwagen burns hotter than the risk of finding another investor. I've never seen Carl more frustrated. Even so, my faith in him is unwavering and I continue to share his dream. But, Sister, that does not stop me wondering, as I have frequently over the years, if it might not be wise for us to sell our home in Mannheim and come to Milwaukee. You, Werner, and Gustav have expressed your doubts about this in the past, but I wonder if things might not have changed. Do you think that Americans might be interested in the motorwagen? Perhaps American businessmen are more inventive and progressive than those in Germany. Write soon, please, Elise. Tell me your news and offer some hope.

I sealed the envelope and placed it on the bureau. I'd ask Eugen to post it on his way to school the next day. When Ava arrived that morning, she noticed it.

"Shall I post your letter for you?" she asked after we'd had coffee.

"Please," I replied. "The sooner it begins its journey to America, the better."

"Does it contain an urgent message?" she asked.

I regularly updated Ava about the lives of my sisters and their families in Milwaukee. She knew how close Elise and I were and how I missed her. However, just as I'd never disclosed my thoughts about moving to America to Carl, I hadn't mentioned the idea to Ava. Now, though, with the stress of having lost Carl's income from the factory and wondering whether we would find new investors or any other way of unlocking the money we needed to build the motorwagen, I felt lonely and longed to reveal my hopes, however tentative they were, to my friend. She understood how worried I was about our current circumstances. Could I tell her what I'd asked Elise? I wanted to, yet it seemed duplicitous to reveal to Ava something I'd kept from Carl.

"No more urgent than my usual concerns about our future," I said cryptically.

Ava arched her eyebrows. "What do you mean?"

I gave in to the urge. "Well, it's just that I've wondered over the years if it wouldn't be wise for Carl and me to move to America. To join my sisters and their husbands in Milwaukee. There might be more opportunity for us there."

Ava sat back in her chair. "Really? I never realized."

"No, I've never told anyone other than Elise," I replied, aware that my heart had sped up. "Please, Ava, don't say anything about it to anyone. I don't… I've never mentioned the idea to Carl."

Her eyebrows rose again. "But you *never* keep anything from Carl. Why wouldn't you tell him? Surely it's something that you should discuss?"

"Yes, but only if it ever comes to anything worth discussing." I felt defensive and already regretted having said anything. "It's just that I've only ever asked Elise what she *thinks* about the idea. Previously, she hasn't encouraged it. I asked again now." I nodded toward the letter. "I didn't think that it would be wise to tell Carl about it unless they—my sisters and their husbands—felt it was a good idea."

"Is that all?" she asked.

"What do you mean?"

"Is that the only reason you haven't said anything to Carl about it?"

Ava knew me well. I looked down, unable to hold her gaze. "I worry Carl might feel that my faith in him is wavering and that by expressing an interest in going to America, I'm edging toward asking my sisters and their husbands for help. Beyond asking for their opinions, I mean."

She took a deep breath. "Carl is a proud man, but you are nothing but supportive."

I nodded, thinking about how difficult it had been for Carl to accept money from Ava for the train fare to Pforzheim and how he'd hastened to repay her. She'd seen firsthand how hard he found it to accept help.

"He might not see it that way. Particularly, if he discovers I've asked my sister about opportunities in Milwaukee more than once since we've been married and yet have never mentioned it to him," I said.

"Only because you want to help him. As I see it, Bertha, everything you do, you do because you think it'll help Carl realize his dream."

She was right. I wanted the project to succeed as much as Carl did and not only because I wanted him to prosper. I'd been involved with it for so long that it had become my life's goal too. We'd worked hard and—despite the ridicule, resistance, and ever-dwindling resources—had kept on working and experimenting with the design. Seeing the motorwagen in operation wasn't just Carl's dream; it was mine too. Yet I couldn't claim it as such out loud, not even to Ava.

"What is it?" she asked.

"Do you know who Caroline Lucretia Herschel is?"

"The astronomer? The woman whose brother went to England and took her with him?"

"Yes. Did you know that she worked as his assistant—he was also an astronomer—for many years but was only recognized for her skills when he got married and she was free to work alone?"

Ava shook her head. "I know she discovered a comet," she said.

"Several comets," I said.

"Why are you thinking about this astronomer?"

"I wondered if it would ever be possible for a woman to work alongside a man and be considered his equal partner."

"Are you thinking of becoming an engineer and working with Carl?" she said, her eyes twinkling.

"No, of course not," I replied, accepting how implausible it would seem to anyone to think of me as Carl's partner in the workshop. Did that prohibit me from revealing how I shared his dream, though? If not, what was it that stopped me from telling Ava how important the motorwagen was to me, not just as Carl's wife but as Bertha, the woman who was intrigued by ingenuity and the business thereof and who worked alongside Carl in the workshop whenever possible?

My friend left, taking my letter to Elise with her, but I continued thinking about what held me back from telling her that I was as driven by the idea of creating a motorwagen as Carl. Was it because it might infringe upon his ambition, thereby reducing the seriousness of his determination? No, that wasn't it. While I worried that Carl would be offended if he discovered that I'd written to Elise asking about our prospects in America without telling him, I didn't believe he would feel uneasy if I spoke openly of my commitment to the motorwagen. He knew how I felt about it. Carl wasn't the problem.

Then I saw it clearly. What concerned me was that other people, even Ava, might think less of the motorwagen if they heard that I, a woman—*only a girl*—was as committed to the invention as my husband. What truly serious project might command the dedication of a woman? Also, even if a woman deserved full credit for creating something new, if she was married, it legally belonged to her husband. A woman was not an equal partner—not in any relationship. Even where her partner might see her as such. Carl attracted enough scorn about the motorwagen without me adding to that by being judged an equally strange wife. It was better for me to say nothing about how I felt about the motorwagen. Just as I had never spoken up about how reading my father's words *Unfortunately, only a girl again* had made me feel, I would not speak freely of my passion for our project.

CHAPTER 18

1883
Mannheim, Germany

A few weeks later, at the dinner table, Carl said that two fellow velocipede enthusiasts had visited that day to express their interest in investing in a new engine-manufacturing company with him. He relayed the information so unenthusiastically that I expected him to follow it up with an explanation about why it wouldn't be possible. However, he continued eating and said nothing more. Eugen was impatient.

"Who are they, Vater? What did you say?" he asked, placing his knife and fork on his plate.

"Herren Rose and Esslinger," said Carl. "You might remember Herr Rose, Bertha. He was the man who was interested in building a tricycle years ago."

"Ah, yes. That's when your father began working on the three-wheel version of the motorwagen," I told Eugen. I glanced at Carl. "Is Herr Rose still in the business of buying and selling velocipedes?"

"Yes, along with several other businesses, some together with his friend Friedrich Esslinger, who is a salesman turned businessman," said Carl.

"What did you say, Vater?" Eugen asked once more.

Carl didn't answer.

"Did you not like what they had to say?" I asked.

Carl shrugged. "The problem is, everyone who wants to start a business with me sounds enthusiastic and their proposals are appealing. I simply no longer trust that the sentiments last. Time has proved that again and again. It makes me wary, and I'm no longer excited by the prospect of having new partners," he said.

"But, Vater—"

"Wait, Eugen," I said. "This is not the time to have this discussion. Neither is it your place to give your father business advice."

Eugen sighed and looked contrite. "But I'm not a child anymore. I understand that we need money if Vater is to build his machine. I wanted to…to encourage him."

Carl smiled at him. "You're wise, my son. Thank you. I'll give it more thought. Eat your dinner, and let's not talk about this anymore tonight."

Later, when the children were in bed, Carl and I discussed his meeting with Herren Rose and Esslinger. The men, said Carl, had told him that they'd heard about what had happened with the Mannheim Gas Engine Factory and were eager to invest in a new engine factory with Carl.

"Naturally, they insisted that I'd be much better off with them than I had been with Emil and Christian. I'd be the director of technology, they said. Our agreement would be in writing," said Carl.

"As you mentioned earlier, enthusiasm flows freely when people want something," I said.

"Ja, but let's face it—it's not just them who want something. We want the investment. We need it. We need it so badly that even our son urges me to accept the offer."

It saddened me to hear Carl sound so dejected.

"Perhaps there's a way we can make this one work for us from the start," I said.

"How?"

"Let's think what we want from investors. We want the money to be able to start production and earn an income again, but there's more to it. Although you know that your livelihood depends on the engines now, they're not what interest you. You want to work on the motorwagen. That's where your enthusiasm lies. When you work on the motorwagen, you hear music, not so?"

He nodded. "Always."

"So let's tell Max Rose and Friedrich Esslinger that you will help them set up a new factory here. You will get it going and ensure that it can build engines, but once that has happened, you'll step aside and focus on building the motorwagen," I said.

"I don't know, Bertha. It worries me to include the motorwagen under the same roof as the engines. Remember what happened with August. How do we know that we can trust Max and Friedrich?"

"You don't have to share the design of the motorwagen with them. Not immediately, anyway. All we need up front is for them to agree, in writing, that the factory will invest in your development of the motorwagen and that you will be given the freedom to work on it once the factory is operating."

Carl sat back. "I cannot see them agreeing to that."

"Then there will be no partnership," I said.

"We need a partnership, or we will go hungry. There isn't enough other work to keep us going," he said quietly.

"I know, but if the partnership fails like the other ones did and you don't have the opportunity to develop the motorwagen, then we'll be worse off than we are now."

"You're the only partner I know I can trust," said Carl, leaning forward and taking my hands in his. "Your opinion is always calm and measured."

I pushed thoughts about what I'd asked Elise from my mind. "When will you see Herren Rose and Esslinger again?" I asked.

"They will come again in two days."

"Then you will be out, and I will be here."

"What? No, Bertha."

"Did you not just say that my opinion is always calm and measured?"

"Yes, but—"

"I know you're not concerned about men criticizing you for allowing your wife to help you, so I cannot see why you will not allow me to negotiate with your potential investors. I cannot sign any agreements without your approval, so there is little risk."

Carl chuckled. "Okay. I'll be out in two days when Herren Rose and Esslinger are due."

—

Two days later, shortly after I'd laid Thilde in her crib for her morning nap, Tappie barked to announce the men's arrival. Hoping to see Herren Rose and Esslinger on their velocipedes, I peered through the window. I was curious about how refined the machines of men in the velocipede business might be but was disappointed to see they had traveled by carriage. Max Rose led the way up the path toward the workshop. He was no longer the athletic young man I recalled but a stocky businessman in a well-fitting black suit. His colleague, though taller and more angular, was similarly attired. Herr Rose was knocking on the workshop door when I opened the front door of the house and called out.

"Good morning. We'll meet in the house today."

The men turned to look at me but made no move in my direction. Tappie bounced toward them, giving a few more innocuous barks before wagging her entire body at them vigorously in welcome. I thought about how she had always growled at Emil, even after seeing him often over time, and tried not to read anything into it. The old dachshund's senses were not as sharp as they had been.

"Frau Benz! Good morning," said Herr Rose, bending to pat Tappie. "It's good to see you again. Is Herr Benz not well?"

He tipped his head toward the workshop. Even he knew how dedicated Carl was to his work.

"He's fine. This way," I replied, turning, walking away into the house and leaving the door open so that they could follow.

Tappie led the men after me into the drawing room. They looked around, presumably for Carl.

"Take a seat," I said once Herr Rose had completed the formal introductions.

As the men shuffled about, choosing their seats, I sat in an armchair, which had as its backdrop the largest window in the room. My father had recounted the story of one of his first clients who had been unhappy with the estimate that Vater—a young, inexperienced businessman at the time—had given him for some work. The man had called a meeting, during which he intimidated my father into reducing his fee significantly. As he'd left his client's study, Vater realized how the man had gained an early advantage by sitting with his back to a large window, which meant, sitting opposite him, my father had had to squint directly into the light. Not only had the glare caused Vater discomfort, but it also illuminated and amplified his client's silhouette, making him seem larger and more powerful than he was. It was a good lesson, said my father, who, from then on, chose his seat with care—particularly for important meetings. Now, while I didn't intend to overawe our potential investors, I strategically positioned myself against the window for our discussion.

"So, has Carl been delayed again?" asked Max. He looked at Friedrich. "Herr Benz has something of a reputation for being late."

"No," I replied. "He's not late. He won't be here today."

They exchanged another look.

"But then—"

"We can go ahead, all the same. Let's begin with you describing what you have in mind," I said.

Friedrich adjusted his position, as if his suit was a little *too* well-fitted for sitting.

"But if we have to have the discussion with Herr Benz later anyway, what's the point?" he asked.

I frowned. "The point is, I am here. My husband is not. If you are serious about the partnership with us, then we should discuss it now—or not at all."

"So, Carl instructed you to meet with us?" asked Max.

Another thing I had learned about business from my father was to never allow others to induce you to disclose anything until you were ready to do so yourself. Vater had said that talking about matters before you were properly prepared put you at risk of misrepresenting yourself and, sometimes, even the truth. One is not, he had advised, obliged to answer questions simply because they are asked.

"Carl explained that you propose the three of you establish a new factory to build and supply gas engines, as he did with the Mannheim Gas Engine Factory, and that he would be the director for technology," I said.

The men nodded in unison.

"We presume he'd be an equal partner and that it would be a formal partnership validated in writing, is that right?"

"Yes," said Max.

"Do you also agree that the exact nature of the role of the director for technology would also be settled upon beforehand and set out in writing?"

The men looked at each other again. Friedrich shrugged. "I can't see why not."

"Do you agree, Max?" I asked.

"Ja, sure," he replied, in an offhand manner that made my scalp prickle. What did I need to do to get them to take me seriously?

"Good," I said, determined not to reveal my irritation. "Then you should know now that, although we might agree to establish a factory whose initial business will be to manufacture stationary gas engines, that will not be all that the director of technology will be responsible for."

Max looked up. I finally had his attention.

"What do you mean?" asked Friedrich.

I leaned back and laced my fingers across my abdomen. "Carl is an engineer, yes. But he's more than that; he's an inventor. Although there might be some things he can do to fine-tune the engine and certainly he can help keep its production going, he has outgrown the engine. His real interest lies elsewhere."

Max snorted. "You don't mean the horseless carriage, do you?"

I ignored him. "He wants to work on the motorwagen."

"Motorwagen," said Max. "That's what he calls it now?"

I was not swayed. "Carl wants to develop the motorwagen, and his role as director of technology at the new factory will *have* to make provision for this. That's a fundamental requirement if we are to reach an agreement."

"Really?" said Max, slapping his thighs so loudly that Tappie, even with her aging ears, slunk from the room. "A 'fundamental requirement'? I had the impression that Carl was desperate for investors. Is he not renting out part of his workshop so that *you* can put food on the table for your four children, Frau Benz?"

My shoulders tensed. "We are doing what we can, and what we *can* do is try to ensure that any agreement Carl enters into is the best one for all. We need investors, yes, and you and Friedrich might be suitable, but it would be unfair for us not to explain, before signing, everything that we want from the agreement."

I paused to emphasize the point. The men stared, silent.

"It's essential that Carl be given the time and resources to work on the motorwagen, and if what you're offering cannot provide that, then we cannot accept it," I said.

"But this horseless carriage...I mean...motorwagen," muttered Max. "It's a far-fetched dream, Frau Benz. Nobody but Carl, and perhaps you, believes in it. The idea of replacing horses with a noisy, stinking engine to move around town is laughable."

"That's what people said about trains," I said.

"Ja, but trains are different. They are large machines that run on tracks. They carry many people, and the carriages are pulled by one massive steam engine. They are nothing alike," he said, shaking his head vigorously.

"Except that no one believed that they were possible until those who were passionate enough about developing them showed that they were," I replied.

"You can't compare horseless carriages or motorwagens with trains," said Max quietly.

"You just did, Max," I replied. "And they are similar. Both transport people and both elicit scorn and disbelief. A chief difference is that the motorwagen hasn't yet been able to prove its worth. That's what Carl plans to do."

Max rolled his eyes toward the ceiling. Friedrich examined his hands, which lay on his lap.

"There's one more thing," I said.

They looked at me once more.

"Since the engine is Carl's and he will be director of technology, the new company should include the name Benz in it. We like Benz & Co. Gas Engine Factory."

Max emitted a long sigh, after which the room was quiet for a moment. Eventually, Friedrich leaned forward and adjusted his trousers beneath his thighs. They were definitely too tight.

"Frau Benz, if I may ask, why is your husband not here today? Surely he should be laying out these requirements himself. We expected him. Why has he left it to you?" he asked.

"Because I asked him to," I replied matter-of-factly. "I'm not an engineer and, while I like making suggestions and supporting my husband's work in whatever way I can, neither am I an inventor. However, I do know Carl, his business, and what is best for them and for the Benz family."

The men stared at me. I heard the tentative whimper of the baby waking up in the girls' room. Thilde would be crying in a matter of minutes.

"Also, I like negotiating," I added with a smile.

"That, I can see," said Max, almost smiling himself as he got to his feet. "We will discuss it and let you know what we decide on Monday. Will you be here? Or will we see Carl?"

"One or both of us will be here," I replied as I saw them to the door.

—

Max and Friedrich met Carl the following week to discuss their counteroffer. Carl and I agreed that I would not attend the meeting and that he would continue discussions without apology or explanation about his absence the previous week. We wanted the men to know that Carl and I were unified, not only by marriage but also in business. Since I'd updated Carl, there would be no need to rehash my discussion with Max and Friedrich. That didn't stop the men from passing comment about me, though.

"They were impressed with you," said Carl after they'd left. "Friedrich described you as the 'ace up my sleeve,' but Max argued you were my 'secret weapon'."

"Not powerful enough, though," I replied.

The men's counterproposal was disappointing. They said the company would only undertake to invest in developments and products other than the stationary engine once the profits of the new factory exceeded the full investment they had made, plus costs. It was not what I'd proposed or what we'd hoped for.

"At least they know what we want," Carl said, placing a consoling hand on my shoulder. "We'll have it in writing, and no one will be surprised when I make space in the factory for the motorwagen. You did that, Bertha. It's progress. It's positive."

"But what if the market for engines dips, like it did suddenly when you were with the Mannheim Gas Engine Factory? It could mean you're locked in there for years without any hope of working on the motorwagen," I said.

"It's a risk, but I have several ideas about how I could make the stationary engine even quieter and cheaper to run. That'll give us a big advantage over the competition and, I believe, help us achieve a profit sooner," said Carl.

"If they know that, then Max and Friedrich should be willing to let you work on the motorwagen sooner. Why must you shoulder all the risk?"

"I'm not. They're risking their money. I'm investing my expertise and knowledge."

He was right, but I regretted not having insisted that I attend the meeting about the counteroffer. It seemed to me that Max and Friedrich had convinced Carl that he needed them more than they needed him. I'd wanted Carl to wield the power for once.

"How did you end the meeting?" I asked.

"I said they should return with a firm offer in writing within a week, which you and I would discuss," he said.

"So there will be no further discussion with them about the terms of the offer?"

Carl shook his head. Then his eyes brightened.

"Ah! There is something I almost forgot to tell you," he said.

"Go on," I said.

"They propose the new company be called Benz & Co. Rhenish Gas Engine Factory."

"Rhenish?" I echoed.

"They couldn't let you have it *exactly* as you wanted," he replied.

CHAPTER 19

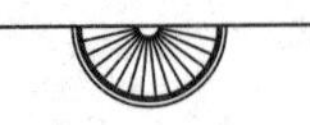

1884
Mannheim, Germany

With Carl having recently set up a similar factory and Max and Friedrich's money and fresh enthusiasm, the Benz & Co. Rhenish Gas Engine Factory was in operation within a few months. In redesigning the engine, Carl discarded the air pump that had previously been necessary to supply the most accurate proportion of air and gas. He also did away with the slide-valve gear, using a poppet valve for the gas inlet instead. The new engine was quieter and more economical than the model he had produced at the Mannheim Gas Engine Factory. This gave the new business an immediate advantage. Among others, Friedrich found new favor among printers and textile factories, who bought engines to drive their presses and looms.

Before long, the business employed twenty-five people. There was such demand for the new engine that Max, Friedrich, and Carl agreed to grant licenses to other workshops to build it. The additional income generated by licensing agreements boosted the factory's coffers at no additional cost. For the first time after twelve years of marriage, the Benz family could afford household help. I employed Fräulein Frida Ziegler, the daughter of one of the factory mechanics, to relieve me of some of my household chores.

In his workshop in the evenings and over weekends, Carl had been working on the wheels for the motorwagen. Because they were strong but lightweight, the wire spoke wheels used by many velocipedes at the time were our first choice for the machine. Carl bought the rims, which he fitted with wire spokes. With the help of Eugen and Richard, he added a solid layer of rubber to the outside of the wheels. This would protect the metal and help cushion the motorwagen from bumpy surfaces. Carl hung the wheels against a wall in the workshop. They looked good.

"We're getting there," I said as we stood back and admired them one evening.

Carl smiled and put an arm around my shoulder. I knew he wished things could move faster, but there was quiet satisfaction in seeing components built one by one and set aside, ready for assembly.

In fact, things were going so well at home and at work for Carl that I was able to convince him to leave his workshop one Saturday. He agreed to join me and the children on the proposed site of a new water tower in town, where the forthcoming development would be celebrated.

"There'll be music, Vater, and food stalls," said Clara, skipping ahead of him as we walked to the door on our way to the celebration. "Mutter has a rug so that we can picnic."

Carl looked at me, smiling. "Ah! I like picnics. I met a very important young lady on the way to a picnic once. Did I ever tell you that?"

Eugen caught Richard's eye, and they grimaced. Carl wasn't one to say much about personal matters, but he'd told them how he and I met—more than once. The boys had fidgeted awkwardly, unsure how to respond. Now their father threatened to tell the story again—this time with their seven- and two-year-old sisters present.

"No. Who was she, Vater?" sang Clara, running backward in front of him now.

"Wait! You have to hear the whole story," said Carl. "Right. Here goes... I was just a poor engineer who needed a ride to a picnic because I was hungry. I was a little late—how that happened, I don't know—and there was only one carriage left, and I had to run to catch it ..."

I laughed as Eugen and Richard sped ahead, out of earshot.

By the time we arrived at the event, Clara—disappointed by Carl's disclosure that the woman he met on his way to the picnic was only her mother—had lost interest in his story and ran to join her brothers. Carl carried Thilde, whose little legs had soon grown tired of walking. Tappie took up the rear, panting steadily as she trotted along. It was a warm day, and we'd need to ensure the old dog drank enough water.

Several colorful stalls had been set up over a large patch of lawn that nudged the edge of the woods, the shade of which looked enticing. The air was dense with the smell of sizzling sausages and the malty aroma of beer as groups of people milled around, talking and laughing. A wooden cart stood to one side of the arena. Marking the spot where the water tower would eventually be built, the cart was filled with flowers of all kinds and colors, which seemed to tumble out in every direction. Clara stood between Eugen and Richard, her mouth open in wonder as she stared at it.

We walked on. The sense of amicable joviality between friends and strangers reminded me how it felt to be at the Christmas market in Pforzheim as a child, except now it was a summer's day and not an icy evening. It was particularly pleasing to be out and about with Carl and the children. We'd lived in Mannheim for twelve years, and yet I didn't know the town and its people that well. That's what happened when you lived on the outskirts and when your husband was considered unconventional. I hooked my arm through Carl's. Perhaps opinions about him would change now that the factory was doing so well. Once he began working on the motorwagen with Max and Friedrich's support, the townsfolk would realize the importance of the machine and give him the respect he deserved. Things were working out.

"Everyone is out to celebrate the announcement, it seems," said Carl as he put Thilde on the grass and we watched her toddle to her siblings. "Though there's no indication of exactly *when* the water tower will be built."

It had long been understood that the quality of groundwater available to Mannheim was not acceptable. For decades, the town had struggled to improve matters, examining various options, including channeling water from the river and from mountain streams. It was decided that a water tower would be a necessary part of the solution to achieve the required standards and steady water pressure. While it was not yet clear when construction of the waterworks would begin, the site for the tower had been proposed. Thus, the early celebration was organized.

"It seems to me the authorities want to show us that better times lie ahead," I said.

"Better water is what we hope for," replied Carl.

I was about to suggest to him that we buy something to eat and drink, find a spot in the shade to spread the rug and enjoy it, when, with a sudden spurt of energy, Tappie ran ahead. She'd seen another dog and seemed unusually eager to introduce herself. We watched as she approached, her tail raised and wagging fast. Clearly, she knew the dog and he knew her. It was Titus, the puppy Ava had bought after old Marta had died. He had visited Tappie frequently with Ava. I looked around for her.

Standing alone several meters behind her dog, Ava lifted her eyes from Tappie and Titus. She looked up, directly at me. I smiled and waved. She looked around uncertainly before lifting her hand in a reluctant gesture. It might've been a wave of acknowledgment but could also have been a lethargic flap of the hand to chase off an insect. Was something wrong with her?

I turned to Carl. "There's Ava. I'm going to say hello."

When I looked back, I saw that my friend was no longer alone. A slight man and a girl were standing on either side of her. They were looking in the other direction, and I was unable to see their faces. The girl pointed and took Ava's hand to lead her away. Ava glanced over her shoulder at me as they walked away.

"Who is she with?" asked Carl.

"I don't know."

"She might not have realized it was you," he said. "Did she know we might come today?"

"No," I said, too distracted by my friend's behavior to describe how our eyes had met. There was no doubt that she'd recognized me. Even if she hadn't, Tappie's incontestable presence—nose to nose with Titus at her feet—would have provided evidence of who was waving to her across the grass.

I didn't see Ava again that day. When the children joined us in the cool spot we'd found on the edge of the field, Richard mentioned that he'd noticed Ava and Titus leaving the grounds with two other people. It seemed they'd gone almost immediately after we'd spotted one another. I tried not to fixate on what might have caused Ava to snub me. It was a lovely day, and the Benz family was enjoying an outing together. Moreover, we were celebrating with other citizens of Mannheim.

Was that why Ava hadn't said hello? Was she embarrassed by her friendship with me and Carl? It was, after all, the first time we'd encountered each other in public. Did she think that others might find it odd that she was acquainted with the family of the eccentric engineer? Was she protecting her reputation?

It was a ludicrous notion, which I banished from my thoughts, giving my full attention to my husband and children instead.

—

The children had barely left for school on Monday when the Ritter carriage drew up at the gate. I looked out the window as Titus hopped down the carriage stairs and sped up the path to greet Tappie. There was no awkwardness between those friends. It was another warm day, and I'd left the door ajar. Whereas previously Ava would've glided into the house, calling my name, this time she paused behind the dogs, gave two hesitant knocks, and waited for me to come to her.

"It's early, I know, but I couldn't sleep," she said, pushing a few wayward strands of hair from her forehead. She seemed to slump and looked uncharacteristically disheveled in a misbuttoned coat and dusty boots, both of which seemed incongruous, given the summery weather.

"Coffee?" I asked.

She gave a small smile, which could've been a grimace and did nothing to ease the tension in her face. I led the way to the kitchen. It was the room in which Ava and I were most comfortable. We'd sat there countless times over the years, drinking coffee and talking with ease about almost anything. The kitchen was the place we'd learned to like and trust each other, to recognize our connection, and, eventually, to take the bond for granted. What had happened to change that?

"You're angry with me," she said as I placed the coffeepot on the stove. "You have every right to be."

"No. Not really. More than anything, I'm confused," I replied.

"I didn't expect to see you there. It didn't seem like an event you'd attend."

I shrugged but didn't speak. What was there to say? Did she want me to explain why I'd attended a public event with my family on a weekend? Were we not entitled to do so simply because it wasn't ordinarily something we'd do? Did Ava want me to apologize for being there?

She continued. "I didn't know what to say."

"A brief 'hello' would've been fine," I said, unable to conceal my hurt. "What stopped you from doing that? Why did you run away?"

"I didn't run away. I… Bertha, will you sit down, please? Can I explain?"

I pulled out a chair and sat down heavily. My conduct was churlish. I would've reprimanded them had one of my children behaved as I was, but I was too wounded to care about etiquette.

Ava's eyes were on the table between us. "As you probably fathomed, the man I was with was Herr Adler," she said.

Herr Adler? Of course! I should've guessed as much, given the age of the girl with them. However, it hadn't crossed my mind. Why would it? There was no reason for me to believe that her former suitor and Ava would be together after she'd offended him by suggesting they get to know each other before settling on marriage. Then the pieces fell into place: It had nothing to do with Carl and what others might think about her being associated with him and his family. Ava was ashamed to be seen with Herr Adler by me. That's why she'd fled in the opposite direction when she saw us at the celebration.

"No, I didn't realize it was him," I said. "But even so, Ava, you could've greeted us, introduced us to Herr Adler and his daughter. Hannah, isn't it?"

"Yes, Hannah," she said, her voice quiet.

I stood up and gathered the coffee things. Perhaps coffee would make things easier. I poured and placed a cup in front of her.

"Thank you," she said, almost whispering.

We sipped quietly for a moment. Then she placed her cup in its saucer and looked at me.

"Herr Adler asked me to meet him less than a week after he stormed out of my parents' home when I'd angered him."

"Less than a week? But that was ages ago."

"Yes. We've been courting for months," she said. Her eyes were steady now.

"Courting? But you—"

"No, I never said anything to you. I was ashamed, and at first, I thought I'd wait and see whether anything came of it. Of me and him. We… You and I agreed that Walter—that's his name—was unworthy. We laughed at him. Remember how furious he was when he told me that any other woman would be grateful for his attention?"

I nodded.

"We mocked him. You said that his passion was not the kind I needed and that it was fortunate that I found out what he was like before it was too late," she said.

"Yes, but—"

She ignored me and continued. Her lower lip was trembling. "When he asked if we could talk again, I agreed. I told myself it was simply the polite thing to do. That I should allow him to apologize. There was nothing wrong with that. But it wasn't true, Bertha."

Ava sniffed. A large tear collected in the corner of her eye before spilling down her cheek. She wiped it from her jawline with her fingers. More tears followed. She dug about in her coat pocket, pulled out a crumpled handkerchief, and dabbed her eyes, talking all the time.

"Even after his outburst, I wondered if I'd made a mistake by rejecting him. Even after you consoled me and told me I'd done the right thing, I wondered. What you have with Carl is different from what most wives have with their husbands. If I wait for that, I might never leave my parents' home."

I tried to interject. "I didn't—"

"I wish I was strong like you, Bertha, but I'm not."

Strong like me? Ava was one of the most confident, determined people I knew. Had she forgotten how she'd convinced August to withdraw his claim for more money from me and Carl? Had she forgotten how we'd become friends despite the animosity between the Benz and Ritter families?

"I don't want to end up alone because no man can offer me what Carl gives you." She blew her nose. "I've agreed to marry Walter in autumn."

"That's—"

"It's done! I've given him my word. My parents are delighted."

"Wait, Ava, please. Let me speak. This is a great deal to take in. Can we slow down?"

She nodded.

I took a deep breath as I considered my words.

"If marrying Herr Adler is what will make you happy, what does it matter what I might've said about him months ago? What kind of friend would I be if I couldn't celebrate this with you?"

"Thank you."

"But after all this time? When were you going to tell me?" I asked.

"The longer I kept it from you, the harder it became to tell you," she said, dabbing more tears with her damp handkerchief.

My confusion had been replaced with a dull throb of remorse. Ava hadn't kept her renewed relationship with Herr Adler from me because she was deceitful; she'd withheld it because she was worried about how my reaction might ruin it for her. Elise had done the same years previously. She'd kept her news about marrying Werner and moving to America from me until the last moment. What was it about me that made the people I loved keep things from me? I'd never met Herr Adler. My sentiments about him were based entirely on what Ava had told me. I tried to quash the tiny prickle of resentment over the fact that what I'd believed to be support had been interpreted as criticism.

I thought about the news I'd shared with Ava over the years. Good or bad, I'd rarely withheld my thoughts from her. I'd told her about my pregnancies immediately after I'd informed Carl. She and I had celebrated the good times relating to Carl's work and lamented the bad. It had never occurred to me not to tell her about matters that were important to me. Sharing news deepened our bond. Wasn't that what friends do? Share good and bad news, if only to affirm that we care about what happens to each other? What was it about me that made it difficult for her to tell me that Herr Adler had apologized and she'd given him another chance? Was I so judgmental and self-assured that Ava, like Elise, felt she couldn't trust me to celebrate things that made her happy?

I lifted the coffeepot and glanced at her. She nodded. I filled her cup but didn't have the stomach for more myself. Ava drank, her eyes on my face. What was I to say to her to make her feel better? Make *me* feel better? How could I protect our friendship?

"Where will you live when you and Herr Adler are married?"

"In his house in town," she replied. "He has no plans to move us from Mannheim."

"Do you like it? His house, I mean?"

"Very much," she said. "I like his house and his daughter. Him, too, naturally."

She was smiling now, her eyes still wet.

"Can I visit you there when you are Frau Adler?" I asked.

Ava blinked, her smile widening. "I cannot tell you what joy that would give me," she said.

CHAPTER 20

1885
Mannheim, Germany

It was our housemaid, Frida, who a few months later told me that Ava and Herr Adler were married. Her mother had been among the staff serving the bridal meal. I told myself it was no surprise that I'd not been invited. The wedding, the second for both bride and groom, was no doubt a small family affair, which, shaky Benz–Ritter relations notwithstanding, made my attendance unlikely. All the same, I wished I'd heard about the wedding directly from Ava. It seemed, despite our efforts, our friendship hadn't entirely recovered from the incident at the water tower celebration.

A few weeks after Frida told me about the wedding, I received a note from Ava inviting me to visit her at her new home. As I stood at the large, vaulted door that granted access to Haus Adler, my breathing quickened. The house bordered a cobbled square in the center of town in a fashionable neighborhood that I'd never visited before. There was nothing there that spoke to me. No blade of grass, trunk of tree, or tiny bloom. No children played. Nor did any carriages or velocipedes trundle by. It was a fine day, and yet all the windows, including Ava's, were closed. There was no laughter or talking to confirm anyone lived there at all. There was nothing familiar about the place or anything that reflected Ava.

I wanted to be happy with anticipation about seeing her, but all I felt was apprehension. How things had changed, I thought as I raised my hand to tap the large brass knocker against the door. It opened almost immediately, as if Ava had been leaning against it, waiting for me. Was she also anxious?

"You didn't bring Tappie. Titus will be disappointed," she said after we'd exchanged greetings and I followed her to the drawing room. The house might have been slightly smaller than her parents' home, but—complete with thick, velvety draperies; padded upholstery; and a crystal chandelier—it was as luxuriously furnished.

"No," I replied. "She's no longer walking very far." I looked around. "Where *is* Titus?"

"He's probably with Hannah. They're very fond of each other."

We spoke a little more about the dogs; Ava sympathized with me when I explained how quiet Tappie had become and how she slept most of the time. It seemed like a lifetime ago that Ava had placed the puppy in my hands.

I admired a large floral tapestry draped against the wall, which Ava explained was her mother-in-law's handiwork. She told me how conveniently close the house was to Walter's office and asked after the children. I ran through a list, giving a fair account of each one. I asked about Hannah. A maid bustled in, carrying an ornate silver coffee set on a matching tray. We watched silently as she poured the coffee.

"So, do you take Tappie out at all?" asked Ava when we were alone again.

"Just into the yard," I said, wondering how long we could sustain a conversation about the dogs and whether we might have to start up on the children again.

"Hannah and I take Titus out twice a day," she said.

We could've been strangers on the train who, bored by the scenery and without anything to read, felt compelled to chat and were relieved to find a common interest in dogs. Our conversation stuttered, started, and died like one of Carl's old engines. Even though the coffee was hot and plentiful, there was nothing warm and intimate about the visit. Everything had changed. The air between us was charged with caution. We were not ourselves. I left earlier than planned, insisting that I needed to get home to Thilde, whom I'd left in Frida's care. Ava didn't try to persuade me to linger.

As I made my way home, I told myself that time would bridge the fissure in our friendship. Ava would adapt to being Frau Adler and stepmother to Hannah. The novelty of her new home and family would wear off. She'd miss me and visit. We'd talk about what had happened and how we felt. Perhaps we'd even laugh about it. I'd understand why she'd felt she couldn't tell me about Walter. We'd reminisce, forgive, and learn to trust each other again. Things would go back to the way they were.

—

My mood lifted when I arrived home. I scooped Thilde up from the floor and laughed as she wrapped her arms around my neck. For once, Tappie wasn't sleeping in the kitchen. She stood in the doorway, watching us, her tail twitching with a speed long since gone from her legs. I'd barely been gone two hours, but I'd been missed. It reminded me where I belonged and how unreservedly adoring children and dogs could be.

"There's a letter for you, Frau Benz," said Frida, tilting her head toward the bureau.

It was from Elise. My day was improving. I longed to read it but sat with Thilde for a while as she told me about her morning with Frida, who had cleverly turned cleaning the house into a game with the little girl. Finally, with my daughter playing with a toy velocipede Carl had made Eugen years previously, I sat down to read Elise's letter.

She wrote about a recent visit to the Milwaukee Industrial Exposition Building, which had been opened with a fair in 1881. Since then, the building had been used for several different events. Most recently, it had housed an art exhibition, at which Werner had purchased a painting for their recently redecorated hallway. On the final page, she finally responded to my questions about whether conditions in America might favor Carl and whether she thought we might consider moving there. Although years and several other letters had passed between us, my sister had not, until now, touched on the subject. Our situation had changed as the redesigned engine and new factory took off, and I couldn't remember the last time I'd wondered about going to America. Nonetheless, I was interested in what she thought.

It pleases me to read how well business is going for Carl. His genius deserves to be rewarded, as does your faith in him. When things went badly with the Bühler brothers and the new investors at Mannheim Gas Engine Factory, and you wrote again asking about Carl's opportunities in America, my heart sank. It was not just that I was saddened to read of your renewed troubles but also that you were again hopeful that Werner and I might encourage you to come to Milwaukee. I don't have to tell you how I have skirted the issue up until now. You have received enough subsequent letters in which I said nothing on the matter. However, after all this time and the consistently good news you have written about Benz & Co. Rhenish Gas Engine Factory, I feel I can be frank.

You described in what I think of as your "approaching doom letter" Mutter's view that Carl might be the author of his own troubles, given how the same difficulties follow him from company to company. I don't know if this is fair, but it seems Carl's temperament inhibits his success, and I cannot imagine that there is a way of changing this. I mean no offense by that. We are the people God created. What I am saying here, Sister, is that I do not think that coming to America—not that you are still considering it—would change your fortune. In fact, Carl might find even less tolerance for his perfectionism, impatience, and pride in this country. Here, influenced by the English, says Werner, people approach topics more cautiously than we are accustomed to in Germany. Whereas we are accustomed to direct, unambiguous communication, Americans often use euphemisms and jokes, and consider indirect speech to be polite and effective. It is not always easy to understand what they mean or want. Reaching agreements sometimes requires many discussions—even when both parties want the same thing right from the start.

I'm writing this relieved that it doesn't matter anymore. Carl seems settled with his new partners, and the business is prospering. Forgive me for taking so long to have the courage to be direct with you. Perhaps I have become more American than I realized.

My eyes skimmed the rest of the letter. Elise sent her best wishes and urged me to write soon. I folded the letter and slid it back into its envelope.

The heaviness in my chest that I'd felt as I left Ava earlier had returned. I didn't want to go to America. We didn't need to. But Elise's assessment of Carl—whom she'd never met—stung. What annoyed me more, though, was that my sister was unable to tell me how she felt until she was sure that we wouldn't come. Just as I had been excluded from Ava's world, I was excluded from Elise's. I placed my elbows on my knees and rested my head in my hands. I felt strangely alone. Something touched my head and rested there. I looked up. It was Thilde, who had placed her hand on my hair.

"What's wrong, Mutter?" she asked. "Are you sad?"

I looked at her. "No. Why would I be sad?" I wrapped an arm around her warm torso and drew her closer. "I have you."

"And Tappie and Eugen and Richard and Clara," she said brightly. "And Vater."

I laughed. "Yes. I have all of you, and we have dreams to make come true."

CHAPTER 21

1885
Mannheim, Germany

It wasn't only Elise's criticism of Carl that intensified my desire to work on the motorwagen alongside him. The renewed focus also helped take my mind off the relics of my friendship with Ava, which I couldn't help but picture as a rose wilting in a vase. It helped that Thilde was an independent toddler. Even when her brothers and sister were at school, she entertained herself, chatting incessantly to a toy or Tappie, the latter of whom was inevitably curled up asleep nearby. It meant I had more time to myself. Despite Carl being at the factory during the week, thoughts of the motorwagen were never far from my mind, as was the case when Frida arrived late for work one morning.

"I'm sorry, Frau Benz," she said, puffing as she removed her coat. "There was a fire at my aunt's house yesterday, and she asked me to help her move some stuff this morning. I thought it would take less time than it did."

"Was it a big fire? Is everyone okay?" I asked, knowing that Frida enjoyed a little morning tête-à-tête before she began work.

"Everyone is fine, ja. The kitchen was badly damaged, and one of the other rooms needs repair too. My cousins were able to confine the fire and get it out before it spread further. But my aunt is very upset. Particularly since she caused it herself and can't blame anyone else," said the girl, unable to suppress a giggle.

"What happened?"

"She was trying to remove stains from her gloves using ligroin. She'd poured some into a bowl and placed the gloves in it. The oven was burning some twenty feet away. She left the room briefly and has no idea exactly how it happened...insists that there were no sparks, but somehow the ligroin and gloves exploded and burst into flames. 'A single sea of fire,' said my aunt."

"Ligroin?" I said, more to myself than Frida.

She looked at me. "Ja. Ligroin. You can buy it from the pharmacy."

"Yes," I said. "I know it. It's useful to get fat and oil out of clothing, tablecloths, and so on—easy to find too."

Frida frowned, puzzled by my preoccupation with the ligroin, no doubt. "Ja, from the pharmacy," she repeated. "I'd better, erm, get to work."

She left the room, where I stood for several minutes, deep in thought. Carl's stationary engine was powered by coal gas, which—as my father had told me—had been piped into homes to use for lighting and cooking since the first municipal gas-distribution company was established in Germany in 1826. Coal gas was also supplied to factories and other businesses for various purposes, including—more recently—operating engines. For obvious reasons, the engine for the motorwagen could not be heated using piped coal gas. Carl had spent hours contemplating and experimenting with other fuels. He was certain the engine would best generate power by burning liquid fuel of some description. Had he considered ligroin? If so, he'd never mentioned it to me. I fetched Thilde and, having pulled on our coats, told Frida we'd be out for a while. I didn't add to the young woman's bewilderment by telling her we were on our way to the pharmacy to buy ligroin.

—

"You're right. It could work," said Carl when I told him about the ligroin that evening after supper as we sat in the drawing room with the children.

The substance, he explained, was a form of heavy naphtha, which was the name for various liquid mixtures of hydrocarbons typically made from oil. As Frida's aunt had discovered, it was quick to ignite and left no residue.

"It also has a low boiling point and a higher energy density, which make it particularly attractive for our purpose. I'd have to build a container of sorts to store it," he said, opening the bottle I'd bought and holding it up.

The odor was pungent and powerful. Carl wrinkled his nose and closed the bottle. "It's definitely something that needs to be sealed in the system."

"How will you test it, Vater?" asked Eugen, whose fascination with Carl's work grew daily and whose understanding of the engine was thorough.

"I have something set up in the factory that will help me determine some important issues very quickly," Carl replied. "I'll test it on the stationary engine. It might be a better option than the gas we use now."

I looked up from Richard's sock, which I was darning. "The factory? Do you think that's wise?"

"It's a good way of introducing the subject to Max and Friedrich again," said Carl. "Things are going well, and I can't see why they should stop me working on the motorwagen during work hours. It would help to have the assistance of some of the workers too."

"They should be honored," said Richard, who was his father's greatest supporter, even though I suspected he preferred playing football to working with Carl.

"Perhaps it would strengthen your position if you examined the accounts and showed them that the factory's profits now exceed their investment," I said. "That's the agreement, after all."

Carl didn't respond.

"They do, don't they?" I asked, looking up again. Carl was still holding the bottle of ligroin, examining it as if looking for something in the liquid. I spoke a little louder. "Profits do exceed Max and Friedrich's investment, don't they?"

He looked at me. "What? Yes. They're very pleased by how things are going," he said.

I wanted more. If the children weren't in the room, I would've asked Carl when last he looked at the accounts and whether the figures would confirm that his partners would allow him to work on the motorwagen at the factory. Max and Friedrich being "very pleased" wasn't the same as presenting them with numbers that matched the relevant clause in the agreement. We typically discussed Carl's work and the factory freely within earshot of the children; it's how they knew so much about it. In fact, the motorwagen was as much a part of our family as Tappie was. However, Carl's detachment and vague response stopped me from pressing on with the discussion. I'd keep it for later, I thought, when we were alone. He, however, felt differently.

"I'll be forty years old in November," he said, finally putting the bottle of ligroin down. "The motorwagen has been in my head and in various forms on paper for decades. I won't wait any longer. We know what it'll look like. We have the wheels and other components. The engine is ready. It's time to put it all together."

"But, Vater," said Eugen. The boy's voice was high, as it was inclined to be when he was anxious. It wasn't the first time this had occurred to him. "If you do it at the factory, we will probably be at school and won't be able to help you."

"There will always be things to do, my son," said Carl. "There's a great deal of work still to be done."

"I want to be there for the testing," said Eugen.

"Me too," said Richard.

"And us," called Clara from where she was playing with Thilde on the carpet.

Carl caught my eye and smiled. The annoyance I'd experienced earlier disappeared. How I loved my family.

"It'll be a while before we get to that," said Carl. "But I promise you that when the motorwagen is driven for the first time, it'll only happen when you are *all* there to see it."

—

I was surprised to see Carl walk into the workshop an hour or so earlier than usual the next day. I was accustomed to him being late, never early. I wondered what might've happened. When, several minutes later, he still hadn't appeared in the house, I went looking for him. He was sitting on the three-legged stool in the middle of the room, staring at the wheels he'd hung on the wall. Elise's comment about his perfectionism nudged its way into my thoughts, and I hoped he wasn't reconsidering their design after we'd agreed they were perfect.

"There's coffee," I said. "Can I bring you some?"

He shook his head without looking at me. It was unlike Carl to ignore me. I went to his side.

"What happened? Did you speak to Max and Friedrich about working on the motorwagen in the factory?"

Still, he didn't look at me. Instead, he put his elbows on his knees and his head in his hands. "They're no different from the others," he said.

I pulled an empty wooden box closer and sat in front of him. It was typical of Carl to initially withdraw when he was frustrated. He hadn't been raised with siblings to whom he could freely express his emotions like I had. He wasn't used to it and had told me shortly after we were married how he didn't tell his mother anything he thought might add to her woes. I'd learned what questions to ask and how to be patient with him. I liked to think that he'd discovered how useful it could be to discuss his feelings with me.

"Why are you home early? Tell me about your day," I said.

Carl was more reluctant to talk than I'd seen him for years. Slowly, though, and in starts and fits, he described what had happened.

He, Max, and Friedrich had an afternoon meeting in town with a French client, Monsieur Emile Roger. Monsieur Roger had visited the factory the previous month to examine the engine, which he planned to resell in France. The aim of the meeting was to confirm his order and agree on a price. It had gone well; the Frenchman ordered twelve engines with the promise of more in forthcoming months.

"We saw Monsieur Roger off at the station, and Max proposed we have a beer to toast the deal," said Carl. "I wanted to get back to work, but it occurred to me it might be a good opportunity to talk to him and Friedrich about the motorwagen. It was my plan to do it as soon as possible, anyway. With the French deal looking so good, I thought the mood and timing were perfect."

I nodded, thinking how unusual it was for Carl to consider things like mood and timing when it came to business. His decisions were typically made for clear, logical reasons that had nothing to do with emotions or what was taking place at the moment. His experience with unpredictable partners and colleagues had, it seemed, encouraged him to assess situations more cautiously.

"However, mood and timing have no influence on Max and Friedrich's opinion of the motorwagen. It doesn't matter how they feel about anything else; they made it clear that they are set against me working on *anything* but the engine in the factory," he said.

Not again, I thought. After everything we'd done to avoid this happening!

"Did you remind them about the agreement?" I asked, trying to remain calm.

"I did. Max was quick to respond to that one. Apparently, not all the costs have yet been covered."

"That can't be true," I said. "The costs referred to in the agreement are the setup costs of the factory, not the running costs. Surely the business doesn't still owe Max and Friedrich setup costs."

Carl looked at me and shook his head. "I don't know how it is possible, but Max insists it is so."

"That's a claim that needs to be proven. Until Max produces evidence that the setup costs have not been recouped, the discussion is pointless," I argued.

"It's not pointless," snapped Carl.

He seemed angry with me now, as if I were the one who was blocking progress on the motorwagen.

"If you saw the incredulity in Max's face when I raised the subject of the motorwagen, you, too, would know that it doesn't matter what the financial situation of the business is. Max thinks the motorwagen is a laughable project. He insists that no one will ever take it seriously and that if people discover I'm working on it at the factory, they will stop taking the engine seriously too," he said.

"That's nonsense. We know that and so does Max. We must fight him on this, Carl. The clause in your agreement with him and Friedrich was included specifically to avoid this argument," I said.

He snorted. "Agreement!"

"Yes, agreement," I replied, feeling overcome by frustration. Why hadn't Carl argued these points with Max and Friedrich earlier? Why hadn't he insisted that they show evidence of the costs they claimed were outstanding before taking the discussion further?

"What did Friedrich have to say during the discussion?" I asked.

"He agrees with Max. As always," said Carl, head in his hands again.

"You mean, he didn't say anything beyond nodding his head."

"He didn't have to say anything. It was clear that he feels the same way about the motorwagen as Max does. They are no different from anyone else," he repeated.

I leaned forward and tried to take his hand, but Carl twisted his body away from me. He was furious, but it was unlike Carl to reject my gestures of comfort. We were silent for a moment.

It occurred to me to comment on how unsurprising Max's response to Carl's request was. We shouldn't have expected anything else. Max had been disparaging about the motorwagen when I brought it up in my meeting with him and Friedrich before they reached an agreement with Carl. They'd only agreed to include a clause about it in the agreement because we insisted. We should have anticipated their resistance now. I didn't mention it. Carl was distressed enough without me appearing to downplay his disappointment. The only thing to do would be to insist that Max and Friedrich *prove* that the setup costs had not been recouped.

"It doesn't matter how Max and Friedrich feel about the motorwagen," I said quietly. "They need to provide evidence of Max's claims about the costs. If he's wrong or lying, your agreement allows you to work on the motorwagen at the factory. It's that simple. Ask him tomorrow."

Carl was silent.

"Will you come inside? Perhaps we can take the children for a walk before it gets dark. It's not too cold today," I said.

"Or perhaps you would like to go to America," said Carl quietly. At first, I thought I had misheard him.

"What?"

"America. Apparently, you believe that I cannot succeed in Germany and have been asking your sisters to find opportunities for me in Milwaukee for years," he said dully.

I stared at him. My mouth was dry, and my heart raced. So, it wasn't only Max's response to his request that had upset him.

"No! I didn't. Why do you think—"

"After a good start, my day fell apart this afternoon. I left Max and Friedrich in the tavern after they'd practically laughed at me and was about to get on my velocipede to come home, when Ava walked down the street. Needless to say, it was a bad time for her to ask me how things were going," he said, glaring at me.

"But she—"

He ignored me, his voice rising. "She no doubt thought she was consoling me when she said that if I couldn't work on my project here, I should simply do what you had hoped for years and go to the land of opportunity. After all, why struggle in Germany, where not even my wife believes I can make it, when I might succeed in America?"

"That's not—"

"Have you asked your sisters and brothers-in-law to find me work there?"

"No!"

"So, like Max, Ava is lying?"

Finally, Carl allowed me to explain. It was—just as I had feared when I told Ava why I hadn't told Carl that I'd asked Elise about work opportunities in America—difficult to convince my husband that I'd not betrayed him. I was, I insisted, simply trying to find out whether America might not present better opportunities for him to develop the motorwagen.

"If that is all it was, then why didn't you discuss it with me?" he asked.

"Because on the occasions that I wrote to Elise on the subject, we were struggling to keep the businesses afloat. I didn't want to add to your worries," I replied.

"But if you believed America might offer opportunities, why would that add to my worries?" he asked.

Because you'd react exactly as you are now, I thought.

"I didn't tell you because I felt it would be better for me to establish what Elise and Werner thought before talking to you about it," I said instead.

"What did they say?" he asked.

"That Germany is a better country in which to build the motorwagen," I replied.

—

We left the workshop and went to the house together, where Carl greeted and played with the children. At supper, Eugen asked if he'd spoken to Max and Friedrich about the motorwagen.

"Briefly," said Carl, glancing at me. "I'll have a full conversation with them tomorrow. There's nothing to report yet."

After supper, he told me he wouldn't require my help in the workshop that night. It was the first time he'd ever discouraged me from joining him there. I didn't insist otherwise. Nor did I hear him come to bed that night.

When I awoke, Carl was, as usual, dressed and ready to leave. I sat up in bed and looked at him, trying to gauge his mood. He smiled, walked over to the bed, and gave me a light kiss.

"I'm ready to have a proper discussion with Max and Friedrich today," he said. "I shall first insist on seeing the accounts; you're right about that. There will be no discussion if Max is being insincere. I will go ahead and work on the motorwagen in the factory. And—in case you ever wonder again, Bertha—I have no desire to go to America."

"I understand," I replied.

After the older children had gone to school and Frida arrived, I left Thilde with her and made my way to town. I'd thought a great deal about Ava's revelation to Carl before I fell asleep the previous night and had decided to confront her about it. I wanted to give her a chance to explain why she'd told him when I had expressly asked her not to. It didn't make sense. Even though our friendship had faltered, I couldn't understand why she'd betray my trust.

She didn't answer the door this time and appeared breathless when she arrived in the drawing room, where the maid had taken me.

"Bertha! What a surprise!" she said. "You're lucky to find me home. I'm afraid I must go out shortly." She glanced around as if looking for an escape route. "I can offer you something to drink, but I won't be able to stay and enjoy it with you."

"It's okay," I said. "I don't think this will take long."

I was still standing. She didn't invite me to sit, nor did she take a seat herself.

"How are you?" she ventured.

"Why did you tell Carl that I'd written to my sister about opportunities for him in America? I'm sure you remember me asking you not to," I said.

"Did you?" she stammered. "I don't recall you, erm, asking that. And—well, it just came out when Carl said how angry he was that he couldn't trust people."

"Couldn't trust people? What do you mean?"

"Well, he said he had trusted that his new partners would support him and his horseless carriage, but then—"

"So my husband expresses his frustration about mistrustful people, and you add to his misery by mentioning something I have done—which, as I explained to you, he might interpret as me doubting him."

Ava glared at me. "Why did you do it, then? If you have such faith in your brilliant husband, why did you write to your sister, looking for help?" she asked.

"Because—"

She wasn't finished. "And why be secretive about it? You and Carl talk about everything else—why not America?"

For a moment, I was too dazed to respond. I'd come to confront Ava, and she'd lobbed the accusation back at me, forcing me to defend myself. If I'd told Carl that I'd asked Elise about America right from the start, none of this would have happened. Or if I hadn't confided in Ava, there'd be no secret for her to spill. She was right: it was my fault. I shouldn't have asked her to hide the truth.

I took a deep breath, ready to acknowledge my role in what had happened. "I should've told him. It was particularly unfortunate that he found out yesterday after discovering that—"

Ava wasn't listening. "I told him because you are always so *smug*. I thought it was time that you feel what it's like not to have the perfect life," she said, her mouth twisting into a shape I didn't recognize.

I was stunned. "Smug?"

"Yes, smug. With your perfect marriage and perfect children."

"What do mean? When did our lives turn into a competition? You have Hannah, Herr Adler…all of this." I gestured around the room. "Why would you want to hurt Carl? Me?"

"Because, because you…"

Her shoulders drooped, and tears coursed down her cheeks. It was as if she'd melted.

"I'm sorry, Bertha. I didn't mean to tell him. It's just that…that…Walter and I… I mean, Hannah is a lovely girl, and this home is beautiful, but we don't have what you and Carl have. We are two lonely people who came together because…because of the loneliness." Her voice quivered. "When I saw Carl yesterday, I was on my way home, and I realized that I felt no excitement about seeing my husband after he had been at work all day. No anticipation about our life together. I've tried to talk to Walter about his work. Tried to find common interests, but beyond Hannah, there are none. I've settled. Nothing more and nothing less. You tried to warn me not to, Bertha, but I didn't listen. I was weighed down by the heaviness of the life I've chosen when I spotted Carl yesterday. When he mentioned his frustration, it felt good. I saw that your life was not perfect. I wanted to make it less perfect. So I told him…about America… even though you asked me not to. Perhaps *because* you asked me not to."

I didn't know how to respond. Moments ago, I'd been ready to accept that I shouldn't have kept the truth from Carl or expected Ava to guard it. Now, though, it didn't matter. Her vindictiveness was shocking. Was this the friend I had trusted so dearly? The woman I'd imagined I was as close to as I'd been to Elise? Even if she was dissatisfied with her life, how was she capable of such meanness?

"Please forgive me," she said.

I stared at her, trying to understand. Ava's reasons for not telling me about her reconciliation with Herr Adler and then snubbing us at the water tower celebration were plausible. It was upsetting to hear that she thought I might disapprove and find her lacking in some way or another, but I'd accepted her reasons and wanted to rescue our friendship. Right now, I doubted her honesty. Were envy and bitterness at the root of what had cracked the foundation of our friendship then? Was there a way to forgive such spite? Could I ever forget it? I couldn't see how.

"I should go," I said, making for the door. "Goodbye, Ava."

—

I took the long way home, walking beyond the bridge, along the river, and through the trees. It was the quieter, cooler route. I wanted to be alone with my thoughts, hoping that I might unravel them and settle my mind. Not for the first time since my friendship with Ava had faltered, I longed to talk to Elise. How I missed my sister!

Elise knew practically everything about Ava. My letters to her over the years had been infused with stories about our friendship, how our lives were intertwined and how important Ava was to me. Yet when last I wrote, I didn't tell Elise about our uncomfortable encounter at the water tower celebration or how Ava had withheld news of her relationship with Herr Adler from me. Now, as I made my way along a narrow, muddy path across a field, I realized why I hadn't mentioned to Elise what had happened. It wasn't just that I didn't want to face the truth that our friendship might be over—but also that I couldn't help wondering if I was somehow to blame for what had happened. What did I do wrong? What could I have done differently? I tried to imagine what Elise might say if I put the questions to her.

It wasn't unprecedented for friends to be jealous of each other. My mother had told me how more than one friendship she'd treasured for decades crumbled when Vater's business grew. Some people found it difficult to celebrate their friends' happiness. It didn't make sense for Ava and me. My circumstances hadn't really changed since we'd known each other. I was with Carl from the start. Certainly, things had improved for us financially since Max and Friedrich had invested in the factory with Carl, but Ava had always been wealthier and remained so. Then I thought about the children and Ava's determination to be a mother to Hannah. Was that the problem? Was Ava jealous of my children? Or was it, as she'd claimed, because Carl and I were happy together and she and Herr Adler had little in common? That's when I heard Elise's voice in my head.

"It doesn't matter what it is that she's jealous about. If Ava can't celebrate the things that make you happy with you, you are not to blame and there's nothing you can do about it. Should you pretend *not* to be happy with Carl and your children to make her feel better? Should you not express the pleasure you get from your family and the motorwagen to prevent her from feeling insecure about her life and thinking of you as smug? No. You are not responsible for her emotions. If you cannot express your happiness to your friend, you need to accept that your relationship is not what you thought it was."

I let my tears flow as I made my way up the final hill home. I missed Elise, and now I'd miss the friendship Ava and I had once known.

CHAPTER 22

1885
Mannheim, Germany

It was only three-year-old Thilde who said anything about Ava's absence from our lives—and even her reference to my old friend was oblique.

"I think Tappie is pleased Titus doesn't visit anymore," she said when we returned from church one Sunday.

"Why?" I asked, feeling Carl's eyes on me. I hadn't told him about my visit to Ava but assumed he'd worked out what might've happened.

"Tappie finds his games too rough."

Our daughter was probably right: Tappie was growing increasingly fragile, but I said nothing. I didn't want to pursue a conversation about Titus, because it made me think of Ava, which I was determined not to do. It had helped that Carl returned from the factory the evening after I'd seen Ava with good news about his business partners. Max must've realized that Carl would want to see proof of his claim that the setup costs of the factory hadn't yet been recouped. Before Carl had an opportunity to demand a meeting, Max had appeared in his office and laid out a new proposal.

"He said he'd given it some thought overnight and changed his mind," Carl had explained. "While he insists that he doesn't believe in the future of the motorwagen, he concedes that I 'have a brain like no other he has encountered'—those were his exact words—and because of that, he and Friedrich agree that I can have space in the factory, time, and the assistance of ten men to work on the motorwagen for six months."

I'd clasped my hands together. "Six months?"

"Max insists, though, that the engines should still take precedence and said if work on the motorwagen causes a dip in profits or quality, it'll have to stop immediately. Six months is not a long time. I asked for more, but he wouldn't budge."

"We'll do it!" I'd said, delighted to hear good news for a change. "If we keep working after hours, too, we'll have a motorwagen assembled and ready for testing in time. It'll work!"

For a long time, I'd wondered if it might be beneficial for Carl to have to work to a firm deadline. That he was ingenious was irrefutable, but even brilliant people needed definite goals. Elise was right when she'd said he was a perfectionist. Carl held himself to high standards and was determined to get everything just right. He didn't like to rush decisions, and even when he had worked out how to do something, he wanted to examine alternatives before moving on. Carl's perfectionism was one of the things that convinced me he would succeed with the motorwagen. It was also a characteristic that slowed the project.

Max's six-month deadline was an opportunity to speed things up. While it was possible the time limit might make Carl more anxious, I hoped that his overriding reaction would be to move ahead more quickly. It was time to assemble the motorwagen and begin testing it as a complete machine.

Now, as we exchanged our church finery for our work clothes, I smiled to myself. Eugen and Richard chatted while they waited for their father in the hallway. Carl was testing the smallest version of his engine, which he'd built at the factory. The boys were excited because despite the engine's size and reduced weight, it ran at a considerably higher speed than any previous engines we'd seen.

"Two hundred and fifty revolutions per minute!" said Richard, repeating what Carl had told us earlier. "That's more than double the speed of the other engines."

"Ja," said Eugen, his voice deeper and calmer than his brother's. "And it's a four-stroke machine but still so small."

Carl's stationary engines operated a power cycle of two strokes—that is, up as it compressed and down as it powered each revolution of the crankshaft. However, because the motorwagen would have to change its speed continuously, he decided that a single-cylinder four-stroke system would work better for it. Our sons were itching to see it in operation.

"I'll call you when it's ready to start so you don't miss it," said Clara, running to be with her father and brothers as Thilde followed me to the kitchen to prepare lunch.

While we were most certainly not a very typical family, we did gather at the table for Sunday lunch. It was one of the few Ringer traditions I'd brought with me from Pforzheim. I wondered what my father would've thought if he knew that not only did Carl work before and after church every Sunday but also that the children and I spent most of the day in the workshop alongside him. Even at his busiest, Vater had never worked on Sundays.

I'd just put the potatoes in the oven when Clara appeared. "Come, Mutter. Quickly," she said, her face rosy with excitement.

Scooping Thilde up into my arms, I followed her sister into the workshop. Eugen and Carl stood alongside the engine. Richard was at the door, hopping from foot to foot.

"They're here," he shouted. "Start it up, Vater!"

Carl had spent many days trying to improve the ignition system he'd developed for the stationary engine. While the dynamo was reliable for the engine in stationary and stable conditions, Carl realized that on bumpy roads—such as the engine in the motorwagen would encounter—the current brushes he used would be so shaken that the ignition current would be interrupted and fail. Finally, he had come up with an electric technique using a battery and a spark plug. I had wound the metal for the induction coil. Now Carl was about to test it on the small engine he'd created for the motorwagen.

—

It took me a while to herd Carl and the children into the house for lunch that Sunday. After the excitement of hearing the engine start immediately and run smoothly, Eugen and Richard were full of questions.

"How will you secure the engine to the wagon, Vater?"

"Where will you store the ligroin?"

"Where will Mutter, Clara, and Thilde sit?"

I had a question, too, which I kept until we were seated at the table and the children finally stopped talking to eat.

"Will you take the engine to the factory, complete the assembly, and test it there during the week?" I asked.

Carl put his cutlery down and swallowed. "No," he said. "It wouldn't be fair on you and the children not to be there for the first test."

"Ah, so it has nothing to do with you wanting to be solely responsible for putting it together?" I teased.

"No, no! Nor does it have anything to do with me wanting to test it alone before Max and Friedrich see it in action," he joked.

"You accept, though, that it will be necessary to demonstrate the motorwagen to all who are interested in it eventually, don't you?" I asked.

"Certainly," he replied. "I'll gladly show it to those who understand engineering and anyone else who might acknowledge what an important invention it is."

"Perhaps initially, yes," I said. "But eventually, you'll have to show it to everyone. How will people learn how important it is if they don't see it?"

"Everyone? You're getting ahead of things again," he said, taking up his knife and fork to resume eating the roast pork on his plate.

I knew it wasn't going to be easy for Carl to show off the motorwagen. As much as he believed his invention was something everyone could enjoy using one day, he wanted to be certain that nothing would go wrong before he presented it to anyone. What made it more difficult for him was knowing that some imagined it was the work of the devil. Doubt and ridicule aside, for the motorwagen to have the effect Carl and I believed it was capable of, it had to be put on display. If the world didn't know about it, the world wouldn't miss it. People were accustomed to walking when they went about their business. Some rode horses and a few velocipedes. Sometimes they used carriages and carts. A few took the train. We'd have to tell them about the alternative that we had created. I'd long ago accepted that I would make it one of my responsibilities to ensure as many people as possible saw the motorwagen when the time was right.

"Perhaps the newspaper will write an article about it," I mused, not meaning to say it out loud.

Carl heard. "We are a long way off from being ready for *that*," he said, giving me an unusually stern look.

CHAPTER 23

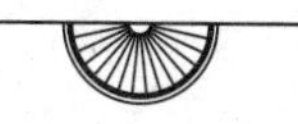

1885
Mannheim, Germany

One cold but clear Sunday in January, almost four months to the day after Max had told Carl he had six months to complete the motorwagen, Carl stepped away from the machine in the workshop and handed Eugen a small metal hammer.

"You put the first one in, and now it's time affix the last one," said Carl with a nod at the seat, which required a final stud to pin the cushion and leather onto the wooden bench.

I involuntarily flexed my fingers. They were still a little stiff from a few days earlier, when I'd spent hours triple-stitching the leather. Carl had insisted it was essential to bolster the cover so that it would withstand the use it would have to endure.

Eugen gave a small, nervous smile as he took the hammer and placed his foot on the step to climb onto the platform of the motorwagen. On the other side, Richard rubbed his hands together and pulled himself up so that he could watch his brother closely. They leaned over the seat, and Eugen tapped the stud into place.

I glanced at Carl. His eyes were fixed on Eugen's hands, as if a moment's distraction might ruin everything. Or perhaps he was simply memorializing the undertaking. After all, it was the final of more than four hundred components that had been installed to complete the machine. The few parts that had not been made by Carl in his workshop were crafted under his direction at the factory. There wasn't a piece of the machine that did not, until they were polished away, have imprints of my husband's fingers on it. Eugen gave the stud a final solid blow. He and Richard brought their heads together as they leaned in to check that the stud was secure. I put a hand on Carl's shoulder. He turned to me.

"We've done it," I said. "With two months to spare, it's done!"

Carl nodded. "Now to see how it moves."

The boys jumped down. Clara, Thilde, and Tappie joined us as we stood, silently staring at the motorwagen, with its spidery three wheels, gleaming tubular steel chassis, wooden slats, leather-padded seat, and back rail with a chain drive and large spoke wheels. The sketches we'd pored over for years and years, the drawings of parts and pieces, and the eventual illustration of the motorwagen in its entirety had finally assumed a tangible, viable form. It had, said Carl, been lifted out of the realm of thoughts and pages and placed in the real world.

Thilde, who, along with her sister, had fallen asleep exhausted every night for weeks after all the polishing of the machine they'd done, took her father's hand and looked up at him.

"Richard says you will take it outside, Vater," she said.

"Ja, he's right. It's the perfect time," said Carl, craning his neck to look into the yard. He had told me earlier that we'd test the car on Sunday at dusk, when it was most unlikely that anyone would pass by.

Thilde frowned. "But how will we keep the rubber on the wheels clean, then?"

Her brothers and sister laughed, but Carl only smiled.

"That's a good question but not something to worry about. If the wheels get a little dirty, it won't upset the machine. It's built to drive over dirt, just as my velocipede and carriages are," he explained. "Come, let's push it outside and see what happens when we start the engine and get it moving. Will you and Clara open the doors?"

The girls ran to unlatch and open the double doors of the workshop. Tappie, awake for once, chose a calculated position just inside the building where she could keep an eye on us without getting underfoot. For years I'd admired how perceptive and calm the little dog was in the workshop. Even when testing the engine was exceptionally raucous, Tappie was unflustered.

With the boys pushing the motorwagen from behind, Carl released the brake and steered it into the yard. I followed, enjoying the sight of the children bustling around the machine. Their excitement and energy reminded me of that which I'd seen in Carl when we met seventeen years ago. It was one of the reasons I'd fallen in love with him. That the children had inherited the same enthusiasm—or perhaps they had learned it—filled me with joy. What more powerful force might anyone need to propel one through life? What further vigor might compel one to dream and to pursue that dream? I loved the idea of our children being as inventive and determined as their father.

Carl maneuvered the motorwagen to the far side of the yard, pushed the shift lever forward to stop it, and turned to me.

"Will you steer?" he asked.

"But don't you—"

"No. I'll start it. If anything goes wrong, I'll be right here," he said, turning to the boys. "Eugen, you stay at the front, to the left. Richard, you come with me. I'll let you know if you need to do anything. The main thing is to look out for anything that might seem wrong."

"What should we do?" asked Clara.

"You and Thilde need to stand back and watch from a distance. This is an important test. I need everyone to watch everything carefully so that if anything looks even a little bit wrong, we can fix it before anyone else sees it or it does any damage," Carl said.

The children nodded, their faces solemn now. Carl took my hand as I placed my foot on the step and climbed onto the motorwagen. It sank slightly but silently as I lowered myself on the seat. Carl was determined that the machine should not make any unnecessary sounds. He argued that if it creaked or squeaked when it was mounted, the motorwagen would be disparaged as fragile and unsafe, particularly by detractors who would inevitably already be dubious about or fearful of the invention.

It wasn't the first time I'd sat on the machine. I'd been there to test the width of the seat, the distance between lever and driver, and the space for legs and feet. I'd climbed on and off countless times to confirm the platform wasn't too high and that the step was correctly positioned. I'd even sat on the motorwagen when Carl started the machine to give my opinion on the extent of the vibrations from the engine. However, we had not applied power to the wheels before. This was the real test.

"Ready?" asked Carl.

My heart thumped with excitement. I wasn't afraid; there was nothing to fear. We'd run the engine and spun the wheels so many times I couldn't imagine anything going wrong. I simply needed to steer the machine across the yard. I knew how to apply power, shift the lever out of gear, and engage the brake. I understood how the tiller worked to steer the front wheel. All I needed to do was aim the pointer to the left for the front wheel to turn left and point it to the right for the same to happen in the other direction.

"Yes," I said, tempted to add that I had been ready for this moment ever since we'd met.

Carl went to the back of the motorwagen and swung the flywheel back and forth once, twice, three times, and four. Then he gave it a firm swing and released it. Exactly as we'd anticipated, the engine *doof-doof-doof*ed to life before hissing, popping, shaking, and finally settling into its regular chugging.

"Apply power," said Carl, returning to the side.

Holding the steering lever with my right hand, I leaned forward and reached for the long shift lever with my left hand. As I pulled it into position to power the back wheels, I heard the chains click, and the motorwagen rolled forward over the cobblestones. The vibrations of the engine reverberated through my body. There was nothing alarming about the sensation. It was like a soft, regular pulse. The motorwagen was moving just as it had been designed to do. I wanted to shout my excitement, but I knew that it was too serious an undertaking for early celebration. The children understood the same and were quiet as they trotted alongside their father, mirroring his intense concentration as all eyes scanned the machine.

Stay focused, I told myself, looking forward once more. Just in time, I noticed a dip in the cobblestones ahead of the front wheel and turned the steering lever to the right. The small wheel responded immediately, missing the bump by a much greater distance than I had planned. The steering lever, I realized, needed a gentler hand when the machine was moving. I applied less force to straighten the wheel once more. There was nothing wrong with the system; the operator was simply a little heavy-handed.

What a sensation! I thought. *Here I am, being powered across the earth, not by the energy created by my legs or those of a horse or because I'm in the carriage of a train but by riding the machine we invented and built.* Where there was once nothing more than an idea, there was now a powerful, practical vehicle. I'd never felt more triumphant.

"Shall I turn and go back?" I called out as I neared the end of the yard, having traveled about fifteen meters.

"No," said Carl. "There's not enough space to turn, and anyway, it'll be out of ligroin." He held up his hand. "You can stop."

I leaned back to push the lever forward to apply the brakes. The motorwagen stopped immediately, and when I turned the knob below my seat, the engine died as it was designed to do.

The yard was quiet until Thilde, her voice high in its earnestness, said, "Vater, I can't think what to tell you because I didn't see anything wrong."

We laughed as one, the tension gone, the joy unleashed. I climbed down and joined the children as they mobbed Carl, all talking at once.

"Did you see how quickly it responded when Mutter pushed the lever?"

"The chains ran so smoothly, Vater! Just the way you wanted."

"Did you see how the engine powered the wheels over the cobblestones?"

"What was it like, Mutter? Tell us!"

Carl looked over the children's heads at me. His smile was wide, and his eyes sparkled.

CHAPTER 24

1886
Mannheim, Germany

The Benz family test of the motorwagen couldn't have gone better. Even when I described how sensitive the tiller was, Carl wasn't perturbed. It seemed he agreed with Thilde's assessment that there was nothing to report. Everything had gone exactly as we hoped it would. Anyone else would've invited Max, Friedrich, and others from the factory to see it in action the very next day, but Carl wasn't like anyone else.

"We'll test it alone here again next weekend. If all goes well then, I shall apply for a patent. Only then will we show it to others," he said that evening at supper, in reply to a question Eugen had asked.

"A whole week. Why not sooner?" I said. "Why will you first apply for the patent? Once he sees it, Max is more likely to agree to spend additional money and time on its development, don't you think?"

But Carl was adamant. "I want to examine it closely this week to see if the test shows up anything that might be problematic. I need to be sure everything operated exactly as it seemed and that nothing has come loose or rubbed against any other part. We still have time. And the patent? Well, that'll secure ownership of the design."

His logic was sound, but I worried that Carl would continue to stall the demonstration. He remained convinced that the motorwagen's first public field test should be witnessed only by those who understood what a mechanical feat it was and how it could change the way we got around.

"But how will people know what an incredible invention it is unless you tell them and show them?" I asked.

"I've told Max and Friedrich repeatedly," he replied.

"And yet they remain skeptical."

He shrugged and sighed.

I went on. "We *have* to tell more people about it. We must explain how it works and why it's exciting. Then we need to show them."

Carl continued eating. I understood his frustration. My husband wanted everyone to miraculously *know* his thoughts and plans without him having to explain them. He forgot that no one but Carl Benz lived in his head. The motorwagen had occupied his thoughts for so long that it was inconceivable to him that the machine might be considered bizarre and even menacing to others. Was it arrogance that prevented him from seeing things from the perspective of others and for acknowledging that we needed to court interest? Certainly, Carl could be impatient and intolerant, but I didn't believe that he was arrogant. However, I saw how others might feel otherwise. What could be done to change their perception and encourage them to see the motorwagen through Carl's eyes? Richard might've been reading my mind.

"Perhaps we could arrange a celebration," he said.

Five pairs of eyes turned toward him.

"Like the city did to announce the site for the water tower," he explained. "Do you remember how everyone complained before? I mean, about how long it was taking the city officials to agree on what they were going to do about the water problem?"

There were murmurs and nods.

Richard went on. "Then they decided where they would build the tower and organized a day of celebration there. Everyone came and they were happy. The water tower isn't even built yet, but no one complains anymore. Well? Do they?"

"No," I said. "They do not."

My younger son smiled at me. "We should arrange a celebration to show off the motorwagen, and everyone will be excited and encouraging and eager for more motorwagens to be built," he said.

Laughter and commentary erupted from around the table.

"That's a silly idea. It's not the same thing at all."

"That could be fun. Would it work, do you think, Vater?"

"What happened at the celebration? Was I there? I don't remember."

Carl held up his hand to quiet the children and smiled at Richard. "That's a novel idea, but I think Eugen is right: it's not the same," he said.

No, I thought, it wasn't the same, but the motivation was similar. The celebration at the water tower had informed the residents of Mannheim about the city officials' plans to solve the water problem. The event had told us where the tower would be located, how it would be fed with water, and how that would change our lives. Richard was right about how the residents had welcomed the news and how, with a plan in place and an official celebration to mark the development, people were content. Even though it would be a while before the tower and the associated channels and pipes were ready to distribute water, the citizens were satisfied and happy to wait for construction to be complete.

A celebration in town might not be a plausible way to present the motorwagen to people and, certainly, it was highly unlikely that Carl would agree to it, but there might be another way of doing the same thing. A way of getting the information to people so that they didn't simply think of the motorwagen as the weird creation of an eccentric inventor with a supportive family—or worse, the work of the devil. I smiled at Richard. He and I thought alike.

—

It seemed impossible, but Carl was more dedicated to the motorwagen than ever over the week that followed. Insisting he needed quiet, he asked us not to come to the workshop. It left me and the children adrift. After the excitement of the test ride and the weeks leading up to it, the anticlimax was hard to bear. The children were accustomed to hurrying to the workshop after school to find out what Carl had achieved the night before or in their absence if he hadn't gone to the factory that day. Now, essentially shut out by Carl, they were bored and restless. Eugen and Richard were uncharacteristically quarrelsome, and on two occasions I had to mediate peace between them. I couldn't help harboring resentment toward their father, and after five days and another argument between the boys, I strode over to the workshop to voice my annoyance.

"I understand your reticence to exposing the machine to strangers, Carl, but I don't understand why you have suddenly decided to deny your family access to it," I said, having burst through the closed doors noisily.

Carl was not examining or working on the motorwagen, as I had envisaged, but was sitting at his desk. He turned to look at me, eyebrows raised.

"It's not as if they get in your way," I continued, my voice lower now. "It's unfair to bar the children from the workshop where we... *they* have spent so many hours with you over the years. They want to help. They are your only—your greatest—supporters. It's unsettling for us all to have to stay away."

"I've been preparing the patent," he said, standing and walking over to me. "It's boring work, and I didn't think you and the children would want to be here. I thought you might like to be free of the workshop, the motorwagen, and me for a bit."

"The patent? But I thought—"

"I believe it's ready," he said, smiling now. "Come and have a look. I was about to bring it to you."

He gestured to the desk. I sat down and looked at the document. Drawings of the motorwagen—both from the side and from above—were familiar to me, as were the images of parts Carl wanted to patent. I had seen countless renditions but none as precise and clean as the ones on the pages before me. They were pristine, and I held my hands up as I scrutinized them so as not to sully them in any way.

Carl chuckled. "Turn the page."

I did so with the utmost of care and read the text. It was headed *Vehicle with Gas-Engine Operation* and continued as follows:

"The present design serves for the operation of mainly light vehicles and small boats, such as those used for the conveyance of one to four people. For whichever system, power is provided by a small engine. The engine is fed with gas that is vaporized from ligroin or other suitable substances by means of an apparatus carried on board. The engine's cylinder is maintained at a constant temperature by the evaporation of water."

"What do you think?" asked Carl after I had examined each page multiple times.

"I wouldn't change a thing," I replied.

"Nothing?"

I shook my head and got to my feet. "It's ready."

Carl exhaled. "Yes, I believe it is."

"So, you are determined to get the patent before demonstrating the machine to anyone? You won't even show Max and Friedrich?"

"No," he said, putting his arms around my waist. "After all these years and all this work, I don't want to risk it. Others have taken me for a fool before, people I should have been able to trust. This time, I want to be sure. We—all of us—have devoted so much time and effort in the motorwagen. I don't want to disappoint you and the children again."

It occurred to me to say that it would have been easier for us all if he had simply told us that that was why he didn't want us in the workshop, but I didn't want to spoil the moment. Having the application for the patent ready for submission was a big step for Carl. It was a big step for all of us. I laced my fingers behind his neck.

"Congratulations, Herr Benz," I said, before he brought his lips to mine.

—

On January 29, 1886, the Imperial Patent Office granted Carl the German patent for the motorwagen. Patent number 37435 was issued for a "functional unit of an engine with a chassis, the Carl Benz Patent Motorwagen." The time had come to show the machine to people outside the family.

"Yes, I know that's what was planned, but there's a good reason to delay it," said Carl when we gathered around him that evening.

"Delay it?" wailed Eugen and Richard, as if they'd practiced their duet.

Part of me had anticipated that Carl would find a reason to put it off. He hadn't stopped talking about how he might improve things, even on the very morning he submitted the patent. Even so, I was disappointed. He caught my eye.

"Let's sit down so that I can tell you why the test will take place in summer," he said, gesturing to the chairs around the table.

There was a collective sigh as we sat. The business, Carl explained, was doing so well that he, Max, and Friedrich had agreed they urgently needed to expand the manufacturing capacity. They had found a large property on Waldhofstrasse 24, which they planned to purchase.

"We'll not only build larger workshops and offices for Benz & Co. there but also a house for us," he said, looking at me.

I stared at him, dumbstruck. That he and his business partners had bought property so that they could expand the business and he hadn't mentioned it to me was one thing, but to decide that we would also build a new home and move there was another. I swallowed, not trusting myself to speak. Carl recognized my expression.

"That depends on your mother's agreement," he said, glancing around the table now. "We'll visit the site together, discuss the plans, and then decide."

"We'll move?" said Clara. "But we've always lived here."

Thilde slid off her chair, came to me, and tucked herself beneath my arm. I felt her little body tremble as her sniffing revealed that she was crying.

Carl cleared his throat. "It's good news," he said. "Change can be frightening, but it can also be good. We know that better than many other people. How can we get ahead in life without accepting change? How will the motorwagen ever be accepted if people don't welcome change?"

"Can we come and see the new site in Waldhofstrasse, too, Vater?" asked Eugen.

Carl looked at me. "Well—"

"Yes, we'll all go," I said, tightening my grip on Thilde.

Alone later, Carl and I discussed the move to Waldhofstrasse again. He apologized for not having spoken to me about it before springing the news upon us all.

"Everyone was so excited about the patent and the idea of demonstrating the motorwagen that I felt cornered and was overhasty," he said. "It was my intention to speak to you about it before announcing it to the children."

"It sounds like the decision has been made," I replied, unable to shake off the displeasure I felt over the fact that he would even consider something so significant without first discussing it with me. "Does it matter what I think at this stage?"

"Of course it matters," he argued. "The company will most certainly buy the land, and we'll establish the business there, but if you don't want to live there, we won't."

"We've never discussed moving," I said.

"Only because it hasn't made sense before."

I sighed. "And now it does?"

"I believe so, and I hope you will when you see the place and the plans."

"So this is not only about you wanting to live close to where you work?" I asked.

He smiled. "That's part of it. It's more than that, though, Bertha. We've been happy here, yes, but finally we can afford a better home. It is a beautiful part of Mannheim. The children will be closer to their schools and their friends. You'll have the kind of home you deserve."

"And the motorwagen will have the kind of address it deserves," I said, almost giving in to a smile myself.

Carl chuckled. "I'm excited to show you the site, and when the master builder shows you how we hope to lay it out, we can discuss what the new Haus Benz should look like. Eighteen eighty-six is a good year for us, Bertha. Let's not be afraid to make the most of it."

It was unusual for Carl to be so eager and confident about the future. It was generally me who highlighted the green shoots on the trees in the final weeks of winter and reminded him about how far he had come since moving to Mannheim and discovering August in the workshop showing a stranger his drawings of the motorwagen. His comment to me and the children earlier about welcoming change was uncharacteristically buoyant and daring. It was good.

"You're right," I said, determined to shake off my resentment and be open-minded about the potential move. "I look forward to seeing the new property and your plans for it."

—

I saw immediately that Carl was right about the property at Waldhofstrasse 24. Not only was it a respected address, but it was also located on a wide road in a stylish part of town on the other side of the Neckar River. My first thought when we arrived to see it was that I could explore the riverbank with Tappie and the children. Then I remembered that the little dog's joints were too swollen and sore for her to walk anywhere beyond the garden. Even so, I was quickly won over by the idea of living there. We'd been happy at Square T6, Number 11, but the move signified progress. Carl's business was doing well, and soon he'd be able to focus on the motorwagen. My pleasure grew as Carl and I discussed the specifications of our new home with the master builder.

With building of the factory soon underway, we once again looked forward to the day that Carl's colleagues would see the motorwagen in action. As the weeks ticked by, the children and I thought of little else.

"Are you nervous about what people will think about the motorwagen, Mutter?" asked Richard as he accompanied me to the market a few weeks before Max, Friedrich, and several of Carl's other colleagues were due to see it in operation.

"A little," I conceded. "But mostly I'm excited. It's a big but essential step. If Vater is to create a business building motorwagens, he must get others interested. We need as many people as possible to see it and want to own such a machine."

We arrived at the market square, which bustled with farmers off-loading produce and stallholders arranging their wares. As we made our way around the rows of horses and ponies still attached to carts and tethered to a long rail, I breathed in the smell of sweat and leather, and imagined a row of motorwagens in their place—the ones that Carl and I had discussed would one day be powerful enough to tow carts.

It was not yet nine o'clock, but on a day that confirmed summer had arrived, the marketplace was already full of customers skirting around and reaching across one another to select what they perceived to be the biggest, freshest crop or cut available. Richard walked alongside me, seemingly oblivious to the chatter, earthy scent of freshly dug potatoes, and elbowing crowds. His mind was on the motorwagen.

"Do you think Herren Rose and Esslinger will invite others to see the motorwagen on Wednesday?" he asked as I stopped to buy some radishes. "Even if we don't organize a celebration like the one the city held for the water tower, it would help if Vater's partners asked others to watch the test."

"Ja, I agree," I replied, handing him the basket. "It would help. I don't know how many will come. The problem is, your father is not patient with people, particularly those who don't have any knowledge of his work. I think he'd be frustrated by trying to explain the motorwagen to a large group of excited people."

"Maybe he could show it to a few people at a time," suggested Richard, trotting to catch up with me as we made our way to another stall.

"You mean, day after day, presenting it to different groups? Hmm, I can't see Vater agreeing to that either."

Richard frowned at me. The expression reminded me of one of Carl's typical looks of frustration. "What, then? You've said yourself we must make people understand the motorwagen and what it is capable of for it to be accepted. How will that be possible if we don't invite them to see it?"

I stopped to examine a tray of cabbages. "We might try and get someone to write about it for the newspaper," I said, lifting a cabbage to confirm that it was as heavy as it looked.

"How?"

"That's something I'm still trying to work out," I replied.

"Do you know anyone who works at a newspaper, Mutter? Someone who might come and talk to Vater about the motorwagen?" he asked.

I turned to answer him, but my words vanished. Standing behind Richard's right shoulder, her eyes on me, was Ava. For a moment, I forgot that we were estranged. A sense of familiarity and connection washed over me, and I smiled. She blinked and her mouth lifted at the edges. Richard narrowed his eyes at me and turned to see what had caught my attention.

"Tante Ava!" he said, his joy pure. "It's been so long! How are you?"

A few seconds of small talk was all it took to awaken the unease between Ava and me. Richard, however, remained unaware. Almost breathless with excitement, he told her about the motorwagen, patent, and imminent test.

"We were wondering how to get someone from the newspaper to come and see it," he said.

"Oh? The newspaper? That sounds like a good idea," said Ava, giving me a quick glance.

I wanted to ask her if things had changed and whether she'd found joy with Herr Adler. Perhaps time had revealed they had more in common than she'd thought when I last saw her. I'd been so determined not to think about her that it surprised me to find Ava's happiness was still important to me. The bitterness she'd demonstrated hadn't changed that. What had changed, though, was how easy I'd once found it to talk to her. That had been replaced by tension so taut it seemed to pull the breath from me. Had she heard about the land Carl and his partners had bought in Waldhofstrasse and our pending move? If she had, would the news fan the flames of her resentment?

I felt Richard's eyes on me, willing me to add to the conversation.

"It's good to see you, Ava," I managed.

She looked at me and I saw she understood. She lowered her eyes.

"Yes, you too," she said quietly. "I'm sorry…"

Richard glanced from her to me and back again. What would a boy, not yet twelve years old, understand of the situation?

"I'm sorry it's been so long," she said.

"Me too," I said. "I'm sorry too."

"Are you taking it or not?" came a voice from behind me.

I turned. The stallholder glared at me over his vegetables. I was still holding the cabbage.

"Yes," I replied, rummaging in my purse and then paying him.

When I turned back, Ava was gone.

"She said to say goodbye. She had to rush," said Richard.

CHAPTER 25

1886
Mannheim, Germany

Tappie and I were home alone one morning the following week when I received an unexpected visitor.

"Frau Benz?" said a short, dark-haired man when I opened the door to his knocking. "I'm Herr Benjamin Stern of the *New Baden State Newspaper*."

"Newspaper?" I echoed inanely.

He nodded. "Frau Adler told me that your husband, Herr Benz, has a patent for a horseless carriage and—"

"The motorwagen," I corrected him. "Ava—I mean, Frau Adler told you about the motorwagen?"

Herr Stern crouched and scratched Tappie behind the ears. The dachshund looked up at him, her eyes milky with age. "Yes. She visited me at my office last week. She said, erm, *assumed* that since a patent has been granted, the news is official and that Herr Benz wouldn't mind me calling on him to ask about it," he said.

I wondered how it was that Herr Stern and Ava were friends. She'd never mentioned knowing a newspaperman. Perhaps that was simply because the subject hadn't come up. On the other hand, as I'd discovered in recent months, I didn't know Ava as well as I once thought I did.

"My husband isn't here at the moment," I said. Carl was inspecting the new factory. "Perhaps you can tell me what information you need so I can pass it on to him. Would you like to come in?"

"Thank you," he said, standing up and following me into the house. "Frau Adler told me that he's the hardest working man she's ever met. Perhaps I should visit him at his place of work?"

"This *is* his place of work," I replied. "Not this house, but the factory and his workshop are, at present, on the property. However, he's in town today."

Herr Stern declined my offer of coffee, and we settled in the drawing room. Tappie, clearly taken by the newspaperman's ear-scratching skills, curled up at his feet.

"What else did Ava tell you about my husband?" I asked, unable to curb my curiosity.

He chuckled. "That he's an extraordinarily clever man—and single-minded."

"Ah, so you *have* come to the right house," I said.

Herr Stern laughed again. It was a deep, sincere laugh that shone in his eyes, which were so dark it was difficult to discern whether they were brown or black.

"Have you known Ava for long?" I ventured.

"Her husband—the first one, Rudolf Fischer—and I were close friends from childhood. I met her the day he and she met. So, ja, it has been many years."

It reminded me how little I knew of Ava's life beyond our friendship. After she'd outwitted her father and brother and won my trust, it was as if we'd put the Ritter connection into an ampoule, sealed it, and set it aside. The difficult history between August and Carl, followed by her father's involvement in their failed partnership, had induced us to separate our friendship from everything that came before we met. It hadn't occurred to me until now that that included Ava's first marriage. She had rarely spoken about Herr Fischer or their life together. Was that why she'd never spoken about their friend Herr Stern?

"You're wondering why she never mentioned me?" he asked, his eyes still twinkling.

"Well, I—"

Herr Stern stopped smiling. "We argued after Rudolf...Herr Fischer died. I hadn't seen her since. Until the other day. It was a surprise, her visit."

So, I wasn't the only friend who'd been on the receiving end of Ava's unpredictable behavior. The thought didn't comfort me. Despite my curiosity, I was uneasy with such intimate disclosure from a stranger. Herr Stern recognized my discomfort.

"So, the motorwagen! I'm interested in writing an article on it for the newspaper. Frau Adler told me that there will be a demonstration of the machine soon," he said. "If it's possible, I'd very much like to attend."

"That could be arranged," I replied, wondering how I'd broach the subject with Carl. "I'll send you a note confirming the place and time."

Herr Stern asked me several questions about the motorwagen, making copious notes in a book with a short pencil. His manner was curious and warm. His queries were considered, and there wasn't a moment that I had the sense he might think that anything about the motorwagen was outlandish. I wished Carl was there to see how someone—other than an engineer—was interested enough in his invention to pay the attention required to understand it. Herr Stern was the kind of person I'd imagined informing the world about the motorwagen. His questions were relevant, and he quickly grasped how the machine worked. I felt confident that he'd accurately report on it. We spoke so long and easily that I was surprised to hear Frida return from her errands. When I looked at the clock, I saw we'd been talking for more than two hours.

Herr Stern stood up. "I've kept you too long, Frau Benz. I apologize," he said, misinterpreting my glance at the timepiece.

"Not at all," I said. "It's been a pleasure. As you can see, the motorwagen is of great interest to me."

"Indeed, I'd be surprised if your husband could tell me more about it. You certainly pay attention to his work."

It occurred to me to explain how much pleasure the children and I got from helping Carl, but Herr Stern had already tucked his notebook away. I walked him to the door and said goodbye. Tappie stood at my feet, wagging her tail slowly as we watched him walk away.

"I agree. He's a nice man," I said, bending to pat her and thinking about how much I had enjoyed telling him about the motorwagen. It was the first time I'd had the opportunity to discuss it in such detail with a stranger. Herr Stern's interest and appreciation of the invention were encouraging. His reaction was the kind we needed if the motorwagen was going to be widely accepted. I was eager for Carl to get home so that I could tell him about my morning, which I did as soon as I saw him that evening. His response pulled the clouds from beneath me.

"No, definitely not," he said. "Your newspaperman cannot attend the factory test."

"Why not?" I asked.

"Because it's not a public test. It's a demonstration for my partners and colleagues. What do you think Max and Friedrich will say if we invite others to see it at the same time as them?" he said.

I sighed. I should've anticipated his resistance. Carl disliked surprises—even those that others might believe were good ones.

"Will you think about it overnight?" I asked, hoping that once the idea settled in his mind, Carl might see the advantages.

"There's nothing more to think about," he said. "You didn't tell him when and where the test would take place, did you?"

I shook my head.

"Then it's simple: he won't have to alter his plans. You can invite him—"

"Herr Stern," I said curtly. "His name is Herr Stern."

Carl tilted his head. "You can invite *Herr Stern* to the public demonstration to be held at a later date."

One morning the following week, Carl returned to the house having only left for the factory about an hour earlier. He was carrying a copy of the *New Baden State Newspaper*, which he handed to me and pointed at an article.

"You were right," he said. "Herr Stern understands the motorwagen."

I sat down, unable to resist smiling as I read the first paragraph:

"Enthusiasts of the velocipede may be interested to learn that great progress has been made in this field following an invention by the local firm Benz & Co. Currently, the aforementioned company, which has already gained some reputation through the manufacture of gas engines with a recently patented form of ignition, is building a three-wheeled velocipede powered by an engine similar in design to a gas engine."

The article went on to accurately explain the mechanics of the vehicle.

"There can be no doubt that this motorized velocipede will soon make many friends, since it will probably prove itself to be extremely practical for use by doctors, travelers, and sportsmen," concluded the piece.

I looked up from the newspaper. Carl was smiling too. "Will you reconsider? Can Herr Stern attend the factory test?" I asked.

"No," he replied. "This changes nothing. I will, however, be pleased to make his acquaintance at the public demonstration."

—

As was the case when we'd tested the motorwagen with the children, Carl insisted the factory test take place at dusk. Although I believed it was time to show everyone the motorwagen, Carl remained determined to guard the vehicle from as many "arbitrary eyes" as possible.

Everyone who worked at Benz & Co. was invited to the demonstration. However, not all attended. Whether this was because it was held after work and several employees worked far from home or because they were disinterested in the vehicle was unclear. Either way, little over half of the fifty employees gathered with Max and Friedrich to watch Carl drive the motorwagen.

I stood back with Clara and Thilde at my side as Carl, Eugen, and Richard rolled it out of the workshop. We'd agreed that Carl and the boys would manage the test without us. The spectators, we'd reasoned, would enjoy sufficient novelty from the vehicle and didn't require any additional entertainment they might garner from seeing the skirted members of the Benz family running alongside it.

Once the motorwagen was in the center of the yard, Carl pulled the lever to apply the brake. Eugen hopped on board. Although Carl would drive the machine for the test, he wanted Eugen to be in place while he started it.

The spectators drew closer. There were a few sniggers, but most of the men chatted quietly to one another. The tone of their voices suggested curiosity, suspense, and even anticipation. Although the vehicle had been assembled within meters from where they worked, it was kept in a separate room. Few men, aside from Max and Friedrich, had seen the motorwagen fully assembled before. Now they walked around it, pausing, bending, pointing, and examining it. Carl stood back, enduring his colleagues' inquisitiveness for a few minutes before he looked at the sky. The light was fading.

"Step away," he said, approaching the vehicle. "It's time to get started."

The men withdrew and Carl put his hands on the flywheel. As the wheel spun the fourth time, the engine thudded to life, causing some of the men to take another step back. I suppressed a smile. They built engines every day and yet found the little one attached to the motorwagen startling.

Eugen climbed off and Carl pulled himself onto the motorwagen and sat down. The spectators watched intently. Carl twisted his torso to check the engine, turned, and looked left and right before leaning forward and reaching for the shift lever. I took a deep breath as he pulled it into position. The chains clicked and the motorwagen bumped forward over the cobblestones.

For a moment, the spectators stood still, watching it go. Then, divided into two groups on either side, they walked, following the motorwagen as if mesmerized or towed along by the machine. I studied their faces, recognizing astonishment, appreciation, and incredulity. The vehicle moved exactly as designed. The engine *chugg, chugg, chugg*ed. It propelled the chains, and the chains drove the wheels. I'd never felt prouder. The excitement among the men seemed to grow. Their voices rose above the rhythmic thumping of the engine. They pointed at various parts, and the groups split again as some men ran ahead to watch the motorwagen from the front and others went behind it.

One of them called out to Carl, "How far will it go?"

I looked at Carl and saw that the tension stretched across his face earlier had gone. He was almost smiling as he looked at the man. "It'll—"

It was at that moment, with Carl distracted, that the front wheel jolted as it connected with a raised cobblestone. Taken by surprise, Carl wound the lever fast. I wanted to cry out and warn him to be gentler. But it was too late.

The motorwagen veered to the left, vaulting over the cobblestones and across a small ditch. The men scattered, shouting.

"Hey! Careful!"

"Stop the thing!"

"Move! Move!"

Carl had lost control and, with the gradient adding speed, hung on to the steering lever with one hand and the seat with the other as the motorwagen bounced down the slope before it plowed to a stop against the workshop wall. Flung forward, his sternum striking the steering lever, Carl groaned loudly. Eugen and Richard ran to him and switched off the engine. By the time I got there with the girls, the three of them were standing alongside the machine. Carl was pale.

"Are you all right?" I asked.

He nodded, not meeting my eye.

The men from the factory gathered around.

"Well, Carl," said Max, "it's all very well to design a horseless carriage, but I don't think many people will buy one if they have to drive it into a wall whenever they want to stop."

The comment was met with howls of laughter. Max roared the loudest. Carl's face was stony as he turned to inspect the buckled front wheel with his sons.

—

The yard cleared quickly as the men left for the evening. Without speaking, the children and I helped Carl push the motorwagen back into the workshop. Fortunately, the front wheel was only slightly buckled, and with Eugen and Richard supporting it and the rest of us pushing, we were able to move the vehicle easily. Once we'd parked it in the center of the room where it always stood, I glanced at Carl, trying to read his expression. Was he angry? Disheartened? He caught my eye and, to my astonishment, smiled.

"You tried to warn me," he said, rubbing his chest where it had hammered into the steering lever. "I didn't listen."

He registered my amazement and went on. "When you drove it, you said the steering was sensitive. You were explicit. I didn't heed your warning, and look what happened."

"It wasn't your fault," said Clara, taking her father's hand. "I saw the wheel clip a cobble and then—"

Carl put his arm around her, still looking at me. "It was my fault. I'm embarrassed and annoyed with myself for making a mess of the test in front of the others, but it's all right. The motorwagen did exactly what it was meant to do, and even though Max and Friedrich might think otherwise because of my mistake, it's a great machine."

I nodded, smiling now too.

"I'll repair the wheel and we will take it out… No, not just out but into the street for another test. We'll go to the center of town, somewhere where there is more space and the road is smoother," he said.

"The center of town!" said Clara and Richard in unison.

It surprised me too. Less than an hour ago, Carl had been worried about anyone other than his colleagues seeing the motorwagen in action. Now, after a less-than-perfect test, he wanted to take it into the center of Mannheim.

"Yes," said Carl. "Why not?"

"When?" asked Richard, ever impatient.

"As soon as possible," said Carl. He looked at me, his eyes bright. "And this time, you can invite others too—even your newspaperman."

I opened my mouth. "But—"

"I didn't drive it far today, but when I saw the expressions on the faces of the men watching, I realized that you're right, Bertha: the motorwagen is ready for the world, and it's time to see whether or not they're ready for it."

CHAPTER 26

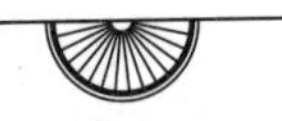

1886
Mannheim, Germany

It was still dark on Saturday the third of July, 1886, when I held open the workshop doors and Carl, Eugen, and Richard rolled the motorwagen through the gates, down the road, and onto the streets of Mannheim. Determined not to draw attention to the vehicle until they'd parked it at the designated starting point on the market square, they remained—Carl told me later—as silent as cats on the hunt the entire way.

By the time Clara, Frida, Thilde, and I had arrived about an hour before the appointed starting time, a crowd of men, women, and children had congregated around the machine. Their chatter was animated and unintelligible, like that of a pack of children playing in a fountain on a hot day. Carl and Richard stood on either side of the motorwagen; Eugen sat on the seat behind the wheel. Their stern expressions and rigid stances could've been those of a trio of royal guards. I caught Carl's eye and waved. He acknowledged me with a terse bob of his head.

"I hope no one touches it," said Clara with a grimace.

"That's unlikely," I replied. "Have you ever seen your father and brothers look as threatening?"

Frida chuckled as I led the way across the road to the median strip that separated the two wide lanes leading to the square. We stood beneath the trees, which created a shady, green avenue on either side of the clipped lawn and colorful flower beds. The Mannheim gardeners had created an eye-catching display of low-growing annual plants.

With the pavement higher than the road, we had a clear view of proceedings from our shaded perch. It was a warm day. I was pleased I'd persuaded Clara and Thilde to leave Tappie at home. Even when the girls carried her, the old dog panted heavily and was uncomfortable outdoors, especially on hot days.

Max, Friedrich, and several other men I recognized from the factory gathered on the other side of the road far from the motorwagen. The machine was built by Benz & Co., but Carl's partners and workers kept their distance. Were they ashamed to be associated with so novel a contraption? Undoubtedly, the fact that Carl guarded the motorwagen so closely fed their detachment.

Max was talking to a man with remarkably thick, glossy gray hair. There was something familiar about him. Did I know him? He wasn't from the factory; I would've recognized him if he were. Anyway, his suit was too stylish for a factory worker. I couldn't place him. Perhaps he reminded me of someone I'd known in Pforzheim.

I was still staring at the man when Max turned his head, saw me, and tipped his hat in my direction. I wondered whether he hoped that Carl might once again drive into a wall or endure some other such humiliation during the test. Although they hadn't stood in Carl's way when he told them about the public test, Max and Friedrich remained deeply skeptical about the vehicle. The day after the factory test, Max again insisted that Carl was "wasting his time and energy" on an invention that wouldn't amount to anything. Buoyed by his faith in the motorwagen, Carl was presently remarkably indifferent to Max's pessimism.

The crowd swelled as those on their way to market or out to enjoy the sunshine gave in to their curiosity and jostled to catch a glimpse of the machine. I was pleased when two policemen approach and ushered the group back a little. Carl smiled at one of the policemen, and they exchanged words. It was clear, even from a distance, that he and the boys were relieved to have a little more space between them and the mob.

As I looked on, I saw a familiar blond head moving across the road toward us. It was Ava, accompanied by Herr Stern. Clara and Thilde ran to greet her.

"Hello," she said, smiling at me over their heads. "What an exciting day! I couldn't miss it."

"I'm glad you didn't," I said. "I wanted to thank you for telling Herr Stern about Carl and the motorwagen."

"Oh, that. Well, I didn't—"

"Thank you for inviting me, Frau Benz," Herr Stern said. "But please excuse me! I'm going to get closer to the action. Perhaps we can talk afterward and, if possible, you might introduce me to Herr Benz."

"Yes. It would be my pleasure," I replied.

I turned to Ava, wanting to avoid what had happened at the market when she'd left before we'd had a chance to talk properly.

"It's a pleasure to know Herr Stern," I said. "He's already written an article about the motorwagen."

"Oh, I hoped you would feel that way!" She beamed. "When Richard mentioned it would help to get an article in the newspaper, I thought of Benjamin immediately."

"His visit was a surprise."

Ava looked away for a moment. "We hadn't seen one another for several years. I… Benjamin was a friend of my first husband. They were… I, erm, lost contact with him. We had a… Well, it doesn't matter. I knew I had to swallow my pride and contact him when I bumped into you and Richard." She reddened. I recalled Herr Stern's reference to their argument. Ava went on. "I wanted to do something for you. To try and make up for what happened. For my stupidity."

She didn't say the words *I'm sorry*, but I thought it was what she meant. It didn't matter. Sometimes, the less said, the better. I'd missed our friendship. She'd introduced us to Herr Stern. The motorwagen was the focus of attention in the center of Mannheim. The dream had never been closer. It was a good day, so I ignored the tiny voice reminding me that Ava had apologized before. She'd asked forgiveness for snubbing me at the water tower celebration before she'd gone on to betray me to Carl. I felt a tug on my arm.

"Look! They're starting," said Clara.

Sure enough, with the boys standing on either side at the front of the motorwagen and the spectators ushered farther away by the policemen, Carl was spinning the flywheel. The engine blasted, hissed, and spat to life on the fourth swing, as I knew it would. There was a cry of astonishment from the crowd. People, including the two policemen, reeled backward. A man fell as he tripped on the pavement. There were shouts and at least one scream. Dogs fled and children wailed. Two horses harnessed to a stationary carriage behind the trees on the far side of the road balked and reared. Someone hurried to placate them.

"My God!" said Ava. "Is it meant to sound like that?"

Clara frowned.

"Naturally, Tante Ava. That's how it goes," she said in a mildly patronizing tone.

A large woman ran past us, dragging a young boy by the arm. "It's the devil's work!" she shouted. "Can't you smell it? I told you not to leave my side! It could've killed you!"

"A gimmick," said a man, standing near us. "A gimmick that is nothing and will amount to nothing. The man belongs in a circus, not on the streets."

In retrospect, we should've anticipated the shock unleashed by the commotion of the motorwagen when it was started in public for the first time. Years in the workshop with Carl meant the children and I were accustomed to the exploding and clattering sounds of the engine. The people of Mannheim were not.

Carl lifted his hands, palms facing forward as if to say, *Stop. Calm down.* His expression was remarkably neutral and showed none of the irritation I imagined he might feel. Perhaps the crowd's reaction hadn't surprised him. Finally, with people quieter, Carl climbed on to the seat and released the brake. There was another slightly less panicky outcry as the engine spluttered, the chains turned, and the motorwagen rumbled down the road.

"Oh my!" said Ava, accepting Thilde's hand as the little girl led my friend into the road to join the procession.

Eugen and Richard ran alongside the vehicle, the former holding a bottle of ligroin to replenish the engine should it run out. Carl looked ahead. He wasn't going to be ambushed by any obstacles in the road this time. The motorwagen moved just as we knew it would.

That afternoon, Herr Stern's second article about the motorwagen was published in the *New Baden State Newspaper*. He wrote: "A velocipede powered by ligroin gas (benzene), constructed at the Benz & Co. Rhenish Gas Engine Factory and about which we have already reported in these pages, was trialed earlier today in town. It created great interest and passed the test satisfactorily."

CHAPTER 27

1886
Mannheim, Germany

Indeed, the motorwagen's first public trial was a success. Not even the mutterings of those in the crowd who said it would "never catch on" and how Carl would "ruin himself and his business" if he continued with his "crazy idea" dampened our pleasure about how well the vehicle had performed. In fact, we laughed as we regaled one another about what we'd seen and heard that morning.

"One man asked another how Vater imagined *anyone* would sit on such a miserable, noisy machine when there are enough horses in the world for us all and so many elegant carriages and cabs to choose from," said Eugen as the boys and I followed the motorwagen home across the bridge over the Neckar River that afternoon.

Carl was driving the motorwagen. Clara and Thilde sat alongside him, still and straight and smiling like princesses on their way to a ball.

"That man probably still reads by candlelight!" chuckled Richard. "Vater says some people will *never* accept progress but that we shouldn't worry about them because there are more people in the world who are excited by it."

"He's right, but some people simply need more time than others to get used to new things. Horses have drawn carriages for as long as we can remember; it's hard to imagine something else doing the work," I said, thinking about my mother's aversion to seeing horses harnessed, whipped, and worked. Even she, I knew, was doubtful that the motorwagen would ever be taken seriously.

As we approached home, Eugen and Richard ran ahead and opened the gates to allow Carl to park the motorwagen in the workshop. I followed, trying to ignore the twinge of nostalgia I experienced when I thought about leaving our old home to move to Waldhofstrasse. The new house would be grand by comparison, and we'd have every modern convenience available. Even so, it would be hard to leave the home we'd always lived in in Mannheim and the only place the children knew. Carl was right: change was difficult. I increased my pace, went into the workshop, and, as Carl switched off the machine, helped the girls from the motorwagen. Their eyes were bright with excitement.

"Did you see, Mutter?" said Thilde. "The children were waving at us as we drove by."

"Only those who didn't run away," teased Carl. "What a day!"

I smiled at him. What a day, indeed. After all the years of dreaming, hoping, and working, we'd finally presented the motorwagen to the people of Mannheim, and while it was scorned and mocked by some, the machine had performed as we hoped it would. People had stopped in the street to marvel and examine it. Some had run away in horror. A few might've gone to pray about it. Many had gathered to smile, laugh, and shake their heads in wonder. Whatever emotions it had stirred, the motorwagen hadn't left anyone unmoved. The people of Mannheim had something to talk about. We were on our way.

"Come," I said, waving my arms toward the workshop door as if hoping to herd my family away from the motorwagen, if only for an hour or two. "Let's go to the house and have something to eat. We can talk about it there."

"Mutter! Wait!"

It was Richard. He was in a dark corner at the back of the workshop, looking down.

"What is it?" I asked.

He knelt on the ground. "Tappie," he said. "She's not moving."

—

Later that evening, after we'd buried her alongside the silver birch tree in the garden, Carl tried to comfort me. That Tappie, who was fourteen years old by then, had died on so auspicious a day was, he said, a good sign.

"She's been with us for as long as we've lived here. She's watched us work and worry, and she's been here to see the children born and grow. Tappie waited with us until she knew we were going to be okay. She waited until we took the motorwagen out of the workshop and into town. She knew it was safe to go," he said, stroking my hair.

I couldn't stem my tears. "But we left her," I replied. "She was alone. What if she went into the workshop to try and find us, hoping we could help her?"

"She went into the workshop because it was quiet and dark, and she knew we'd find her there," he said. "Even if we were here, she would've found a peaceful place away from us to take her last breath."

Carl was right, but still I was sorry that Tappie had been alone when she died. I'd known her time was near, but, as I wrote to Elise a short while later, I had hoped that I'd have the chance to say a final goodbye.

Perhaps because I didn't comfort Affie in her final hours and arrived too late in Pforzheim to say goodbye to Vater before his death, I'd hoped to encounter death more gently from then on. I imagined stroking her ears and holding Tappie's paw as she went to sleep for the last time. Now I accept that death is not like that. It comes without notice or fanfare. There's no protocol to guide us or magic to make it easier. So, Sister, my little dachshund companion is gone, but life goes on. Carl says we shouldn't mourn her but celebrate her life and the pleasure she gave us. He's right. We should celebrate, particularly at this time, when things are going well with the motorwagen.

—

Indeed, things were going well with the motorwagen. With the factory having relocated to Waldhofstrasse—the house would take another year or so to complete—Carl traveled from home to work in the vehicle almost every day. It didn't seem that long ago that we'd celebrated when it drove a hundred meters without unscheduled stops or breakdowns. Now Carl was driving it over several kilometers at a time.

"Each ride is nothing more than a test drive," he said, as if I might accuse him of having too much of a good time. "Every drive brings new gains, new improvements and advances. Also, once it's at the factory, the motorwagen must work too. We use the engine to pump water into the basin for the gasometer."

As if his rides to work during the week weren't enough, on weekends, Carl, the children, and I regularly took the motorwagen to the Ringstrasse, a road that ran around the city. The sandy road, which was bordered on either side by two roughly stacked stone walls, was rarely used at the time and, particularly on Saturdays and Sundays, was an excellent place to drive the motorwagen. The countryside, with its soft meadows and shady enclaves and peaceful backdrop (once we'd shut off the engine), was perfect for picnics. It was on the Ringstrasse that Eugen, Richard, and I became competent, experienced drivers, getting the vehicle up to its thrilling speed of sixteen kilometers per hour.

—

Having noted Herr Stern's articles on the motorwagen, other newspapermen approached Carl for interviews. He obliged, and reports about the vehicle multiplied, including an article published by *Mannheim General News*. Below the headline "Streetcar Powered by Gas Engines," the report read, "Herr C. Benz, co-owner of the Benz & Co. Rhenish Gas Engine Factory and inventor of gas engines with electric ignition, constructed a road car powered by a gas engine and patented this invention. We heard about the first vehicle being built months ago and were certain that Benz's invention solved a problem of using elementary power to produce a road car. However, as was to be expected, there were still many deficiencies that could be remedied by continued trials and improvements. This work, just as difficult as the invention itself, may now be regarded as completed, and Herr Benz will now begin with the construction of such vehicles, calculated for practical use.

"We believe that this vehicle will have a good future because it can be put into use without much trouble and because it will become the cheapest means of transport for business travelers and possibly also for tourists."

Reports were not limited to daily newspapers. A scientific journal, *The Wildermann Yearbook of Natural Sciences*, reported on the motorwagen's engine as follows: "The motor from Benz & Co. is not only designed for ships but also for cars and especially bicycles (velocipede). The piston is driven by the explosion of a mixture of air and ligroin gas, which is generated almost automatically in an onboard device, that is, without the driver having to supervise it."

It was, however, during a conversation with Herr Stern that the idea of exhibiting the motorwagen at a trade fair arose.

"Your newspaperman called on me at the factory today," Carl told me one evening after supper. "I believe he might be as fascinated by the motorwagen as we are."

"Does he want to write another article?" I asked, pleased by the news of Herr Stern's continued interest.

"Yes, but he's eager to write something new. He wanted to know when we will start mass production."

"Mass production? Are you ready for that?" I asked.

"I'm ready. The factory is ready, but we need to know we'll sell them as fast as we can build them. That's the dilemma. And there's Max."

"Oh, yes. Max," I said.

Carl grimaced. "Even with the trials having proven it works and several rides on it himself, the motorwagen fails to impress him. He insists that it will not find favor among enough buyers to prove successful. As you know, if we are to build more to sell, I need his agreement."

"We are back to that," I said, weary at the thought.

"Max says that if I want to shift the factory's focus away from stationary engines and onto the motorwagen, he will sell his shares."

"To you? But can we—"

"No, we can't afford to buy Max's shares *and* invest in producing more motorwagens. We need him."

"What about trying to find buyers before you build more?" I asked.

He smiled. "That's exactly what Herr Stern suggested when I explained the situation. He also told me about a trade and industry fair that will take place in Paris next month."

"Paris?"

"The French, I believe, will be more eager to adopt the motorwagen than our countrymen. It was, after all, Jean Lenoir who manufactured the first internal combustion engine in numbers. And look how well our stationary engine has done in France. The French will recognize the motorwagen and see how important and transformative it will be for transport and economic life. Paris is the perfect place to show it," he said.

"But you've demonstrated it here and you manufacture it here. Doesn't it make more sense to keep demonstrating it in Germany? At least for a while. Find buyers here, and then go to France," I argued.

"Buyers will come to me at the fair," he said.

"Will you be able to demonstrate the motorwagen there? Drive it? You saw how amazed people were when they saw you driving it in Mannheim. You know how people respond now when you drive it in town. The motorwagen *must* be driven to be fully appreciated."

"The event is in an exhibition hall. It won't be possible to drive it there," he said.

"But how will people at the fair know how it works if they can't see it in action?"

He stood. "I'll tell them," he said with a sigh.

It was true that Carl had grown accustomed to talking to people about the motorwagen, explaining how it worked and what it offered the world, but he was better at demonstrating it than he was at talking about it. I worried that he'd grow impatient at a fair where he was unable to start or drive the machine and had to repeat himself all day.

"Has Herr Stern been to the fair in Paris before? Could he describe what it was like? Give you some idea of what to expect?" I asked.

"No. He simply told me that he believed a fair might be a good place to find buyers. I asked him if he knew of any such events taking place soon, and he mentioned the one in Paris."

"So he didn't recommend the Paris fair in so many words. Carl, perhaps you need to give this more thought."

Carl placed a hand on my shoulder. "It's bedtime. Let's not argue about this. This will appease Max. I'll take the motorwagen to Paris, come back with orders, and he'll agree that we can start building more of them in the factory."

CHAPTER 28

1887
Mannheim, Germany

ALTHOUGH THE LITTLE DOG HAD BEEN GONE FOR MONTHS, TAPPIE LINGERED large in my thoughts. I still expected to see her when I awoke every morning and looked for her when I got home after running errands. So strong was her presence that once or twice I was sure I'd seen her toddle in or out of a room, tail flicking and eyes bright. I missed her. I missed having a four-legged companion, but I couldn't imagine introducing a new dog to the house. It was too soon—but Lupin knew none of this.

The tall, lean shepherd dog introduced himself to us while Carl, the children, and I were picnicking alongside the Ringstrasse one Sunday.

"Look!" said Richard, jumping to his feet and approaching the dog, who seemed to have appeared from nowhere and stood, observing us from the edge of the woods several meters away. "He looks like a black wolf."

"Careful, he might eat you," teased Eugen.

We watched as Richard walked slowly toward the animal. He held out his hand, palm upward. The dog didn't flinch. His tall, pointy ears were pricked and his eyes unblinking. Richard stopped and placed his hand millimeters from the animal's muzzle. Boy and dog stood like statues. Eventually, the dog stretched his neck and sniffed Richard's fingers. His tail lifted and he began wagging it slowly.

"The lupus smells roast fowl," said Carl, his voice low.

It's possible he did and that was what had lured him to us.

"We mustn't feed him," I said. "It'll confuse him and give him the wrong idea."

"What's a lupus?" asked Clara.

"It's Latin for *wolf*," I said.

"Lupin is a good name for him," said Thilde as we watched Richard amble back across the field to where we sat. The dog was at his side, where he stayed until we packed up to leave.

"He can't come with us," I told Richard. "He probably belongs to a farmer out here. He must stay."

"But, Mutter, he's thin. I don't think anyone owns him," said Richard.

"He's not a stray, Richard. Look how tame and relaxed he is, and he doesn't appear hungry. He's a lean, fit dog, that's all."

To Richard's credit, he tried to dissuade Lupin from following us when we left. The boy scolded the dog, telling him to stay in a low, unfriendly voice. However, every time we watched him skulk away and thought he'd finally left us, he'd reappear from behind the wall or between the trees, his eyes fixed on Richard.

"There's a farm up ahead," Carl said after the dog had followed us for a couple of kilometers. "Go and ask if they know the dog, Eugen."

We waited while Eugen ran up a short road and disappeared around the corner and into the farmyard. He wasn't gone long.

"The farmer says the dog is a stray. He's seen him in the area for several days and has chased him from his house. He doesn't want him around because of what he might do to his hens. He says we should take him to town with us and sell him at the market," said Eugen.

"Can we?" said Richard, who stood with Lupin back at his side. "Can we take him to town but not sell him at the market?"

Carl looked at me. I shrugged. Lupin came home with us and stayed.

—

The following week, Carl told Max and Friedrich that he'd load the motorwagen on the train and take it to Paris for the week-long trade and industry fair Herr Stern had told him about. Max was livid.

"If you insist on making decisions like this without discussing them with your partners first, then you can pay the train fare and exhibition costs yourself," he said.

"Then I shall keep the profits from the motorwagen to myself too," Carl had responded.

"What profits, Carl? We've not seen a single mark from your ridiculous machine," said Max. "For an intelligent man, you can be astonishingly stupid when it comes to this invention. We have a perfectly good product in the stationary engine. The Benz engine is considered the best around, but you want to risk it all! If, after your adventure to Paris, you continue this way, I *will* sell my shares in the company. I don't want to see everything we've built here disappear in a whiff of smoke and dust as your three-wheeled machine forces our collapse."

My stomach roiled when Carl recounted the conversation. It did so again when I stood, Lupin at my side, and waved goodbye to Carl as he drove down the road to the station to leave for Paris.

"He'll be back next week," I told the dog, who'd taken Tappie's place as my larger furry shadow while Richard was at school.

What worried me was whether his time in Paris would be worthwhile or if it would elicit a new episode of uncertainty and drama at the factory—and in our lives. I wanted to believe all would be well and that my doubts were unwarranted. If Carl returned with orders for the motorwagen and could say, "I told you so," I'd rejoice. I wanted to be wrong about doubting him but couldn't stop fretting.

—

Perhaps, I thought two days after Carl's departure, Herr Stern might have knowledge of the fair that would reassure me. After all, he was the one who'd told Carl about it. I pulled on my coat and headed to town.

"Frau Benz! This is unexpected," said Herr Stern, having been called to the front office at the building that housed the newspaper business.

When I saw him, I felt silly, and I regretted having come. He was a busy man and I nothing more than a fussing woman who wanted to share her concerns. I needed a friend, not the counsel of a newspaperman. If things had been easier with Ava, I would've visited her, but I'd not seen her since we'd watched the motorwagen demonstration on the market square. I'd hoped I might hear from her; perhaps she hoped to hear from me. Neither of us had taken the step.

"I'm sorry to disrupt your day, Herr Stern. It's not… Well, I'm not here on an urgent matter, and I'll understand if you don't have time. After all, news waits for no one," I said with a nervous laugh.

He frowned. I wasn't doing well.

"I have time, Frau Benz. In fact, it's my coffee break. Let me get my coat, and we'll go to the café on the corner. I'll show you where we reporters find inspiration," he said with a smile that reminded me why I'd warmed to him when we met.

"So," he said a while later in the café. "What's on your mind, Frau Benz?"

I explained, telling him how eager Carl had been about exhibiting at the Paris fair and how I'd tried to persuade him not to go. However, I didn't mention Max's displeasure or his ultimatum. Herr Stern listened silently.

"I'm here for your counsel, Herr Stern. To get your opinion. You were the one who mentioned the fair. I want to know if I'm worrying unnecessarily," I said.

He looked at his coffee. I'd made him uncomfortable.

I emitted a short, joyless chuckle. "Indeed, I'm sorry. I'm looking for reassurance, and I see you cannot give it to me."

Herr Stern took a deep breath. "It's true, I *did* talk to your husband about fairs and exhibitions and how useful they might be to him. You see, I think the motorwagen should be demonstrated as widely as possible. Exhibitions provide opportunities to do this. Herr Benz asked me for a list of imminent events. The newspaper has one, which I gave to him. However, I didn't specifically propose that he attend the fair in Paris. In my opinion, the ideal exhibition for the motorwagen would be an event focusing on machines that allows exhibitors to demonstrate inventions. I told him as much but, as you know, Herr Benz was eager to participate in a fair as soon as possible."

"Did you propose any other exhibitions?" I asked.

"We spoke about the Munich Exhibition of Engines and Working Machines, which takes place next September."

"Does it allow demonstrations of machines?" I asked.

"Yes, but only stationary demonstrations. No one expects exhibitors to want their machines to move about in the exhibition halls. The motorwagen is an exception," said Herr Stern.

I didn't respond. Presenting the motorwagen in Munich made sense. Carl had already established his reputation as the creator of one of the finest stationary engines in Germany. It was possible that people attending the exhibition might already have heard or read about the motorwagen. Their curiosity would already have piqued. Perhaps there was a way of convincing the Munich exhibition organizers to allow Carl to drive the vehicle at the event. There was still time to petition them.

Herr Stern took a sip of coffee and placed his cup in its saucer. "I understand your concern about what little impression the motorwagen might make as it stands quietly and immobile in a hall somewhere in Paris this week, Frau Benz. It's at its most impressive on the road, where it hisses, rumbles, roars, and moves, but that doesn't mean your husband won't find success with it in Paris," he said.

I tried to smile.

"That's not what you wanted to hear, is it?" he asked.

"No, but it's what I expected. I've wasted your time."

"No, Frau Benz, not at all. It's a pleasure to talk to you. It's seldom that one meets such visionaries as you and Herr Benz. I'm honored that you sought my counsel. It gives me an opportunity to talk about the motorwagen. There's nothing I enjoy more," he said.

"What a refreshing thing to hear," I replied, feeling lighter than I had in days. "Herr Benz told me you regularly visit the factory, eager for news on the motorwagen. We're grateful for the attention."

"I'm intrigued by the machine and what it might—no, what it *will*—mean to the future. I meant what I said about how I believe it should be demonstrated as far and wide as possible. Germany needs to see what a genius it has in Herr Benz and what magic he has created. Mannheim is too small to appreciate it. Imagine if people in the countryside could see it," he said, his dark eyes bright with excitement.

"Imagine how they would run, screaming in fear," I said. "As some did when they first saw it travel across the market square."

He laughed easily now. "Yes, they might. But then, just like the people of Mannheim, they would grow curious and watch it more closely. They would grow accustomed to it, and eventually the brave, forward-thinking ones among them might buy a motorwagen of their own."

"I wish *you* were a partner at the factory," I said without thinking.

Herr Stern's brow wrinkled again. "Herr Benz's partners do not see the future of the motorwagen the way he does?"

This time, I gave my words more consideration. "Let's just say that they are not as enamored by it as Herr Benz and I are. Or you, for that matter."

CHAPTER 29

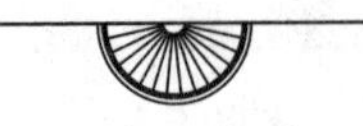

1887
Mannheim, Germany

"I could've been a violet blooming in secret," said Carl when he returned from the Paris exhibition. "I stood alongside the motorwagen, hidden away between the horse-drawn carriages, all of which were taller, broader, and shinier than the motorwagen. I was buried and overlooked. Nobody paid me or the motorwagen any attention."

He raked his fingers through his hair. "It wasn't the machine's fault. It was my own. You said it, Bertha: the motorwagen's most striking feature is that it is self-mobile. It's this characteristic that must be demonstrated. No journey with the motorwagen—real or philosophical—can be taken without movement. It's horselessness must be presented for it to be understood. Forgive me for not listening to you."

It wasn't for me to forgive Carl; he hadn't wronged me. However, I didn't deny the glimmer of relief that washed over me. Despite it being unsuccessful, the experiment of Paris had shown Carl what I believed to be true: the motorwagen *had* to be driven to be fully appreciated. The idea of it was too outlandish for many to imagine—even when they saw it. Something useful had been achieved in Paris. Max was less magnanimous than I was.

Carl and I had a meeting with the master builder working on the house in Waldhofstrasse at the factory the day after he returned from Paris. As such, I was there when he told Max and Friedrich about the fair.

"Not one order!" fumed Max. "You spent a week in Paris and returned without a single order for your machine? Bah!"

He strode to the other side of the office and spun on his heels to glare at Carl. "I shouldn't be surprised. No, I'm not! But I hope you finally see what I've known all along. This bloody carriage will end us! You must give up on it, Carl. It's a worthless gimmick, which only *you* take seriously."

"That's not true," said Carl. "Wherever the vehicle is driven, it attracts interest and awe. You've taken trips with me yourself, Max. You've seen the excitement it stirs. The mistake I made in Paris was to participate in an event during which I was unable to drive it. I won't do that again."

"No, you won't," said Max. "You won't take it anywhere at the company's expense."

"I covered the costs in Paris myself."

Max's face was red. "You spent a week away from the factory. Benz & Co. paid the price of you not being here. Drive it? Excitement in the streets isn't the same as money changing hands, Carl. The motorwagen is not a viable product."

It was then that Friedrich, who was leaning against a desk, contemplating his shoes, came to life. "Actually, while Carl was in Paris, France came to Mannheim," he said.

I watched as the other men looked at him, bewildered.

"Monsieur Emile Roger was here last week," said Friedrich, referring to the French customer who'd purchased several stationary engines from Benz & Co. over the years. "He ordered four new engines and asked where Carl was. I told him about the motorwagen. He wants to test it."

Max and Carl stared at their partner.

"You didn't mention this last week," said Max, pulling at his collar.

"I didn't think to," said Friedrich with a shrug. "Neither Carl nor the motorwagen was here. There was nothing to show Monsieur Roger."

Carl rubbed his hands together. "It's a pity he didn't come to the fair."

"He didn't know you were going," said Friedrich. "And by the time he got back to Paris, the fair was over."

The men were quiet for a moment. I spoke up from behind them.

"Invite Monsieur Roger back again. Take him for a drive," I said.

Max turned and stared at me. He might've forgotten I was in the room. "This changes nothing," he snarled. "If Carl spends any more time on the motorwagen, I will sell my shares in the company. I will not wait until they are worthless. I've already had interest from a prospective buyer. I will take steps to sell immediately, if necessary."

Carl placed his hands on his head. "Please, Max, be reasonable. If you sell your shares, it'll disrupt production. We'll have to get used to working with a new person. Give me some more time...another year to prove to you how worthwhile the motorwagen is," he said.

"Another year? No! It's too risky, Carl. How will you prove that the motor carriage is worthwhile? The only way you can prove that is by selling it," said Max.

"Yes, but to sell it, I need to publicize it. I need to continue working on the motorwagen so that I can improve it, show it off, and allow others to drive it."

"You mean, spend more of the company's time, labor, and money on it? No, that I will not accept. If that's your plan, then—"

I'd had enough and stepped forward. "I don't understand why you think that you can lord over us, Max. Have you forgotten that you, Carl, and Friedrich are equal partners in this business? Have you forgotten that your partnership agreement stipulates that Carl has the right to pursue interests in other products if he so wishes?" I demanded.

"I haven't forgotten, *Frau Benz*," said Max. "But our agreement doesn't say I have to accept it, which is why I *will* sell my shares in the company if this madness continues. That's my final word on the matter."

—

Carl and I didn't discuss Max's ultimatum for several days afterward. In fact, we didn't talk about Benz & Co. or the motorwagen at all. His experience in Paris had knocked the wind from him, and he was brooding. Or perhaps he was plotting. Either way, I didn't press him to share his thoughts with me. He'd do so when he was ready, I thought. Eugen wasn't as patient.

"What will you do about the motorwagen now, Vater?" he asked at supper one night.

"Do?" said Carl, in what seemed like an uncharacteristically obtuse way.

Eugen shifted uncomfortably on his seat. "To find buyers, I mean."

"Well, I'll show it to Monsieur Roger when he comes to Mannheim next month," he said. I looked at him, surprised that he'd not mentioned the Frenchman had agreed to come back to examine the motorwagen.

Carl ignored my glance and went on. "I wrote to him with details. He said he's interested and looks forward to seeing it. However, he did say he was concerned about its reliability over long distances. He doesn't want a motorwagen to drive around town. He wants something that he can use to travel between his apartment in Paris and his house in the country. He's not the only one who doubts the motorwagen's ability over long distances. I've had similar comments from others."

"But Monsieur Roger hasn't even seen it yet," said Richard.

Carl shrugged. His despondence was pitiful. I put my knife and fork down. "Take Monsieur Roger for a long drive," I said.

"Yes, perhaps," he replied.

Later, as we lay in bed, I rolled toward Carl and put an arm around him. "It's not like you to stop fighting for the motorwagen. What are you thinking? Tell me," I said quietly.

He turned to face me. "I haven't stopped fighting for the motorwagen," he said. "I've stopped fighting Max."

"Isn't that the same, given his demands?"

"No."

"What do you mean?"

He looked away. My scalp prickled, as if I'd braided my hair too tightly.

"What is it?" I asked.

He didn't reply. My mouth felt dry.

"After everything we've gone through, surely you know that I'm on your side whatever happens. I'm at your side always, here, at the factory, on the motorwagen…" I said.

Carl nodded without speaking. I sat up.

"Tell me, please."

He sat, too, and we faced each other as he spoke.

"You're on my side, but we don't always see things the same way, Bertha. This is difficult for me to tell you."

"Why? You can tell me anything. You know that. We—"

"Wait, please. If you want to hear what I'm planning, you have to let me explain without interruption."

I tried to smile.

Carl took a deep breath and cleared his throat. "I can't proceed with the motorwagen at Benz & Co. I need money to invest in it. Money to develop and build more. Money Max will not release from Benz & Co. So I have no choice. I need to find another investor for the motorwagen. Once I've found someone and we have our plans in place, I'll sell my shares in Benz & Co. and invest that money in the motorwagen. I'll start again. This time, I'll focus entirely on the motorwagen—just as I have always wanted," he said.

I felt faint with panic. "No, Carl! Why should you leave Benz & Co.? Let Max go if someone must. Someone will buy his shares. He said he has someone interested. He should go! Not you. After everything—"

"Wait, Bertha! Please listen to me. I've thought about this. There is more value in selling my shares in the company and combining those with the money of another investor than Benz & Co. will have to invest in the motorwagen. Benz & Co. must look after the stationary engines too. It's become too complicated. It makes sense to separate the business of the stationary engines and that of the motorwagen."

I shook my head. I couldn't believe that Carl would contemplate starting all over again. The expense and effort of setting up a new business would be immense, not to mention the energy it would require from Carl. And what about our house that was being built at Waldhofstrasse? It would surely have to be put up for sale if Carl sold his shares in Benz & Co. I couldn't imagine us living alongside a factory in which we no longer had shares. My head whirred.

"Why haven't you discussed this with me up until now?" I asked, wondering if this was how Max had felt when he found out that Carl had already decided to take the motorwagen to Paris.

"I wanted to find an investor before I did," he replied, not meeting my eye. "I thought it would be easier for you if I'd already taken that step. Also, I don't want Max and Friedrich or anyone else to know my plans. It's important that Benz & Co. continues as it is and that there is no uncertainty about its future. I want my share of the company to be as valuable as possible when it is time for me to sell it."

I threw the blankets aside, stood up, walked to the foot of the bed, and glared at Carl. Anger coursed through me like a river in flood.

"No!" I said through gritted teeth. "This is unacceptable, Carl. You're treating me the way *other* men treat women. It's not our way! I'm your partner. I've been on your side from the moment we met. You *cannot* make this decision without my agreement, and I do not agree. It's not fair. I'm not only a girl; I'm Bertha Benz, and I will not stand by while you put everything we've worked for at risk because another one of our business partners is threatening to let us down."

Carl leaned toward me. "What do you mean? I'm not putting it at risk. Quite the contrary: I'm protecting the motorwagen."

"If you sell Benz & Co., we'll have to start all over again. It doesn't matter that you still have the motorwagen. There won't be a factory. Your tools and equipment will be gone. You'll leave behind the engineers and workers who you've trained and trust. You'll start all over again, the way you did when August let you down and the Bühler brothers sold you out. Let Max go, Carl. Don't let this happen again," I pleaded.

"If Max goes, my days will be consumed by work on the stationary engine once more. Even if there is money to invest in the motorwagen, I won't have the time to use it," he said, his voice low and quiet now.

"Then we will find another way to convince Max to allow you to focus on the motorwagen. There must be another way," I said.

Carl lay back on his pillow. "If there is, I cannot see it."

I climbed back into bed alongside him. "I saw Herr Stern while you were in Paris. He told me about the Munich Exhibition of Engines and Working Machines that takes place in September next year."

"Yes, he mentioned it, but after Paris—"

"It's different from Paris because demonstrations are permitted," I said.

"You mean, we could drive the motorwagen around the exhibition?"

"I don't know, but we could apply for permission to do so."

"It doesn't matter. Max wouldn't permit it."

"If we don't tell him, he won't be able to do anything about it until it is too late," I replied, not daring to think how that very tactic had infuriated Max previously. "I'll take care of matters so that he cannot accuse you of spending company time and money on the exhibition."

Carl sighed. "Even if the organizers grant us permission to drive the motorwagen at the fair and we are able to get there without Max finding out, will it be enough?"

"I don't know, but we have to try. If the exhibition is a success and we get orders for the vehicle there, I'm certain Max will change his mind. Please, Carl, put aside the thoughts of giving up Benz & Co. and starting all over again. It's not a good idea, and it's not necessary."

"I've thought about nothing else since my return from Paris," he said. "I'm certain my plan is the best one. I accept it might be difficult for us again for a while, but it'll mean I can finally work only on the motorwagen."

"That could also be possible if we give the motorwagen a little more time to prove its worth to Max. If you must do it alone again, you'll have to take several steps back before getting on track. Don't rush into anything, please."

He sighed again. "Here's what I will agree to: if you can get permission for me to drive the motorwagen at the Munich exhibition, I will wait until then before looking for a new investor," he said, then lay down and turned his back to me.

CHAPTER 30

1888
Mannheim, Germany

My second visit to Herr Stern was not unannounced. This time, I'd written, asking for an appointment. He responded promptly, saying he looked forward to it. When I arrived at the agreed time, he was waiting for me at the door of the building.

"It's such a lovely morning, I wondered if you'd like to take a walk rather than be inside?" he asked after we'd exchanged greetings.

"I'd love to walk," I said, thinking about how much I'd enjoyed walking along the Enz River with Affie, Elise, and later with Carl when we'd lived in Pforzheim. Then how I walked along the Neckar River with Ava, Tappie, and the children here in Mannheim. "If I'd known, I would've brought my son's dog, Lupin. I feel guilty walking without him."

"I won't tell him if we meet," Herr Stern joked.

We walked down a steep, narrow road, which led to a path along the Neckar. Despite the sunshine, it was soothingly cool at the riverside, and several others were taking advantage of the fine weather. I'd indicated in my letter that I wanted to ask Herr Stern about the Munich Exhibition of Engines and Working Machines. However, because it was important that Max didn't find out about our hopes for Munich, I needed to tread carefully.

"You probably heard about Paris," I said.

"Yes," he replied. "Herr Benz told me it was not a success. I'm sorry."

"Do you ever speak to Herren Rose or Esslinger when you visit Carl at the factory, Herr Stern?"

"No. I greet them if I see them, but because my interest is the motorwagen, I visit to see your husband," he said. "Why do you ask?"

After Ava had betrayed my confidence about America to Carl, I was anxious about asking Herr Stern to keep a secret, but I couldn't see a way around it if I was to get his help.

"I want to investigate the Munich exhibition with the idea of exhibiting the motorwagen there, but I don't want anyone at Benz & Co. to know that I'm doing it until...well, until I'm ready to tell them," I said.

Herr Stern raised his eyebrows and smiled at me. "You don't want them getting their hopes up," he said.

"Yes, something like that," I replied. "It would make things easier."

"I can assure you, Frau Benz, I will have no cause to say anything to anyone about it," he said firmly.

There was something convincing about Herr Stern's manner, and I felt my shoulders relax.

"Thank you, Benjamin," I said. "Do you mind if we use our first names? I'm Bertha. If I'm not mistaken, we're friends, after all."

"We are and it's my pleasure, Bertha," he said with a playful bob of his knees. "Now, tell me how I can help you with your investigation into the exhibition in Munich."

It was unusual for me to collaborate with anyone other than Carl, but it was also a relief. Carl and I had agreed that we'd not talk about the future of the business and motorwagen until there was something new to discuss. We'd reached something of an impasse. On the one occasion I'd tried to revive our discussion, he'd shut me down. He would, he said, honor his promise not to do anything until I'd petitioned the organizers of the Munich exhibition to allow him to drive the motorwagen there. Before that, it was better not to rehash the subject. Now, as Benjamin and I walked along the river, I was happy to be able to talk about the motorwagen freely once more. I described my plan.

"Yes, I'll do whatever I can to help you get permission to drive the motorwagen at the exhibition. But I'm not sure that I can do anything that you can't do alone," he said.

"Oh, I disagree. You're a skillful writer. You could help me word the application in such a way that the exhibition organizers will *beg* us to attend and drive the motorwagen in Munich. I'm counting on your experience as a news reporter to help me persuade them that driving our vehicle at their event will draw more crowds than any other exhibition has ever seen," I said.

Benjamin laughed. "You are even smarter than I thought."

That evening, I couldn't help but tell Carl about my meeting with Benjamin. It was news, after all, I thought. I explained why I'd asked for the newspaperman's help and offered to show Carl a draft of the letter we'd written. He smiled and, to my surprise, took me in his arms even though the children were in the room.

"No, I don't want to see it. For the time being, I'd like to pretend I know nothing about it," he said quietly. "But I do appreciate your efforts, Bertha. I always have. I should tell you that more often."

"Did you have good day?" I asked.

He stepped back, his eyes no longer on me. "Yes, yes. It was a good day. I'll wash my hands and we can eat," he said before leaving the room.

—

The exhibition organizers were quick to respond to my letter, and their reply was explicit: No, it would not be possible for us to drive the motorwagen anywhere within the exhibition hall or nearby. It would pose a danger they were not prepared to risk.

I met Benjamin at the café near his office and showed him the letter. "They leave no opening for further appeal, do they?" he said, grimacing as he handed it back to me.

"Actually, I think they do," I replied. "They write that the motorwagen poses what they believe to be a risk that *they* are not prepared to take. What about if someone else took the risk?"

"What do you mean?"

"Well, what if we apply to exhibit at the event and also write to the chief of police in Munich, asking for permission to drive the motorwagen on the streets of the city while the fair is taking place?"

Benjamin chuckled. "Well, that's a different approach," he said. "Do you think the police chief will be more amicable to the idea than the exhibition organizers?"

"I don't know, but it's worth a try."

"Yes," he said. "I believe you're right. I shall find out who the chief is and get his address for you when I get back to the office. Do you want my help with the letter?"

"Thank you. Yes, but I have another idea I want to discuss with you too. It's something of a backup plan in case we cannot convince the police chief to welcome us on the streets of Munich," I said.

He leaned forward. "Do tell me."

In fact, the idea came from Eugen and Richard. Like me, the boys were suffering from their father's downcast mood. After the excitement of working on the motorwagen for so many years and its successful presentation in Mannheim, Carl's apparent apathy for the vehicle was a sizable comedown for us all. I'd overhead them talking one day.

"Vater says one of the doubts about the motorwagen is that it won't endure long trips," Richard had said. "Do you think that's why he's worried about it?"

"I know, but it's not true. It's just that no one has taken it on a long trip," Eugen had said.

"We should tell Vater that! Encourage him to do it," his brother had replied. "Not only would it prove that it can travel a long distance, but more people will see it."

"Ja, but I don't think we should say anything to Vater. Not now, anyway," Eugen had said quietly.

I'd wanted to run from the hallway and into the drawing room where they were and urge them to repeat what they'd said to Carl. I wished they could dispel their father's inertia, rekindle his fire, and encourage him to chase his dream once more, but that wasn't our children's responsibility. It was mine. That didn't mean I couldn't use their idea, though.

"A long-distance drive. Hmm, that's a good plan," said Benjamin after I'd told him about the boys' idea. "Particularly if Carl chooses a route that takes him through the countryside and several villages and towns where many people will see it in action."

"Yes," I said. "But I didn't say anything about Carl driving the motorwagen."

Benjamin's eyes widened. "Your sons?" he asked.

I said nothing.

"You?" he said, his eyes wider still.

"Yes. With my sons," I replied. "Imagine what an impression the motorwagen would make if a woman with two boys drove it a hundred kilometers across the countryside. It would show the world that not only is the motorwagen *the* transport of the future but also that anyone can operate it."

Benjamin clapped his hands and laughed. "It'll be the news event of the year, and I'd like to be the first to report on it. Is that possible?"

"It's all yours," I replied. "But first, we'll write to the chief of police in Munich. Carl has agreed to the proposal about Munich. It might be more difficult to get him to agree to the idea of me and the boys driving the motorwagen to Pforzheim."

"Pforzheim? Ah! To visit your family."

"Indeed," I replied.

"It's an excellent idea. Tell me when you plan to go, and I'll take the train and meet you in Pforzheim. You can tell me all about the trip, and I'll immediately write an article," said Benjamin, shifting about in his chair as if I might leave any moment.

"Let's not rush things. There's still a chance we can attract all the attention we need by driving the vehicle in Munich."

The first letter I wrote to Herr Reimann, who Benjamin informed me was the acting chief of police in Munich, received no response. After three weeks, I wrote another, pointing out to the chief that, with the exhibition fast approaching—I had confirmed the motorwagen's appearance at the event in another letter to the organizers—I required an urgent response. This time, the police chief replied, saying he didn't understand exactly what I meant by "self-moving carriage" and that if I required a legitimate response, I should come to Munich to explain it to him in person.

"Would you like me to come with you?" Benjamin asked when I told him the news.

"Thank you, but I think I'll manage," I replied, reluctant to appear before the policeman with a man whose involvement in the petition might not be clear.

"Perhaps Eugen should go with you," said Carl when I told him that I'd be going to Munich for an audience with the police chief.

I glanced at my son. He smiled. "I'd like to go," he said.

"Can I come too?" asked Richard from where he sat on the floor with Lupin's head in his lap.

"I'd like Eugen to come," I replied. "I'm sure there'll be some other way you can help soon, Richard."

So it was that Eugen and I caught the train to Munich early one morning the following week. It was unusual for me to be alone with just one of my children for an extended time, but he was easy company. As the carriage swayed gently across the countryside, we spoke about the motorwagen and how disappointed Carl had been by its showing in Paris. Eugen was measured in thought and speech. He'd never been one for outbursts or spontaneity. I realized how much our older son had matured in recent months and was touched by how perceptive he was about what Carl was going through. Carl and I hadn't discussed his thoughts about leaving Benz & Co. with the children and had been careful not to allude to the possibility when they were around. It seemed, though, that Eugen might understand more than we realized, and now, on the train, I wished I could discuss it with him. But it wouldn't do to worry my son with matters he didn't have any control over. So I said nothing. He, however, brought up the idea of a long-distance trip.

"Do you think Vater might consider taking the motorwagen on a long journey?" he asked, unaware that I'd heard him and Richard talking about the idea. "It could be a good way of showing it off to more people."

I sighed. He misunderstood it as my rejecting the notion.

"You've always said that the more people see it, the more intrigued they'll be and more accustomed to it they'll become," he said. "Wouldn't it be a good way of attracting prospective buyers?"

"It *is* a good idea, I agree," I replied. "But let's see how things go in Munich before we suggest it to Vater."

—

Herr Reimann wasn't in his office when we arrived at the station for the appointment. We were told the police chief had had to attend an unexpected meeting with the mayor. As I watched the hours tick by in the large, cold waiting room, I wondered if Eugen and I might have to find a hotel and spend the night in Munich. We were set to get home after dark even if the meeting had taken place as scheduled—the train ride between Munich and Mannheim was well over three hours—but I wasn't prepared to go home without seeing the policeman.

Finally, hours after the appointed time, Eugen and I were ushered into an office. The blond man behind the desk was younger than I'd expected, but the expression on his face was not one of youthful hopefulness. Herr Reimann's eyebrows, which were surprisingly dark for someone with hair so pale, hung low across his eyes, and his mouth was set in a firm line. The chief seemed irritated or tired. Perhaps he was both.

His greeting was cursory, and, as we gave him our names, I saw immediately that he favored addressing Eugen. Even when a woman was accompanied by a fifteen-year-old boy, the male was considered by other men to be superior. I stepped toward the desk in front of my son and led the conversation.

"You have my letter, Herr Reimann, requesting a license to drive a motorwagen on the streets of Munich during the exhibition, which takes place here in September. I traveled here at your bidding from Mannheim to discuss the matter," I said.

"Ja, ja. I remember," he said. "So, this motorwagen. Tell me exactly what it does and why you want it on the street."

I handed him a copy of the leaflet Carl had had printed for the Paris fair. It featured an illustration and information about the motorwagen.

Herr Reimann's irritability indicated that he wasn't in the mood to read, so I explained what the machine was and how it was operated while he examined the drawing.

Finally, he put down the leaflet. "It moves without a horse or tracks? It must be unsafe. How could I possibly allow it on the streets?" he said.

"It's powered by an engine but will be driven by my husband. He has complete control of it. It's not dangerous," I said.

"How do I know that?"

"My husband drives it in Mannheim. He has for months. Not even a chicken has been injured in all that time."

"Mannheim!" he scoffed. "What do I know or care about Mannheim? My city will be full of visitors during the exhibition. I cannot allow you to run riot in your outrageous machine. No, Frau Benz, I will not take responsibility for what might happen if I permitted it."

Herr Reimann stood up, ready to dismiss us. I knew I had to do something quickly to convince him to change his mind. I remembered my father's words: *"If ever you feel intimidated by someone who seems to wield power, remember they have a heart—just like yours."*

I stood my ground, pretending I hadn't noticed his eagerness to get rid of us. "Do you have children, Herr Reimann?" I asked.

He narrowed his eyes. "Yes. I have a son and a daughter."

"You often wonder what the future might hold for them, I'm sure. Do you picture them living the same lives as your parents did? As you are? Do you imagine… No, I'm certain you hope that your children will experience the same excitement and wonder that our forefathers did when gas was first piped to their houses. You want them to enjoy the thrill that we and our parents experienced when we took our first train ride and read about Herr von Siemens's electric railway in Berlin," I said.

He opened his mouth as if to speak, but I took the leaflet about the motorwagen off his desk, held it in front of him, and continued. "You look like a man of progress, Herr Reimann, and I'm sure you want to witness the unfolding of the future. Most of all, I can see you want your children to be part of it."

The chief scowled and glanced at the door. "Frau Benz—"

I wouldn't hear him. "You want a bright, exciting future for your children, as do I for mine. We are the same, you and me. We want to help bring progress to them, here in Germany. We want to be responsible for that progress. Please, Herr Reimann, don't stand in the way of progress. Don't be the man who blocks the way for an invention that will change the history of transport, that will give mankind—your children—an exciting new way of traveling, the kind of freedom never experienced before. Don't block it. Be part of it by permitting us this small thing."

The room was silent for a moment until I heard Eugen shuffle his feet behind me. I turned and gave him a small smile. His eyes twinkled, the way I remembered Carl's sparkling when he'd first told me about his dream.

Herr Reimann sighed, loudly and deeply. He reached toward me and took the leaflet from my hand. "I will give it some more thought, Frau Benz, and write to you with my final answer," he said.

"I think you found his heart, Mutter," whispered Eugen as we left the police chief's office shortly afterward.

CHAPTER 31

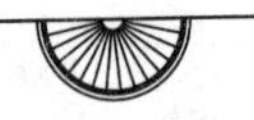

1888
Mannheim, Germany

Eugen and I returned to Mannheim with high hopes. It was late when we arrived home, and the only light came from a lantern Carl had left burning in the hallway. I assumed everyone was asleep and said good night to Eugen. Our bedroom, however, showed no sign that Carl had been there. I took the lantern and went to the workshop. Sure enough, a sliver of light shone beneath the door.

"You waited up for me," I said as I went in.

Carl was at his desk alongside the motorwagen, which gleamed in the center of the room. He closed the notebook in front of him with a snap and slid it into a drawer.

"I was doing some calculations," he said, as if I'd asked. "Well? What happened?"

I explained briefly, thinking I'd leave it to Eugen to give a more detailed account of my conversation with Herr Reimann the next day. Carl stood and placed his hands on my shoulders.

"Did he say when he would make his decision?" he asked.

"No. I thought it better not to ask. I was rather strident to that point and didn't want to overstep any boundaries. He knows when the exhibition is, so he understands the urgency," I said.

"Hmm."

"I'll mail a reminder if I don't hear from him in the next two weeks," I said, disappointed that Carl wasn't more enthusiastic about the idea of the police chief agreeing to give the matter more consideration. "I'm hopeful. I think I might've convinced him. Let Eugen tell you his version of the meeting tomorrow."

"All right," said Carl, taking the lantern with one hand and steering me toward the door with the other.

The speed with which he'd closed the notebook and his eagerness to leave the workshop were unusual for Carl. I tried to tell myself his haste was because it was late and we needed sleep. However, as he opened the door, a wave of apprehension swept over me. I couldn't ignore it, stopped, and turned to face him.

"What calculations were you working on?" I asked.

He hesitated, swallowing so deeply that his Adam's apple disappeared below his collar before fighting its way up again.

"What?" I insisted.

He stepped away from me, his eyes on the ground. "I was, erm… I've had interest—"

"Interest?"

"Yes. Well, a businessman who—"

"You mean interest from a potential partner for the new motorwagen business that you assured me you wouldn't think about until we'd exhausted other opportunities to win Max over? Is that what you're talking about?" I said, barely breathing as I spoke.

"Bertha—"

"I don't understand, Carl. Why are you doing this? Why won't you work with me to find a solution? Why do you want to throw it all away?"

He groaned. "I'm not throwing it away. Quite the contrary. I want to get us to a point where we can devote all our energy, time, and money on building the business around the motorwagen. I don't want to waste any more of my life on other things and on fighting for what I want with Max or…"

"Or?"

"Or you," he said quietly. "I don't want to fight with you. We've never done it before, and I can't think clearly when we don't agree."

Yes, you're right, I wanted to say. You *can't think clearly. That's why you don't see what a disastrous road you're contemplating by wanting to sell your shares in Benz & Co. to start all over again with another partner, who almost certainly will not always agree with you, just as Max doesn't.*

"Who is your prospective new partner?" I asked, feeling nauseous with dread and exhaustion.

"It doesn't matter," he replied. "You're right. I assured you that I wouldn't take any steps until you'd had the chance to find out if we could drive the vehicle in Munich. I will honor that."

If he'd meant to reassure me, it didn't work. The only thing that would put my mind to rest would be for him to agree that his idea was unreasonable and to fight with me to show Max how valuable the motorwagen could be to Benz & Co.

Carl looked at me, expecting a response. I said nothing, and he placed his hand on my cheek, brought his lips to mine, and kissed me gently. "I love you, Bertha. I don't want to chase this dream without you."

—

The next two weeks were interminable. The motorwagen stood in the workshop. Carl went to the factory while the children went to school, and I waited for a letter postmarked *Munich*. It didn't come. The end of the second week heralded the start of the school's summer holidays. Eugen, who'd stopped asking if the letter had arrived the moment he got home from school, brought up the subject of the cross-country drive again.

"It's the ideal time for it," he said. "School is closed, and the weather is good. Everyone will be outside to watch us. Can I talk to Vater about the idea? Or will you, Mutter?"

"Please, Mutter!" said Richard, who stood alongside his brother with Lupin. "Eugen and I could do it! We know how to drive and how to keep it going if anything goes wrong. We could do a round trip through to Weinheim and Ladenburg and be home after lunch. We'll be careful."

I smiled at the boys and looked around to ensure that Clara, Thilde, and Frida weren't within earshot. "Yes, we will," I whispered. "We'll be careful, but we won't take your route, Richard. We need to go further. We'll visit your grandmother in Pforzheim."

"Pforzheim!" said the boys together. Lupin tilted his head, his eyes as bright and eager as ever.

"But that's more than one hundred kilometers away," said Richard.

"Yes. Pforzheim. And we'll have to return. So that's about two hundred kilometers."

The boys stared at me, silent for once. Eventually, Eugen spoke. "When?"

"If you can get the motorwagen ready and I can sort something out with a friend in town in time, we can go next week. We could celebrate Tante Thekla's birthday with her," I said.

Even before I'd heard the boys talk about taking the motorwagen on a long journey and prior to mentioning the idea to Benjamin, I'd fantasized about one day surprising my mother, Herbert, Erwin, Amelia, Thekla, and Julius—all of whom still lived in Pforzheim—by arriving in the city in the motorwagen. In my daydreams, I'd been with Carl. I'd imagined him taking Mutter for a drive and reminding her how she'd dreamed of freeing horses from carriages. Indeed, I had often thought about the trip, but it was the first time I'd resolved to do it.

"Do you think Vater will agree to it? Have you already asked him?" said Eugen, his brow wrinkled with concern.

"No. I haven't. I don't know if he'll agree. We won't give him the opportunity to say no."

Richard's mouth gaped before stretching into a smile. Eugen's frown deepened. "We must keep the plan to ourselves. We'll go in secret," I said.

"Secret?" asked the older boy. "We won't tell Vater. But—"

Richard grabbed his brother's forearm. "He won't let us go, and... Well, it would be a pity because the trip will be good for the motorwagen, and what's good for it is good for Vater," he said. "Not so, Mutter?"

"Yes," I said. "Think about it, Eugen: we haven't heard from Herr Reimann. I'll write to him again today and urge him to respond. However, his silence worries me. We can't keep waiting without doing anything. A drive to

Pforzheim will do at least some of what we hope driving during the Munich exhibition would do. In fact, it will do more! We'll show off the motorwagen *and* prove its reliability over a long distance."

Eugen wasn't convinced. "I know, but surely Vater will understand that. We should get his agreement because—"

"It's the perfect time to go now. We can't risk telling Vater and his saying no or dithering too long so that we miss the opportunity," I said. "We need you, Eugen."

He ran his hands over his head, a gesture typical of his father. Then the boy smiled. "Okay. Our secret. Come, Richard, let's go and start the motorwagen before Vater gets home. He hasn't driven it for a while. We need to make sure it's ready for the trip."

Richard gave a whoop of joy, turned, and ran from the room with Lupin bounding alongside him.

I rested a hand on Eugen's shoulder. "I'll take care of the other plans. We'll make your father proud and happy; you'll see."

—

I understood Eugen's hesitation. When the boys left the room, the magnitude of what I'd proposed dawned on me. It wasn't just that we planned to cover a distance over which the motorwagen hadn't yet proven itself but also that we'd betray Carl to do so. Certainly, I was confident that the trip would help spread the word about the vehicle and Carl's genius. It might also be the catalyst we needed to attract buyers and convince Max to get behind the motorwagen. But I worried about what it might do to our marriage. Carl's decision after Paris had driven us apart. We tiptoed around each other like cats meeting for the first time. Things were even more tense than they'd been after Ava told Carl I'd written to Elise asking about America. Even if the trip was a success, would Carl trust me again? On the other hand, if we didn't do anything and Herr Reimann forbade us from driving the motorwagen in Munich, Carl would sell his shares in Benz & Co. to start all over again. Surely the fallout of *that* would be worse for Carl than how he might feel about being misled by me and the boys.

—

Carl saw the envelope addressed to Herr Reimann on the table in the hallway that evening.

"Another plea for the police chief, I see," he said.

"I told you I'd write again if I hadn't heard from him within two weeks," I replied.

"Yes, you did," he said. "It's just that I can't see why he'd decide differently simply because you ask again."

"I haven't heard anything from him. He hasn't given me a decision."

"Don't you think his silence says it all?" he said quietly. "You've done everything you can, Bertha. We're not going to be permitted to drive the motorwagen on the streets of Munich."

Carl's surrender—or perhaps it was his unusually condescending manner—made my eyes burn. I turned away, determined not to cry. Tomorrow, after I'd posted the letter to Herr Reimann, I'd visit Benjamin to confirm whether, as he'd proposed, he'd be able to take the train to Pforzheim to meet the boys and me there after our trip and write about it for the newspaper. Carl's most recent show of hopelessness hadn't only made me want to weep in despair—it had also solidified my decision to drive the motorwagen from Mannheim to Pforzheim as soon as possible.

—

Their father had barely left for the factory the next morning when Eugen and Richard found me in the kitchen, where I'd gone to speak to Frida. I needed to be sure that she'd be available to look after Clara and Thilde in my absence the following week.

"The boys and I will take the train to Pforzheim to see my family for a few days," I told her. "Clara and Thilde have some events in Mannheim that I know they'd be disappointed to miss. So they'll stay here, and I'd like you to take care of them."

It wasn't entirely untrue. Our daughters had been invited to two birthday parties the following week, and while I suspected they might not have complained about missing the festivities to visit their grandmother and cousins, the prior arrangements were credible and practical explanations for leaving Clara and Thilde in Mannheim.

"Yes, that'll be fine," said Frida, looking curiously at the boys and Lupin, who'd rushed into the room and were clearly impatient to speak to me.

"What's going on?" I asked, leading them away from the kitchen.

"We wanted to tell you the motorwagen is in good order," said Richard, hopping from foot to foot.

I looked at Eugen. He nodded. "It's as ready as it will ever be. What have you told Vater?"

"I mentioned last night that I planned to go to Pforzheim next week and that you two wanted to come. We'd take an early train, I told him, and be gone for a few days," I said.

"When?" said Richard. "When will we go?"

I explained that I'd confirm that after I'd seen Herr Stern that morning, which prompted my youngest son to hand me my hat.

"Don't forget to tell Herr Stern not to tell anyone about our plans until we're gone," he said, also giving me the envelope to post to Munich.

CHAPTER 32

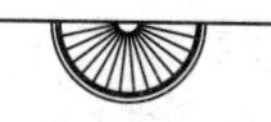

1888
Mannheim, Germany

Carl didn't question me the next week when I told him that Eugen, Richard, and I would leave to catch the train while it was still dark the following morning. In fact, he provided an explanation for our early departure.

"You want to be there when Thekla wakes up, I suppose," he'd said. "She'll be delighted and surprised to see you on her birthday."

"Yes, it will be a surprise," I replied, not without a twinge of shame.

I could see Carl was aware that I wasn't entirely myself. Although he hadn't apologized directly for the way he'd dismissed my repeated attempts to get Herr Reimann to allow us to drive the motorwagen in Munich, he knew he'd upset me. He'd been gentle and more attentive afterward, going as far as buying me some chocolate. I tried to ignore the thought that rather than wanting to make amends, he might be compensating for the fact that he intended to go ahead with his plan to find a new partner despite my objections. I didn't want to think about it and decided I'd focus on the trip. If need be, I'd take up the combat to retain the Benz & Co. shares when I returned.

So it was that Carl and the girls were still asleep when my sons and I opened the workshop doors and rolled the motorwagen out of the yard and down the road. We'd agreed the day before that we'd wheel the vehicle well beyond town before starting it. We didn't want to risk waking anyone who might be angered enough by the disturbance to rouse Carl. It was not, Richard had pointed out, as if anyone else might be running an engine down the road other than a member of the Benz family.

Finally, having headed south, away from the houses, over a hill, and with no lights indicating there might be a farmyard nearby, we stood for a moment to recover our breaths. But who was breathing so heavily? We looked at one another. The breathing, we realized, was actually panting. I made out the wave of a tail alongside Richard. It was Lupin!

"I told you to leave him in the kitchen," I said.

Richard crouched and put his arms around the dog. "I did."

"The window was open," said Eugen quietly. "I noticed it before we went to bed last night but didn't think about it this morning. What'll we do?"

"There's nothing we can do," I said. "If we take him back, your father will almost certainly wake up. Lupin will have to come with us."

The dog panted and wagged his tail so enthusiastically I wondered if that's what he'd planned all along.

"He'll run," Richard said, stroking the dog's head. "He's very fit."

"It's too far, no matter how fit he is," I said as I climbed onto the motorwagen and Eugen went to the back to spin the flywheel. "He can ride with us when he gets tired."

The engine spluttered to life, and the motorwagen vibrated as if eager to get going.

"Come, all aboard," I said, moving over. "You drive first, Eugen."

—

Although I'd traveled the road between Mannheim and Pforzheim in a carriage previously, most of my journeys had been by train, and I'd certainly never navigated the route myself before. Benjamin had drawn a rough map, which he'd checked with a coachman before giving it to me. How fortunate I was to have so resourceful a newspaperman as a friend, I thought, making a mental note to thank him for his help once more when he met us in Pforzheim.

The road to Weinheim was smooth and wide and, with a thin strip of daylight touching the horizon, easy to follow. For a while, the boys and I were silent, as if, despite the loud chugging of the engine, we feared we might wake up the farmers in the vicinity if we spoke. Our silence was finally broken when Lupin sped past us in pursuit of a hare and Richard shouted, "Hey, Lupin! Not so fast! You're meant to be getting tired," which made Eugen and me laugh.

"Do you think Vater is awake yet?" said Eugen. "Will he have noticed the motorwagen is gone?"

"He might be awake. You know what an early riser he is. But I can't say when he will realize that we've taken it."

Up until he went to Paris, Carl went to his workshop before leaving for the factory every morning. Inevitably, he'd tinker on the motorwagen, forever looking for ways of improving it. Or he'd sit at his desk and work on new designs for improvements. Recently, though, he'd begun leaving for work without even opening the workshop doors, as if seeing the motorwagen would spoil his day. I had no idea when he'd realize that it was gone.

It was still so dark that most of the villagers were sleeping as we chugged through Weinheim. However, several curtains swooshed open when we passed beneath their windows, and we heard a man shout, "It's that crazy Benz guy on his carriage with the engine," confirming that we were still close enough to Mannheim for people to recognize the motorwagen.

It was near Dossenheim that we began encountering others on the track. The first to approach was a farmer on a small cart pulled by a gray pony. We saw him coming toward us in the distance. For a while, it seemed he was untroubled by our advance, and I hoped, as I always did when I was in the motorwagen, that his pony would be calm enough to let us pass without incident. We'd learned from experience that it was impossible to predict animals' responses to the vehicle. Many horses were so well trained and accustomed to unusual encounters that they were nonplussed by it, despite the machine's unfamiliar noise and form. A few cattle and sheep were curious enough to approach the motorwagen, necks stretched and nostrils pulsing. Most, though—horses, dogs, cats, cattle, sheep, pigs, geese, chickens, rabbits, and deer—fled as soon as they caught wind of the strange smell and clatter.

This time, it wasn't the pony that reacted but the farmer. He suddenly sat tall, as if only now noticing us, and tugged at the reins. The pony lifted her head and stopped, and the farmer got to his feet and stood on the toe board. We were about fifty meters away when he began shouting and waving his arms.

"The Lord is on my side. He will protect me. Go hence, you devilish thing!" he bellowed, so loudly that his words were easily understood above the noise of the engine. "The Lord is on my side. He will smite you! Be gone, you fiend of the earth!"

"Stop," I told Eugen, who did so immediately but not without rolling his eyes heavenward.

It would've been unwitting of us not to have expected to arouse such reactions in people during our trip. However, I knew that my sons, like me, hoped that we wouldn't lose too much time to the terrified and cynical as we drove.

I climbed down and walked toward the cart. The man, who'd paused his hollering when the motorwagen halted, started up again.

"Stay away from me! Don't take another step," he said.

"Good morning," I called, standing still. "I'm sorry to have startled you. I am Frau Benz of Mannheim, and those are my sons. The machine—it's a machine, not a monster—is the Benz motorwagen. It's—"

"Where's the horse?" he shouted.

"It doesn't need a horse; it has an engine to turn the wheels. Come and look at it. I'll show you how it works."

He stared, wide-eyed and incredulous. "Never! I won't come near you and your trickery. You are the devil…the she-devil. What carriage moves without a horse? You are not of this world! You are a demon!"

"No, I'm a person of flesh and blood, like you," I said as calmly as I could. "I'm a mother and the wife of inventor Herr Carl Benz. This is his machine."

"Inventor! Bah!" he shouted. "Only God invents!"

"Yes, he does. But he's equipped us to create too," I replied. "I mean, your cart, for example."

"Bah!"

I sighed. "If you don't want to look at our machine, please move aside so that we can continue our journey."

"Move aside? No! I will turn around and ride back to Dossenheim to rally the villagers. We will be ready for you there. You will not pass through on your—"

He stopped talking mid-sentence, fixated by something at my side. I looked down. It was Lupin, who'd hopped off the motorwagen where he'd been sitting with Richard and come to me. I placed my hand on his head.

"Is that your dog?" asked the farmer.

"He's my son's."

"Is he traveling with you?"

I chuckled. "It was not the plan, but he followed us when we left Mannheim earlier."

To my surprise, the farmer climbed down from his cart and walked toward me slowly. He stopped a few meters away. "What's his name?"

"Lupin."

"Lupin! Come here," he called.

The dog trotted to him, tail wagging. The farmer reached out and placed his hand on the crest of Lupin's skull. As he touched it, his eyes met mine. Until that moment, he'd believed us to be spirits of the underworld, but phantoms, he seemed to have reasoned in that instant, didn't travel with real dogs.

—

So it was that the farmer and his pony led us into Dossenheim, where he invited us into his home on the edge of the village for coffee. While we drank, he sent his children into the streets to spread the word so that he could show off the motorwagen to the other villagers. By the time we got back to the machine, it was surrounded by curious people, many of whom were rubbing their eyes and yawning as if they'd just been roused from their beds.

"We should get going," said Eugen as a new group of people gathered around and Richard launched into another description of the motorwagen. "We have a long way to go."

"Yes, we should, but we shouldn't forget that this"—I gestured to the crowd around us—"is exactly what we hoped to achieve on the trip."

Finally, Richard, Lupin, and I climbed aboard, and Eugen swung the flywheel. The gathering retreated, startled, when the engine fired, but many followed us, waving and calling goodbye for some distance as we headed out of the village in the direction of Heidelberg.

The road to Heidelberg remained smooth and fast, and although we came across several carriages, carts, and people along the way, none of the encounters gave us cause for much delay. It was as we crossed the Neckar on the Friedrichs Bridge that we spoke about how easy it was to travel on the motorwagen and how well the machine was performing.

"It goes so well that I wish Vater was here to see it," said Eugen, as if reading my thoughts.

With the sun rising, it was getting warmer, and with every kilometer, I grew more confident that the journey would provide the testimony Max needed to accept that the motorwagen could become Benz & Co.'s primary product. That, I hoped, would encourage him to back the vehicle and agree to invest more time and money in it at Benz & Co. rather than sell his shares in the company. Could I have convinced Carl to agree to the journey if I'd had more faith in him? Might he have even undertaken it himself? It no longer mattered; the boys and I were on our way, and it was going well.

Richard drove for about ten kilometers from Heidelberg to Nussloch over a road so even that Lupin lay down and curled up near the driver's feet for a while.

"We should tell Vater he might have to add some extra space for sleepy dogs," said Eugen.

"Perhaps he could attach a basket to the back of the seat to keep them from falling out," said Richard, laughing as the motorwagen bumped unexpectedly and Lupin scrambled to his feet.

South of Nussloch, we encountered our first real climb. The coachman Benjamin had spoken to had warned him about the hills approaching Wiesloch, but we'd not anticipated how the engine would struggle on such steep inclines.

"We'll need to push," said Eugen. "Mutter, you drive while Richard and I get behind."

I shook my head. "No, Richard is the lightest. He must steer while you and I push."

Lupin helped by hopping off the carriage and trotting alongside us as we struggled up the steep, rocky incline.

"Let me do it," said Richard at one point as he glanced over his shoulder and saw the perspiration dripping off my face. "Come. Have a rest, Mutter."

However, we were almost on the top of the hill above Wiesloch. I shook my head and put all my weight behind the motorwagen, silently thanking Carl for working so hard to ensure that it weighed so little.

We rested for a moment at the top of the hill. It was then that Eugen realized our shortcoming: we'd drastically miscalculated how much benzine we'd need for the trip, and the second bottle we had with us was almost empty.

"What will we do?" asked Richard.

I pointed down the hill. "We'll visit the druggist in Wiesloch. And every druggist necessary along the way to buy as much ligroin as we need."

Our troubles were not, however, limited to a shortage of fuel. As we bounced down the hill toward the village, we heard the loud scraping of the leather-covered wooden brakes. They'd never had to endure such friction before. Would they last? If the leather wore away, the brakes wouldn't hold, and the motorwagen would hurtle down the mountain unrestrained. It was one thing to risk Carl's ire by taking the motorwagen on the trip but another to risk his son's lives, not to mention mine. As we made our way down the hill, I told the boys we'd also need to check the brakes in Wiesloch.

A group of children were playing in a river near the village. They shrieked in fright and fled in all directions when they saw us. However, by the time we arrived in Wiesloch, most of them had reappeared to escort us into the village. I was driving, which allowed Richard to answer the many questions the youngsters had as they ran alongside us with Lupin bounding between them.

"No. It's not magic," said my younger son. "It's science. My father is an engineer and an inventor in Mannheim. Not a wizard."

"No, you can't just drive it. You have to learn how, and we don't have time to teach you. We're going all the way to Pforzheim."

"Why not? My mother can do anything she wants to."

"No, you can't have a ride. It's not built to carry more people."

"He's my dog and he's not for sale."

"We are not princes. My father is not royalty. He's clever, that's all."

The children were joined by others when we stopped and switched off the engine in Wiesloch. It was a smaller village than I'd expected, and I wished we'd realized that we'd need fuel when we were in Heidelberg, which had many more people and shops.

"Good morning," I said, greeting a stern-looking woman, who had the expression of someone who knew whatever there was to know about the village and its inhabitants. "Can you tell me where to find the druggist, please?"

"The druggist?" she asked, looking even more severe. "What business do you have with the druggist?"

Any other time, I might've explained, but it seemed to me that telling her about how the engine worked would only lead to more questions, and I was eager to find ligroin.

"I need to make an urgent purchase," I replied.

"From the druggist?" she said.

A boy, one of those who'd accompanied us into the village, was standing behind her. He caught my eye and tilted his head to the right, mouthing, "Follow me."

"Eugen," I called, wanting to distract the village keeper so that I could go with the boy, "tell this kind woman and her friends about the motorwagen."

My son looked at me, momentarily confused. Then he caught on. "Come to the back of the motorwagen and I'll explain."

The boy led the way past a bakery and two houses, and into a narrow street, where he pointed to a door. I thanked him and went in. He followed closely, as if his help had given him proprietorial rights. I made my way to a large counter in the dimly lit, windowless shop. Two men, one young and the other a generation older, looked up from behind the worktop.

"Can I help you?" asked the younger of the two.

"Yes, please. I'd like some ligroin."

The older man picked up a lantern and walked around the counter, holding the light at shoulder height. He looked me up and down.

"You'll need more than ligroin to clean that skirt," he said.

I glanced down. He was right; my dress was filthy. It wasn't only smeared with mud but also featured patches of oil. I'd deliberately chosen a dark-colored outfit to travel in because I thought it would show less dirt, but I had underestimated just how filthy pushing the motorwagen, with its struggling engine, would make me.

"It's not for this," I replied, indicating my skirt. "How much ligroin do you have?"

The man with the lantern ignored me. "What I would suggest is that you first soak—"

"Thank you," I said. "I appreciate that you know how I should treat my skirt, but that's not what I want the ligroin for."

He looked at the younger man, who was leaning on the counter. "Some women don't want advice—even when it is offered for free," he said.

The young man slapped the counter and laughed. I felt the anger rise in me like frothing milk on the stove. Why was it that some men felt that they always knew what women needed to hear, even when women were explicit? Would this man have taken it upon himself to tell Carl, or even Eugen and Richard, why they didn't need what they asked for? I was tempted to confront the druggist and his colleague with these questions but didn't want to anger them. All I wanted was ligroin. I was still choosing my words when the boy spoke.

"She rides a noisy carriage that moves without horses," he said.

"What are you saying, boy?" asked the older man.

The boy shrugged. "It's in the street. I ran into the village alongside it. It's...it's...it's science made by an inventor, not a wizard, in Mannheim. There's a dog too."

I smiled at him. He'd paid good attention to Richard. "That's right," I said. "I need ligroin for the...science."

CHAPTER 33

1888
Wiesloch, Germany

Finally, with the tank full and two spare bottles of ligroin—which was all the druggist had had—Richard started the engine, and Eugen steered the motorwagen over the dusty road that us led us away from Wiesloch. We'd checked the brakes and had two sets of leather strips cut by the cobbler, which we'd use to replace the worn leather at the bottom of the hill on the other side of the village.

The boy who'd taken me to the druggist was the last of the children to tire of running alongside us.

"I'll be here when you come back!" he shouted, waving goodbye to us. "And I'll remind the druggist to order more ligroin."

"Thank you!" shouted Richard before turning to me and adding, "That boy has more energy than Lupin. I thought he might run the whole way to Pforzheim with us."

I laughed. How grown up he seemed.

"The cobbler said we should make sure we're well beyond Singen before dark," said Eugen. "He said the hills between there and Pforzheim are even steeper than these ones."

The warning corresponded with what the coachman had told Benjamin. It was almost midday, and we were approaching halfway.

"That shouldn't be difficult," I said, taking account of the long daylight hours we'd have to our advantage, given that it was summer. "As long as we're quick with the brake replacement, we'll have plenty of time."

It would've been the case if it weren't that by the time we reached Mingolsheim, we realized we'd have to find a blacksmith to adjust the chain. With the steep, lengthy ascents it had endured, the chain had stretched, which meant it frequently fell off the gears, forcing us to stop to put it back on.

The blacksmith in Mingolsheim was intrigued by the motorwagen. "Does it work like a clock?" he asked, looking at the gears.

It wasn't an entirely unreasonable question, since they looked like clock gears. Carl often spoke about how his early interest in clocks and watches had helped him understand how gears would work for the motorwagen.

As Eugen described the mechanics of the engine and how it turned the wheels, I felt warm with pride. That our sons understood the motorwagen so well was something I'd known for years, but that they told their father's story so carefully and kindly to strangers was freshly endearing. So fascinated was the man by the vehicle—and, I suspected, charmed by Eugen's manner—that he set aside the work he was busy on and immediately attended to the chain.

"My sister lives in Munich," said the blacksmith when Richard told him how we hoped to drive the motorwagen in the city the following month. "I shall visit her during the exhibition so that I can meet your father. What a genius! And to think that he and I share a lifetime."

We left Mingolsheim with the chain shortened and secure—and a new friend—and were making good time toward Bruchsal when, on a particularly dusty stretch, a procession of large, shiny carriages drawn by magnificent, matching horses approached at speed. I steered the motorwagen onto the verge and stopped, pulling my hat down and my scarf up to keep as much dust at bay as possible. We watched the carriages thunder by.

"Where are you going?" shouted Richard as the third coach passed.

"It's the count's wedding party!" came the coachman's call.

I stopped counting at eight, and still they raced by in clouds of dust, which made it difficult to see. Peering through the powdery dirt, I was able to discern several elaborate hats, tall and adorned with colorful feathers, and many bright buttons on glossy fabric. The count's guests, it seemed, were a moneyed lot.

With the last carriage in the procession gone and the dust settled, Richard hopped off to swing the flywheel. For the first time that day, the engine didn't start as usual by the fourth swing. Eugen glanced at me. Richard swung the flywheel again. This time, the machine responded, and we drove on, but all was not well. It seemed to have developed a cough. We said nothing, hoping perhaps that ignoring the strange sound would make it go away.

We'd barely driven a kilometer when, on the tiniest of inclines leading out of a stream, the engine stuttered and died.

"Let *me* do it," said Eugen, as if Richard hadn't started it properly earlier.

This time, though, even after several attempts, the engine didn't murmur.

"What could it be?" asked Richard as we gathered around the engine.

I looked at Eugen, hoping he had an idea. He scratched his head. "I don't know."

There was a splashing sound. I looked around to see Lupin at the stream. It was hot, and he'd had a drink and was pawing at a stone on the water's edge, his eyes on Richard. He wanted the boy to throw the stone for him.

"Lupin! No time for games now!" shouted Richard.

As Lupin trotted back to us, I noticed how dusty his coat was. I patted the fabric of my skirt. Billows of dirt rose with every smack.

"It's the dust," I said. "I think the fuel supply is clogged."

—

It was the dust, but although we determined the cause quickly, remedying the problem was slow. We didn't know where the obstruction was, so, using the pin I took from my hat and Eugen's scarf, we methodically worked our way through the system, detaching each relevant and accessible component, pushing the pin through holes, polishing the parts, and carefully reassembling them. We worked on the roadside for more than an hour before the engine obliged with a sneeze and a blast, and finally, we set off once more.

In Bruchsal, while I bought bread and Eugen nailed the second set of new leather strips onto the brakes, Richard explained the workings of the vehicle to a large group of villagers.

"My horse is getting old," I heard a man ask as I returned from the bakery. "Could this thing pull a cart of hops to the brewery?"

When the roar of laughter that ensued died down, Richard answered, "This particular engine might not be strong enough to pull your cart, but my father will build a more powerful one. Come and visit us at Benz & Co. in Mannheim in a year or two, and I'm sure you'll find we have what you want."

The mention of Benz & Co. reminded me afresh of my hopes for our journey. How proud I was of our sons, their faith in their father and Benz & Co. Eugen interrupted my musings.

"We'll need at least one more set of leathers for the brakes," he said.

I sighed, frustrated by the thought of another delay. We'd lost time unclogging the system, and I worried we might end up traveling in the dark if we encountered further interruptions. Richard eyed the bread.

"We'll stop in Durlach and get more cut," I said.

"But there's a shoe shop over there," said Eugen, pointing across the street.

Perhaps I was also hungry or tired. Either way, I didn't listen to Eugen or reason. If I had, I would've acknowledged my father's maxim that *to have is to have*, and where chance presents itself, it's always wiser to take advantage of it. Instead, I hoped chance might show itself again, and we left Bruchsal without spare leather for the brakes.

As we departed the village, a pair of mares and their foals grazing in a field alongside the road lifted their heads and stared at us, snorting as we approached. We'd barely passed them when they kicked up their hooves, squealed in excitement, and galloped along the wooden fence that followed the road. We laughed as they bucked playfully. I thought about my mother's description of horses unencumbered by bridles and harnesses and frolicking freely in the countryside. I was eager to get to Pforzheim and tell her that I finally knew exactly what she meant.

The drive to Weingarten was without incident, and we covered the twenty-seven kilometers in little over two hours, eating the bread as we traveled. With about thirty kilometers separating Durlach and Pforzheim, I was confident we'd reach our destination well before dark. My assurance was buoyed by the fact that one of the first signs we saw as we drove into Durlach was that of the cobbler. We stopped at his door.

"There's no one here," said Eugen, who'd hopped off to order the leather strips but found the door barred.

I looked around. "Perhaps he's somewhere nearby."

"He's gone to a funeral in Singen," said a woman, who was among those who'd gathered to examine the motorwagen. "He'll be back tomorrow. Do you need shoes?"

"Is there another cobbler in town?" I asked.

She shook her head. "Only in Ellmendingen."

"That's not too far from here," said Richard, squinting at Benjamin's map.

Indeed, Ellmendingen was little over halfway between Durlach and Pforzheim. What worried me was that there were two particularly hilly sections before Ellmendingen. I looked at Eugen, ashamed for not having heeded him and getting the leather in Bruchsal.

"It should be all right," he said generously as he pulled himself back onto the motorwagen. "Next stop, Ellmendingen!"

—

The coachman who'd helped Benjamin with the map hadn't exaggerated about how steep the hills between Singen and Ellmendingen were. Eugen and I climbed down to push the motorwagen several times. After the sixth or seventh incline overpowered the engine, Richard insisted I drive while he help his brother push.

"It's not that you're not strong, Mutter, but so am I," he said. "And what will Vater say if we tell him that you had to push the motorwagen while I only steered?"

I was too tired to resist and almost as grateful for his offer as I was a little later when we found a cobbler willing and able to provide us with fresh leather for the brakes in Ellmendingen.

"All the way from Mannheim on this machine?" said the cobbler as he helped Eugen nail the strips to the wood. "It's like something that has been dropped from the sky!"

Richard caught my eye, and we shrugged in unison. Indeed, we'd heard many curious comments about the motorwagen that day, but this was the first time anyone imagined it was heaven-sent.

"Will you tell the people of Pforzheim that I was responsible for repairing your carriage when you arrive there?" said the man as we prepared to leave. "They should know that a shoemaker from Ellmendingen made this journey possible for Frau Benz."

Too weary and eager to get going to engage in further conversation and aware of the lengthening shadows, we simply nodded, smiled, and thanked him. As we left the village, Richard turned to Eugen.

"Did you get the name of the cobbler?" he asked.

"The man we saw now?" said Eugen.

"Ja."

"No. Why?"

"Because now we don't know the name of the man who made the journey possible for Frau Benz," said Richard, imitating the man.

We laughed until, turning a corner, we saw how steep the road ahead of us would shortly become. Richard groaned.

"According to Herr Stern's map, there are only three more hills between us and Pforzheim. It'll be over soon," I said, as much to reassure myself as to encourage my sons.

With the sun low, it had grown cooler. Lupin's energy, which had flagged for a short time during the early afternoon, returned. He sniffed about as we pushed the motorwagen up two large hills and ran alongside the vehicle as we bumped down the other side. Pforzheim was, by my estimation, about seven kilometers away, with only one hill separating us from the city lights.

As we motored across a smooth, flat section, during which the engine seemed to thud with rhythmic relief, I began planning what I'd say when Mutter and my siblings found us on their doorstep. I knew that, as was family tradition, they'd gather at the family house to celebrate Thekla's birthday that evening. What a surprise it would be when they found us there—not to mention their awe when we told them how we'd covered the distance between Mannheim and Pforzheim. I described my thoughts to the boys.

"Perhaps you should knock on the door, Richard," I said. "Eugen and I will hide. They'll be alarmed to see you there alone. Then we could—"

My words were interrupted by silence. The engine had died again. The motorwagen gradually rolled to a stop. No one said a word as Eugen went to the flywheel. Aside from the brief whirring of the flywheel and Eugen's grunts of exertion, there was no sound. He tried again. Twice. Thrice. Four times.

"Is it clogged again?" asked Richard, his voice abnormally small.

"I don't think so," I said. "Try again, Eugen."

The engine was still. I climbed down and walked over to Eugen. Richard lay on the seat, curling his legs toward his chest. He suddenly seemed so small. Lupin hopped onto the platform and licked the boy's face.

"What do you think?" I asked Eugen.

His shoulders drooped. "I think it's a long way to push it to Pforzheim."

I smiled. "Swing it again. Let's listen and watch."

Eugen sighed and swung the flywheel. The engine didn't respond.

—

It was dusk by the time we got going again. Richard and Lupin were asleep. After lengthy searching, Eugen and I discovered that some electrical wires had shaken lose and the ignition was shorting. We needed something to isolate two wires and insulate the current. I was about to tear a strip of fabric from my underskirt when it struck me that one of my garters would be ideal.

Eugen blushed and looked away as I slipped it from my leg and wound it around the wires. If Carl had been there and not my sons, I would've told him, "Save your blushes and spin the flywheel." Instead, I looked at Eugen and said, "Let's give it a try."

Richard and Lupin were startled awake, and with the engine thumping happily once more and the light fading fast, we headed off.

We didn't talk as Eugen and I pushed the motorwagen over the steep sections of the final hill and Richard steered. It was dark by then and, without a lantern to light the way, slow going. The younger boy didn't offer to get behind the vehicle again. It had been a long, exhausting day, and as I looked at his face, drawn and pale now, I reminded myself that he was not quite fourteen years old. Would I have managed what Richard had achieved today when I was his age? It was my father's voice I heard when the reply came to me: *"Of course you would've."*

"Look," said Eugen as we reached the crest of the hill, where we would climb back onto the vehicle for the final descent.

The lights of the city spread out below us, making the place seem much larger than I remembered it. I walked to the front of the car, trying to get my bearings.

"Pforzheim," I said.

"Let's keep going," said Richard from the driver's seat. "You drive, Mutter. I'd like to sit and think about what our grandmother will serve us to celebrate Tante Thekla's birthday."

CHAPTER 34

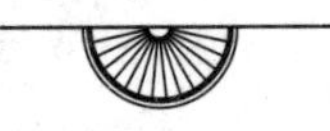

1888
Pforzheim, Germany

The dark road leading into Pforzheim was bare as I drove into the city. Earlier in the day, I'd pictured throngs of people lining the streets to welcome us. Someone, I'd imagined, might've ridden ahead during the day and told them about our journey. People who'd known me years ago would want to see if it was true.

"The third Ringer girl married an inventor and is driving his masterpiece from Mannheim to Pforzheim with her young sons and a dog. You have to see it to believe it!" they might've said, pushing and shoving one another aside to catch sight of us.

Instead, the town was empty. Streetlights flickered, a cat slunk into the shadows, and a carriage clattered across the cobblestones in the distance. Then a man stepped onto the road in front of us beneath a streetlight and held up his arm.

"I didn't want to doubt you, but I *was* beginning to wonder!" he said, walking toward us.

It was Benjamin.

I laughed in relief. "You're here, at least!"

"Come. Follow me," he said. "I have the perfect place for you to park. We want everyone to see the motorwagen in all its glory in the morning."

I wanted to remind him that I'd grown up in Pforzheim and that I knew the place he meant but said nothing as we followed him two blocks to the fountains in the marketplace.

"I'm staying at the hotel over there," he said, pointing to the building nearby. "I'll be close by to take care of it."

"Must we walk to our grandmother's house?" asked Richard as we switched off the engine for the final time that day. "Is it far?"

"No, silly," said Eugen. "It's just around the corner. Don't you remember? Come."

The boys walked ahead, their energy replenished by thoughts of a warm house and birthday dinner. Benjamin fell into step with me, and I told him briefly about our day.

"Incredible! But you're tired," he said as we rounded the final corner before the house. "I'll come by tomorrow, and you can give me all the details. I want to write the article for the afternoon edition."

"I'll meet you at the square after breakfast," I said. "I need to send Carl a telegram as early as possible. He might've noticed the motorwagen is gone and be concerned. I don't want to worry him—well, unnecessarily."

Benjamin chuckled. "I saw him this morning on my way to the station. I was worried that he might see me and start a conversation. I wasn't sure that I'd be able to hold my tongue, given how excited I was. Fortunately, he didn't spot me. He was too engaged in conversation with Herr Adler."

I stopped and turned to him. "Herr Adler? Ava's husband?"

Benjamin nodded.

I had to be sure. "Carl was talking to Herr Adler?"

"Yes, they were at a café. It seemed they were having a meeting. Carl was showing him something in his notebook. I mean, it *looked* like a business meeting. I didn't linger because, well, I didn't want him to see me. It could've just been two friends having coffee," he said.

"They're not friends. I didn't know they knew each other," I replied.

I was cold, much colder than I'd been on the motorwagen an hour previously. My mind buzzed. Was Walter Adler the partner Carl had in mind for the new business he imagined starting when he sold his shares in Benz & Co.? How had they met? Did Ava have something to do with it? How much had Carl and Herr Adler discussed?

Benjamin looked at me. "Are you okay?"

"Yes. Yes. I'm…I'm just tired." I tried to smile. "And curious about what Carl was talking to Walter Adler about."

Benjamin glanced away. "Well, perhaps it has something to do with Benz & Co."

"What do you mean?" I asked, even colder now.

"One of my colleagues—he writes mainly about business—mentioned to me recently that he'd heard a rumor that August Ritter was hoping to buy shares in Benz & Co."

I felt faint. "August Ritter? Ava's brother?"

"No, no, her father. August Ritter Senior." He peered closely at me. "Bertha, what's wrong?"

I shook my head. "It's just that I don't know anything about this. Or Herr Adler. I'm worried—"

"Wait! Bertha, I'm sorry. I shouldn't have said anything. Not now, when you're barely awake on your feet. These are all just rumors. But I did see him—Herr Ritter—with Max Rose at the public demonstration of the motorwagen. I wondered at the time why they were together. When my colleague told me about Herr Ritter's interest in Benz & Co., I thought it might explain things," Benjamin said.

So August Ritter Senior was probably the man I'd spotted with Max. He'd seemed familiar because he reminded me of his son and daughter. The only thing worse than Max selling his shares in Benz & Co. was Max selling those shares to August Ritter. I shouldn't have left Mannheim without talking to Carl. I should've insisted he tell me who he was talking to about a new partnership. We should've had another meeting with Max to try to regain his support for the motorwagen. I had to get back as soon as possible. I had to return to Mannheim as soon as we'd rested.

There was a call from across the street. Eugen and Richard had reached my mother's house. Richard waved his arms, urging me to hurry. My thoughts whirled and I became flustered.

"I don't know what to think anymore. It's too much."

Benjamin placed his hand lightly on my arm. "It'll all be all right, Bertha. You've had an exhausting day. Go to your family. Rest. I'll see you in the morning."

—

After the initial excitement of surprising Mutter, Herbert, Erwin, Amelia, Thekla, Julius, and their extended families had died down and we'd reshuffled the place settings and squeezed three more chairs around the dinner table, Richard demonstrated his storytelling skills as he described our journey. His account, I thought as I glanced at the enraptured faces around the table, was the one Benjamin should hear and write about. Eugen caught my eye and smiled. He was proud of his brother too.

Finally, with dinner over, the boys headed to bed.

"Don't worry, Grandmother," said Richard as Lupin followed him upstairs. "He won't sleep on the bed."

Mutter glanced at me and called after him. "Ja. The same way Affie never slept on your mother's bed. Only your grandfather believed that."

We laughed and, for a moment, were quiet with Vater on our minds. What would he have thought about our journey? What would he advise if I were able to tell him about Carl's predicament and how he and I were unable to agree on a solution?

"You should go to bed," said my mother. "Tomorrow I'd like you to take me for a drive so that I can show all of Pforzheim how it is possible to free their horses from harnesses."

"Remind me to tell you about the mares and their foals tomorrow," I said as I headed upstairs.

Despite my worries, I fell asleep quickly and woke refreshed at first light. As is often the case with anxieties that one experiences at night, my concerns were offset by the sunshine, and I went about my morning business calmly. By the time I met Benjamin in the square, the motorwagen was surrounded by people. Eugen had already taken his grandmother, aunts, uncles, and cousins for drives, and I'd been to the post office to send Carl a telegram.

"What did you write?" asked Benjamin as we sat on a low wall near a fountain some distance away from the hubbub at the motorwagen.

"'Arrived safely in Pforzheim,'" I replied.

He frowned.

"There's so much to say. So much to ask. None of which is suitable to write in a telegram. So I thought I'd keep it simple," I explained.

Benjamin nodded. "Can you tell me? I mean, why you're so worried about Benz & Co. and Herr Adler? Not for the article but as one friend confiding in another."

It was a relief to talk about my worries, and I told him everything, beginning with Max's ultimatum when Carl had returned from Paris and Carl's frustration. I explained what Carl planned to do if we were unable to drive the motorwagen in Munich and how he'd lost hope that we would be given permission to do so.

"Carl conceded that he has had interest from a potential investor, although he assured me that he wouldn't do anything until we were *certain* that we couldn't drive in Munich. His idea is to establish another company, one that would focus entirely on the motorwagen," I said. "When you told me you'd seen him with Walter Adler, I wondered if he was the man. The notebook you described could be the one that I saw Carl making notes in about the possible new business recently."

Benjamin let me talk without interruption, but his knitted brow showed concern. Finally, I reached the end of my explanation.

"What is it?" I asked. "You look as worried as I feel. Have I burdened you with my problems?"

"How well do you know August Ritter Senior?" he asked.

"Ha! I don't know him at all. We've never met. However, Carl and I have something of a history with the man," I said. "But it predates our time with Max. I don't think Max is aware of how appalled Carl would be by the idea of Ritter's involvement in Benz & Co."

"That may be so, but there's something I need to tell you about him. About Herr Ritter, I mean. Something that might explain Ava's second husband's meeting with Herr Benz," he said.

I listened with growing dread as Benjamin elaborated. Years previously, shortly before had Ava married her first husband—that is, Benjamin's closest friend, Rudolf Fischer—Ava's father set his sights on a building in Pforzheim, which was up for sale. However, the seller was a man who'd fallen out with August Ritter Senior over a business deal. It was widely understood, said Benjamin, that Herr Ritter had abused the man's trust and caused him great financial loss. (*Was that where his son had learned to deceive Carl?* I wondered.) Given their history, the seller of the building refused to consider Herr Ritter Senior's offer to buy. He would never, he said, trust Ritter again.

"But August Ritter Senior is not one to stand down," said Benjamin. "He convinced Rudolf to go in as his front man and buy the building. Obviously, the building wasn't for Rudolf; it was for Ritter. When Rudolf told me what he'd been bullied into doing, I was furious. Rudolf was an honest, kind man. He was deeply troubled by what he'd done. His future father-in-law gloated in triumph and boasted around town how he'd fooled the seller by using Rudolf. That made things even worse for my friend."

"That's why you and Ava argued, isn't it?" I asked.

"Yes. I was furious. However, Rudolf loved Ava and begged me not to talk about the incident. He didn't want her and her father to know he'd unburdened himself to me. I didn't say anything until after Rudolf died, when I accused Ritter of causing my friend such misery in Mannheim that he'd sought to redeem himself by going to fight a war. I might've even accused Ritter of causing my friend's death. Ava stood up for her father, insisting that it was 'simply business.' We didn't talk again until she arrived in my office a few months ago to tell me about the motorwagen."

"And now you think that August Ritter is using Ava's husband to weasel his way into Carl's business. But what about his interest in Benz & Co.? Do you think he wants to have ownership in both businesses?" I asked, wondering whether Ava knew about her father's dealing or, worse still, if she might be involved.

"I don't know," said Benjamin. "All of this is speculation."

"We have to get back to Mannheim. We need to leave today," I said, getting to my feet.

"Wait. Let's give this some thought."

"But—"

"Please, Bertha. Sit."

Every inch of me was ready to get on the motorwagen and race back to Carl and tell him everything I knew. But Benjamin was right: I needed to calm down and think clearly.

Carl wasn't, I rationalized, going to finalize a deal with Herr Adler or anyone else immediately. If he was, indeed, going to start another company with a new investor, he'd first need to sell his shares in Benz & Co. That would take time, and if he discovered that August Ritter was eager to get involved in the company, he would surely decide against it.

There was no need to rush back today. We needed to finish what we'd started when the boys and I undertook the journey to Pforzheim. Benjamin deserved our full attention so that he could write the best-possible article about the motorwagen's long-distance journey. He needed to write the kind of article that would convince Max to hold on to his shares in Benz & Co. and allow Carl to focus entirely on the vehicle. Benjamin needed to write an article that reminded Carl how brilliant he was and how I believed in him.

CHAPTER 35

1888
Pforzheim, Germany

RICHARD AND I TOLD BENJAMIN ABOUT OUR JOURNEY SEPARATELY. AFTER HEARing my son describe our adventure the previous night, I knew he'd provide all the color Benjamin needed for his story. My account, I hoped, filled in the detail.

"Are you sure Eugen shouldn't tell you his version of events? He has an excellent understanding of the motorwagen," I said as Eugen and I walked Benjamin to the station, where he'd catch the train back to Mannheim.

Eugen laughed. "What else could there possibly be left to say, Mutter?"

"I would be happy to hear what Eugen has to say, but I have to get on the train and write the story now if I am to get it to the newspaper this afternoon," said Benjamin.

After we'd said goodbye to our friend, my older son and I walked back to my mother's house, where we'd moved the motorwagen. Now, in a quieter part of town, the curious crowds were gone, and it stood unattended in the street.

Eugen ran his hand along over the back wheel as we walked by. "When will we leave?" he asked.

"Tomorrow," I said, unable to completely quell my impatience to get back to Carl.

We hadn't reached the door when it was flung open. Richard stood there, Lupin at his side. The boy was holding a piece of paper. "A telegram from Vater," he announced.

I took it and read the words:

`Send the chains back immediately. Express.`

"What?" I whispered.

Eugen took the telegram from me and read it. "He must need them for the other motorwagen. The one they were building at the factory but stopped work on when things went badly in Paris," he said.

I stared at him. Other motorwagen? How was it I didn't know that there was another one so near completion that it only required the chains? Was this how poorly Carl and I had communicated in recent months? Why the urgency to complete the other motorwagen now? Did this have anything to do with the new partner? The man who might be Herr Adler—or probably August Ritter?

Eugen walked back toward the motorwagen. "Where are you going?" I asked, feeling dazed.

"To take the chains off and send them to Vater," he said.

"But—"

Richard put his arm on my shoulder. "He'll send more chains as soon as he can," he said.

"How do you know?" I asked dully.

"Because he's Carl Benz—and my father," he said, giving my shoulder a light squeeze before going to help his brother.

—

I didn't leave my childhood home for the next two days. Once, looking out of the window, I saw the motorwagen in the street: chainless, ignored, abandoned. I chastised myself for being melodramatic when it occurred to me that I, too, had been abandoned. Whereas once I'd believed that Carl and I were happily bound to one another by our dreams and our family, it seemed he had now forsaken me. Although we were the ones who'd left him in Mannheim, he'd now deserted us.

Eugen and Richard made me feel ashamed of my misery. Full of energy and enthusiasm, they spent their days out and about with their cousins. I regularly heard them talking about the motorwagen and our journey to strangers who visited to see it.

"My father will send us replacement chains as soon as he can," said Richard. "Then we can show you how it works."

Carl had sent no further word, and yet the boys were certain of his plan. I, on the other hand, had begun wondering whether it would be possible to find someone in Pforzheim skilled enough to make new chains. Not even Benjamin's article—he'd sent us a copy of the newspaper—cheered me. He'd written a lively full-page story about our adventure, praising the motorwagen for its reliability and durability, and concluding that "Frau Benz and her sons have emphatically proven once again that not only is Carl Benz a genius but also that the Benz Motorwagen is the future of travel."

On the morning of our fourth day in Pforzheim, my mother called me from the hallway. The boys, who were reading in Vater's old study, followed me down the passage.

"It's very heavy," said Mutter, pointing to a package on the console.

Eugen put a hand on either side and picked it up. "At last!" he said. "The chains!"

He carried the box to the dining room, where he placed it on the table and began unwrapping it. Carl had, indeed, sent a new set of chains. There were also two envelopes in the package. The first, addressed to Carl and postmarked *Munich*, had already been opened. I slid out the letter and read, my pulse racing. It was from Herr Reimann.

I write in response to Frau Benz's visit to me in Munich and her subsequent letter about the possibility of you driving your machine, the Benz Motorwagen, in the streets of my city during the forthcoming Munich Exhibition of Engines and Working Machines. I have given the request much thought, and while I cannot give you a license to freely drive it during this time, I can also not find it in myself to stand in the way of progress.

As such, I have notified my officers that you will be permitted to drive the machine on the streets of Munich for two hours a day for the duration of the exhibition. If, during this time, there are any incidents during which your machine harms residents, animals, or any property in the city, this privilege will be withdrawn immediately. Neither will I, my office, nor any of the city's authorities accept responsibility for any damages that might occur due to this exceptional permit. I wish you success with your motorwagen and might, if you agree, accept a ride on it during the exhibition.

"Why are you crying, Mutter?" said Richard.

I'd not noticed until then that my tears were flowing.

Eugen gently took the letter from me. He read silently for a while but then out loud: "'You will be permitted to drive it on the streets of Munich for two hours a day for the duration of the exhibition.'"

He looked up, first at me and then at Richard. "We're going to Munich! The motorwagen is going to Munich!" he said.

Richard whooped and the boys danced around the table, Lupin bounding and barking at their heels. My mother looked amused but also baffled.

"You're going to drive it to Munich now?" she asked. "But that's a great distance."

"No, Grandmother," said Richard. "We're going to drive it at the Munich fair."

"I see," said my mother, sounding unconvinced.

Richard turned to me. "What does Vater say in the other letter, Mutter?"

The second envelope was addressed to me in Carl's hand. I walked to the window, tore open the envelope, and read the letter silently.

Darling Bertha,

I was shocked to find the motorwagen also gone the morning you and our sons left for Pforzheim. At first, I was confused. It was only when Clara and Thilde awoke and insisted that you had most certainly taken the machine that I accepted it. "Lupin wouldn't go on the train with them, Vater," said Clara, with one of her most condescending sighs.

I won't pretend I wasn't angry. I spent the day arguing with you in my head, but when I got home that evening and found the letter from Herr Reimann, I began cooling down.

By the time your telegram arrived, I'd decided to get the second motorwagen ready for the exhibition. Max argued briefly against it when I told him I'd need help to work on it. He was, however, won over by the police chief's letter. Then, the next day, I received word from Monsieur Emile Roger from Paris. He has buyers for the motorwagen in France and wants to discuss setting up an agency for it there. Then came Herr Stern's article. Max is almost as thrilled as I am. In fact, so optimistic is he that he has now decided that he will come to the exhibition too.

The second motorwagen will be ready for Munich, but to test it, I needed the chains urgently. Hence my telegram. It was terse, I know, but I was still simmering about you and the boys having driven to Pforzheim without discussing it with me.

Am I less heated now? I am. When I read Herr Stern's editorial, my annoyance was replaced with pride. I saw that your experiences will help me build a more powerful, capable motorwagen that will get over the hills without you having to push it. I will improve the brakes so that you don't have to call on the help of village cobblers. I will change the wiring to avoid interference and will create a cover to protect the fuel system from the dust.

Come home, Bertha, and tell me what else I can do to improve our motorwagen and your life with me.

Your loving husband,
Carl

CHAPTER 36

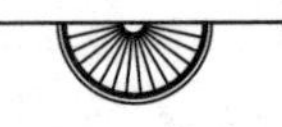

1888
Mannheim, Germany

We took a different route back to Mannheim, traveling through Bretten, Hockenheim, and Schwetzingen. We carried with us spare leather strips for the brakes and extra bottles of ligroin. Although we were eager to get going and keep moving, the idea was that going another way would give new groups of people the opportunity to see the motorwagen. There were as many hills on our return as there had been on the way to Pforzheim. However, this time they appeared in the early part of our journey, so we pushed earlier in the day while we were still fresh. Even so, it was a relief to get home that evening.

With Lupin having leaped off the motorwagen and bounded ahead to alert them of our arrival, Clara, Thilde, and Frida ran to the gate to greet us as we chugged toward Square T6, Number 11. Despite the warmth he'd shown in his letter, Carl was less demonstrative, waiting in the doorway as Richard switched off the engine.

"I'm glad you're home safely," he said, briefly catching my eye as I climbed off the vehicle.

Before I could respond, Thilde enveloped me in her arms and squeezed me tightly. I watched over her head as Carl circled the vehicle, flanked by Eugen and Richard, whose smiles had been replaced by scowls that mirrored their father's expression. Carl walked to the back. With one hand on the flywheel, he leaned over the engine, his head rising and dipping as he methodically inspected each component. He ran a finger along the chain we'd replaced in Pforzheim. Eugen gave Richard a nervous glance. The younger boy shrugged.

I should go to them, I thought. Shield them from their father's silent scrutiny. Instead, I reached for Clara and drew her into my embrace.

Satisfied, it seemed, with the state of the engine, Carl continued his inspection. The boys crouched alongside him as he examined each of the wheels. Finally, after a lengthy look at the brakes and steering, Carl drew back and smiled at his sons. I exhaled.

"Come," he said to Eugen and Richard. "I want to show you what I plan to do to improve the things that troubled you."

He slung an arm across each of their shoulders and steered them toward the workshop. Lupin, who'd stretched out on the path while the examination was underway, scrambled to his feet and trotted to Richard's side. I watched them go, too weary to follow but certain of Carl's pride in his sons. Frida, who'd been watching with me, touched my arm.

"There's hot water if you'd like to bathe before dinner," she said.

It was exactly what I desired.

—

I didn't see Carl again until a while later, when Frida served dinner. He and the boys were still talking about the improvements as they walked into the dining room. Carl's eyes met mine and he smiled.

"Dustless, I see," he said.

I nodded. "That's something you might need to find a solution for too. It's not only the fuel system that suffers from the dust," I said, returning his smile.

"All in good time," he replied, taking his place at the table.

Carl looked down to examine the plate of stew before him, gave a short nod of approval, and raised his eyes. "The other motorwagen is ready for Munich. It'll go next week," he said.

The children and I stared at him, anticipating more information.

Carl glanced at his place again. "Shall we eat?" he asked.

No one moved.

"Will we *all* go to Munich?" asked Clara, staring pointedly at me.

"No," said Carl.

I glanced at the boys. Clara and Thilde glared at their father.

"Lupin will stay with Frida," he said, unsuccessfully trying to hide a smile beneath his mustache.

There was a moment of silence before the children grasped their father's joke. Then, as one, the girls squealed, and Eugen and Richard spoke over one another.

"Are you sure it's ready, Vater? What about the—"

"Who will drive it in Munich? Can I?"

Carl held up his hands, trying to restore calm. The children ignored him, chattering and laughing. I heard Frida chuckling from the kitchen. Carl's eyes met mine, and he smiled again, shaking his head. I'd been on a journey, but our love hadn't gone anywhere. It was here, at home with us.

I looked around the table, examining each beloved face. How lucky we were. I was eager to tell Carl what Benjamin had revealed to me about August Ritter Senior, how the older man had coerced Ava's first husband into misleading another Mannheim businessman years previously, and how he and Herr Adler were related through Ava. I hadn't spoken of it to anyone aside from Benjamin. Carl needed to know urgently, but it wasn't a conversation for the children to hear, and I didn't want to spoil the joy of the moment.

Finally, the youngsters were in bed, and, with Lupin stretched out in front of the dying embers in the fireplace, Carl took me into his arms.

"Bedtime for you, too, Frau Benz," he said. "I'm surprised you aren't asleep already."

I wrapped my arms around him, resting against his familiar chest, and then stepped back. "First, there's something I must tell you," I said.

Carl sat and let me talk without interruption. I'd expected fury and a barrage of questions, but although he frowned and his eyes flashed, he remained calm. When I'd relayed the full story, he shook his head in disbelief.

"But Walter Adler said he learned of the motorwagen at the public demonstration here in Mannheim," he said.

I shrugged. "It's possible he was there, but there was much more to it. Maybe he was there with Herr Ritter."

He ran his hands over his head. "He's such a reserved man, Adler. Meek, almost. A gentleman, I thought. I can hardly believe it."

"Benjamin said his friend, Ava's first husband, was browbeaten into misleading Ritter's former business partner by his father-in-law. It's possible Adler was pressured the same way," I said.

Carl sighed. "Yes, it's possible. He never mentioned Ava or Ritter, and it didn't occur to me that there was any association." He stood up and began pacing between the fireplace and the door. "But how could I have missed it? You must've mentioned Ava's husband to me at some stage, but I didn't recognize the name Adler. Did we never see them together? How is it I didn't make the connection?"

"I don't remember mentioning it," I said. "Things were difficult between her and me when she got married, so it's possible you didn't know. When I saw them together at the water tower celebration, I barely glanced at him, and there was no reason for you to have known him."

"I should learn to pay more attention to people," he said.

It was something I'd thought often ever since I'd known Carl, but it didn't seem like a good time to agree with him. I said nothing.

"Do you think Ava is behind this?" he asked.

"I don't know. I want to believe she isn't, but I also lack the courage to find out," I admitted.

"Perhaps Herr Stern will confront her," said Carl.

"Or not. It doesn't matter. She and I are no longer friends."

"But Herr Stern and Ava are. He's also your friend. It might be important to him," he said.

Carl was right. Benjamin would want to know if Ava was part of the deceit. He was a man of principle, who deserved the truth. He'd want to know if she'd misled him—again.

"What will you do about August Ritter Senior and Max?" I asked.

"I'll tell Max what you discovered. Your trip, the news from Paris, and promise of the Munich show have changed his mind about the motorwagen. Even if, after all that, he reconsiders and once again thinks of selling his shares,

Max won't do business with someone who is dishonest. He can be difficult, but he's honorable."

"It's good to hear you say that," I said, aware of a peace within me that I hadn't experienced in months. Or was it exhaustion?

"What's good is to have you home, my darling," said Carl, his voice low. "I'm full of admiration and gratitude. Your determination and intelligence are extraordinary. Who else could persuade a police chief to allow us on his city's streets? Or foresee the consequences of driving the motorwagen across the country? I'm in awe of you—but more than anything, I'm happy you're home. Your absence reminded me that I'm adrift without you. People believe that I'm driven by the motorwagen. I know that if you are not at my side, my world stops turning."

CHAPTER 37

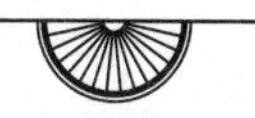

1888
Mannheim, Germany

Carl drove to work early the next morning. In case they had any doubts, Max and Friedrich needed to see for themselves how well the motorwagen had fared, he said. Eugen, Richard, and Lupin left the house shortly after breakfast. The boys told me they were going to join their friends, ostensibly for a swim in the river, but I suspected they were eager to tell the others about our adventure. Their departure gave me a chance to ask Clara and Thilde how they were enjoying their summer break.

"Vater took us to see how the new house is progressing," said Clara.

"And?" I asked. "How is it?"

"We won't be moving soon," she replied.

"He showed me where my room will be," said Thilde, the most resistant of the children to the move.

I looked at her, trying to gauge her feelings. "What do you think?"

"It looks onto the street," she replied. "I'll have the best view. I wish we could move soon."

I caught Clara's eye. She smiled and shrugged, recognizing my relief at her sister's change of heart.

"Vater said that you will finally be able to use all the things you've been hiding in the table," added Thilde.

"Hiding in the table? What do you mean?" I asked.

"It's not a table, Thilde. It's *used* as a table," said Clara, pointing at the large chest against the wall containing my trousseau, most of which had never been used or even unpacked.

I laughed, amused by the fact that Carl had thought about it while I had not. "Ah! Of course. We'll have to invite your grandmother to the new house once it's decorated so that she can see everything in its rightful place," I said.

Clara raised her eyebrows. "Do you think that's a good idea? She might want to see what Thilde and I are working on."

"That's all right," said her sister. "We'll show her the motorwagen!"

We were still laughing when I heard a knock at the door. It was Benjamin. He'd come to ensure that we'd arrived home safely. I invited him in and asked Frida to make coffee. After the girls had agreed with him that it was good to have me home, they excused themselves and left the room.

"I have good news," I said, going on to tell him about the letter from Munich, order from Paris, Max's turnaround, and Carl's response to the information about August Ritter Senior and Walter Adler. As I spoke, it occurred to me how quickly things had changed and what an important role Benjamin had played in the developments.

"Your article couldn't have come at a better time," I said. "It verifies Herr Reimann's, Monsieur Emile Roger's, and, finally, Max's decisions to support the motorwagen. Thank you, Benjamin. Without your friendship and interest in the vehicle and your—"

"It's my work and you're a friend and—well, it's been a pleasure," he said.

We were silent for a moment, suddenly shy. Then Benjamin spoke again, quietly this time. "I visited Ava when I returned from Pforzheim."

"Oh."

"The more I thought about it, the angrier I became. I had to know if she knew anything about her father's plans for Benz & Co. and her husband's alleged interest in the motorwagen," he said.

"So you confronted her?" I asked, aware of my pulse racing.

Benjamin sighed. "Yes. She denied it outright. Whereas, when her father bullied Rudolf, she said it was 'just business,' this time she said she had no idea and was appalled by the idea. She didn't know her father was hoping to buy Benz & Co. shares, and she had no idea Walter knew Carl."

"Do you believe her?"

"I wasn't sure. I'm still not entirely convinced. But then she called on me yesterday and told me something that made me think that she might be telling the truth," he said.

"Oh?"

"After I'd been to see her, she challenged her father and her husband. They confessed and indeed, once again, Ritter had badgered his son-in-law to deceive someone, this time Carl. Ava was in shock. She said she can only imagine what you and Carl think of her."

"Yes," I said, feeling a little ill, as if I'd had too much coffee, even though it sat untouched on the table.

"She told me that Walter has agreed that they'll leave Mannheim as soon as possible. Says she's too ashamed to stay and *has* to get away from her father," said Benjamin.

"Leave Mannheim," I echoed.

"Yes. Apparently they've discussed it previously. They're going to—"

"America," I said.

Benjamin stared at me. "How did you know?"

I shrugged. "It's where they all go."

CHAPTER 38

1888
Munich, Germany

The motorwagen was the foremost attraction at the Munich exhibition. After the excitement and success of its demonstration at the fair and—for two hours every day—on the streets of the city, the vehicle was awarded the 1888 Munich Exhibition of Engines and Working Machines Gold Medal.

The Munich Daily News commissioned Benjamin—it was no surprise that he was considered the expert reporter on the vehicle—to write about the motorwagen's showing at the event.

In the article, which was published on September 18, 1888, Benjamin wrote, "Without the kind of power we are familiar with from heating steam or from our legs, as in the case with velocipedes, the carriage rolled through the streets of Munich without fuss. As it moved, it took in all the curves and dodged oncoming carriages and pedestrians. Throughout its journey, the motorwagen was pursued by large numbers of people who followed, breathless with excitement. The admiration of all passers-by, who could barely contain themselves at the sight of the wondrous machine, was enormous. The petrol engine mounted behind the seat is the driving force and, as seen with our own eyes, is surely the most thrilling invention of our lifetime."

Max, who joined us in Munich for the duration of the exhibition, bought a sizable pile of newspapers containing the article to distribute to people who showed interest in the motorwagen. For the first time, Carl's business partner was proud to be associated with it. As we'd anticipated, Max had been appalled to discover that the man who'd been harrying him to sell him his shares in Benz & Co.—that is, August Ritter Senior—hadn't been sincere in their discussions.

To his credit, Walter Adler had called on Carl at the factory before we left for Munich to confirm that his father-in-law had coerced him into proposing a partnership with Carl to get his hands on the motorwagen. Herr Ritter Senior, it seemed, was determined to make us pay for what he believed we owed his family after his son and Carl's partnership failed.

"But Adler absolutely insists that, as she told Herr Stern, Ava had nothing to do with her father's interest in Benz & Co. Neither was she aware that Ritter had bullied her husband into pretending he was interested in investing in the motorwagen," said Carl.

I wanted to believe it was true but couldn't quell my doubts. Even if she didn't know about her father's plans, our friendship had soured, though I couldn't help wondering why. Had Ava always been envious of my life? Why had she so actively pursued a friendship with me if it didn't bring her joy? If she was as sickened by her father's behavior as she'd indicated, why didn't she call on us to explain? Why was she running away? I tried to tell myself it didn't matter. The Ritter family had brought anxiety, doubt, and double-dealing to our lives before. It was better to have nothing to do with them. Instead, I'd focus on the success of the motorwagen in Munich and celebrate our triumph with my family.

—

Gold medals, mesmerized crowds, burgeoning orders, and expressive newspaper articles notwithstanding, it was what the police chief, Herr Reimann, said to me when I bumped into him at the exhibition that stood out for me during our time in Munich.

"How good to see you, Frau Benz," he said, surprising me with a broad smile as I stood outside the exhibition hall, enjoying the sunshine on the penultimate day of the event. "Congratulations! I've taken not one but three rides on the motorwagen with Herr Benz since it has been in the city. What a machine!"

"Ah, so you're pleased that you decided not to stand in the way of progress, then?" I replied.

"Very pleased. Your visit to my office to petition for the machine had a great effect on me. I will never forget that day," he said.

"Because you want your children to enjoy an exciting future, I suppose?"

"That's part of it. Indeed, when I got home that evening, I told my children about your visit. I described the motorwagen and showed them the picture. They are Munich's most informed children when it comes to the machine. But that's not what I'm referring to," he said.

"Oh?"

"I told my children how Frau Benz bravely walked into my office and persuaded me to change my mind, not because she argued well—although she certainly did—but because she showed me that women can do anything they set their minds to. I told my children that even though your husband is the engineer and inventor of the motorwagen, I saw that day that you are the wheels that have made it possible for him."

I felt myself redden. "Thank you. I—"

But he wasn't finished. "You didn't only change my mind about allowing the motorwagen on the streets of Munich, Frau Benz, you also changed my mind about women and their power in this life. I told my daughter that just as the world lies at her brother's feet, it lies at hers."

My smile was so broad that made it difficult to speak. "What you mean, Herr Reimann," I said finally, "is that there is no such thing as *only a girl*."

AUTHOR'S NOTE

It's only in recent decades that Bertha Benz's 1888 journey from Mannheim to Pforzheim and back began receiving the attention it deserves. The Bertha Benz Memorial Route, which traces the trip, was unveiled in Baden-Württemberg, Germany, in 2008. After over a century of being considered little more than the wife of "the Father of the Automobile, Carl Benz," Bertha's part as his business partner is now increasingly celebrated. While the Benz family no longer has operational interests in Mercedes-Benz AG, the company applauds the legacies of both Carl and Bertha, with growing emphasis on Bertha's role as an entrepreneur, innovator, and all-round extraordinary woman—era notwithstanding.

However, in most cases where Bertha's name is recognized, it's typically because of what's become known as "the world's first long-distance test drive." In fact, as I've sought to show in *The Woman at the Wheel*, that's only a small part of her story.

Bertha's devotion to Carl's work and what became the motorwagen began before they were married. She wasn't only intrigued by the young engineer's dream; so determined was she to be part of the invention and business that went with it that when the first of Carl's partnerships failed, she invested her dowry and inheritance in his company. This was only possible at the time because she was unmarried. In other words, Bertha was not only deeply committed to her betrothed but was also an astute, tenacious visionary and businessperson.

When I read how, as a ten-year-old, Bertha read the words *Unfortunately, only a girl again* alongside the record of her birth in her beloved father's handwriting, I couldn't stop thinking about it. What were the consequences of an educated, intelligent, curious, and driven girl reading those words? She was fascinated by her father's work as a master builder and intrigued by how things were made and what the future would bring. Did her father's words incite Bertha to prove that she wasn't "only" anything? Or was she destined to be a trailblazer regardless?

As she matured, Bertha grew more perceptive and shrewder. Although her parents were determined to match her with a man of affluence and reputation, Bertha was set on finding a partner who interested her and treated her as an equal. When she met Carl, she recognized his brilliance, was excited by his dream, and saw how equitable a partnership with him might be. But she also saw his shortcomings and understood the part that she could play to help realize their ambitions. Bertha wanted to live a life of innovation and purpose in an era when women were expected to be grateful to do nothing more than keep house and raise children.

These were some of the things that fascinated me and made me love Bertha. And when an author discovers she loves someone from history, what's she to do but write a novel about her?

The Woman at the Wheel is based on the biographical facts as they're known about Bertha's life between 1859, when she was ten years old, and 1888, when she undertook the famous trip at thirty-nine years old. However, it is a work of fiction. While the trajectory of her life before and with Carl is based on the facts as they're known, I've taken liberties with characters and characterizations. Where they're not publicly known, I've imagined the characters' thoughts, conversations, emotions, and relationships.

In researching as much as I could about their early lives, I tried to understand what shaped Carl and Bertha. The Bible incident, Bertha's education, and the immigration of her siblings to America are based on truth. Bertha and Carl did indeed meet on an outing to Maulbronn Monastery, which is today a World Heritage Site.

The record of Carl's childhood, education, employment, and failures of his various partnerships are also fact. Learning about how difficult he found it to work for others, the family's financial struggles, and the challenges Carl faced as a businessman helped me understand him. It also allowed me to hypothesize about the emotions experienced and decisions taken by Bertha.

I based my account of Carl's work on the stationary engine and the motorwagen largely on what he wrote in his autobiography, *Carl Friedrich Benz—Lebensfahrt eines deutschen Erfinders (Life Journey of a German Inventor).*

While my story of Bertha ends with the success of the motorwagen at the Munich fair, which took place shortly after the legendary drive, it was by no means the end of her and Carl's story. They continued to develop the motorwagen, adding a fourth wheel and refining it while patenting new technologies along the way.

In 1889, Emile Roger set up the first foreign sales office for Benz & Co. in Paris. Emile went on to successfully race various Benz models in some of the world's earliest car rallies over the years.

Bertha and Carl's fifth child, Ellen, was born in 1890. The same year, despite evidence to the contrary, Max Rose and Friedrich Esslinger's doubt about the motorwagen's prospects resurfaced, and the men sold their shares in Benz & Co. When he left, Max told Carl, "Don't waste your time on motor cars." Three years later, Carl invented double-pivot steering. This solved the challenge of steering four-wheeled vehicles, and in 1894, Benz & Co. built twelve hundred units of the Benz Velo. The model is considered the world's first production car and was a commercial success. By then, both Eugen and Richard worked alongside Carl at Benz & Co. Shortly after the Benz Velo was introduced, the company launched a model of a bus and a truck.

Between 1890 and 1899, the number of employees at Benz & Co. increased from 50 to 430, and the company became the world's leading automotive manufacturer. Carl and Bertha's dream of seeing horseless, trackless carriages rule the road became a reality.

The damaging effects of World War I saw Benz & Co. enter a joint venture with its competitor, Daimler Motoren Gesellschaft, in 1924. Two years later, Daimler-Benz AG was established. The new company presented the inaugural Daimler-Benz models at the 1926 Berlin Motor Show, unveiling the first car under the Mercedes-Benz brand name. (Mercedes was the daughter of Daimler-Benz vehicle designer and automobile entrepreneur Emil Jellinek.)

Although Carl remained a member of the Daimler-Benz board for the rest of his life, he, Bertha, and their sons also founded a private company,

C. Benz Sons, and began building cars independently. Known for their reliability, C. Benz Sons cars were used as taxis in London in the 1920s.

Carl died in 1929 at age eighty-four. In 1944, to mark her ninety-fifth birthday, Bertha was named honorary senator of the Technische Universität Karlsruhe. She died two days later.

Although there are no formal records of Bertha's involvement in the family's business from 1888, Carl's dedication to Bertha in his autobiography stressed the vital role she played as his partner in business and life. He wrote: "Only one person stayed next to me in the little ship of life in the days when the sinking was approaching. That was my wife. She did not tremble before the onslaught of life. Brave and courageous, she hoisted new sails of hope and support at a time when no one else believed in the dream."

Carl understood that the "sails of hope and support" hoisted by Bertha were expansive and abiding and that they began well before and continued long after the journey she undertook in the motorwagen with their sons during the summer of 1888.

Bravo, Bertha Benz!

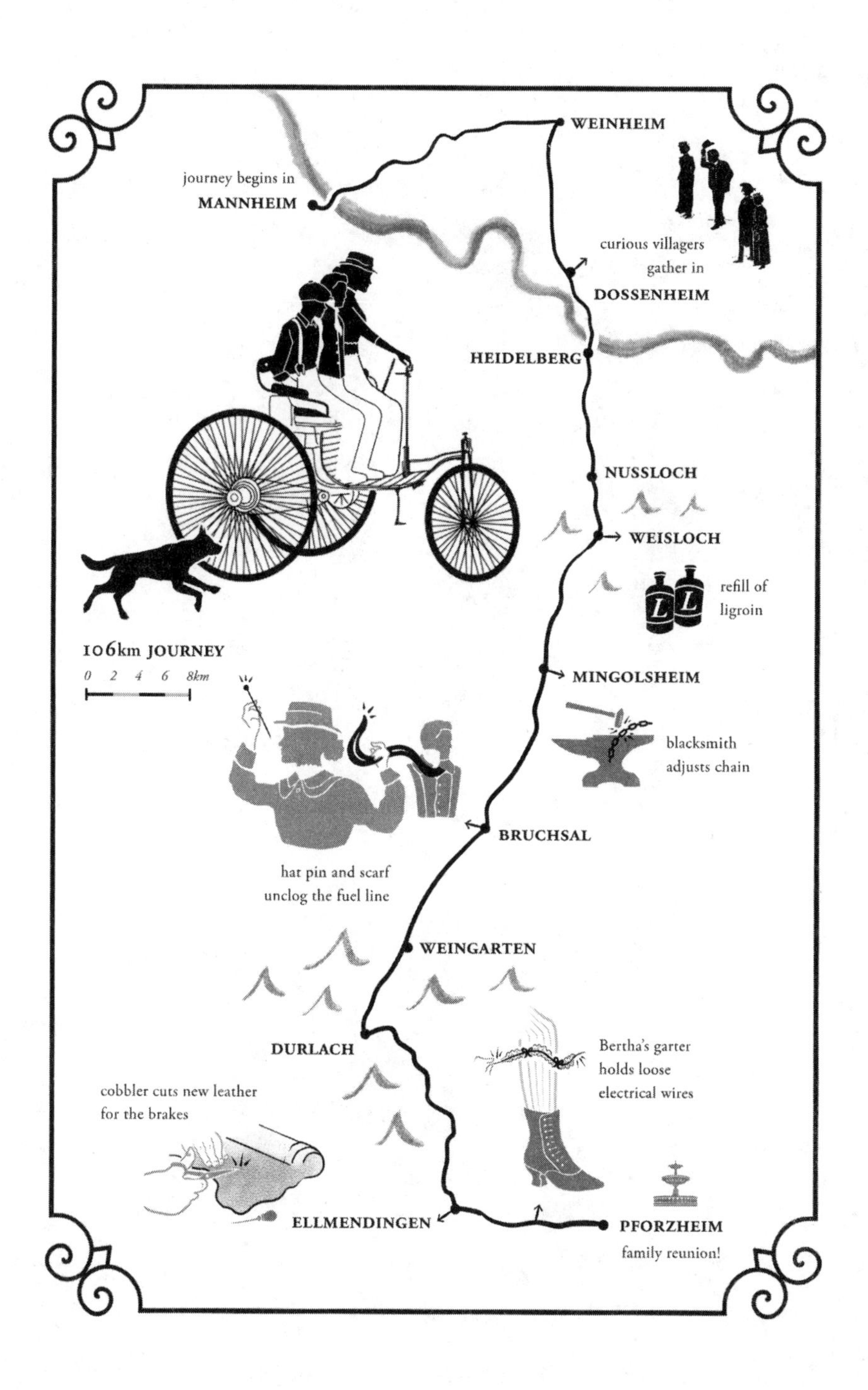
WEINHEIM
journey begins in
MANNHEIM
curious villagers
gather in
DOSSENHEIM
HEIDELBERG
NUSSLOCH
WEISLOCH
refill of
ligroin
106km JOURNEY
0 2 4 6 8km
MINGOLSHEIM
blacksmith
adjusts chain
BRUCHSAL
hat pin and scarf
unclog the fuel line
WEINGARTEN
DURLACH
Bertha's garter
holds loose
electrical wires
cobbler cuts new leather
for the brakes
ELLMENDINGEN
PFORZHEIM
family reunion!

READING GROUP GUIDE

1. How did Bertha's seeing her father's inscription next to her birth information in the family Bible—"Unfortunately, only a girl again"—impact Bertha's later years?

2. How did Bertha's sisters marrying and moving to America affect Bertha?

3. What do you think were the primary reasons why the partnership between Carl and August Ritter did not work out (beyond the obvious betrayal that occurred)?

4. "It would take more than being a genius to realize a dream." What did Bertha mean when she said this, when referring to Carl?

5. Bertha and Ava were never able to recover their friendship, which sadly does happen from time to time. Have you ever had a falling out with a friend that you weren't able to reconcile? Do you think Bertha was at all to blame for their friendship crumbling?

6. Not many people besides Bertha believed in Carl's dream of building a horseless carriage. Have you ever been faced with skepticism for your dreams? How did you persevere?

7. Bertha's mother says that Carl was "the author of his own troubles" when it came to making bad business decisions. Do you agree with this? Or were there other factors at play?

8. Why do you think Elise was reticent to share her news with Bertha about marrying Werner and moving to America, and similarly, why did Ava hesitate to share with Bertha that she was marrying Herr Adler?

9. Do you think it was wrong of Bertha to ask her sisters what they thought about Carl's prospects in America without Carl's knowledge?

10. Why do you think inventors, such as Carl Benz, are so often labeled "eccentric" or "crazy"?

11. The creation and success of the motorwagen were truly a family affair, with everyone—even the dog—playing a role. What were some of the most important lessons Bertha and Carl taught their children—either consciously or inadvertently?

12. If Bertha hadn't been there to support and encourage Carl in his endeavors, do you think he still would have invented the motorwagen?

A CONVERSATION WITH THE AUTHOR

What compelled you to write about Bertha Benz?

I came across information about Bertha Benz's cross-country drive in the motorwagen with her sons when I was working as a journalist on an article about women and technology in history years ago. It occurred to me at the time that there must have been a great deal more to the story than what was recorded in most places. It was unlikely, I thought, that Bertha would've undertaken the journey without there being a compelling reason for doing so. Neither would she have set off without a good understanding of how the vehicle worked. I was curious, and when I had the opportunity to look deeper into the story, my suspicions were confirmed. Bertha Benz was an ambitious, wise, and energetic woman. She was entrepreneurial and an astute businessperson at a time when women were expected to manage the family home and raise children. I was fascinated by her, and when the opportunity arose to learn more and write about Bertha, I was delighted to do so.

The wives of famous men are so often overlooked despite how involved and responsible many of them are for their husband's success. Why is it important that these stories be told?

Recorded history provides little evidence of the important roles women have played in all aspects of life, both in relation to their husbands and as individuals. It's not only because of gender inequality but also that history was written primarily by men. Even today when people trot out the adage "Behind every successful man there stands a woman," they typically mean that she's there in a supportive, auxiliary role. They imply she does things like press his suits, heat his soup, and comfort him when things get hard. The reality is that without their wives' involvement in various aspects of their lives at home and work, many well-known men would not have succeeded. Where this is the case, it's important to celebrate the women's achievements. It's not only valuable to have the facts, but it also reminds us that women have always accomplished remarkable things—even when the odds were more heavily stacked against them than they might be today.

Carl and Bertha's story is one of persistence. How does this relate to your own personal story of becoming a published author?

I love the idea of being passionate about something and working hard to realize one's dreams. That's part of what drew me to Bertha and Carl's story. They were visionaries and didn't allow their detractors to dash their dream. I love telling stories and writing. After working as a journalist for decades, I wanted to write fiction and be published. Even when I discovered how difficult it can be, I was determined to get better at it and find a way. I didn't accept it couldn't be done. One of the most exciting things about being a writer is that you can always improve. Just as Bertha and Carl worked on the motorwagen for years, overcame failed partnerships and ridicule, and found a way to show the world the motorwagen, I've kept going. I'm just as passionate about writing as Bertha and Carl were about the motorwagen. My story is like theirs and akin to those of most other published authors: it's one of persistence.

What was your favorite scene to write?

When I read about Bertha's mother's love for horses and how appalled she was by how many were treated, I was intrigued. Theirs was a time when horses were relied upon heavily for transport, farming, industry, and battle. I understood the thrill and wonder of seeing horses run free, but it seemed odd at first to me that Frau Ringer would wish horses freedom in the 1800s. Surely, she took for granted the essential services they provided? Then I thought more about it and pictured her growing up in the country as she did. I imagined her there and saw how she might feel the way she did. Why wouldn't Frau Ringer have watched horses at play in the fields and wish they could always be as free? At that moment, I knew I'd write a scene during which Bertha's mother would watch a horse break free, celebrate his power, and tell her daughter how she felt. I too love animals, including horses. I enjoyed writing every word of *The Woman at the Wheel*, but I got special joy creating the scene at the equestrian center when I imagined how, even if Frau Ringer couldn't imagine Carl's horseless carriage when they first met, she liked the idea of the horses being free of harnesses.

What is your advice for new writers?

Write about what brings you joy and try to focus on what makes you happy about the process. When things get difficult—as they do—and you wonder if it's worth continuing, focus on what gives you pleasure. There are times when the pleasure only comes when the hard work is done. Look ahead to that and keep working toward the reward. One of the things that I enjoy about writing is the idea that it's always possible to improve and do things differently. It's not work. It's creative, and being creative should be fun and bring you joy.

Do you ever get stuck while writing? How do you work your way out of it?

The most effective way for me to get out of a writing bog is to…get out of the bog. It helps me to step away from the story and do something different for a moment. Or, if deadlines mean I must keep writing, I go on to another scene. Somehow, when I don't think about the problem and forget that I'm looking for a solution, it comes to me. Much of my writing inspiration comes while I walk my dogs. So, I guess my advice to get out of the bog is go outside with a dog!

BIBLIOGRAPHY

Benz, Carl Friedrich. *Lebensfahrt eines deutschen Erfinders.* Leipzig: Kohler und Amelang, 1925.

Dormeyer, Recca. *Education of Women in Germany.* The University of Chicago Press Journals, 1906.

Elis, Angela. *Mein Traum ist länger als die Nacht.* Deutscher Taschenbuch Verlag, 2011.

Mercedes-Benz Group. *Historical articles.* https://group-media.mercedes-benz.com.

Nixon, St. John C. *The Invention of the Automobile.* Edizioni Savine, 1936.

ACKNOWLEDGMENTS

It's sometimes said that the life of a writer is a lonely one. I've found the opposite. There's a proverb—from my continent, Africa, I believe—that says, "It takes a village to raise a child." In recent years, I've seen that it takes a world to create a book—particularly if you consider the whereabouts of those who have worked on *The Woman at the Wheel*.

I'd like to thank my editor, Erin McClary at Sourcebooks Landmark, for her calm wizardry, wisdom, and guidance—all of which were steadfastly forthcoming while she led the life of a digital nomad, traversing the United States of America with her mini goldendoodle, Cheddar. It is a joy to work with you, wherever you are!

Huge thanks too to the rest of the Sourcebooks Landmark team, including Anna Venckus, who keeps a stream of exciting publicity flowing from New York City; Jessica Thelander, who steers the production ship from Chicago; art director Heather VenHuizen; design lead Stephanie Rocha; copy editor Rachel Norfleet; cover designer Chelsea McGuckin; and proofreader Sara Walker. I have loved every moment of the publishing process and am deeply grateful to you for your creativity, keen eyes, expertise, passion, and kindness.

Thank you, too, to my marvelous agent, Jill Marsal in San Diego, who, despite living in a time zone that lags mine in South Africa by ten hours, responds to my missives as if she never sleeps. It's such a pleasure and reassurance to have you at my side—despite the miles and hours that separate us.

Back in South Africa, I'm certain my family didn't anticipate the long-term ramifications of their urging me to turn my hand from journalism to fiction years ago. They've endured the ensuing prattle about my books ever since without discernible dissent. For that, I thank you, Jan-Lucas, Sebastiaan, and Claudia—with special thanks, regarding *The Woman at the Wheel*, to Jan-Lucas for helping me understand combustion engines, torque, tillers, and the like. I'm also grateful to him and Claudia for helping me translate several German resources.

My friends, too, are consistently patient and attentive. I am particularly grateful to those in my writing group who are always the first to read what I write and offer their opinions and direction. Thank you, Gail Gilbride, Paul Morris, Peter Horszowski, and Joelle Searle for your support, acumen, and generosity—and all the laughter that comes with it. To Karina Szczurek, thank you for your largesse, friendship, and help and for making me feel so much a part of the South African literary community.

Aside from my family and writing friends, there are arguably no others who know as much about each of my books than Marianne Marsh, Sue Dods, and Karen Stark. Marianne hears it all as we walk our dogs while, as my running muse, Sue, gets the huffing and puffing version. Karen and I talk about the business of books and baking—and pretend that we'll one day stop working. Thank you all for being such great listeners, friends, and inspiration for my writing.

Indeed, it takes a world to create a book, and my appreciation knows no borders. Thank you.

ABOUT THE AUTHOR

© J-L de Vos

Penny Haw worked as a journalist and columnist for more than three decades, writing for many leading South African newspapers and magazines before yielding to a lifelong yearning to create fiction. Her stories feature remarkable women, whose achievements, determination, and fortitude demand celebration. They also illustrate her love for nature and animals and explore the interconnectedness of all living things. She lives near Cape Town with her husband and three dogs, all of whom are well walked.

THE INVINCIBLE MISS CUST

a novel

"Inspiring, heartwarming, and ultimately triumphant."
—LISA WINGATE, #1 *New York Times* bestselling author of *The Book of Lost Friends*

PENNY HAW

ALEEN CUST HAS BIG DREAMS. AND NO ONE—NOT HER FAMILY, SOCIETY, OR THE LAW—WILL STOP HER.

Born in Ireland in 1868 to an aristocratic English family, Aleen knows she is destined to work with animals, even if her family is appalled by the idea of a woman pursuing a veterinary career. Going against their wishes but with the encouragement of the guardian assigned to her upon her father's death, Aleen attends the New Veterinary College in Edinburgh, enrolling as A. I. Custance to spare her family the humiliation they fear. At last, she is on her way to becoming a veterinary surgeon! Little does she know her biggest obstacles lie ahead.

The Invincible Miss Cust is based on the real life of Aleen Isabel Cust, who defied her family and society to become Britain's and Ireland's first female veterinary surgeon. Through Penny Haw's meticulous research, riveting storytelling, and elegant prose, Aleen's story of ambition, determination, family, friendship, and passion comes to life. It is a story that, even today, women will recognize, of battling patriarchy and an unequal society to realize one's dreams and pave the way for other women in the face of seemingly insurmountable odds.

"INSPIRING, HEARTWARMING, AND ULTIMATELY TRIUMPHANT."

—Lisa Wingate, #1 *New York Times* bestselling author of *The Book of Lost Friends*